THE MELTED SEA

BOOK TWO IN THE TREE OF AGES SERIES

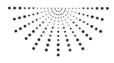

SARA C ROETHLE

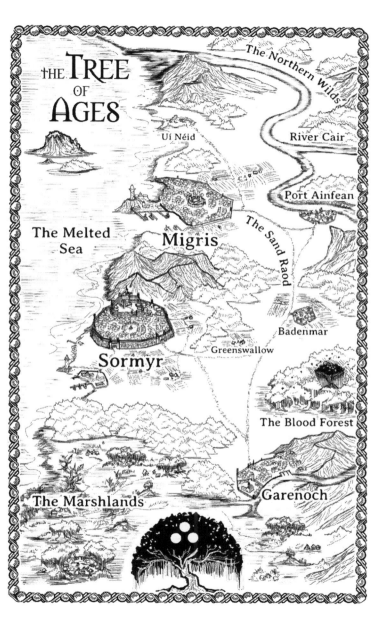

ᴛʜᴇ TREE ᴏꜰ AGES

The Northern Wilds

Uí Néid

River Cair

Port Ainfean

The Melted Sea

Migris

The Sand Raod

Badenmar

Sormyr

Greenswallow

The Blood Forest

The Marshlands

Garenoch

PROLOGUE

The man's icy eyes stared forward as he rode his horse full speed down the Sand Road. He would make it to Migris within two days, and there he would earn the largest bounty of his life. His silver hair blew back in the breeze generated by his galloping horse, but the lines of his aged face remained impassive, as hard as the stone that composed his heart.

Óengus smiled coldly as he thought back to the previous night. The night a sorceress made him the offer he'd been waiting for, for a very long time . . .

He'd been eating his supper near his fire when she'd appeared. She was as tall as any man, but thin as a rail, with wild, fiery red hair that reached her waist. She'd approached his fire without hesitation, then eyed him coolly as the flames reflected in her bright blue eyes.

"Óengus," she'd purred, "It's been far too long."

1

Óengus had quirked a silver brow at her in response. It *had* been a long time. He'd met Keiren when he was just a lad, and they'd traveled together for a time. She'd made him the man he was today. A heartless killer.

"I have a job for you," she'd said, which coming from Keiren, meant she had a *demand.*

Óengus had snorted in reply. "Knowing you, you're either after the Faie Queen's Shroud, or the tree girl."

Keiren had looked momentarily surprised, then quickly schooled her face back into its haughty expression. "Given that you already know of these things," she'd said, "that will make your task simple."

He'd shook his head. He wasn't sure if she'd called the girl a *thing* on purpose, but it was a fitting statement coming from Keiren. People were her pawns, nothing more. He easily related to the sentiment. "Last I heard, the girl and her companions were on their way to Migris," he'd explained. "I will meet them there, though I can't quite decide if I should sell the girl, or allow her to lead me to the shroud."

"You will acquire them *both*," Keiren had snapped, but Óengus had only smiled. He'd known this girl when she was less sure of herself, and knew those insecurities still lurked within her depths.

He'd smiled up at her. "Something protects these *items* from you," he'd mused, knowing it was the truth. Keiren possessed the *sight*. She could see the future and past, and could find any person she wanted in the blink of an eye . . . though she hadn't bothered with finding Óengus in many years.

She'd glared at him. "I'll give you back what I stole from you," she offered.

There had been no need to elaborate. She'd known that was all it would take.

"I'll reach Migris in two day's time," he'd replied simply, agreeing to her deal without giving her the satisfaction of acknowledging her offer.

"I'll be in contact," she'd said simply, then melded back into the darkness like a ghost.

As far as Óengus was concerned, that's exactly what she was. A ghost from the past, come to haunt his dreams, one last time.

CHAPTER ONE

$\mathcal{F}$inn was bruised, sore, and lying in a ditch. She reached a shaky hand to dab at the blood on her forehead, then listened for signs of pursuit. Her waist-length, light brown hair hung loosely around her, adorned with broken twigs, grass, and dirt. One of the trees blocking her view of the far-off path shifted slightly. The minute movement of the branches would be perceived as wind catching the leaves, but Finn knew better. These *trees* protected her from her captors. . .

SHE HAD GONE to sleep beside Iseult, the night after they'd left Port Ainfean. She was restless with excitement for the journey ahead, but at the same time was troubled with thoughts on what Gilion had revealed to them. Àed had hoped that his one time friend would have information on who Finn really was. Unfortunately, it was not information that any of them had chosen to accept.

Gilion had implied that Finn and Iseult were enemies, or at least they should be. He'd also made it clear that Finn would likely turn on Iseult, once she remembered who and what she was. Yet, Iseult clearly did not believe that Finn would turn against him, else he wouldn't sleep so easily beside her. His black hair, flecked with gray surprising for a younger man, glinted in the moonlight. She almost wanted to reach out and touch it, reassuring herself that this man who'd done so much to protect her was real, but she didn't want to wake him.

She sighed. She would feel better in the morning once Iseult and Àed were awake, and the three of them could have breakfast together. It was that thought alone that allowed her to finally drift off to sleep, and it was the first thought on her mind as she woke gasping for breath.

Leathery appendages entwined around her body, nearly crushing her, but not quite. Soil scratched against the back of her scalp as she struggled to free herself, but it was no use. Suddenly sunlight stung her eyes as whatever entrapped her began to loosen its grip, moving away from her face and neck. Now that she could see, her pattering heart sank. Massive roots were slowly peeling away from her body to return to the earth. They were the same roots that had crushed a man to death before her very eyes. The man had been attempting to kill Kai, but that didn't make the roots any less frightening.

Her eyes searched frantically for Iseult or Àed as the roots retreated, or perhaps even Kai, come to find her after she ran away from him in Port Ainfean. What she hadn't expected was Branwen. At first, Finn was filled with excitement to see her friend alive and well, but that excitement was soon dampened as she took in the blankness in Branwen's honey-colored eyes. The young woman stared down at her apathetically, her tawny red hair hanging matted and dirty down the sides of her angular face. The noonday sun illuminated Branwen's hair so that it looked like fire.

It was only when Branwen turned to look over her shoulder that Finn noticed the creatures gathered around them. Their lower bodies looked just like horses, with fur done in grays and muddy whites, but it was their upper bodies that held Finn's attention. They looked almost human, but with gray, bloodless skin. Gaunt faces were dominated by uptilted, pure red, pupilless eyes. The creatures appeared to be male, and had an eerie *sameness* to them, down to their lank, silvery hair.

One spoke to Branwen in a language that sounded familiar to Finn, though she didn't understand it. Branwen nodded, then silently helped Finn to her feet and brushed the loose soil from Finn's burgundy skirts. Branwen's deep red cloak was tattered and full of burs, but she didn't seem to notice. She looked like she had been crawling through the underbrush for a week, and it appeared that she'd had very little food in the process, judging by the gauntness of her face and the thinness of her limbs.

"Branwen," Finn whispered, "where are Iseult and Àed?"

Branwen stared at her as the half-man half-horse creatures shifted impatiently. Finn thought that Branwen might not answer, but then she licked her dry, cracked lips and said, "Gone."

Finn inhaled sharply. "What do you mean, *gone?*"

One of the creatures stepped forward and stomped its front hooves inches from Finn's boots. It said something in its guttural language while it gazed down at Finn with a sneer on its thin lips. A moment later, hands wrapped around Finn's upper arms, lifting her to standing, then all the way off her feet. She didn't resist as she was put upon the back of another one of the creatures, given that her only other choice was to stay dangling in mid-air.

Her skirts hiked up around her legs, she placed her hands against the creature's back to steady herself as the one who had grabbed her let go. She was surprised by the velvety texture of the creature's fur, many times softer than that of a horse. Giving Finn no time to recover, the creatures began to trot in a cohesive unit, jostling her senses, and taking her away from any clues as to how she'd arrived in that place to begin with. She leaned forward and squeezed her legs around the creature's equine back for dear life, not daring to wrap her arms around the humanoid torso.

Panicked, she looked around, hoping for some sign to tell her where she was. The trees here were tall, with broad, star-shaped leaves instead of needles, and the ground was more loamy and green, nothing like the rocky landscape she'd gone to sleep in.

The creature carrying Branwen on its back hurried to catch up to Finn's creature, allowing the two women to ride side by side.

Finn looked over at Branwen silently, afraid to ask her more questions that would garner no real answers. "Where is your brother?" she asked finally. "We left you in his care, but when we returned from the Blood Forest, you were both gone."

Branwen's expression didn't change in the slightest at the mention of her brother. Instead, she pointed to a structure in the distance.

There was ample moisture and fog in the air, making it difficult for Finn to see the structure clearly, but it looked like it had once been a castle, long since fallen into disrepair. The towers that she could see were partially crumbled, leaving only the lower part of the structure possibly inhabitable. They were several miles off, so she could not distinguish whether or not anyone currently dwelled there.

Finn gulped as her brain rattled from the creature's continued trot. "Is that where we're going?"

"Cavari," Branwen stated.

Finn's thoughts came to a violent halt at the name of her tribe. She had little information on them, and was beginning to strongly suspect that they were the ones who had turned her into a tree, leaving her with few memories, and no explanations. They had also eliminated Iseult's people.

As far as Finn knew, she had aided in the slaughter, at least in the beginning. Then, one hundred years ago, she was left alone in a field as a tree. Could the Cavari be the ones responsible for taking her away from Iseult and Àed? If they had left her as a tree, why would they want her now? Finn shivered. Perhaps they just wanted to root her back in the ground. Weeks ago, she would have accepted such a fate willingly, but now, she was unsure.

"Branwen," Finn whispered, not wanting to draw her captor's attention, though she doubted the horse creatures spoke her language, "I do not think we should go there." She subtly gestured to the castle in the distance.

Branwen glanced at her, then turned to stare straight ahead, dismissing her. Finn searched around for some way to escape, or to at least slow their progress. She wasn't ready to face her people, especially when she didn't know where Iseult and Àed were, or if they were even still alive.

As Finn scanned her surroundings, something caught her eye. It was just the barest hint of movement in the trees. She would have passed it off as nothing, but then she saw it again. The trees along the path they followed were moving in.

Some of the man-horse creatures realized something was amiss, and began barking orders in their strange language. They halted their forward progress and closed in around Finn, though whether they were protecting her, or just preventing her escape was unclear. Whatever they were doing, it obscured Finn's view of the moving trees.

Tension was thick in the air as they waited. Finn's heart thudded in her chest, making it difficult to focus. She sat up as straight as she could, trying to see what was happening. Her panic grew until it felt like she could no longer breathe. The cold air that did find its way in stung her lungs. If she was going to escape, now would be the time, but how?

Her question was answered a moment later as the ground began to tremble. Finn screamed as massive roots shot up from the earth, scattering dirt throughout the air and tossing her equine captors aside like they weighed nothing.

Finn was knocked from her perch to the ground, and would have been trampled by the horse-creature's hooves if one of the roots hadn't darted in to fling her aside. She flew through the air, then hit the ground hard, several feet away. She huddled on the ground for a moment as she tried to regain her breath, then knowing she might soon run out of time, she rolled to the side away from the chaos caused by the roots.

She forced herself to continue rolling, and soon hit a downhill slope. She picked up momentum, hitting painfully against rocks on her way down until she landed in a heap at the bottom of the gully. The trees around her quickly uprooted, then moved on spindly, wooden limbs to replant themselves in front of her, blocking her view of the road. She could hear shouting in the distance, and the thundering of hooves as the man-horse creatures stampeded across the countryside, looking for her. She held a hand to her head, and came away with blood, as a group of the creatures trotted merely twenty feet away from where she was hiding, within the tightly packed group of trees.

Once they'd passed, she quickly returned her hand to her side. It was important to be still. She closed her eyes and gripped her fingers in the damp grass as the shouting continued, and hoof beats thundered all around. The sounds surrounded her for what felt like ages, but eventually they grew distant as the search party deemed the area clear. When the hoof beats could no longer be heard, one of the trees near her bent itself in half, bringing its upper branches toward her face.

The Trow opened its eyes and smiled down at her. It looked much like the Trow she had met in the Blood Forest, with its rough bark and spindly limbs, but she was very far from that place. The Trow's deep green eyes grew concerned when Finn did not return its smile. The jagged crevices in its bark flexed in and out as it took long breaths through its knobby, wooden nose.

"What has happened, Tree Sister?" the Trow inquired kindly in a voice that sounded like bark scraping over rocks.

The other Trow that had helped conceal her all turned curious gazes down to where she still lay.

She shook her head minutely, having no idea how to answer the question. What *had* happened? She'd been stolen away by roots while she slept, but now the same roots had just saved her.

Taking her silence for fear, the Trow comforted, "The Ceinteár are gone now. You're safe."

Finn wiped at the tears streaming down her cheeks as she tried to rise, only to double over in pain. A large rock had jabbed into her ribs on the way down, and it felt like one might be cracked or broken.

"The roots," she began, gritting her teeth against the

pain as she forced herself to standing, "they've saved me before, yet they also brought me here. Do you control them?"

The lead Trow seemed confused. "My lady, only one of the Dair can control nature in such a way."

Finn shook her head, spilling her long hair forward over her shoulders as she panted in pain. "I was being taken to the Cavari. Why would my people save me from themselves?"

The Trow looked confused again, until another one stepped forward. This one seemed older than the rest, with large lumps and gray areas mottling its bark. "My lady," it began in a gravelly voice as it gazed down at her, "only one of the Dair could accomplish such a feat. We simply stepped in to shelter you."

"But the roots that brought me to this place . . . " she trailed off, not understanding why some roots helped, and some hurt.

The Trow shrugged, if the awkward creaking of the bark on its shoulders could be called a shrug. "Perhaps you saved yourself, or perhaps you have friends you've yet to be made aware of. Not all Dair are Cavari."

Finn's head began to spin. She sincerely hoped her skull hadn't suffered any damage. What the Trow said about her saving herself couldn't be correct. She couldn't control anything in nature, especially not without meaning to. Yet the thought of other Dair involving themselves was no more comforting. She knew the Cavari had not been the only tribe involved in the world of man. There were others, at least at one point in time. Whether they were friend or foe, she did not know.

The Trow around Finn waited patiently while she attempted to gather her wits about her, but said wits were nowhere to be found.

KAI HAD BEEN FOLLOWING Finn and the others since they'd departed from Ainfean. At first he'd thought he'd never find them, as there were many tracks leading out of the port town, but sticking to the Sand Road had proven the correct choice. By sleeping little, and taking no time to rest during the day, he'd eventually caught sight of them, only to fall behind before he was spotted in return.

When Finn had left him, Kai had been at first relieved to learn that she had rejoined with Iseult and Àed, but then he'd also learned that they were being followed by a silver haired man. Kai had little doubt that the man in question was Óengus. He'd been curious about Finn back in Badenmar, which meant he was likely out for the bounty on her head. Óengus was an exceedingly dangerous man, and Kai wouldn't mind being the one to keep Finn from him, if only to prove that he wasn't the man she thought he was. He was sure that once he proved her wrong, he could let her go and move on with his life.

He liked to think that he had rescued her from trouble the first time too, never mind the fact that he was the one that put her in said trouble to begin with, stealing her away from Iseult and Àed in an attempt to gather the same bounty that Óengus was likely after. He sighed as he thought back to the moment she awoke, realizing that he and Anna had betrayed her. Oh, how angry she had been.

Kai could admit to himself now that half the reason he took her was because she intended to branch off with Iseult and Àed the next day, leaving Kai and Anna behind. He wasn't sure why he couldn't just let her go. He was good at letting go. In fact, it was what he did best. Anna wouldn't hear of it though, and after what she had been through in the Blood Forest, he hadn't the heart to tell her no. Plus, it delayed his parting with Finn.

After the initial sighting, he'd continued to follow them, leaving enough distance that they would not catch sight of him. In the evening, they'd made camp, and he'd listened as Iseult and Finn had a rather odd conversation about things out of legend. They'd spoken of the Archtree, and the Faie Queen's shroud, objects straight out of Faiery stories for children. Yet, they'd spoken of them as if they intended to *find* them.

Kai crouched in the darkness as the party's conversation died down, and they eventually crawled into their bedrolls. Finn lay between the two men, who were understandably fearful of losing her again. He waited a while longer, until the night grew still, and the party fell into the gentle rhythms of sleep. Hoping that his movements would not wake anyone, he stood to retreat back to where he'd left his horse, but a sudden movement caught his eye in the darkness. Something serpentine was creeping up near Finn's feet. At first Kai thought *snake*, and was about to rush forward, when countless other *snakes* appeared. They writhed upward in the moonlight, and Kai suddenly realized what they were. *Roots*. Just like the roots that had crushed a man to death in front of Kai while he traveled alone with Finn. He'd speculated that *she* had called those roots forth, but there was no way she had called these. Her small form was perfectly still, deep in the throes of sleep.

He ran forward to save her, pushing aside the memory of the mangled corpse that had been left behind on the previous occasion. He couldn't seem to run fast enough as the roots multiplied and swarmed, fully covering Finn's body, and the bodies of her two companions. Reaching her, he pulled a knife from his belt and hacked away at the vine-like tendrils. The roots coated his hands in their sticky blood as he cut and pulled them away, but the more he removed, the more quickly the roots swarmed. He continued cutting frantically until he reached bottom of the mass to reveal only bare ground. Finn was *gone.*

Panting with exertion, he turned to the other two root-covered mounds, illuminated by the moonlight. With grunts of panic and frustration, he began to chop away at one of them, all the while glancing back at where Finn should have been. Àed gasped for breath as Kai revealed first his head, then his chest. Tears stung at the back of Kai's eyes as Àed struggled free from the rest of the roots, then aided Kai as he freed Iseult. Once

Iseult could breathe, Kai fell back, feeling numb and shaken, and let Áed help the other man with the rest of the vines around him. Finn was lost, and it was all Kai's fault. If only he'd been faster. If he hadn't stood gawking when the roots first appeared, he could have saved her.

Once free of his trappings, it didn't take Iseult long to recover. Instantly comprehending Finn's absence, he jumped on Kai like a ravenous beast, knocking him to the ground as he pressed a knife to his throat. Exhausted from his efforts against the roots, Kai barely reacted, not that Iseult had given him much of a chance. Kai felt himself once again in awe of how fast the man could move.

"Where is she?" Iseult growled into his face. His black hair, flecked with gray, tousled from sleep, gave him a wild appearance to mirror the intensity in his grayish green eyes.

"Gone," Kai rasped against the pressure on his throat, "but through no doing of my own." He wouldn't have minded if Iseult had stabbed him right then. He felt little fear at the notion.

Iseult's face crumbled slightly, but his anger was back in the blink of an eye. "Why did you help us?" he asked, his voice barely above a whisper. "Why not simply leave us to die?"

"I'd answer you," Kai managed to grunt, "if I could breathe." He could feel blood welling on his throat as Iseult pressed the finely-honed knife against his skin. Kai was quite sure that he was about to die.

"I should kill you now," Iseult stated coldly, affirming Kai's suspicions.

"Iseult," Àed said calmly, standing back while he brushed the dirt and sap from his ragged clothing, though Kai could make out little else in the darkness. "Let the lad go."

The stinging at his throat made Kai grateful for the interjection. Unfortunately, he was not sure Iseult was going to listen to Àed's advice. More pressure was applied to the blade, to the point where he thought it might cut through more than just skin. The rage in Iseult's eyes spelled the end for Kai.

"*Iseult*," Àed said more firmly. "Finn wouldnae want the lad harmed. I can assure ye of that."

Before Kai could even blink, Iseult was off him, stalking away into the dark trees like an angry predator. Kai had just gathered his wits enough to rise, when Àed's face came into view above him. He offered Kai a hand up, which Kai took appreciatively.

Once he was on his feet, he dabbed at the blood on his throat and looked down at the aged conjurer who'd rescued him. Àed still wore the tattered gray robes that he'd worn when Kai first met him, topped with a burlap cap in even worse shape than the robes. Though his long, silvery hair was matted from sleep, his sky blue eyes were as sharp and clear as ever, looking almost eerily bright in the moonlight.

Those aqua eyes watched Kai steadily. "What did ye see?" he asked suspiciously.

Kai's thoughts raced. He wasn't exactly sure *what* he'd

seen. The roots had been just like the ones that killed one of the thugs that attacked him and Finn in the woods, but in that instance, a body had been left behind. No one had been sucked into the earth like Finn.

Kai gestured with both hands to the dismembered roots strewn all about them, oozing dark fluid into the soil where Kai's knife had sliced them. "They covered her like a mass of snakes," he explained. "I did my best to cut them away and free her, but when I reached the bottom, she was gone."

He felt a sudden jolt in his gut at his own words. The roots had taken her, but that didn't mean she was dead. He had suspected that Finn had somehow summoned the roots that killed the thug that day, what seemed like ages ago. She was of the Dair, after all, though he wasn't quite sure what that meant. All he knew for sure was that she wasn't entirely human, and had been trapped in the form of a tree for nearly a century. Still, despite what magic she might possess, he highly doubted that she would summon the roots to steal herself away while she slept. She had been searching for Àed and Iseult, and Kai saw no reason for her to leave them.

Àed muttered under his breath and examined the severed roots. He picked one large chunk up off the ground and held it up to his nose, then dropped it as his lined face crinkled in disgust.

"It's a good thing she's been shining brighter than the sun," Àed said more to himself than to Kai. "She should be easy enough to find."

Hope welled up inside Kai. "So she's alive?"

Àed spat on the ground. "Aye, lad, though what state she's in, I cannae say. I imagine we'll want to be leavin' as soon as Iseult returns."

Kai felt sick again. "We?"

Àed chortled. "Ye've been following us for a reason, and I'm not about to suppose ye've fallen in love with *me*."

Kai's mouth went dry. "I haven't fallen in love with anyone. I followed out of curiosity, nothing more."

"I'd call you a liar," a voice called from out of the darkness, "if I thought you'd take offense."

Kai backed away as a now-calm Iseult approached, but Iseult paid him little mind. Instead he went to stand beside Àed. The two of them peered off into the darkness together, looking odd with the great difference in their heights.

"How far is she?" Iseult asked.

Àed left Iseult's side to untangle their bedrolls from the dead roots. "Far enough, lad. I can sense the direction, but little else. She seems to be on the move."

Iseult finally turned back to Kai. "I imagine you have a horse hidden somewhere around here?"

Kai nodded. He'd left his horse hidden in a copse of trees, fearing the animal would snort or whinny, alerting those he was spying on of his presence. "I'll be out of your sight in no time."

He turned to make his escape, but stopped in his tracks as Iseult said, "I don't think so." Kai turned back around as Iseult continued, "I will not kill you for Finn's sake, but I will not let you run free where you may harm her again. You will travel with us, and perhaps Finn will let me kill you once we find her."

Kai took another step back. "You caught me unawares the first time, but if I choose to leave, I'm not so sure you could stop me."

Àed, who had set to saddling both his and Iseult's nervous horses, if Àed's small, shaggy mount could be called a horse, chuckled to himself. "Yer just going to follow us anyhow, so ye may as well do as Iseult demands."

Kai's mood soured at that, because it was the truth. He knew he couldn't just let her go. He had to at least know what had happened to her, even if he chose to never see her again after that. Finn thought that he was a bad man. A liar, and a thief. She was right, but it didn't make him want to change her mind any less.

FINN STUMBLED THROUGH THE WOODS, carrying herself in the opposite direction of the ruined castle as quickly as possible. She knew she would need to face her people at some point, but she would do it on *her* terms. She would not let them treat her like an object, something they could stick in the ground, then summon when it suited them.

She shivered as she thought back to the roots *she* had allegedly controlled, though she'd consciously done nothing to call them. The only explanation was that someone else had controlled them, someone who might be watching her, even now.

If the roots were controlled by someone else, she had no idea of their intentions. Even with that distraction, her escape would not have been successful without the help of the Trow, so what was the point? Had whomever summoned the vines known the Trow would step in to aid her? Had the Trow lied when they claimed they didn't know who summoned the roots?

Finn shook her head, unable to believe the Trow had deceived her. She had given them her thanks before departing, but it didn't seem like enough. Trow had helped her in the Blood Forest too, and once again while she was held prisoner by Anna and Kai.

Finn's thoughts trailed off on that recollection. What she wouldn't give to be back in one of the warm taverns of Port Ainfean with Kai. As quickly as the thought had come to her, she shook it away. It was a product of her cold hands and empty belly, nothing more.

She looked down at the hem of her dirty burgundy dress to her oversized shoes. Neither offered much warmth, and it seemed much colder in this new region, compared to where she had left Iseult and Àed. It didn't help that she had appeared without her bedroll or any provisions. The Trow had helped to conceal her, but they couldn't keep her warm.

Even though every step was painful, her body bruised and sore, she'd had to leave the Trow and their offer of aid behind. She couldn't help regretting the decision. The Trow couldn't provide her with food and warmth, but they at least offered company. Being alone in the woods, with the strange trees and unrecognizable vegetation, she found herself more frightened than she had been at any point in the Blood Forest. She had no way of finding food or water, and the only shelter she'd seen was the ruined castle, which she wanted to stay away from at all costs.

Her fears grew as the sun inched steadily toward the horizon, threatening to leave her alone in the dark. She quickened her pace, though her ribs ached and she felt dizzy with exhaustion.

Eventually, despite her efforts, Finn's fears were realized. Darkness came, and still she walked, panic blossoming inside her. As the last hints of sunshine disappeared, Finn thought she heard an animal growl somewhere to her right. She froze, struggling to see anything within the trees. When no further sounds emanated, she started walking again, repeating in her head that she would be fine, as her breath fogged the chilly night air.

Some time later, panting and drenched in a cold sweat, Finn caught sight of the moon. Its full light swept across the open expanse between the trees. Though the light made Finn's surroundings seem eerie, she was still relieved. The night she'd been taken was a full moon, which meant she hadn't lost much time unconscious. Perhaps only a single night.

She increased her pace, not sure where she was going, but knowing she didn't want to remain in the forest. If the Trow had made it this far, it was likely that other Faie had too. She didn't fancy another encounter with the Grogochs, tiny, rock-like creatures with bat wings, that sung their victims into madness or sleep, and the thought of encountering any of the Travelers, the Ceàrdaman, made her sick.

She stumbled over a rock and had to brace herself against a tree to keep from falling. As she huddled against the rough bark, surrounded by a veil of her long hair, she almost thought she saw a flicker of light, too bright to be caused by the distant moon. It had to be a fire. She straightened and tried to find the light again, but it was gone.

Not willing to let her slim hopes of a warm fire go, she pushed away from the tree and stumbled onward, doing her best to head in the direction of where she'd seen the light. Sounds of wildlife seemed to be all around her, spurring Finn onward. The loud hoot of an owl in a tree directly overhead made her jump. She lost her footing and fell to the ground, then heard a low growl somewhere beside her. Acting purely on instinct, she scrambled to her feet and began to run toward an upward slope. She crested the small hill, and relief flooded through her like lightning. She could see the light again.

Finn couldn't make out much through the trees, but she felt sure that the light emanated from a campfire. It was risky approaching a campground without knowing its occupants, but she found she had little choice. Even if they attacked her, well, she'd surely freeze to death in the woods regardless. The sound of a branch breaking echoed behind her, solidifying her decision as she darted forward.

A few minutes more, and the campsite came clearly into view. As far as she could tell, there was only one figure sitting near, absorbing the fire's warmth. Finn guessed the person was female, or otherwise a slender young man.

She closed the rest of the distance, feeling like she might collapse as soon as she reached the fire. The figure looked up from the light, scanning the darkness.

Finn halted a few feet away from the fire, then collapsed to her knees as her heart caught up with her. As soon as she was able, she lifted her eyes to observe the person still seated on the other side of the campfire.

"You scared me half to death," the woman commented, though she didn't seem frightened in the slightest. In fact, she didn't seem surprised by Finn's sudden appearance at all.

Still, Finn let out a sigh of relief. A single woman was much preferable to a campsite full of Ceàrdaman. "I apologize," Finn panted, forcing herself to her feet to take a few steps closer to the fire. "I'm lost, so I followed the light of your fire."

The woman nodded, shaking her loose, shoulder-length brown hair. She smiled warmly. Finn couldn't tell for sure in the dim light, but she thought the woman's eyes were a deep amber. She wore a heavy traveling cloak, obscuring any other details of her appearance.

The woman lifted her hand and gestured for Finn to

move closer. "Come and warm yourself before you catch your death. You're lost, you say? Are you hungry?"

Every muscle in Finn's body relaxed with relief. She was saved, at least for the night. She did as the woman bade her, taking a seat on the opposite side of the fire. The warmth seeped into Finn's bones, which remained cold and achy despite her exertion. Finn lifted her hands to the flames as the other woman began pawing through her nearby satchel. A moment later, she produced something wrapped in cloth. She tossed it to Finn, who fumbled it with her cold fingers, dropping it into her lap. Laughing softly at her own shaky movements, she retrieved the package and opened it, revealing dried meat, and hard, crumbly cheese.

"I can't thank you enough," Finn said, looking up from what seemed like a feast. "I was worried I wouldn't last the night."

The woman smiled softly as she held her hands up to the fire. "It's nothing. I thought I might go mad soon without anyone to talk to, so really, it is you who is saving me."

Finn chewed on a piece of the meat and smiled. "My name is Branwen," she lied, not knowing if there was still a bounty on her head, or if anyone would have even heard of it in these parts.

"Bedelia," the woman replied happily.

Finn took another bite of the tough meat, and Bedelia handed her a water skin to wash it down.

"Forgive me," Finn said after taking a hearty swig of water, "but you don't seem terribly surprised to see me."

Bedelia smiled again. "I heard you running from aways off. I was just debating whether I should flee when you appeared. You looked frightened, so I guessed you weren't barging into my camp to rob me."

Finn nodded at the explanation, though Bedelia's attitude still seemed slightly off. Regardless, her best chance of survival was to remain where there was warmth and food.

Finn scooted a little closer to the fire, feeling safe for the first time that day.

CHAPTER TWO

*T*hey had been riding together since the early hours of morning, though Kai felt no less uneasy now that the sun had reached its apex. Any time they dismounted, he expected to suddenly find a knife in his chest. The knife never appeared, but he would have almost preferred it to the sullen faces of Iseult and Àed.

He looked forward at the backs of the men in question, pushing his shoulder length, chestnut hair behind his ear. Both of them rode on as if Kai wasn't even there, though they were the ones that insisted he come.

He stared at Iseult's tall, slender back, clad in black as usual. They'd spent the morning traipsing through the woods in a frenzy. Àed had acted like a hound with a scent, making a beeline toward Finn, and not caring if the path took them far from roads and through dense forest. Kai had followed willingly at that point, elated by the idea that perhaps Finn was not as far off as they'd thought, even though her location seemed to be changing every moment.

After a time, Àed began to seem confused on which direction he should go. Then, with a look of resignation, he had guided them back in the direction of the Sand Road. When asked where they were going, he answered Migris. When asked if Finn was there, he simply shook his head. Kai suspected that the hound had lost his scent.

He glanced at Iseult again as they continued to ride. He'd shown no signs of worry when Àed had given up his search, though Kai knew he likely felt more than he was letting on. The cut still stinging on Kai's throat was there to prove it.

Since they'd reached the road, they'd seen no other travelers, an unusual occurrence for a normally busy trade route. To make matters more unusual, all of the small burghs they'd passed along the way had been recently abandoned, though many belongings had been left behind. The only explanation Kai could think of were the recent Faie sightings, but it was still surprising for entire villages to clear out on rumors alone.

Kai shook himself out of his fugue as the thatched roofs of another burgh came into sight. Iseult and Àed veered from the road to investigate, though Kai wasn't sure what they hoped to find. The settlement was quiet and still, abandoned like all the rest. Giving in to the situation, Kai tugged his reins to the right, instructing his horse to follow the others.

As he left the road, movement caught his eye near the first buildings of the settlement. Whatever moved out there was too small to be human. Kai gulped. He didn't care what it was, as long as it wasn't Faie. Iseult and Àed rode on ahead of him, unperturbed. He continued on reluctantly.

As he neared the settlement, the source of the movement became apparent. *Ravens.* The glossy black birds flew to the rooftops, startled as the other two men reached the burgh ahead of Kai. Not driven off so easily, the ravens soon returned to picking at things on the ground, then flying back up out of reach. Even from a distance, Kai knew that ravens were not a good sign. His two companions dismounted their horses ahead of him, taking the time to tie their reins to a post before leaving the mounts behind.

As Kai's horse neared the first homes and his companion's horses, signs of struggle became obvious. Upturned and broken furniture could be seen through the windows of the houses, sometimes overflowing into the streets. Kai stifled a shiver as he rode past a particularly ruined house. Many of the boards of the wall had been ripped loose like something large had pried its way in, not bothering with the door. He brought his horse to a halt. The ruined house did not compare at all to what lay in front of him. A woman's body, at least what remained of it, blocked the path further into the burgh. Half of the woman's skull had been crushed in, as had half her chest. Her skirts were soaked with blood. Kai looked away as his breakfast threatened to make a reappearance.

Àed came into view around the corner in front of him

with a few sacks slung over his bony shoulder. He seemed unfazed by the carnage. As Kai looked down the streets past the old man, his eyes began to pick out several more bodies. There was even a man, well half of a man, on a rooftop.

Àed hoisted the sacks on his shoulder for a better grip, drawing Kai's attention back to him. "Let's be on our way," he announced.

Iseult walked up behind Àed. He was dragging something heavy behind him. He reached Àed's side and let the object drop. The object, which turned out to be a massive sword, forced up a puff of dust as it hit the stone-strewn earth with a metallic clang.

Àed looked down at the sword with distaste. "Famhair, as I suspected."

Kai turned to look at what Iseult had found. "It's far too large for a human," he observed, doing his best to keep his eyes on the weapon, rather than on the carnage around them.

"A giant sword for a giant hand," Àed grumbled. "The Faie are not the only myths returning to these lands."

"Giants," Iseult said thoughtfully as he looked down at the half-crushed woman in front of Kai's horse. "We should leave this place."

Kai didn't want to believe that giants, or *Famhair*, had returned to the lands either, but the evidence was quite compelling. He was too young to have ever even seen a giant, but that alone was not enough to compel him to wait around.

"Why would one of the giants leave its sword?" Kai

asked, trying to focus on something, *anything* besides the mangled corpses.

Iseult kept his calm eyes on the horizon. "That is a very good question."

The question received its answer quickly. At first it sounded like distant thunder, then resounding thuds began to shake the earth, making the horses whinny nervously. Iseult and Àed jumped into motion, hurrying past Kai toward their mounts. Iseult began untying their reins as the rhythmic thuds grew closer.

It took a great deal of restraint for Kai not to run off and leave Iseult and Àed behind. Instead, he rode out from within the buildings, searching for the source of the thuds. If he couldn't immediately flee the danger, he could at least see how close it was.

Kai scanned the freshly tilled fields, awaiting crops that would never come, until his eyes settled on a massive figure near the road. He'd imagined that a giant would look like a human, only much larger, and he was wrong. The creature that glanced curiously around until its eyes landed on Kai had a humanoid body, but the head was not human at all. Its face was lumpy, the skin thick and shiny with a deep green tinge. The creature looked at him with relatively tiny, pure black eyes as Iseult and Àed rode their horses to stand on either side of him. The Famhair opened a large mouth to reveal rows of broken, jagged teeth. It had to be at least 18 feet tall, and could have lifted a human in one of its massive hands.

Kai's horse began to dance about beneath him,

anxious to get away from the giant. Kai was in agreement with his horse. "We should probably flee," he advised.

Neither Iseult nor Àed seemed worried yet, though the giant was eyeing them curiously.

Iseult squinted his eyes to look past the massive creature. "Is that someone chasing it?"

Kai followed Iseult's gaze, and indeed there was a rider on horseback, galloping straight toward the giant. As they watched, several more riders came into view. They wore matching uniforms, done in dark brown with a hint of red at the chest, but that was all that Kai could distinguish.

The giant turned on the riders, lifting a massive foot to stomp them, since it was without its sword. Several of the riders expertly threw loops of rope around the raised leg, securing them quickly to their horse's saddles. The sound of a war horn echoed across the countryside, then the well-trained horses backed away, tightening the loops like nooses around the giant's leg.

The giant looked down at the ropes in confusion. The horn sounded again, and the riders turned their horses, urging them forward as a unit, tugging the giant's leg out from under him. The creature fell to the ground with a resounding thud, and had no time to get up as the riders rushed him, unsheathed swords raised high.

The entire sight was awe-inspiring, but Kai couldn't help to think what such skilled men might do to a known thief and smuggler. "We should leave."

Iseult nodded, but his eyes remained on the riders. Not willing to wait a moment more, Kai turned his horse to ride further away from the road and the contingent of men. Iseult and Àed soon caught up to him, mumbling about Famhair and the giant-slayers.

They rode away unnoticed, back through the ruined burgh, and deeper into the trees.

Kai felt more morose then ever. He wasn't daft enough to think that the appearance of giants wasn't related to the freeing of the Tuatha from the Blood Forest. Just as he knew that Finn was somehow connected to it all. He was too young to remember the Faie War, but that didn't mean he hadn't heard the stories. The Ceàrdaman had been doing the world a favor in keeping the Faie trapped. Changes were coming. None of them good.

EALASAID WISHED with all her heart that she weren't alone. She would take a bandit, a bard, or even the man who'd crept about outside of girl's windows back in her village, as opposed to being alone. She looked at her skinny, brown horse, feeling defeated. The animal had gotten stuck in a pool of sticky, watery mud that she'd accidentally ridden through. The woods were so dense with grass and vegetation that Ealasaid hadn't seen the patch until it was too late.

Now she was stranded, far from the main road, attempting to tug on the reins of an animal too panicked to move, while her boots and the hem of her pale blue dress got soaked through with mud. She pushed a clump of her curly, blonde hair behind her ear in frustration. She only had a few days worth of food left. She was going to die in the boggy forest all alone.

Just as she had leaned against a nearby tree to rest, the sound of voices caught her attention, filling her heart with elation. Yet a moment later, fear panged through her body. Not all travelers would be friendly, and some fates were worse than starving in the woods alone.

The voices drew nearer, and soon she could make out a group of three riders, taking their time as they rode through the woods. If they were this far off the road, they were either bandits, or they were trying to hide for some other reason, just like her. A black haired man rode in the lead, his upper body towering well above his horse, exhibiting his above-average height. Behind him rode a more slight man with chestnut hair. Bringing up the rear was a small, elderly man, seemingly well beyond his traveling years.

Ealasaid's heart raced as she tried to decide what to do. The riders hadn't spotted her yet, and likely would not with the route they were taking. Yet, friendly or no, they might be her only chance.

"Oi!" she called out, waving at them.

The eyes of the tall rider found her instantly, and she regretted calling out. His expression was cold, like that of a predator. He was *definitely* a bandit, or something far worse.

"Is that a girl stuck in the mud?" the second rider asked as he squinted in her direction.

"Ye need some help, lass?" the elderly man called out.

"Y-yes," Ealasaid called back as she debated whether she should take off on foot. "My horse refuses to budge." She tried to still her breathing. If the men showed any signs of ill intent, she would run.

The riders dismounted and began to close the distance between themselves and Ealasaid. She shifted from foot to foot, resisting the urge to gather her skirts around her knees so she wouldn't trip when she ran. Yet, there was still the chance they might help her. The tall man frightened her, but the elderly one seemed nice enough. Plus, she reminded herself, she was not without her defenses.

The tall man reached her first and she froze. Any decisions about running were stolen from her as she cowered in fear. She flinched as his arm moved, but he simply handed her the reins of his horse. She took the reins with a shaky hand and the man walked past her, doing little else to even acknowledge her presence.

The younger man came next, and handed her his reins too, though this time she was prepared for it. "You might want to move out of the way," he said with a wink before turning his attention to her horse.

Next came the old man, who wasn't even holding the reins of the shaggy mule he rode. The animal seemed to follow him of its own volition. The old man's feet sunk into the mud as he went to stand beside Ealasaid's horse, placing his aged hand against the side of its neck. Instantly the horse's eyes grew less wide, no longer showing white. The harsh panting of its breath slowed.

Both of the younger men took hold of her poor

horse's reins and began to tug, while the old man remained beside the animal, keeping it calm while his feet sunk further into the mud.

With nods to the older man, the two younger men gave a simultaneous tug. Her horse whinnied, then hopped forward, splashing mud all over the old man. Ealasaid stood aside, blushing and feeling like an idiot. They had made it seem so easy.

"T-thank you," she stammered as she handed the two younger men the reins of their horses in exchange for her own. "She had refused to move for over an hour, I swear it."

The old man gave her a crooked smile. "Wasn't yer fault, lass. I've a way with animals."

The younger men guided their animals away from the muddy area, and away from Ealasaid. The tall one climbed effortlessly into his saddle, not even bothering to bid her farewell. The other looked her up and down, then cast a glance at the supplies strapped to her saddle. Seemingly satisfied with Ealasaid's chances of survival, he mounted his horse and followed after the tall man.

The old man hopped up onto his mule, moving like a man of twenty. He began to guide the animal away, then paused to look back at her. Ealasaid felt like the man could see right through her skin and into her soul.

"I'm Ealasaid," she blurted.

"Àed," he introduced. "Now come along, lass. We'll see ye back to the road."

Ealasaid nodded and scrambled up onto her horse. She had no desire to go back to the road, the whole point of leaving her village behind was to not be found, but it was better than getting stuck in the mud again.

～

"I CAN SEE YER MAGIC, LASS," Àed commented as he glanced over at Ealasaid, riding her skinny brown horse beside him.

He hadn't meant to startle her, but she instantly tugged on her horse's reins, bringing it to a sudden stop. They had reached the Sand Road only a short time before, and Ealasaid had continued riding with the party without a word as the sky began to darken. Àed wasn't overly surprised that she'd decided to join them. After all, she'd been riding through the woods alone. The only reason to do that, is if you had something to hide. He suspected that she was afraid of being recognized as a magic user, and her sudden reaction only served to solidify his suspicions.

The look on the girl's face surprised him, however, as her pale gray eyes held unshed tears, instead of fear. "I'll just be on my way then," she murmured.

Àed held up a hand to stop her from riding off. He glanced at Kai and Iseult, who had ridden further ahead. He was glad for the distance. He felt no need to spill the girl's secrets to everyone.

"I wasn't accusing ye," he clarified. "Nor was I tryin' to

make ye leave us."

Ealasaid's expression softened. She seemed very young to be away from home, and perhaps hadn't even reached her eighteenth year.

"I have the feelin' yer afraid of something," he went on as they both nudged their horses back into movement. She was right to be afraid. Since the Faie war, magic users had not been treated kindly.

Ealasaid bit her lip, clearly still nervous. "Have you heard of *An Fiach?*" she questioned.

Àed, recognizing her words, but unsure of her meaning, squinted his eyes at her. "The Hunt?"

She nodded a little too quickly. "They formed soon after the rumors of the Tuatha's return, back when only a few sightings had occurred. As the Faie spottings continued, their ranks grew in number. By now, I'm sure they number in the thousands."

Àed, never slow to figure things out, spat in irritation. Rumors of Faie returning to the land had been circulating for months, but it was nothing compared to the release of the trapped Faie in the Blood Forest, something he'd witnessed for himself. If these men had been gathering power from the start, the sudden influx of Faie would have only increased it. "I'm guessing these men wear uniforms with red crests."

Ealasaid nodded. "So you've seen them. The crests are in the shape of a wolf, the inspiration of the Hunt. An Fiach is meant to track down the Faie, killing them off before they can do the same to us. The thought of another Faie War is in the forefront of everyone's minds."

"Aye, lass," Àed commented distantly. "We saw them take down a giant, one of the Famhair."

Ealasaid nodded, not surprised. "I've not seen any Faie myself, but I've heard awful stories. Recently, An Fiach took to raiding villages, looking for signs of the Faie, and the folk welcomed them. It started because of a village called Badenmar, where several of the townsfolk danced themselves to death."

Àed knew his sharp intake of breath likely gave him away. He had been in Badenmar that night, and had in fact helped Iseult escape questioning for the deaths.

"In the beginning," Ealasaid continued, not put off by Àed's reaction, "An Fiach harmed few, but as the recent chaos ensued, the raids became more intense. They began to persecute simple herbwives and weathermen. Some were burned alive inside their homes, along with their families."

Àed's mood was souring by the second. He hated to think what the Hunt might do should they find Finn before him. "So ye ran," he observed, unwilling to share his more private thoughts.

Ealasaid pushed her curly hair away from her face, but it was too thick and returned instantly. "I have three sisters. I could not let them come to harm because of me. The other villagers knew I was . . . different. It would only have been a matter of time before one of them gave me away."

He shook his head. It was going to be just like the last time the Faie interfered in the world of man. People would be jumping at shadows, more likely to stab their own neighbors than an actual Faie.

"Yer welcome to ride with us," he decided, not liking the idea of leaving an obviously inexperienced young girl on her own. "We'll keep ye safe along the way." Perhaps she could blend in with the large population of Migris. Surely the Hunt would not be able to single her out then?

Ealasaid looked startled once more, but her attention was drawn forward as Kai and Iseult began to argue. Àed couldn't quite make out what they were saying, but he didn't need to. He'd heard the arguments time and time again throughout the day.

"Should we stop them?" Ealasaid asked, looking worried.

Àed shook his head. "It's no use, lass. They'll only start fighting again in a few hours."

Ealasaid glanced at the arguing men, then back to Àed. "Why on earth would they travel together if they fight so much?"

Àed smiled crookedly at her. "That's what happens when two men fall in love with the same woman."

Ealasaid's mouth formed an 'oh' of understanding. "She must be quite the woman."

Àed nodded and looked forward at the arguing men. "That she is, lass. That she is."

They both watched the arguing men silently for several minutes, until Ealasaid cleared her throat.

Àed glanced at her, ready for her to announce that she would part company. It really was for the best.

Dangerous things revolved around Finn, and Àed planned to place himself right back in that danger. Their new young companion was better off being far from all of them, especially Kai. Who knew what kind of trouble that man might get such a naive girl into?

"So say I joined you on your travels," Ealasaid began, surprising him. "Where would we go, and what would we do upon arriving? You know my story now. I have nothing to offer, and nothing to lose."

Àed smiled sympathetically. "There is always plenty to lose. Ye'll learn that in time, probably soon, if ye remain with us."

She looked about ready to cry again. "But you said I didn't need to leave . . . " she trailed off.

Àed sighed. "Ye don't, though ye'd likely be better off if ye did."

"I have no one in this world," she stated, "so I fear I must disagree."

Àed sighed again. He *had* offered, and it was his own fault that he hadn't thought things through. "We travel to Migris," he explained. "It's a large city. I imagine it wouldn't be hard for a girl like ye to find work at an inn. Ye'll have a new life in time if ye try hard enough."

Ealasaid didn't seem thrilled by the idea of working at an inn, but nodded. "I suppose I don't have much choice. A large city is likely the best place to hide what I am."

Àed nodded. It was good that the girl had her head on straight. When you had magic, hiding was essential. Gone were the days when conjurers and sorceresses were sought out for aid. The Faie war had ruined that. Magic was to be feared, and never trusted.

They rode on in silence as Iseult and Kai continued to argue. It would be a long journey to Migris. Àed could only hope that the men's arguing would be the extent of any excitement.

BEDELIA WATCHED her new companion as she slept. The girl had slept through the night, and dozed on as the first hints of morning peeked through the trees. She smiled despite her irritation. Finn had fallen right into her trap, just like Keiren said she would. Keiren knew a great many things. Bedelia had seen her lady use those powers of knowing for many an evil deed, but she was unfazed. She would follow Keiren to the ends of the earth, and would even jump off, if that was what her lady commanded. Now Keiren wanted this long-haired, frail-looking girl, and Bedelia would not question it. Of course, not questioning it didn't help with the jealousy she felt at this girl warranting so much of Keiren's attention.

She watched as Finn tossed and turned in her sleep, mumbling unintelligible things. The girl had thought to lie about her name, calling herself Branwen, but hadn't questioned why Bedelia had an extra bedroll, not knowing that the bedroll was brought along just for her. What a little fool.

She shifted in annoyance, careful not to make a sound

with the leather and metal armor she hid beneath her cloak. She couldn't risk Finn questioning her occupation. She was, after all, a soldier without a contingent, fighting for a cause that did not benefit her country.

Bedelia's impatience grew as the sun slowly moved into full view. Would she sleep forever? Having had enough, she gently cleared her throat. Finn did not stir. She cleared it a little more forcefully.

Finn shot up in her bedroll, looking around frantically as if she had forgotten where she was. She held a trembling hand to her chest as her eyes found Bedelia. With her long hair all mussed, and her dark eyes wide with surprise, Bedelia thought for a moment that Finn was actually quite pretty, for a weakling.

"I'm sorry for sleeping so long," Finn apologized, seeming to have remembered where she was and who she was with. "I must have been more exhausted than I realized."

Bedelia nodded and smiled, schooling her face to show warmth. "I didn't want to wake you, but I really must get moving if I'm to make it anywhere near the Sand Road by nightfall."

Finn's face lit up at the mention of the well-known road, just like Bedelia knew it would. "Would you mind if I joined you?" she asked hesitantly. "I'm sure I'd never find the way on my own."

Bedelia cringed internally at Finn's admission of weakness. One should never admit weakness to a stranger. Bedelia wouldn't even admit it to a friend. "Of course," she replied, smiling encouragingly.

She stood slowly, careful once again to make little noise with her armor. She knew Finn would notice the armor at some point, but hopefully not until Bedelia had gained her trust. Until then, her thick, midnight blue cloak would serve to conceal it.

Finn unbundled herself from her bedding, pausing to roll the blankets into a tight package before excusing herself for morning necessities.

By the time Finn returned, Bedelia had packed up the camp, and snuffed out the fire to the point where no one would realize how recently the spot had been used. She didn't believe anyone would be following them, but old habits die hard, and Keiren had instructed her to be cautious.

She'd also led her black and white dappled mare to the campsite from the well-sheltered thicket where the horse had spent the night. The horse now whinnied, drawing Finn's attention.

"I thought I heard a horse last night," Finn commented, regarding the animal with a smile. She walked straight toward the horse and stroked her hand lovingly across the its nose, something you should never do with an unknown animal, unless you fancied getting trampled. Yet, Bedelia's horse did not seem in the least bit surprised by the act, and in fact, nuzzled against Finn's hand in reply.

Bedelia scowled behind Finn's back, then moved to strap the last of the supplies as well as her bow behind the horse's saddle. "The fire spooks her," she explained, "so I usually tie her a short distance away."

Finn nodded and tossed her long, tangled hair over the shoulder of her dirty green cloak. "I'm not sure I'll be able to keep up with you on foot. Perhaps you could give me directions?"

Bedelia expected there to be annoyance in Finn's expression at the idea of being left behind, but she saw nothing of the sort. Had this girl any self preservation instinct at all?

"We can ride together," she explained. "Rada will not tire from the extra weight." She looked Finn up and down. "Not that you'll really be adding any."

"Rada," Finn said to herself, ignoring the quip about her size while gazing up at the horse in question. "What a pretty name."

Bedelia almost let slip a genuine smile at the compliment, but quickly stuffed it back down. "Shall we?"

Finn nodded, then waited for Bedelia to seat herself in the saddle before climbing up behind her. She tensed for a moment when she thought Finn might wrap her arms around her, thus revealing her armor, then Finn gripped the back of the saddle instead, saving Bedelia from the premature explanation.

They began to ride through the damp, cold forest as the sun shone prominently at the edge of the sky. The happy light was a mockery of the weather as of late, unseasonably cold well into spring.

They rode in peaceful silence for a time, shaded by the broad, star shaped leaves of the trees. There was no path, but Bedelia had an excellent sense of direction, so she knew she was heading straight for the Sand Road. She also knew she should be making conversation, but found acting comfortable difficult. She'd never been one to have *friends*, but knew the best way to gain someone's trust was to make them feel comfortable with speaking candidly.

She guided Rada northeast to cross a narrow stream. "Might I ask you something?" she said finally, tired of waiting for Finn to speak.

"Of course," Finn replied instantly. "I'm very grateful for your help. Ask whatever you like."

I can ask, but you'll likely just lie, Bedelia thought to herself. "What were you doing in such a remote place by yourself?" she inquired. "Not that I wasn't out there myself, but I at least have supplies and a horse."

She could sense uneasiness from Finn as she explained, "I wasn't traveling alone or without supplies. I was separated from my companions. I hope to find them again once we reach the Sand Road."

"Separated?" Bedelia pressed, not satisfied with the vague answer.

Finn was silent for a moment, likely formulating her next lie. "I ventured away and got lost," she clarified.

Bedelia chuckled, though inside she was squirming with irritation. If you were going to lie, at least make it a good one. "I'm sure they are on their way to the road now, hoping to find you."

"I know they will find me," Finn agreed, sounding more like she was speaking to herself than Bedelia. "They did it once, and they'll do it again."

"Oh?" Bedlia said good-naturedly. "So this isn't the

first time you wandered off?"

Finn paused again before speaking. "We were separated for a week the first time, and I traveled a great
distance. I never truly thought they'd find me, but
they did."

"You were lost, and survived on your own for a
week?" Bedelia asked, not having to fake the disbelief in
her tone.

Finn laughed. "Oh, I wasn't alone. I was with a . . .
friend."

Bedelia nodded, wishing she knew what Finn was
going on about. Normally Keiren would have known
everything there was to know about the girl, but something often shrouded her from Keiren's seemingly all-
seeing eyes. With Finn, Keiren was only able to steal little
glimpses of the present and future, like she'd done when
she predicted Finn would come to Bedelia's campsite.
Her lady had flown into numerous fits of rage whenever
she couldn't see Finn, always leaving Bedelia frightened
that the rage would be turned on *her*.

"Well you are with a friend this time too," Bedelia
stated jovially. "I look forward to meeting your companions once they find you."

"I believe I am in much more honest company this
time," Finn replied warmly, "so thank you."

Bedelia smiled ruefully as she watched the path ahead
of them. *Honest.* Finn's company during her previous
bout of being lost must have been the King of Lies to
have outdone Bedelia.

$\mathcal{F}$inn stared into the comforting light of the fire, waiting for Bedelia to return with more wood. They had traveled together all day, talking and getting to know each other. It was different traveling with only a woman. It made Finn feel safe and comfortable in a way much different from the men.

Their conversations had been wonderful. Finn had revealed many of her fears and worries, though she had to put them in a different context so as not to give away who she was. Still, sharing those thoughts had lifted a great weight off her chest. She hated that she'd felt too ashamed to admit them to Iseult or Àed, but there it was.

Bedelia had commiserated, making Finn feel less silly and weak. Maybe all women went through the same internal battles. Perhaps if Branwen ever righted herself, Finn could share such conversations with her.

A scream tore through the shadowy vegetation, paralyzing Finn with fear. They were still far from the Sand

Road and civilization. The scream had to belong to Bedelia.

Finn hopped to her feet and wrapped her tattered cloak tightly around herself. She was shaking like a leaf, but little of it was from the cold. She heard the scream again, then darted off into the night.

She could barely see where she was running and ended up tripping over small rocks and brambles, stinging her cold feet through her socks and boots with the impact, and catching her skirts and the vulnerable skin underneath on thorns.

The screaming had ceased, but she could hear grunts of struggle amidst a chorus of low growls and yips. Finn skidded to a halt in a clearing as several pairs of glowing eyes turned toward her. The shadowy creatures were enormous, likely outweighing Finn and Bedelia put together. From what Finn could see in the moonlight, they were wolf-like, but their faces seemed smushed, their jaws too wide. Their fur was wiry and grew in patches.

Bedelia, who'd been on the ground among the creatures, took advantage of the momentary distraction. She'd left her bow at their camp, but wielded a large knife, its blade glinting in the moonlight. The knife plunged into the neck of the nearest creature. The creature's shrieks echoed around them as Bedelia rose to her feet and stumbled toward Finn.

Reaching her, Bedelia clutched at Finn's arm, obviously having trouble standing on her own. The two women backed away slowly as all but the injured creature began to stalk toward them.

Finn's eyes darted around for something that might save them. If she'd been able to think clearly, she would have at least drawn the small knife at her belt, but her thoughts were solely on the glowing eyes marching toward her.

The creatures had gone silent, except for a few low growls. The one nearest to the women crouched down, preparing to pounce. Finn closed her eyes, her thoughts a jumble, and reached out her hands to ward off the attack. She felt a surge of adrenaline and almost opened her eyes, but felt dizzy with fear and unable to move. The earth shook beneath her feet, surely the thundering charge of the creatures about to eat them. Bedelia shrieked, pulling away from Finn.

The creatures erupted in a cacophony of yips and squeals, while the earth trembled so violently that Finn was knocked to the ground. She fell backward and hit the dirt as a thrill of pain shot through her to mingle with the lingering adrenaline. She waited on her back for the killing blow, but none came. Everything had suddenly gone still.

Finn opened her eyes slowly to find Bedelia panting beside her. She sat up, whipping her head around in search of the creatures. They were gone, and rocky, turned earth was in their place.

Her eyes darted back to Bedelia, who'd scooted away, her jaw slack with fear. "W-what are you?" she whispered. "What did you do?"

Had she made the earth move to swallow the creatures up whole? It couldn't be. First the Trow had accused her of summoning the roots, and now this? Finn gazed back at the turned earth, tears welling up in her eyes as she answered both questions at once. "At this point," she began, "I'm really not sure."

BEDELIA'S LEG WAS INJURED, and she was stuck with this apparent sorceress in the dark woods. Her armor had been fully revealed during the chaos, and Finn eyed it warily as they recovered in the now silent woods. Would Finn kill her now? Swallow her up in the earth like she had done with the wolf creatures?

Bedelia shivered at the thought. One moment, the wolves had been about to pounce, and the next, Finn raised her hands and the earth rose up to swallow them like a giant, hungry bear.

Finn had risen shakily to her feet after the eruption, but Bedelia was unsure if she was capable of doing the same. Finn moved to stand next to her, then crouched down. Bedelia closed her eyes and flinched away, but Finn did nothing to harm her. She opened her eyes to see Finn drop her hands to her sides with a hurt expression.

"You're frightened of me," Finn muttered, the words barely audible.

Bedelia sighed with relief. The girl was more worried about what Bedelia might think of her, than the fact that Bedelia was wearing expensive armor. Armor that only a soldier belonging to one of the most wealthy lords would wear. Finn wasn't even questioning it. She was either very forgiving, or a total fool.

When she didn't speak, Finn looked down at Bedelia's injured leg. "You're bleeding!" she exclaimed suddenly. "We must get you back to the fire to bandage it."

Bedelia nodded numbly, still afraid for Finn to touch her. She'd seen Keiren wield more fearsome powers, but Keiren was in control of her actions. This meek little girl, was not.

Seeing no other choice, Bedelia allowed Finn to slide her arm around her lower back to grip around her waist. Bedelia had a larger frame than Finn, and was several inches taller than her, making the struggle that followed awkward and uncomfortable. Yet, with the use of her good leg, Bedelia and Finn managed to stand together.

They hobbled back in the direction of the fire, Bedelia leaning heavily on Finn's small, bony shoulders as they stumbled across the uneven terrain. She felt blood dripping down her leg to cool and congeal around the edge of her boot.

Once they reached the campsite, Finn lowered Bedelia to the ground, then went to crouch by her injured leg. "I'm not sure how to undo *this*," Finn commented, gazing down at the bronze plate that covered Bedelia's shin above her boot.

"I can explain," Bedelia replied blandly, meaning both why she wore the armor *and* how to get it off.

Finn's eyes met hers, but Bedelia saw no accusation in them. "If you have not been honest about your identity," she began, making Bedelia's heart skip a beat, "I cannot blame you for it. I have not been entirely honest either."

Bedelia let out the breath she'd sucked in. Finn wasn't as foolish as she'd seemed. The armor had made her question Bedelia's identity and motives. She was probably even questioning Bedelia's motivations for helping her. Yet, she wasn't angry?

Bedelia looked down at her injured leg. "There are buckles at the back of my calf," she explained softly.

Finn nodded, allowing the subject to drop, and began searching Bedelia's calf gingerly with her fingers. Her small, nimble hands found the buckles quickly, and undid them while Bedelia cringed against the added pressure to her wound.

Finn lifted the plate away, and both women looked down to assess the damage. Though Bedelia's previously covered shin was unscathed, the wolf's jaw where it bit her had been large enough to encompass the plate, puncturing the back of her calf on either side. The four circular wounds oozed with blood.

"Do you have any bandages?" Finn asked softly, worry coloring her voice as she continued to stare down at the steadily bleeding puncture marks.

Bedelia nodded and pointed toward one of the satchels she'd taken from Rada when they made camp. Without another word, Finn rose and grabbed the satchel, then returned as she pulled out a rolled up wad of fabric. "We should probably clean the wounds first," she commented, hesitating over Bedelia's leg.

Bedelia nodded. "We can use some of our drinking water."

She appreciated that Finn had thought to clean the wound. She was not keen on finding out what a bite from the strange creatures might do if left untreated. Finn stood and walked away from the campsite, in the direction of where Rada was tethered.

Bedelia's heart pounded in her ear as Finn disappeared from sight in the darkness. Had it all been a ruse? Would Finn steal Rada and leave Bedelia to die?

A few minutes later, Finn returned with a small tea kettle and an extra water skin. She held the kettle up nervously. "I thought some tea might calm your nerves," she explained, then frowned as if realizing her idea might be silly.

Bedelia relaxed slightly. Finn set to boiling the water for tea, then gently washed Bedelia's leg with the remaining water in the skin. Bedelia gasped as Finn began to wrap her leg with the fresh bandages. She felt increasingly nervous. Had Finn seen anything else in Bedelia's belongings when she'd searched for the water? There were certain items that her *friend* would likely question. Finished with her work, Finn sat near Bedelia and held her damp hands up to the fire. She sighed in relief. Finn wasn't going to question anything.

"About what happened with those creatures," Finn began, breaking the silence.

Was Finn going to tell her the truth? Did it matter? "You don't have to explain," Bedelia cut in. "You saved me. That's the end of it."

Finn turned to her and smiled. "You don't have to explain either, about the armor I mean. I owed you a saving."

Bedelia smiled too, though she felt sick to her stomach. Keiren had not shared her plans, but Bedelia was beginning to hope that Keiren did not intend to harm Finn. It was odd, but at some point, while Bedelia had been working so hard to gain Finn's trust, Finn had gained hers.

FINN GROANED as the first rays of sunlight hit her face. She felt like she hadn't slept at all. Bedelia had claimed that the fire would keep them safe from any more wolf creatures that might be out in the night, but Finn hadn't been so sure. She suspected that Bedelia's injury was more serious than she was letting on, and it prevented her from wanting to travel in the night.

Still, none of the creatures had returned, so perhaps Bedelia was right. Or perhaps Finn had simply killed them all. She swallowed a lump in her throat at the thought. What had happened to unleash these strange powers that dwelled within her? Thinking of her people, she reminded herself that she should just be glad that they hadn't stolen her away in the night again.

Bedelia groaned from her bedroll, drawing Finn's attention. She looked across the fire at her friend's pale, sweaty face.

"Oh no!" Finn exclaimed as she pulled herself from her bedding. "Is your wound paining you?"

She scurried to Bedelia's side as the sickly woman raised herself up on her elbows. "I just feel a little ill is all."

She reached out to place a hand on Bedelia's forehead. Bedelia flinched away initially, then looked apologetically at her, relaxing against the re-offered touch.

"I'm afraid I know little about caring for injuries," Finn commented, her hand still resting gently against Bedelia's tanned face, "but you feel very warm, and I don't think that's a good sign."

Bedelia shrugged Finn's hand off and sat up fully. "It will be fine. We'll reach the Sand Road today, and from there Migris isn't far off."

Finn looked down at her lap. "I can't go to Migris. I must find my friends."

Bedelia opened her mouth to say something, but Finn cut her off with an irritated huff. "What am I saying?" she continued. "I can't expect you to travel to Migris alone and injured."

Bedelia smiled. "I'll be fine, but you'll have a better chance of finding your friends there, regardless. There is always the chance that they might leave the road to ask after you in some of the smaller burghs. You could very well miss them, then they'd reach Migris before you. If you're not there to meet them, they may move on."

Finn's eyes widened as she continued to crouch over Bedelia. "I hadn't even thought of that. You're right."

Bedelia nodded and crawled out of her bedding,

rising slowly to her feet. With a grimace, she began to roll up her blankets, but Finn eventually had to take over when she noticed Bedelia swaying unsteadily. She was able to stand on the wounded leg, so that wasn't the problem, she just seemed dizzy. Finn feared the wolf's bite had made her friend sick. Her thoughts were verified when Bedelia allowed her to clean up the rest of the campsite herself. She must have really been feeling awful to give away such a large amount of control.

Once everything was packed, the women climbed onto Rada's saddle and rode on toward the Sand Road. After a short while, Finn wrapped her arms around Bedelia's waist to steady her. Bedelia did not protest.

By the time they reached the Sand Road, Bedelia seemed a little more herself. She was still pale and fevered, but at least seemed capable of holding herself up in the saddle. The sky was mostly clear, but the air was icy cold, and Finn could see a distant storm brewing behind them.

They hurried onward, urging Rada to carry them away from the possibility of rain. They didn't get far, however, before they found that the road was blocked ahead of them.

The first of the men to catch Finn's eye stood near to what amounted to a small village of brown and green tents, blending into the scenery. The men wore matching dark brown clothing, though she thought she could make out a hint of red on their chests.

"We should go back," Bedelia warned, spotting the men. She'd drawn Rada to an abrupt halt.

Finn eyed the men warily. "They've already seen us," she whispered. Though the men were still a good distance off, she recognized their motions as they gestured to where she and Bedelia waited. "If we turn from the road now, it might give them reason to pursue us."

"If we walk into their hands now," Bedelia countered, "it might give them reason to keep us."

Finn glanced at the men again. The nearest ones were beginning to walk toward them. "They look like soldiers," she observed. "Surely they mean us no harm."

Bedelia snorted. "You'll find that soldiers are often far more harmful than normal men."

Finn was alarmed by Bedelia's words, but it was too late, two of the soldiers had moved away from the rest of the group to approach them. They wore matching, dark brown woolen breeches, topped by slightly lighter coats, with the symbol of a red wolf stitched over the left side of their breasts.

As the men neared, Finn noted that they had few features in common. One was dark haired and olive skinned, while the other was pale, with reddish blond hair. Despite their dissimilarities, they had a relative *sameness* about them, from their grim expressions, down to the braids holding back the hair on either side of their heads.

"You needn't fear," the red-haired man said, taking in Finn's worried expression as he reached them. She couldn't see Bedelia's face, but imagined it held her usual look of grim determination.

"We are here to protect you from the Tuatha," the darker man went on. "Have you sighted anything strange on your travels?"

"Nothing," Bedelia stated coolly, "and as we'd like to beat the storm, we must be on our way."

Both men turned calculating expressions to Bedelia. Finn found in that moment that she had the slight urge to strangle her friend. If she'd chosen to be polite, they'd likely already be on their way.

"We can offer you shelter for the night," the red-haired man began, "if that is your *only* concern."

Instead of answering, Bedelia flipped her cloak over her shoulder, revealing her armor, and the sword she had begun to wear at her waist once Finn stated that she wouldn't inquire about the armor.

Both men held looks of surprise. "A soldier then?" the darker man asked. "To what lord?"

Bedelia made no further move, except to answer, "One that could easily wipe out your entire contingent, should he find that you *delayed* his general."

The dark haired man frowned while the other looked around nervously. The first thought things over for a moment, then waved Bedelia and Finn away. "Off with you then, and give your *lord* our regards."

Bedelia nodded, then started Rada forward. Finn looked over her shoulder as they passed the men. Both watched the women with a mixture of caution and irritation.

Straightening herself, Finn leaned close to Bedelia's ear to whisper, "They believed you so easily. Why?"

Bedelia snorted, then whispered back. "Look at them," she nodded toward the tents they were now passing, and the uniformed men scattered about. "They're unorganized. Little better than mercenaries. They'd not risk a confrontation with one of the more powerful lords, even if the chances were slim. Calling my bluff would not have been worth the gamble."

"But *who* are they?" Finn whispered, doing her best to avoid eye contact with any of the men they passed.

"It doesn't matter," Bedelia replied. "They've little to do with us, unless you think you'd find your friends among them."

Finn tried to imagine solitary, silent Iseult lounging comfortably and playing cards with some of the men. The thought was almost as humorous as the idea of cantankerous, brazen Àed chumming about with the men who'd questioned them.

"No," Finn replied softly, "I think it very unlikely that we would find them among these men."

"I like your friends more and more," Bedelia mused.

Finn smiled, though as she sat behind Bedelia in the saddle, the other woman couldn't see it. "I look forward to you meeting them," she said happily.

As they continued on in silence, Finn amused herself with thoughts of introducing Bedelia to her friends. Perhaps she would even continue to travel with them, if she had no other place to be. Of course, Finn would need to tell Bedelia the truth about herself first. She felt bad enough for lying to her as it was.

Bedelia had claimed that Migris was only another

day's ride away. The truth would have to come out then, if Finn hoped to maintain her new friendship. Hopefully Iseult and Àed would be there to help Finn explain things. She had no idea where to even start, given that she didn't understand half of what was happening to her.

For now, she'd just have to focus on the first step. Finding Iseult and Àed. She didn't know much about Migris, but she knew that it was very large, and that finding specific people there would be like finding a specific grain of sand in a field. She frowned as a sick feeling settled into her stomach. Making it through wolf attacks and soldier camps was nothing compared to what might be ahead of her.

ANDERS HAD JUST THROWN back his third dram of whiskey, when a group of uniformed men walked into the dank, little tavern residing in the middle of Port Ainfean. He paid them little mind, except to note the red insignia, stamped with a wolf, stitched over their hearts. He thought it an odd insignia for a private militia, but they were not his concern.

"Tell me again how you lost your companions," the little woman behind the bar demanded.

She'd introduced herself as Malida, and though she had many broken teeth, and definitely looked her age, her small brown eyes conveyed a sharp intelligence that Anders found slightly intimidating.

He raked his fingers through his dirty, dusky red hair

in irritation. "I've told you ten times already. The girl's name is Finn. She's small, with light brown hair all the way down to her waist. She was traveling with three men, one around my age, with chestnut colored hair, one a little older, the scariest man I've ever met, and one elderly and short. They also travel with an angry young woman with long, dark brown hair."

"And why do you want to find them?" she asked as she poured more whiskey into his glass.

Anders sighed. "I told you, I've lost my sister to a band of terrifying Faie creatures, and I believe Finn or the old man may be able to help me get her back." He looked down dizzily at his fresh cup of whiskey, then back up at Malida. "You know, if I didn't know any better, I'd say you were trying to get me drunk."

Malida gave him a wry smile. "Your journeys have been long. I'm only trying to help you relax."

Anders looked down at the cup suspiciously, then grabbed it and took another sip. When he'd been unable to find his sister, he'd journeyed to the port. A caravan had been nice enough to pick him up along the way, which was convenient since he'd lost his horse and supplies.

Some of the uniformed men began speaking loudly, drawing Anders' attention back to them. One stood and cleared his throat, then launched into a boastful story, something about defeating a giant, if Anders heard correctly.

Malida's dark haired daughter carried a tray of drinks to the group, then rolled her eyes as she walked away.

Anders shared her sentiments. The man's boasting was obviously a load of drivel.

"Who are they?" Anders asked as he turned back to Malida.

Malida glared past him at the men in question. "They call themselves *An Fiach,* the Hunt. They began to form up once the Tuatha sightings started, though I don't see that they've done much good. Mainly they drive near powerless conjurers and herbwives out of their homes, claiming that they're a danger to their neighbors."

Anders took another sip of his whiskey, though he was already quite drunk. "Do they mean to hunt the Faie? I'd advise them against it. Just look at what happened to my sister."

Malida narrowed her eyes at him. "And what *did* happen to your sister?"

Anders placed his whiskey on the bar and eyed Malida steadily, at least he hoped it was steadily. He felt a bit dizzy. "I've told you ten times already."

Malida leaned forward, but was so short that she had to stand on her tip toes to get closer to Anders over the bar. "I might have seen your friends," she admitted. "They *might* have left here going on several days ago."

Malida's daughter came up behind Anders and grabbed his whiskey, then took a sip. She'd heard his story multiple times as well, since her mother continually made Anders repeat it. "What my mother is trying to say," she began, returning his whiskey to the bar, "is that the little waif Finn left the port with the black haired man and the elderly one. I saw them."

Her mother glared at her. "I hadn't yet decided to trust him," she chastised.

Her daughter snorted. "They've been gone several days already. I don't see that it'll do any harm to let him know."

Anders groaned. He'd never catch up to them at this point.

Both Malida and her daughter's expressions softened. "They can't have gone too far," the daughter comforted.

Anders looked back and forth between the two women, wishing he'd had less to drink so he could leave right that moment. With every second that went by, the hope of ever rescuing his sister dwindled. "Please tell me one of you at least knows where they were heading."

Both looked at him apologetically.

A chair clattered to the ground behind them as one of the uniformed men stood abruptly. It was obvious that the men were not on their first drinks of the night, as the one standing thrust his beverage into the air, declaring that they would hunt the Faie to the ends of the earth. The other men raised their mugs in sloppy good cheer, saluting their comrade.

A thought dawned on Anders, albeit a drunken and not well-planned out one. He stood, excusing himself from Malida and her daughter, then approached the table of soldiers. "*I* know of some Faie that need hunting," he announced loudly.

The men turned toward him as he came to stand, somewhat unsteadily, near their table. "You wouldn't know a Faie if it bit you on the bum," one of the men with a head shaved nearly bald accused with a sneer.

"Not true!" Anders exclaimed, thrusting a finger into the air. "I encountered an entire contingent of creatures that were half horse and half man. They stole my sister."

The man who'd spoken narrowed his eyes at him. "We've heard word of such a force, far west near the Melted Sea."

Anders jaw dropped. The sea was a good week's journey away. He began to feel dizzy, and wasn't quite sure what he was doing speaking to the soldiers.

"That just so happens to be where we're headed," the man went on, "and we could use more able-bodied men."

Anders nodded along with a smile, though the words were all becoming a jumble.

The man stood and offered him a hand. Anders, wondering how the man seemed so steady and well-spoken when too-strong whiskey was floating around the bar, gave the man's hand a hearty shake.

"Welcome aboard!" the man exclaimed, then stood and offered Anders his own seat. "The next round is on me."

He sat down, wondering how he ever thought these men could be blustering fools. He watched his new friend approach Malida at the bar, but the tiny woman's eyes were all for Anders. She looked worried, though he couldn't imagine why.

CHAPTER FOUR

*F*inn craned her neck upward to take in the expanses of the impossibly high city walls as they approached Migris. She was sure she had never seen anything like them, even in her life before she was a tree.

Bedelia glanced around warily as she and Finn walked side by side down the approach to the city, leading Rada behind them. Her condition since being bitten had steadily improved, but she was still weaker than she would admit. Finn could tell by the way she held herself, slightly hunched, and the way her feet lifted off the ground when she walked, as if every step was a struggle.

Bedelia side-stepped a large puddle in the well-worn road. "I've never seen so many refugees gathered before."

Finn observed the clusters of people camped outside the city gates. The camps dotted the landscape for several miles leading up to the city. Most of the people looked cold, tired, and scared. "Where did they all come from?" she whispered, leaning close to Bedelia.

Bedelia shook her head and averted her gaze as they passed a small child playing in the dirt at the side of the road. "It's been ages since I stayed anyplace where I might hear of such news, but I'm sure we'll find out once we're in the city."

Finn's brow furrowed as she watched a group of travelers reach the main gate ahead of them. The gate was lined with soldiers, who all shook their heads tiredly. After a few moments of discussion, the travelers turned away.

"We may not be able to get into the city at all," Finn commented, feeling distressed. Her goal was to ask after her friends in one of the city's inns. Searching through the endless fields of refugees would take weeks.

Bedelia didn't acknowledge Finn's comment, as the rejected travelers passed them by. She instead approached the guards confidently with her bow strapped across her back, and her sword in plain sight.

"No one is allowed entrance into the city," one of the guards stated, not bothering to look up at them.

Bedelia stepped close to the guard, as Finn watched curiously. Bedelia spoke to the man in hushed tones, quiet enough that she couldn't hear what was said.

A moment later, the guard stepped aside and gestured to the man in a lookout post atop the city's wall. The man waved to someone on the other side of the wall, then the gates swung inward to admit Bedelia, Finn, and their horse. Finn tried to catch the eye of one of the guards as they passed through, hoping for an explanation, but the men had already turned back around to meet the next travelers.

Soon Finn forgot all about the strange moment as she was overtaken by the chaos of the great city. Iseult had explained to her that Migris was one of two grand cities, the other being Sormyr, also known as the Gray City. Iseult was from somewhere farther North, but had emigrated from his homeland once it was all but destroyed. Within Migris, Iseult's mother had been executed for an incident blamed on Iseult, though he'd been no more than a child at the time. Finn had a strange feeling of nostalgia as she looked up and down the bustling streets, imagining Iseult running along them as a boy.

Bedelia grabbed Finn's hand, interrupting her revelry to drag her forward. The grasp was necessary. The main street was crammed with people in all different states of dress. Some wore fine winter cloaks, letting Finn know the unseasonable cold had been holding on to the coast just like it had inland, while some wore garb similar to the fishermen and women she'd seen in Port Ainfean, loose, muted fabrics with swatches of cloth used to hold back unkempt hair.

Finn almost stumbled as she took in a woman dressed in strange finery, deep emerald silks with delicate silver embroidery so ornate that Finn thought the clothing must have been created by magic.

Bedelia tugged Finn forward, seemingly unimpressed by the spectacle. Rada pranced nervously behind them, tugging back on the reins in Bedelia's hand, while keeping the city folk from overly crowding the women, lest they get kicked or trampled.

Not wanting to miss a thing, Finn's eyes searched past the people to the buildings. Most were made of heavy, dark wood, and looked like they could withstand the strongest of storms. Many were ten times the size of the largest inns in Ainfean.

A strange bird flying overhead caught Finn's eye. It was pure white with bands of gray, and a thick, yellow beak. It let out a throaty honking sound, soon drowned out by the murmur of conversation in the streets.

"Is the sea near here?" Finn questioned, hoping Bedelia would take the time to answer her, as she seemed to be in a hurry.

Bedelia looked over her shoulder at Finn, startling her with the paleness of her face, and the sweat on her brow.

"Oh you're not well!" Finn exclaimed.

Bedelia cringed, then turned forward to continue walking. "I'm fine, and yes, the sea is near. Can't you smell it?"

As a matter of fact, she could. The chilly air was permeated with a salty, fishy smell. The smell plucked at something primal deep within her, something that cautioned those that thought they might conquer the sea, yet drew them in all the same.

Bedelia began walking again, dragging Finn toward one of the imposingly large inns. The inn boasted a massive, ornate, rectangular sign, with curving waves and ships carved across its surface. More deeply carved was the inn's name, *The Melted Sea*, named after the nearby coast that Finn was finding herself almost desperate to see.

A man dressed more like a fisherman than a stableman stood at attention as Bedelia handed him Rada's reins, giving him strict instructions on her horse's care. She placed several coins in his grubby hand, and he assured her that Rada would be well cared for. As soon as the stableman led Rada away, Bedelia led Finn inside, shoving rudely past the loitering travelers partially blocking the wide doorway.

Finn glanced apologetically back at them as they ventured inside. The inn's interior was no less grand than the exterior, strewn with gleaming wood tables and heavy brass lanterns. The scent of food hit Finn's nostrils, making her salivate after being on road rations for the past few days.

She was forced between a group of women attempting to reach the bar and the presiding innkeep as Bedelia shouldered her way forward. The women were dressed in ornate silks like Finn had seen on the street, and all turned identical, calculating looks to her as she made her way past them. She shivered, uncomfortable with the attention the women were giving her, but then as one, they turned away, dismissing her.

Once at the bar, Bedelia lifted her hand to catch the innkeep's attention. He strode forward, ignoring all of the patrons who'd arrived before them. Finn gasped as the man came to a halt in front of them, with only the narrow bar to keep them apart. He was tall, as tall as Iseult, and had the same dark hair and greenish gray eyes, like those of a large, predatory, cat. He wore a fine, gray woolen tunic, and simple breeches.

The innkeep's eyes landed on Finn for a moment, then moved back to Bedelia.

Bedelia pulled Finn close to her side, then let go of her hand. "We need a room, Maarav," Bedelia stated.

Maarav. Finn wracked her brain for some meaning to the name, perhaps something Iseult had mentioned. They looked similar enough to be brothers. Bedelia obviously knew him. Perhaps Finn could ask her later.

Maarav swept one of his long arms outward, encompassing the tightly packed patrons. "As you can see, we're very busy, my dear ladies."

Bedelia quirked her mouth into a half-smile. "We *need* a room, *Maarav*," she repeated.

He chuckled, then reached underneath the bar. His hand reappeared to produce a key, which he placed on the bar, then slid toward Bedelia. As soon as his hand retreated, Bedelia swiped up the key and strode away, once again leading Finn.

"You didn't pay him," Finn whispered as they pushed their way back through the crowd.

"I will later," Bedelia answered vaguely.

Finn glanced back over her shoulder at Maarav, who watched her with a small smile. Their eyes met, and there was something there, like he knew something she wanted to know, and knew that she knew he knew it. Finn lost sight of him as he moved to help another patron, and Bedelia began leading her up the wide stairs in the far corner of the room.

"We left our supplies on Rada," Finn realized as she tried to keep up with Bedelia on the stairs. Bedelia probably shouldn't have been overexerting herself in her current condition, but Finn knew there would be no arguing with her.

She didn't look back as she replied. "They'll be brought up to our room, don't worry."

Finn *did* worry. She worried about Maarav, looking at her like he knew her, and she worried about the Cavari snatching her away again. Most of all she worried about herself, and whether or not she would panic and cause the earth to come up and swallow the inn whole.

Resigned, Finn followed Bedelia the rest of the way up the stairs to pause in front of one of the first rooms. Bedelia unlocked the door with the key Maarav had given her, then held it open for Finn to enter.

The room inside was simple, with two beds, a table, and a roaring fire already going in a large, stone fireplace. The whitewashed walls made the room seem larger than it was.

"We should let the innkeep know to keep an eye out for my friends," Finn burst out, unable to contain her anxiety as she entered the room and turned on Bedelia.

Bedelia nodded, then shut the door behind them, not doing as Finn asked at all. "Let's have some tea first," she said as she moved to a table near the single window. At Finn's frantic expression, she added, "I'm not feeling well."

Suddenly feeling horribly guilty about disregarding Bedelia's physical state, she rushed over to the table where Bedelia was filling a kettle from a small, clay jug of water. Bedelia ignored her attempt to help, pushing past her to hang the kettle over the fire.

Resigned, Finn slumped down onto one of the beds to wait.

Once the kettle was hot, Bedelia retrieved it with a cloth, then brought it back to the table. She looked over her shoulder at Finn, who was watching her intently.

A knock sounded on the door.

"That's our supplies," Bedelia explained, sounding relieved.

Finn did not question her friend's relief, as she was also worried about their belongings. Finn answered the door, retrieving the saddle bags from a woman dressed in the tight corset and gathered skirts she'd seen some of the barmaids wearing, while Bedelia finished the tea.

Placing their belongings at the foot of one bed, Finn went to sit on the other bed with Bedelia, who handed her a steaming mug.

Finn blew on the hot liquid, then gingerly took a sip. "What type of tea is this?" she questioned, finding the taste strange and bitter.

Bedelia sipped her tea. "It's a restorative. You'll feel good as new in no time." She gestured to Finn's cup. "Drink up."

Finn did as she was bade, sipping the tea as quickly as the temperature would allow. Not long after emptying the cup's contents, she began to feel sleepy. *Very* sleepy.

She turned to Bedelia to once again ask just what was in the tea, then she slumped to the bed, dead asleep.

～

BEDELIA SMILED WICKEDLY as Finn fell fast asleep, just as she'd planned. The powder she'd added to Finn's mug of tea wouldn't hurt her at all, in fact, she'd get a nice, peaceful rest as a result. She couldn't have Finn getting suspicious of her actions, nor could she risk losing her in the city streets.

After placing a blanket over Finn, Bedelia stood and left the room quickly, locking the door behind her. She still felt overwhelmingly ill, but she had things she needed to attend to. It had been Keiren's plan for her to bring Finn to Migris. Now that she'd accomplished that step, she needed to move onto the next.

She descended the stairs quickly, ignoring the throbbing pain in her leg. The common room had grown busy with the evening crowds, making it easy for Bedelia to slip out without drawing any attention to herself.

As she exited, she glanced at Maarav, serving wine to a finely dressed trio of ladies. His eyes didn't rise to notice her, which was for the best. Though Maarav and Bedelia had a business understanding, he did not know the intricacies of her life, and she didn't want him observing her any more than was necessary. It was better that way. Bedelia had many secrets she would take with her to the grave.

She wrapped her cloak tightly around her shoulders

as she hurried out into the cold evening air. The streets were crowded, but Bedelia managed to dart from alleyway to alleyway unhindered. She'd been told that she was to meet someone, but she didn't know who, or *why*.

She had brought the girl to Migris and gained her trust all on her own, and did not feel that a partner was needed at this point, but she trusted Keiren's judgment above all else. She thought back to Finn asleep in their room. She felt almost bad for tricking her, but it wasn't like the herbs would cause any harm.

As she walked she felt eyes on her back, but when she turned around, there didn't appear to be anyone watching her. Ignoring the feeling of unease, she continued on in the direction of the meeting point. She slipped past the happy people hopping from tavern to tavern, down an alleyway that would lead her to a more rundown area of town. The feeling of eyes on her remained. It was not wise for a woman to walk alone at night in the part of town she'd entered. Any number of thieves could be watching her. Luckily, Bedelia was no ordinary woman.

"It's about time," a voice called from the darkness behind her.

She'd left her bow at the inn, but reached her hand beneath her cloak to grip the dagger that rested at her hip. She spun on her possible assailant.

"You!" she gasped.

The man's hair glinted silver in the moonlight. His unusually pale eyes held laughter, crinkling his slightly lined, but handsome face. "Surprised to see me, my lady?"

Bedelia took a step back, her dagger trembling in her hand. "What do you want, Óengus?" she demanded, hating the slight quavering in her voice.

"I'm here to meet you," he explained as he took a step forward, bathing himself further in the moonlight. A black cloak disguised his body, perfect for slipping away unnoticed in the night after committing one crime or another. "I'm told you need help with a rather interesting . . . package."

"You're mistaken," she snapped, backing further away. If she could put enough distance between Óengus and herself, she'd be able to turn her back and flee.

Óengus shook his head and tsked at her. "Two weeks past, I met a fiery-haired woman in the woods, beautiful and tall, with pale blue eyes. She told me many interesting things, then left me with a mission. I was well on my way when she visited again, explaining that I must meet some poor, scared little girl in Migris, who needed help doing her job."

Bedelia felt heat creeping up her face. Keiren would never refer to her in such a way. It was ridiculous. Wasn't it? "You're lying," she accused.

Óengus tsked again and closed the small distance between them. "I've dealt with the tree girl before," he explained. "I've been looking forward to another go at it."

Bedelia felt like she might cry, but she would rather endure torture than give Óengus the satisfaction. "I don't believe you. You're just trying to steal the girl from me."

Óengus' icy eyes glinted in the moonlight as he smiled. "Your lady told me to offer you a message. She said, *Do not argue mo leon baineann. We all do what we must.*"

Bedelia sucked in a breath and held it for so long that she thought she might faint. *Mo leon baineann.* My lioness. It was Keiren's pet name for her, used only in private. Keiren really had sent Óengus to her, but why? She knew how hard Bedelia had worked to escape him, so many years before.

She tensed her jaw in frustration. "What is our plan?"

Óengus bared his teeth in a wicked smile. He knew he had her. Bedelia had a feeling that this time, she might not escape him like she'd managed in the past.

FINN HAD WOKEN to an empty room. She couldn't believe she'd fallen asleep so suddenly. She could tell by the noise of the common room that it was still relatively early, and her suspicions were verified by her missing companion. Bedelia had likely gone in search of supper.

She left her room to creep down the inn's wide stairs, wishing she had something to wear other than her tattered, dirty dress. Unfortunately, she was stuck with it, and she was too hungry to let her appearance stop her.

She reached the landing and was accosted by the din of conversation, flavored with the scent of food in the air. The inn was packed. There were almost enough chairs for most of the patrons, but not quite. A few groups stood off in corners while they ate their meals.

Finn's mouth watered. Everything smelled delicious, but she had no coin. She looked past the many patrons to the bar. Maarav was still there serving wine and whiskey, though now he had several serving maids tending the tables, balancing large trays of food like they weighed nothing.

Maarav glanced at Finn as she approached, then began wiping the bar with a clean cloth. She was hesitant to talk to him, as she knew little about him, and had fallen asleep before she could prod Bedelia for information, but the call of food won out. If Bedelia could pay him later for the room, perhaps Finn could pay him later for food. If she happened to find out some information on him in the process, then so be it.

Before she had moved forward far enough to ask him, his eyes met hers. Not looking away, he raised his hand to catch the attention of one of the serving maids, then pointed to Finn. A moment later, the girl approached and handed Finn a bowl of stew and two fresh slices of bread from her large tray.

Finn took the food in hand awkwardly, then looked around for a place to sit. Once again acting first, Maarav stared down a man who had a seat at the bar, then gestured for him to move. The man did as he was bade, not offering a single argument. Maarav motioned for Finn to take the vacated seat.

Entirely regretting her decision to leave her room in the first place, Finn shuffled forward, bowl and bread in hand. She climbed into the seat and set both on the bar as Maarav placed a pewter mug of wine in front of her.

"Thank you," she muttered.

He nodded. "Any friend of Bedelia's is a friend of mine."

Finn nodded, as her resolve suddenly left her. How had she ever thought to wheedle information out of him? She was a terrible liar, and the only way she knew to gain information was to ask questions directly.

When Maarav didn't walk away, she took a deep breath, summoning her courage, then looked up to meet his intense, gray-green eyes. "It seems you're quite busy," she said politely, hoping he would take the hint to leave her alone.

He smiled wryly. "Though that is true, I'd never leave a woman as lovely as you sitting alone at my bar."

Finn frowned, then glanced down the length of the bar to see several lovely women waiting to be attended, then turned her gaze back to him.

"Eat your food," he instructed.

She did as he asked, though she felt increasingly uncomfortable with him watching her. Unable to take the odd situation any longer, she asked, "Have you always lived in Migris?"

He inclined his head. "For the most part."

"And Bedelia, how do you know her?" she pressed.

He raised an eyebrow. "If she has not told you, then perhaps she doesn't want you to know."

"I'm sorry-" she began.

"My turn," he cut her off.

Finn gasped at the abrupt turn in conversation, then stared back at him, too befuddled to speak.

His black hair fell forward as he leaned over the bar, bringing his gaze close enough that it would have been awkward for her to look away. "I know your face. Normally, I would brush it off as perhaps a family resemblance, but given these times, and the rumors floating about, I do not think your appearance mere coincidence. Now tell me, how is it that you happen to be sitting right in front of me? By the records, you should be long dead."

Finn's head was spinning, and she felt like she might vomit from anxiety. *The records*, he'd said. Iseult had previously explained to Finn that he'd recognized her face from a book his mother had shown him. He'd known who she was, even before she figured it out herself. Could this man, who looked so very much like Iseult, have seen the same book?

"I don't know what you're talking about," she breathed.

He leaned a little closer. "The look on your face says otherwise."

She stood abruptly and pushed away from the bar. The Cavari had eradicated Iseult's people, the people of Uí Néid, from the face of the earth. If Maarav was also from Uí Néid, Finn had little doubt of his intentions. She had learned much on the nature of man over the past weeks. Iseult, who wanted to right his people's wrongs, was a special case. Anyone else would just want revenge upon any directly responsible for their undoing.

Maarav made no move to stop her as she stumbled

away, abandoning her wine and supper. Not looking where she was going in the crowded room, she accidentally ran into a tall, thin man in a neutral gray cloak. Thrown off balance, she fell to her knees. The tall man crouched down to aid her, but her eyes were all for the area where Maarav had stood. He was gone, and in his place was one of the serving maids.

She finally turned her attention to the man she'd collided with as he helped her to her feet. First she noticed his impossibly long, pale fingers that gripped her trembling hand. Her gaze raced upward to take in the translucent skin of his face, and oddly reflective eyes. Most of his head was covered by the hood of his cloak, but she could tell that he didn't have any hair. A few of the inn's patrons cast nervous glances his way, but most quickly returned to their meals.

"*You*," she whispered, with her hand still gripped lightly in his.

The Traveler inclined his head. Though many of the Ceàrdaman looked alike, there was no mistaking *this* man. The last time Finn had seen him, she and Kai were rescuing Anna, at that time known to Finn as Liaden. Finn was pretty sure she'd broken the Traveler's nose that night, but it looked perfectly straight now. Perhaps she'd only bloodied it. She hadn't stuck around to see, as an army of Faie had arrived to slaughter the Travelers, thus releasing the Faie from the Blood Forest.

Still gripping Finn's hand, he turned and led her toward the far side of the room. She tugged back against his grasp, but his grip was iron tight. Unable to free herself, she glanced over her shoulder as she was pulled along, but Maarav was still nowhere to be seen. She wasn't sure why she even looked, as he had no reason to aid her. Still, he'd claimed that any friend of Bedelia was a friend of his. Perhaps that would hold true, to an extent.

Finn moved forward, lest she lose her feet. She might have fought harder if the Traveler was leading her up the stairs or out the front door, but he seemed to be headed toward an empty table against the wall. The empty table was an odd sight, since the rest of the establishment was brimming with people, but she didn't question it. The Ceàrdaman had their *ways.*

The Traveler dropped Finn's hand as they reached the table, then gestured for her to sit. She glanced nervously around, then did as he bade. If he only wanted to talk, she would happily accommodate him. She had no love for the Travelers, but this one had given her information in the past, and he might do so again. Of course, Liaden had been the price for the previous information. She was unsure of what he might want this time.

The Traveler lowered his lanky form into the seat opposite her, then steepled his fingers in front of his face, leaning his elbows on the table. He eyed her for a long while, then opened his thin, bloodless lips to speak. "I've come to offer you a deal."

Finn wasn't surprised. The Travelers were fond of deals. "Will I be told the terms of this deal beforehand?" she asked bitterly.

He inclined his head. "Your people have resurfaced."

She quirked her lip, pleased to know something before the Traveler deigned to tell it to her. "So *that's* who stole me away from my friends while we slept," she said sarcastically. "I had *no* idea."

Finn's satisfaction grew as surprise swept across the Traveler's face. "Then you know why they want you back?"

Her stomach dropped. She didn't know, as she had avoided meeting them.

"Ah," he said at her expression. "Not so knowledge-able after all."

Finn glared at him. "Will you offer your deal, or not?"

He chuckled, but his mirth was soon replaced by a stony expression as he explained, "We would like you to join us against the Cavari."

Finn chewed her lip in thought. "You would ask me to fight against my own people?"

The Traveler rolled his eyes. "Your people would only use you. No one likes to be used, my dear."

She stared him down. "*No,* they *don't.*"

The Traveler looked almost abashed, but Finn doubted it was little more than a ruse. When she didn't buy in to the expression, his face fell back into its apathetic lines. "We offer you a partnership, *this time.*"

Finn scoffed, not believing the offer. Still, she wanted to know why such a proposition was being offered to begin with. "How would such a partnership benefit me?" she asked slyly.

The Traveler cocked his head. "One would think that

rescuing you from your people would be incentive enough."

Finn glanced around the room once again for Maarav, concerned by the meaning of his disappearance. She felt at that moment she needed a lot more rescuing than the Traveler had to offer. "Do they intend to harm me?" she asked, hoping to glean more information.

The Traveler snorted. "The last time they finished with you, they stuck you in the ground for one-hundred years. What do you think they'll do *this* time?"

Finn looked down at her lap. Being a tree hadn't been bad. In fact, she missed the simplicity of such a life every day. Still, she was not sure if she'd taken that form willingly, and could admit that she was no longer sure if she'd like to do so again.

The Traveler smiled, showcasing his perfect, white teeth. "I see I've gained your attention."

He had, but not in the way he thought. She would never enter a partnership with the Travelers, especially not while she still held out hope of finding Iseult and Àed. "What's your name?" she asked, trying to buy time while she thought of how to phrase a more meaningful question.

This time, the Traveler looked genuinely perplexed. "We do not have names among my people," he stated finally, then paused as if deep in thought, "but you may call me Niklas."

The front door to the inn opened and shut with a loud *bang*. Finn whipped around at the noise to see Bedelia standing near the door, scanning the common room. Finn turned quickly back to Niklas, wanting to voice her question before Bedelia spotted her. "Niklas," she began nervously, "why would you offer me partnership? What is my true purpose?"

He leaned in close, as if afraid that someone might overhear. "My dear Finn," he began softly, "you are a weapon."

Finn froze. It couldn't be true. She'd been told she was a high priestess of sorts. She was a person, not a sword. She sensed it the moment Bedelia's eyes found her, and turned in her seat to ward the woman away. She needed more time with Niklas.

Her eyes met Bedelia's. The other woman started forward, but Finn subtly used her hand to shoo her back. Bedelia halted, but looked confused, prompting Finn to look back over her shoulder. Niklas was gone.

She turned back to Bedelia with a defeated expression, prompting her friend to close the rest of the distance between them. As Bedelia neared, Finn finally noticed her puffy, red-rimmed eyes and disheveled appearance.

"What happened?" Finn asked as she stood and took Bedelia's hand in hers.

Bedelia flinched as if Finn had struck her, then shook her loose, brown hair forward to partially obscure her face.

"*What* happened?" Finn demanded more firmly, ready to hunt down whoever had harmed her friend. She had no idea where her courage came from, when just a moment before she had been internally trembling at the Traveler's presence.

Bedelia shook her head. "I'm tired. Did Maarav feed you?"

Finn bit her lip. Had Bedelia asked Maarav to watch over her? "Yes," she replied quickly, glad that it wasn't actually a lie. He *had* provided her with food, she simply hadn't eaten much of it.

Bedelia nodded, a distant expression on her face, then walked past Finn toward the stairs. Finn hurried after her, glancing around for any sign of Maarav or Niklas. When neither man presented himself, she followed Bedelia up the stairs to their room.

Once inside, Bedelia went straight for her bed, curling up with her back toward Finn. Finn shut and locked the door behind them, then approached the bed where Bedelia lay.

"Bedelia, *please*," she pleaded, wanting desperately to know what had happened to her friend.

With a sigh, Bedelia rolled onto her back and looked up at Finn, who stood over her. "Do you remember when I told you that I escaped from my previous lord?"

She nodded, then took a seat on the bed beside Bedelia. "I asked if he'd been a cruel lord, but you never really answered me."

Bedelia closed her eyes for several heartbeats, then opened them slowly. "He was not quite a *lord*, but he was a cruel master. I encountered him tonight."

Finn waited for her to say more, but instead she turned her head to the side, avoiding Finn's gaze.

"Should we leave the inn?" Finn pressed. "Is he after you?"

Bedelia shook her head gently, still not meeting Finn's eyes. "Maarav would not allow such a man inside his inn. We are safe . . . for tonight."

"About Maarav," Finn began, not feeling safe despite Bedelia's assurances. He was the innkeep, and she didn't like the idea of a possible enemy having access to their room.

"I'm tired," Bedelia cut her off. "Tomorrow we will move on from the city. You have nothing to worry about."

Finn felt near tears herself, but didn't have the heart to ask her friend once more if they should leave the inn. More distressing still, was the news that Bedelia wanted to leave the city already. Finn couldn't leave. Being in Migris was her best chance of finding Iseult and Àed. Bedelia had said so herself.

Feeling numb, she stood, climbed onto her own bed, then snuffed out the lantern that rested on a little table beside her. She closed her eyes and tried to rest, but couldn't quite ignore the sniffles and gentle sobs coming from the other bed, just a few feet away.

THE SOLDIER SIGHED. Over the past week the guard in Migris had been doubled, then tripled. He didn't see what good it would do against the Tuatha Dé Danann. If the Faie came for Migris, the city would fall. The extra soldiers would only mean more bodies. He'd heard about *An Fiach*, the Hunt, but doubted half of the stories. Twenty men would stand no chance against a giant.

His comrade, Galen, shifted his weight impatiently. "General Eisen must have been bladdered when he gave his commands," he grumbled. "What good does it do to stare out into the darkness? Why not post a small watch and let the majority rest?"

The soldier turned to Galen, a snide comment on the tip of his tongue, but his eyes were met with only darkness. "Galen?" he questioned.

No reply.

The soldier turned to glance in the other direction, but was interrupted by a sharp pain in his gut. He gasped as he looked down to find a knife protruding from his belly, its pommel gripped by a black-gloved hand. The hand gave a tug, withdrawing the knife as the soldier slumped to the ground.

He tried to look up at his attacker, but the fiend's face was concealed deep within a cloak. "Find the girl," the form whispered in a feminine voice, not to the soldier, but to someone standing behind her.

There was no reply, only the barest sound of soft-booted footsteps as the soldier's vision faded to black.

*A*nders gazed up at the castle ruins ahead of them. His fellow soldiers had not taken long to find the trail of the man-horse creatures that stole Branwen away. Rumors ran rampant through the nearby burghs of murdered travelers, and the pounding of hooves in the night. Tracks had been found, leading them right to this place, far away from the main road.

Though Anders desperately wanted to find his sister, he'd grown increasingly nervous as the hoof prints of the creatures had become more pronounced in the mud. Radley, the leader of his contingent, had remarked that they were nearing their quarry, as the tracks couldn't have been more than a day or two old.

A battle might soon come to pass, but Anders wasn't really a soldier, not like the other men. He was a man of books and logic, and had never even felt the need to throw a punch. He shifted uncomfortably in his dark brown uniform, and nervously stroked the pommel of his newly acquired sword as Radley investigated the final prints.

Said prints ended at the ruined castle, though Anders doubted the creatures had gone inside. He looked up at the crumbling stone, overgrown with foliage in places where the stone had eroded into nothing. The structure seemed like it had been abandoned a very long time ago.

"In we go," Radley remarked, straightening himself from where he'd crouched in front of the prints. He swiped a hand over his close-shaven head absentmindedly as he looked up at the ruins. "Mind your steps as we make our way, lads. I don't want to hear any of you complaining about twisted ankles."

Anders wiped the cold sweat from his brow, and looked back to where they'd tied their horses in a nearby copse of trees. A fast getaway wasn't likely. Radley didn't seem worried, but Anders was quite sure that the man had never felt fear or worry in his entire life.

He did his best to appear confident as he walked amidst his companions toward the castle, though he ran a hand over his hair self-consciously. Most of the men wore braids above their ears, sort of an extension of the uniform, and wanting to fit in, Anders had done the same. He thought it less obvious than shaving his head like Radley.

He'd been told there were much larger factions of An Fiach out there, but Radley claimed most of them were fools and children. Anders would believe most anything Radley told him on that front, the man was capable of bringing down giants, after all.

Radley reached the entrance of the structure first, little more than a crumbling hole in the wall. Whatever door had once sealed it had long since rotted or turned to ash. Radley signaled those closest to him to halt, then journeyed into the dark ruins on his own. A few minutes later his hand emerged from the entrance, waving the men inside.

Torches were lit and one was handed to Anders, marking him as one of the men who would venture inside, though he wasn't singled out. Most everyone filed into the dark building, leaving five or six men outside to stand guard. Anders didn't think it likely that he'd find his sister in the ruins, but a small, nagging sliver of hope guided him forward.

The inside of the building stank like a mixture of chamber pot and rotting flesh, though the floor was clear of debris. The men fanned out in search of the source of the smell, or anything else. It was a truly expansive building, and each of the men were able to move in a different direction without traveling in pairs.

As Anders journeyed further into the building, signs of inhabitance became apparent. He kicked an old blanket aside to reveal several pieces of crumpled parchment, which he crouched to read, but found nothing of value. Mainly they were supply lists.

He stood, holding the small torch in front of him to light his way as he entered a windowless room, less eroded than much of the building. The smell intensified tenfold. Not wanting to be the one who had to examine the source of the smell, he almost turned around, but he forced himself to continue. If there was even a chance that the horrid stench was his sister's corpse, he needed to be the one to find it. She didn't deserve to be gawked at by an entire contingent of men.

Tears threatening at the back of his eyes, Anders held the torch up to the nearest walls to reveal a light splattering of blood. He swallowed and instantly regretted it as the smell that coated his sinuses made its way down his throat. He took a moment to steady himself, then moved his light across the rest of the room. There was a large shape in the corner. The source of the smell.

He edged closer. He could hear the sounds of the other men, exploring the expanses of the castle, but none neared him. With a final prayer, he lowered the light to the shape, then reeled away at what he saw.

It wasn't Branwen. The body at his feet was twisted and mangled, obviously tortured, but it wasn't his sister. It was one of the horse creatures. Its entire form was covered in lacerations, and most of its limbs were badly broken.

Anders took a few steps back, then called out, "I found something!"

One of the younger men was the first to find him, but the lad quickly stepped aside as Radley came charging in. Anders held the torch out at his side to illuminate the corpse for his commander. "This was one of the creatures that stole my sister," he explained, doing his best to not run and vomit.

Radley crouched down beside the corpse. If he was bothered by the smell, he didn't show it. He rubbed his thumb and forefinger across his stubbly chin in thought. After several long minutes, he stood.

Anders and the few other men who had entered the room waited for an explanation, but Radley turned and strode forward silently, leaving the room and the mangled corpse behind.

After a moment of surprise, Anders jogged past the other men now examining the corpse to catch up with Radley as he left the castle. "Where do we go from here?" Anders demanded as he fell into step at Radley's side. "There are still scores of these creatures out there, and they likely still have my sister."

Finally Radley stopped and faced Anders. "Worried about these creatures, are you?"

Perplexed, Anders just stared at Radley slack-jawed. Eventually he realized that the question hadn't been rhetorical and answered, "Yes, of course I am. They kidnapped my sister, and who knows how many others they've harmed along the way."

Radley frowned and sucked his teeth, unimpressed. "I'd say what we really have to worry about, is whatever did *that* in there. These creatures who took your sister might be fearsome in their own right, but imagine a creature capable of mangling one in such a way."

Anders found himself stunned once more.

Another soldier, a man by the name of Wallcot, trotted out the castle entrance toward Radley and Anders, carrying some sort of fabric in his hand. "I think this might be of interest," he commented as he reached them. "The blood on the hem is fresh."

Before Radley could even take a look, Anders snatched the fabric away from Wallcot and examined it frantically. He recognized that burgundy color, and the darker color of the large patch where the fabric had once been torn. The blood on the hem was indeed fresh.

Radley put his heavy hand on Anders shoulder. "I take it this cloak means something to you?"

Anders couldn't tear his eyes away from what he held in his hands. He nodded numbly. "It was my sister's."

"WAKE UP," Bedelia demanded, shaking Finn briskly by the shoulders.

Finn's eyes snapped open as she sat up, freeing herself from Bedelia's grasp. She glanced out the room's small window to see only the barest hint of sunlight. "It's barely dawn," she groaned.

Bedelia stood and began pacing. "I need you to pack up our things, and be ready to leave at a moment's notice."

"Wha-" Finn began, but Bedelia cut her off with a sharp look.

Bedelia approached Finn a little too quickly, making her flinch away from the woman's confusing fervor. Bedelia stopped, and let her hands fall to her sides. "You'll just have to trust me," she pleaded. "And please, don't leave this room. It's not safe. I'll be back to get you as soon as I've secured a ship."

"A ship?" Finn questioned weakly, still sitting motionless in bed.

Bedelia nodded. "We'll not escape any other way. Now promise me you won't leave this room until I return."

Finn's eyes widened, but she nodded.

Seemingly satisfied, Bedelia donned her cloak over her armor and left the room, slamming the door shut behind herself with a loud bang.

Finn jumped at the sound, then sunk back into her bedding, deep in thought. The previous night had been confusing, at best, and now Bedelia wanted to sneak away onto a ship. Finn pawed nervously at her tangled hair. She felt a kinship with Bedelia, and wanted to trust her, but if there was anything she'd learned over the past few weeks, it was that she shouldn't trust anyone . . . except for Iseult and Àed, that was.

She rose from her bed and began to pack Bedelia's supplies. She would wait for her friend to return, then demand an explanation. Even if Bedelia had one, she wouldn't be getting on that ship. She'd come to Migris to find her friends, and she wasn't leaving until she did just that. For all she knew, they could be reaching the city gates at that very moment.

Once she'd finished packing and straightening the room, she paced back and forth across the creaky, wooden floor. Her footsteps seemed to be keeping rhythm with her heart as she tried to focus on *anything* but the unbearable feeling of waiting. Bedelia had been gone over an hour, and Finn had long since lost her patience. While she was packing, she'd eaten some stale bread from their rations, so she was no longer starving, yet remaining in the small room was becoming near impossible, not only because she needed to speak with Bedelia, but because she didn't feel at all safe in the inn. She could just imagine Maarav downstairs, planning some sort of trap while she sat around like livestock waiting to be slaughtered.

A shout paused her mid-pace. She waited, perfectly still, as more shouting ensued, filtering in through the room's small window. She strode forward to look outside, curious about the clamor below. Using the window curtains to obscure herself as much as possible, she glanced down through the opening to see men milling about in brown uniforms, the same sort of men she and Bedelia had encountered on the road. A few of them stood apart from the others, questioning an old woman.

Finn doubted the tiny woman would even reach her shoulder in height, yet her ferocity held the three uniformed men at bay as they attempted to intimidate her. Onlookers had gathered around, yet none stepped in to help.

Sensing an opportunity to get some information, Finn turned and went for the door. Surely Bedelia couldn't be mad at her for leaving to aid an old woman.

Finn left the room and shut the door behind her. Bedelia had taken the only key, so she couldn't lock it, but she'd just be right outside anyhow. She hurried down the stairs and let out her breath when she saw that

Maarav wasn't in the common room. She ventured out of the inn without paying much mind to the few patrons.

She began to feel more confident once exposed to the brisk morning air. Though she'd grown accustomed to human comforts, she still felt more at ease out in the sunlight. She hurried toward where she'd seen the old woman, being careful not to slosh through any mud puddles that dotted the wide, dirt street. The shouting had escalated, spurring her onward.

She rounded a corner and saw a uniformed man take hold of the old woman's arm. The woman continued to screech as he began to drag her away, but the onlookers did not aid her. Finn was surprised to see that even a few of the city guards watched the spectacle, making no move to interfere.

Mustering all her courage, Finn pushed her way through the gawking people, then shoved herself in between the old woman and the soldier.

The man stopped his movements and looked down at Finn with impassive eyes, while the old woman gasped in surprise.

Finn felt like her stomach had turned to mush, but she forced herself to stand tall. "Is there a reason you're dragging this poor old woman away?" she demanded.

The man only stared at her, but one of the other soldiers stepped forward. He didn't look old enough to be a soldier, his scrawny shoulders barely filling out the jacket of his uniform. "We must question any who might be involved with Tuatha magic, lass," he explained with a heavy accent, similar to the way Àed spoke.

"I'm but a simple herbwife!" the woman screeched from behind Finn.

Finn looked at the men like they were being silly. "You truly believe that this old woman could mean harm to this city?"

The younger man blushed, but the other two soldiers just stared at Finn blankly. The rest of their entourage shifted uncomfortably, some of the men looked the other way like they weren't part of the spectacle. The one who'd grabbed the old woman crossed his arms. Once it became apparent that Finn had no intention of moving, he stated, "We are within our rights to question her, and to question you as well for aiding an alleged cohort of the Faie."

Finn's eyes widened and all of her bluster came crashing down. She took a step back, moving the herb-wife with her. The man reached forward to take hold of Finn, then someone in the distance screamed. He hesitated, looking over his shoulder toward the sound.

"A body!" someone else screamed.

The guards who'd been watching the spectacle finally rustled into motion, while the onlookers moved to get a peek at the new spectacle.

At that moment, caring more about her own life than that of a stranger whose life was already lost, Finn turned and pushed the old woman along. They entered the nearest alleyway, opposite the direction of the alleged dead body, then the herbwife took charge.

"This way, lass," she whispered, taking hold of Finn's wrist to hurry her along.

Confused by the sudden trade off, Finn didn't argue.

The herbwife tugged her down another short back road, then turned a sharp corner. Finn's wrist was finally released as the old woman began searching the various pockets of her baggy dress while standing in front of a shabby door. Finn looked over her shoulder for any signs of pursuit, then heard the jingle of keys. She looked back to watch the old woman unlock the door.

"Come inside, lass," she instructed.

Finn took a step back. "I can't. My friend will be looking for me. I wasn't supposed to leave the inn."

The old woman rolled an eye at her. Now that Finn had the time to actually observe the woman's appearance, she noticed that the other eye was clouded over and didn't move with the good one. The woman had a mop of frizzy, dark gray hair, but didn't bother using it to cover the bad eye. She grinned, showcasing the few teeth she had left. "You'll not want to be seen until those men give up searching," she explained. "When they say they'll *question* you, what they really mean is they'll put you in a large iron cage and burn you alive."

Finn gasped, then allowed the herbwife to pull her through the doorway.

She had expected an interior as unkempt as the herbwife, but instead walked into a small, cozy home, squeaky clean and organized. There was a small stove, surrounded by bundles of drying herbs, with a large cauldron of liquid boiling on its surface. Next to the stove were shelves upon shelves of glass vials, and larger containers holding dried roots and herbs.

The opposite side of the room held a small, straw mat for sleeping, a large basin of water, and several other pots similar to the one on the stove, stacked neatly and ready for use.

The space was lit by small windows placed high in the wall, too high to see out of, but expansive enough to let in a fair amount of sunlight. The herbwife had lowered herself into one of the four chairs that surrounded a small, circular table in the center of the room.

"Please sit," she instructed. "You're making me nervous hovering about like that."

Finn sat quickly, blushing with embarrassment.

The silence stretched out, making Finn feel like she might burst with anxiety. "Why were those men hassling you?" she asked suddenly, unable to keep it in any longer.

"They're called *An Fiach*," the old woman explained with a sigh. "They intend to eradicate the Faie before another war can begin, but if you ask me, the war has already started. I've heard many stories, and I've treated my fair share of Faie inflicted injuries. At least, I treated them before the guard closed the gates to refugees and travelers alike."

"Injuries?" Finn questioned distantly, thinking of Bedelia's bite.

The woman shrugged. "Sometimes infected bites or scrapes, but more often they are injuries of the mind. Some I can help, some I cannot."

That gave Finn even more to think about. Perhaps she could fix Branwen . . . if she ever found her. "What about a wolf bite?" Finn asked hopefully.

The woman raised an eyebrow. "Normally I'd ask what a wolf bite might have to do with the Faie, but my guess is you're not talking about ordinary wolves."

Finn leaned forward in her seat. "So there have been others?"

The herbwife nodded. "Several others. Those wolves have invaded the forested regions all around Migris over the past two weeks." She looked Finn up and down. "I take it you're asking for someone else? You don't seem ill."

"My friend," Finn admitted. "She was bitten a few days ago. She claims she's fine, but I can tell she's not feeling well."

"She'll feel much worse before long," the old woman said as she stood. "The bite of the Faie wolves is poisonous."

Finn gasped and stood abruptly. "I must warn her!"

The herbwife rolled her good eye. "Sit down, lass. I'll brew her up a tincture that will make her vibrant once more."

Finn slumped back to her chair in relief as the woman approached her stove. She began to crumple herbs into the boiling pot. "What's your name, anyhow?"

"Branwen," Finn answered, giving her the same lie she'd given Bedelia, a lie she still felt guilty over.

"I'm Venetia," the herbwife replied as she began collecting several small vials from the shelves beside the stove, leaving the liquid to boil, "and since you aided me against *An Fiach*, I will help your friend for free."

Relief washed through Finn. Surely Bedelia couldn't

be angry with her for leaving the inn if she returned with a life-saving tincture. She watched with interest as Venetia poured several liquids from different vials into the cauldron, then added a chunk of dried root, and a few different herbs.

"Won't be more than a few minutes," Venetia explained as she turned back to Finn, wiping her aged hands on her baggy dress. "She'll need to take it all at once. As long as the infection isn't too far along, she should be fine."

Unable to contain herself, Finn stood and wrapped Venetia in a tight hug. "I can't express how grateful I am," she sighed. "Bedelia is the only reason I'm alive right now. I couldn't stand it if she were to die when I could have helped her."

Finn felt Venetia tense, or maybe it was just her imagination. Regardless, she let her go and both women resumed their seats.

They discussed Venetia's business, and the latest happenings in Migris until the cauldron began to emit a thick, earthy scent. Venetia rose and returned to the stove, then strained the liquid into a large bowl for it to cool. They continued their conversation as they waited, and soon Finn had the precious, glass vial in her hands. The vial that would save her friends life.

"I can't thank you enough for this," she said with a smile, gripping the mixture tightly in her palm. "I really should go find her."

Venetia nodded, and opened her mouth to speak, but was interrupted by a knock on the door. She excused herself, slipped out the door, then disappeared into the alleyway where whoever had knocked awaited.

Finn stayed seated, gazing down at the vial in her palm for a moment before securing it within the bodice of her dress. She knew she should leave, but didn't want to interrupt Venetia, especially if she was with a customer. Bedelia would have to wait just a few moments longer.

Eventually Venetia returned, and came to stand in front of Finn. "I'm sorry, lass-" she began, but was interrupted by a second pair of footsteps.

Finn tensed, and prepared to stand, then a hand pressed tightly over her mouth. Rough cloth scratched her nose and lips, permeating her lungs with an acrid, dizzying smell. Her hands fluttered around her attacker's grip like dying butterflies as she felt her senses leaving her.

As her vision faded, the person behind her wrapped an arm around her waist and lifted her to her feet. She couldn't see Venetia as she was dragged away, but thought she heard her mumble, "A Faie girl, right here in the middle of my home . . . "

Cool air hit Finn's face as she was led out into the street, just before she lost consciousness.

THIS WAS a strange turn of events, thought Maarav as Bedelia's unconscious *friend* was dragged away, though he wasn't surprised to see who was doing the dragging.

She'd been in his inn less than an hour before, questioning him about a bounty on a *tree girl*. Maarav knew all about the bounty, and knew that it was for Finn, but that was not why he'd pointed the woman in Finn's direction, nor was it why he'd followed shortly after.

It had all been rather convenient, with Finn running out to protect the herbwife, then following her into her home. It left far fewer witnesses than it would had Finn remained at his inn.

As he hid in the shadows of a nearby alleyway, the herbwife peeked out into the street warily, then shut her little door. Maarav could hear the lock sliding into place as he approached.

At his feet was a small, glass vial. Something Finn had carried. He crouched to retrieve it, then scrawled a mark with black coal on the herbwive's door. The mark would tie up *that* loose end nicely, as he didn't have time to take care of the old woman himself.

He strode away with a spring in his step. Everyone had their part to play in the grand dance of war, and Maarav had never missed a single step.

THE NUMBER of refugees camped outside the gate had Kai feeling jumpy. Many of them had already awoken, and stared longingly at the sun as it made its slow progress over the horizon. It had been a cold night for all, and Kai could not blame the destitute people for craving the sun's warmth.

He turned his attention forward, feeling a sickening kinship with the poor, skinny children asking their parents why they weren't allowed into the city. He'd been one of those poor, skinny children, lorded over by the wealthy people of Sormyr, the Gray City, with their fine homes and warm winter clothes.

He looked forward to the imposing gates of Migris, as yet another family was turned away. People had fled the smaller burghs, abandoning their farms and possessions, in hopes that the larger cities would protect them from the Faie. They were fools to believe that the rich cared for their well-being, even as they depended on the food from the now abandoned farms.

Iseult rode next to Kai silently. He glared coldly at the city walls, like the stones and mortar were something living that he could fight. Àed and Ealasaid rode behind them. Kai still wasn't sure why the old man had invited Ealasaid along, but he didn't really mind. You never knew who might prove useful.

Kai almost voiced his opinion that they shouldn't bother with the guards at the gate, but Iseult appeared so frighteningly determined that Kai thought he might actually stand a chance. He would let Iseult try his way to get into the city, then Kai would try his own.

They reached the end of the line of folk waiting before the gates. Kai shifted atop his horse as his stomach growled. Though he wasn't looking forward to spending time amongst the higher classes, he wouldn't mind a day without riding, and a night with a proper bed. He briefly thought back to his time in Malida's home with Finn, back in Port Ainfean, then shoved the memories away. He was there to prove Finn wrong, nothing more.

The line moved quickly as the poor folk were turned away before they could even speak. Four riders on horse-back would not be deemed poor, but they might be turned away for other reasons. It probably wouldn't help that Iseult looked like a tall, dark, killer, ready to take the city by force all on his own.

Soon they were next in line. Kai observed each of the guards in turn, then tensed as his eyes landed on the one actually speaking to those who approached. He'd encountered that guard before, which might have helped them gain entrance to the city if Kai hadn't been doing something illegal at the time. Gambling was frowned upon in Migris. Organizing an underground, gambling empire got you thrown in the stocks. Kai had escaped his misdeeds unscathed, but had avoided Migris for several months afterward, as rough drawings of his face were hung in most of the larger inns. The incident had occurred nearly a year ago, but Kai had no doubt the one guard would still recognize him. A man would not readily forget the face of someone who'd escaped arrest by tying his pursuer's boot strings together, tripping him up and humiliating him in front of several women.

Kai tried to gain Iseult's attention, but it was too late. He'd already dismounted to lead his horse forward. Needing to act fast, Kai dismounted, shielding his face as much as possible, to lead his horse away with the latest group of rejected refugees.

Àed and Ealasaid didn't seem to notice, as they had

ventured forward to stand at Iseult's side, the three of them intent on the guards before them as the next group moved away.

Wiping the nervous sweat from his brow, Kai led his horse further away before remounting. There was more than one way to get into the city, and Kai would likely reach it while Iseult was still arguing with the guards.

He kicked his horse into a gallop as he rode the length of the city gates, far off enough to not draw any attention to himself. The smell of salt in the air grew thick as he neared the sea. Soon he reached another gate with different guards. Guards who had nothing to do with the Lady of Migris, and those who obeyed her laws.

He dismounted and approached this new gate with a spring in his step. Being recognized here was a good thing, at least for Kai.

Past the gate were the docks, which dominated the coast, all sturdy wood and rope railings. As he reached the *guards*, he discreetly slipped the thuggish men several coins then smiled, waiting. One brute gave a wave of his hand, then suddenly the gates swung inward of their own volition, though really there were several hidden lookouts manning them.

Kai took a deep breath as he led his horse through. The docks were an ideal location for information gathering, as the men of the docks knew more than any innkeep or stableman around, but it would still be difficult to find information on one woman in such a large city, if she was even there at all.

He'd just ask around until Iseult finished his argument with the guards. Then, if Iseult managed to not get arrested, and actually made it into the city, he would lead him and the others to the docks. It was tempting to move on and scour the city on his own, but four sets of eyes were better than one, and Iseult would be handy should Kai encounter any trouble.

He walked along casually, leading his horse as its hooves echoed on the thick, wooden planks of the docks. There were ships moored all the way down the long stretch, some being loaded with supplies for export, as others expelled their goods into the city. Kai had just decided to question a few sailors waiting for their ship to load, when he was interrupted by a familiar face.

"Kai!" the man exclaimed in a voice like gravel falling down a hillside. "It's been many a moon since I've seen ye in these parts."

"Sativola," he replied, genuinely pleased. If anyone had the information he sought, it would be Sativola. He would keep quiet about seeing Kai as well.

Sativola swiped his meaty palm across a fresh, red scar, spanning the width of his forehead, then up into his curly, blond hair. He'd aged poorly over the past several years, but still looked sturdy for a man of around fifty years.

"What are ye doing in these parts?" Sativola questioned, drawing Kai aside from the busy walkway. "Last I heard, ye were with Anna in the Southlands. She said she left ye there."

Kai shrugged, trying to play off his surprise. Sativola made it sound as if he'd recently spoken to Anna, which perhaps meant she'd beaten him to Migris. If she was already within the city, she might have tracked Finn down.

"I've seen a bit of travel over the past month," Kai explained, leaning back against the railing in an attempt to appear relaxed. "I'm actually looking for Anna," he added.

Sativola clapped him on the back, nearly knocking him over. "Yer in luck lad. I'm crewin' this here ship for her."

Kai looked past Sativola to the small ship. It hardly seemed seaworthy, but if Sativola supported its use, Kai knew that it would sail, and if Anna was preparing to sail, she had a very good reason.

"Anna? Taking to the sea?" he said jokingly. "She must really want something to engage her deepest fear."

Sativola chuckled and slapped Kai on the back again. "Don't let her hear ye sayin' that!" he laughed. "She'd throw ye overboard." He leaned close again, conspiratorially. "Just between us," he whispered, "I hear she's plannin' on kidnappin' a girl. Never knew Anna was into that sort of business."

Kai's heart gave a shudder, but he did his best to act unsurprised. "Ah," he began, "I might know a little something about that, but if I told you, Anna would have my head."

Sativola grinned, exposing rotten, blocky teeth.

"Do you think I could wait on the ship for her?" Kai went on. "Scare her out of her wits upon entering her cabin?"

Sativola's grin widened as he nodded excitedly. "Oh, I'd pay a good deal of coin to see that." He held his hand out to take the reins to Kai's horse.

Kai handed his horse off, trusting that Sativola would stable him. Horse in hand, his friend stood aside and gestured to the narrow, temporary walkway that led up to the ship.

Kai eyed the walkway, suddenly regretting his plan, but knowing he had no choice but to ascend it. As Sativola had suggested, Anna *wasn't* in the kidnapping business, and had only entered it the first time they stole Finn. He had little doubt that the human package to which Sativola referred would be the girl he'd come all this way to find.

Kai started toward the ship, wishing he'd brought Iseult along from the start. He wasn't looking forward to facing down Anna and an entire crew of men. He'd only thought to ask questions at the dock, so he might return to his companions with a plan of action. Now that he knew Anna intended to sail away with Finn, he couldn't risk both women slipping right through his fingers.

Once on board, he walked casually by several more crew members who paid him little mind. The ship likely had multiple main cabins below deck, but only one above that he could see. *That* would be Anna's cabin. Perhaps he could confront her in private, and convince her to let him take Finn back to her friends.

He entered the unlocked cabin, then shut the door behind him, prepared to wait, but the sight of a quill and ink brought a plan to the front of his mind. He hurried to the small desk, built into the wooden wall, and picked up the quill, and a rough sheet of parchment. He began scrawling a hasty message.

There were still so many things that could go wrong, but he couldn't help his elation as he placed the final words upon the page. He could at least account for certain outcomes. He grinned as he allowed himself to fully process his conversation with Sativola.

Finn was alive. She might hate him, and she might tell him to crawl back to whatever hole he came out of, but at least she was alive, and he'd just come up with a brilliant plan to save her. It was the best news he'd heard all week.

His letter finished, he rushed out of the cabin to hand it to Sativola, knowing the man wouldn't fail him in delivering it. Sativola might be a criminal, but he was a reliable one.

That task done, Kai went back to Anna's cabin to wait. Some time later, he lounged casually on her bed as the sound of footsteps approached the cabin door. Hearing grunts of struggle, he stood quickly, feeling suddenly unprepared for the meeting that was about to take place.

The door swung open, revealing Anna. Her black, pin-straight hair whipped about in the salty ocean breeze as she peered inside the cabin, not seeing Kai right away. Her dark, hawk-like eyes held satisfaction as she stepped inside to make room for one of her crewmen to carry a very angry human package inside.

Finn still wore the dress Kai had last seen her in. The

deep reddish purple hues still suited her creamy skin tone, and her hair was still the wild, long mess that he remembered. He felt like it had been years since he'd last seen her, and he for some reason had expected her to look far different. Yet, she hadn't changed at all, down to the angry scowl on her face, and the sudden ire lighting up her dark eyes as her gaze found him.

"You!" she exclaimed, fighting against her brutish captor's grasp.

Anna turned quickly to see what Finn was shouting about, and took on an almost identical expression to the one Finn held. She moved to slam the cabin door shut behind the brute holding Finn, then turned to Kai with her hands on her hips. He noticed two sheathed daggers cinched to her belt, one near either hand. Times must have been tough if she was wearing weapons openly.

Finn began to scream for help, but the brute clamped his dirty palm across her face. She thrashed about, but he was large enough, and she small enough, that it did little good. Though he knew it would ruin his plan, Kai tensed, prepared to cut off the hand that covered Finn's mouth, but Anna moved in front of him.

She crossed her arms, clad in a billowy white blouse that rested beneath a tight, black vest, lying snugly against her lightly-muscled frame. "Give me one good reason to not throw you overboard this instant," she demanded.

The brute grunted behind her as Finn bit his hand. "You fiends!" she shrieked, but her mouth was soon covered again.

Ignoring the commotion behind her, Anna stared Kai down patiently.

He took a step back to lean against the cabin wall, doing his best to appear at ease. "I was under the impression that we were in this together."

At that moment Finn kicked the brute in the shin so hard that he dropped her, and she scurried away toward the bed. She eyed each of them in turn as everyone's attention fell on her, but she didn't try to run. Likely because the brute's body blocked the entire doorway.

"I *knew* I was right for leaving," Finn rasped, speaking to Kai while still looking at the brute who blocked her way.

Kai frowned, but turned back to Anna, ignoring the feral woman in the corner. He was about to take a gamble. If Anna just wanted the bounty on Finn, she would have no need to sail the Melted Sea. She was after something else, perhaps something out of legend. "So are you looking for the shroud, or the Archtree?" he inquired.

Anna glared at him. "How on earth do you know about either of those things?"

Kai smirked. "I could ask you the same question."

"So that's what this is all about!" Finn exclaimed before Anna could answer. "I've been drugged, kidnapped, and manhandled, all over a silly piece of fabric!"

Anna shrugged and turned back to Kai. "As far as I've been able to discern, Finn knows how to find it. *That's* why everyone around is so keen on gaining possession of her."

Finn laughed bitterly, drawing everyone's attention back to her. She looked downright evil as she stated, "I don't know how to find the shroud. Your efforts have all been a waste."

Anna turned to fully face Finn. "What do you mean," she began slowly, her voice barely above a growl, "you *don't* know *how* to find the *shroud*? The entire reason that bounty was placed on your head was to find it!"

Kai was genuinely surprised. "You found the bounty's backer?" he questioned in astonishment. He'd tried to find that information himself while he was in Ainfean.

"You're all a bunch of fools!" Finn shouted before Anna could answer.

As the women continued to scream insults at each other, the brute slipped out the door, shutting it quietly behind him. Kai couldn't blame him.

He cleared his throat to get the women's attention, but they were both too caught up flinging curses to notice. He cleared his throat more loudly, then waited patiently as they both turned their angry expressions to him.

"What!" they shouted in unison.

"*I* know how to find the shroud," he announced.

Finn suddenly seemed confused, while Anna gave him a calculating look. When she realized that Kai wasn't joking, a superior smile crossed her face. "Perhaps I was a little hasty in threatening to throw you overboard." She turned back to Finn, "You on the other hand . . . "

Kai grunted in irritation.

Anna rolled her eyes at him. "I'm not *really* going throw her into the sea, though I would like to. She's still a part of this, and the only way we come out on top is to have all of the pieces."

Kai nodded in acceptance, hating the way Finn was looking at him. She thought he was betraying her all over again.

"So what is our next step?" Anna asked curiously.

He pulled his eyes away from Finn, and forced a mischievous smile onto his face. "We set sail for the Archtree."

Anna smiled, though there was little warmth to it.

Finn growled in annoyance at being ignored. "*How* do the two of you know about the Archtree?" she demanded.

Kai was suddenly embarrassed. "I might have followed you after you left Ainfean," he admitted. "I overheard many of your conversations with Iseult."

Finn gasped. "You followed me? Was it not apparent that I was trying to get *away* from you?"

Kai rolled his eyes. "Yes, your point was well made, but you were also being followed by Óengus."

"What?" the two women asked in unison.

"Is he still after the bounty?" Anna added.

Kai shrugged. "I didn't bother asking him."

Finn almost seemed to doubt her anger toward Kai for a moment . . . but it was a short moment. "That doesn't change the fact that you eavesdropped on my private conversation!"

Ignoring her, Kai turned back to Anna. "Now tell us,

how did *you* come to find out about both the shroud, and the Archtree?"

Anna's face went rigid at the question, making Kai want the answer even more.

"That's private," she snapped.

Kai lifted a hand to his chest and pouted, feigning hurt feelings. "But I told *you*," he protested.

Anna glared at him. "Gobán!" she shouted suddenly.

A moment later, the thug came back into the room.

Anna looked up at her minion. "Take the girl below deck," she demanded. "Keep her under lock and key."

CHAPTER SIX

*I*seult clenched and unclenched his fists while he waited for the guard to change his mind. If he knew what was good for him, he *would* change his mind. Àed felt sure that Finn was within the city walls, and he trusted his judgement. Now, if only the insufferable guards would step out of his way. They had already waited too long in line, and he refused to let that time be a waste.

Kai had disappeared, of course, leaving him, Àed, and Ealasaid to deal with the guards on their own. Iseult had hoped that the girl would be of some use, she was pretty, after all, and most of the guards were men, but she stood back meekly, covering her face with her curly hair.

"I don't care if you're the Lady of Migris herself," the guard spat, "*no one* is allowed entrance. The city is full, and there have been multiple killings."

Iseult finally shook his head and backed away, lest he lose his temper and end up in the stocks. Ealasaid hurried out of his path as he turned and stormed away from the gates, his horse in tow behind him.

They walked off the road, further away from the gates, to a secluded area where refugees were yet to set up camp. Iseult stopped and waited for the others, then handed his reins to Ealasaid.

"Surely she'll come out of the gates eventually," Ealasaid comforted. "We can just wait for her here. She won't be able to slip by."

Àed had obviously filled her in, as Iseult and Kai had spoken to her very little during their journey. Unfortunately, the girl knew little of the outside world. There were many ways to leave a city, and if someone found Finn before him, she wasn't likely to exit by way of the gates.

"Migris is the largest port this side of the Melted Sea," he explained gruffly. "I'm not worried about missing her at the *gates*. She'll be impossible to find if she boards a ship."

Ealasaid's face crumpled into a dejected expression that Iseult had no time, nor desire, to remedy. He turned to Àed. "I sailed these seas as a boy. The gates were simply our first option for entrance. I'll find another way in, and I'll bring Finn back out to meet you here."

The old man glared, just as Iseult knew he would. "I'll not wait around like a useless stump while ye venture off into the city," he growled, blue eyes blazing with ire.

"And what if she *does* come through the gates?" Iseult replied calmly as he unclasped his black cloak. He handed the item to Ealasaid, who took it silently.

Àed spat onto the ground near Ealasaid's feet. She jumped aside, tugging both her and Iseult's horses along with her. She glanced down at the spit, then over to Àed. "I'll wait with you here. If you tell me what she looks like, I can keep an eye out while you rest."

Àed's expression softened, though he grumbled something about not needing any rest. Satisfied that the pair would be there when he returned, Iseult left them without another word.

His boots sank into the loamy earth as he ventured back toward the road. He crossed it, then continued walking through the congested area of refugee camps while he considered his options.

The docks would have fewer guards, but there would be other sorts watching over things, and he hadn't spent enough time in the city to make connections. In fact, he'd only been there once or twice since he first left.

When he was young, he'd avoided Migris because his mother had been killed for his alleged crimes. Though the thought of death at the time was a welcome idea, he wouldn't give the city the satisfaction. If he died, it would be with his sword drenched in the blood of his enemies. In later years, when he would no longer be recognized, he could admit that he'd stayed away out of guilt. He couldn't face the city where his mother had died because of him.

Now he would finally return. He would find Finn, and she would help him right the wrongs of his people, his mother's lifelong wish. His people had been cursed to destruction, and he was the only one left to lift that burden. Perhaps once that was done, he could rest easy for the first time in his life. Then again, perhaps not. He was not a man accustomed to a normal life, and was not sure inaction would ever suit him.

He passed through the refugee camps unhindered as his long legs carried him toward the distant coast. He didn't need the salty air, or the distant call of sea birds to tell him the ocean was near. He felt it in his bones, an exhilarating mixture of fear and feeling utterly at home.

It wasn't long before the water came into view. The sea pounded the shore angrily, displaying its deep green and blue tones that shifted to white froth upon impact. The texture of the earth changed beneath his feet as he continued to walk, from slippery grass to soft, damp sand. Though he had spent years away from the ocean, it still felt like home to him. His people were sailors. The sea was in his blood.

He looked to his right at the empty expanse of coast, then to the South, where he could barely see the busy docks. He knew that past the docks, was a coastal inlet inside the city walls. Beyond that, the gates butted up against jagged rocks, too high to climb, and if you somehow managed it, an abundance of rope would be needed to lower yourself down the other side. The inlet was his aim.

He double checked that his weapons were all secure, and his boots tightly laced, then he approached the frothy water's edge. He entered the freezing cold water without hesitation. The waves crashed around him as he dove forward, propelling himself past the violent waves toward calmer waters. Once he was far enough out, he began swimming South. He knew it would be a long swim, but an easy one. The cold barely touched him, and he had no fear of the creatures that lurked in the depths. The sea was in his blood, after all.

He swam on, never tiring, thinking of what might come next. He had a sea map to the Archtree, which he'd left strapped to his horse back with Àed. Once they had Finn, they would need to find a ship, not an easy task. Hiring enough crewmen to make the journey would be expensive, and hiring men that would be trustworthy was nearly impossible. Still, it had to be done. He'd believed Finn when she said she had no idea where the shroud of the Faie Queen was, so they needed the Archtree to find it. Once they had the location, they could hunt down the shroud, and Iseult could bestow it upon Finn. Perhaps then, his curse would finally be lifted.

Before he knew it, he'd reached the inlet. The chilly air was a shock as he climbed out of the water, but he barely noticed, so intent was he on his mission. He ignored the nagging anxiety of returning to the city of his childhood as he left the shore and progressed to the nearest buildings, mainly middle class homes. Once amongst the homes, he began to jog, unwilling to waste an unnecessary second.

His black clothes began to dry with the added move-ment as he made his way through the streets of Migris, doing his best to ignore the sights and sounds around him. He needed to reach an inn if he wanted to gather information. He was *so* close.

He wound his way to the inner city, dominated by shops and inns rather than residences, not acknowledging the curious glances of passersby. He had begun to approach an inn named *The Melted Sea*, when something stopped him. There was a man watching him from a few paces away, not with the subtle glances of the other city folk, but with an intent, knowing gaze. Iseult eyed him directly. The man nodded to him, then turned to walk into a dark alleyway.

The man's face had been partially shadowed by the hood of his black cloak, but there was something naggingly familiar about him. Unable to shake the feeling that this mysterious person might have information about Finn, Iseult veered from his course and followed the figure into the alleyway.

Moments later, he was face to face with a man who looked alarmingly like . . . well, like *him*.

"It's good to see that the blood is still around. I was beginning to think that I was the last one left," the man stated.

Iseult's fingers twitched around the short sword at his hip, but he did not draw it. "The blood?" he questioned.

"Of Uí Néid," the man went on. "I'm thinking that seeing *you* here means that you've come to the same conclusion as I."

He'd mentioned Uí Néid, Iseult's homeland. It had been a long time since he'd heard a stranger mutter that name, let alone a stranger that others might think kin to him, based on appearance.

"And what conclusion is that?" Iseult asked apathetically.

"That the Cavari have returned along with the Faie" the man answered.

Iseult glanced about them, but they were completely alone. He drew his attention back to the man before him. The Cavari were, of course, of great interest to any who hailed from Uí Néid, but few would know such a thing.

"How do you know me?" he demanded.

The man smiled, but the gesture was neither warm, nor reassuring. "It would be a shame for a man not to recognize his own brother."

Rage overcame Iseult. How dare this imposter claim to be something he was not? "My brother is *dead*," he growled.

The other man did not falter. "My name is Maarav Mac Aodha, son of Brógán Mac Aodha, and I am very much alive."

"How?" Iseult asked, taken aback. His older brother had fallen ill when they were children, and had passed long before their mother had. Many children died during that time.

The man who claimed to be Maarav clapped him on the back. "That is a story for another time. Right now, we must catch a ship."

"I don't have time for this," Iseult growled. "I'm looking for a girl," he added, just in the off chance this imposter might have information regarding Finn.

The man calling himself Maarav grinned. "What a strange twist of fate. So am I. Actually, I was just heading off to find her."

Iseult couldn't help his surprise. This man couldn't be his brother, but he was still clearly of his blood, however distantly. Could he have recognized Finn, just as he had? If that was the case, he likely intended to harm her. Few hailing from Uí Néid would suffer one of the Cavari to live, even if she came in the form of a pretty, young girl.

"If you intend to harm her . . . " Iseult warned, letting the threat hang in the air.

His alleged brother grinned. "Now, now. I was simply following her out of curiosity. She doesn't seem the type to murder women and children, and so I would not harm her, unless she offered me violence to begin with."

Iseult felt like electricity was filling his body, coursing down to his fingertips that itched to retrieve his sword. Making an impulsive judgement, he forced himself to relax. "Lead the way."

The Maarav imposter grinned, then took off running down the alleyway, his cloak billowing behind him. Iseult followed. Eventually it became clear that they were heading toward the docks. Those milling about in the street cleared a path, not used to seeing two unusually tall men, dressed in black, running as if their lives depended on it. The distant crash of the ocean resonated with Iseult as he ran. He was *so* close.

He pushed onward, and the docks came into view. Following the billowing black cloak ahead of him, he bounded down the city steps until his feet met with the wooden planks suspended above the water. He halted suddenly beside his guide and looked to him for information. There were several scores of ships, and he did not know which one he needed.

His *brother* scanned the row of ships as he panted. "We are too late. I thought to simply retrieve some supplies before attempting to hire on as one of the crewmen. I did not think they would depart so hastily."

Iseult followed *Maarav's* gaze as he watched a ship disappearing over the watery horizon. Iseult took a step forward, prepared to swim after it, but *Maarav* took hold of his arm.

Iseult eyed him coldly.

"Think, brother," the imposter cautioned. "Even if you were able to catch them, you would be half dead by that point. They would have to haul you on board, and you'd be in no position to rescue anyone. We must be smart about this."

Not acknowledging anything *Maarav* was saying, Iseult continued to stare. "*Where* are they sailing?"

Before Maarav could answer, a child came to stand before them. He couldn't have been more than six or seven, but his jaded, ruddy brown eyes made him seem much older. Those eyes held experiences that no child of that age should know.

"Can we help you?" Maarav asked, still gripping Iseult's arm tightly.

The child looked like he might flee at the sight of the two men, one still slightly damp from the ocean, but he held his ground. "I was asked to deliver a message to a tall man in black, with eyes like a cat. I'm not sure which of you it is meant for."

Iseult held out his hand for the message, but the boy dropped it to his side. He looked down at the ground, obviously nervous. "I was told I'd be paid for my trouble," he muttered quietly.

Maarav chuckled, in much better spirits than Iseult, and searched his pockets. A moment later he produced several coins and handed them to the boy.

The boy snatched the coins, then handed the parchment to Iseult. As soon as the paper was relinquished, he turned and ran. Iseult unrolled the letter and read it quickly. Soon, a wry smile crossed his face.

"Now that's a scary smile if I've ever seen one," *Maarav* commented, but Iseult did not reply.

Not all was lost. Perhaps, in the end, he might be able to let Kai live. That was, if the letter was not a lie.

FINN THREW herself against the wooden door frantically, but it wouldn't budge. After Kai and Anna had revealed their plans, she'd been thrown into a cabin below deck. The heavy door was bolted from the outside, and no matter how many times she attacked it, it would not budge.

She'd screamed for help as the ship began gently rocking, and could hear men yelling, preparing to leave the port. Then she'd thrown herself against the door repeatedly, but it was no use.

She had tried to remember what it felt like when she'd called the earth to save her and Bedelia from the wolves, but she'd felt no returning call. She was surrounded by water. It simply didn't resonate with her like the earth did. She'd then collapsed in a heap and began to cry. Iseult and Àed could have been reaching the city at that very moment, and Bedelia, *poor* Bedelia would be arriving to an empty room. Finn wouldn't be able to tell her that she needed medicine for her injuries. Without Finn to help her, she would die.

The anguish was too much for her as the ship reached deeper waters and calmed its motion. Her chance to escape was gone, but that didn't mean she would give up on escaping her cabin. She glanced around the room for something to aid her, and almost considered using the small hanging lantern that lit her room to start a fire, but she soon dismissed the idea. It would do her no good to burn herself alive.

She wiped at her puffy, damp face in irritation. She might have considered stabbing Kai several times over the course of their relationship, but the next time she got the chance, she would not throw it away.

Feeling weak and powerless, she crawled to the nearby straw mat with a pillow, and curled up in the bedding to cry. The ship's rocking lessened as time passed, and utterly exhausted, she drifted off to sleep.

THE NEXT MORNING, at least she thought it was morning, Finn awoke to find her entire body ached from her efforts against the locked door. Her lantern had burned out, leaving her in utter darkness. When the door suddenly opened of its own accord to let in a sliver of light, she thought perhaps she was dreaming.

The relatively pleasant dream was shattered as a man with curly blond hair, and a fresh red scar across his forehead stepped into view, a new lantern illuminating his face, as well as a measure of sunlight streaming in behind him. In his free hand, he carried a tray of food that looked minuscule in his meaty palms. His smile for her seemed genuine.

"I've brought ye some breakfast, lass," he announced.

Finn eyed him cautiously as he entered the room and set the tray down beside her on the straw mat where she'd slept. She looked down at the food, an assortment of small, preserved fish with bread and fresh butter, then looked back up to the man numbly as he replaced her lantern with the new one.

"It's not poison," he encouraged, glancing down at the food. "There's no use bringing someone on board a ship just to poison them, though I do suppose the ocean would make disposin' of the body an easy task."

"Was that supposed to be comforting?" Finn asked weakly.

The man chuckled, then moved to sit in the only seat the room had to offer, a short, wide stool, perfect for maintaining balance in choppy waters. "Once ye've finished eating, I'll show ye around the ship."

Finn's eyes widened in surprise. "So I'm not to remain in this room the entire journey?"

The man laughed again. "What's yer name?"

Seeing no reason to lie, since Kai and Anna already knew her true identity, she answered, "Finn, and yours?"

"Sativola," he replied.

Finn smiled, though she knew it held little warmth. Still, she wasn't about to alienate the only person who was attempting to be nice to her. She picked at her breakfast, not wanting to eat, but would, knowing she'd need strength when the time came to fight. There might be little she could do on the ship, but they'd have to dock at some point. She'd sooner die than help Kai and Anna do *anything*. Perhaps if she was nice enough, she could even persuade Sativola to help her escape.

"Did they tell you where we're going, Sativola?" Finn asked slyly while she rearranged the fish on her plate.

The large man shrugged. "Searching for an island in the North, apparently."

Finn nodded, realizing she'd have to give information to get it. "They want the shroud of the Faie Queen."

Sativola burst into laughter, slapping his knee at the *joke*. He waggled a sausage-like finger at her. "Yer a fun one, ye are. The shroud is just a myth. A faiery story told to young children."

Finn gave him her best blank expression.

His look of consternation wrinkled the scar on his forehead. "Yer not jokin', are ye?"

Finn shook her head as she lifted one of the fish to take a bite. It was horribly salty.

"Then where do ye come in?" he pressed. "Why would Anna need a pretty little lass like yerself to find a shroud of legend?"

She shrugged and lounged back on her straw mat, attempting to act casual. "I've no idea, really."

Sativola grunted. "How am I supposed to get paid, when the valuable item we search for doesn't exist?"

Finn smiled, proud that she was managing such a clever manipulation. "I've better things to do with my time as well."

Sativola leaned back on his stool, balancing precariously with two of its pegs off the ground. He seemed deep in thought for a moment, and Finn thought she might have found an ally, but then he shrugged. "I trust Anna to pay me, one way or another. Even if it's from her personal purse."

Finn's hopes deflated. She pushed the barely eaten breakfast away from her.

Watching her movements, Sativola raised his bushy eyebrows. "Ready to see the rest of the ship?"

Finn sighed. She might as well. "That would be lovely," she said graciously as she stood.

Sativola was up in an instant, holding the door open for her to walk through ahead of him.

First he showed her everything below deck, though it held little of Finn's interest. It was all just wooden walls and storage. She could barely pay attention to any of it, as she was overcome with a much more pressing concern. Her legs weren't working properly, and she felt a peculiar queasiness. She had felt ill lying in bed too, but she'd passed it off as her body reacting to her devastation. Now the sickness was increasing with every step, and she felt almost as if her body was leaning sideways while she walked.

She stopped moving, feeling about ready to lose the small amount of breakfast she'd eaten.

Sativola took one look at her and frowned. "Looks like yer yet to find yer sea legs, lass."

Finn closed her eyes against the dizziness, but it only made things worse. The next thing she knew, Sativola had scooped her up in his arms. She had the sensation of moving upward as the sound of Sativola's footsteps became more hollow, then she was hit with the refreshing sea air. She opened her eyes slowly, assaulted by the brightness of the sun reflecting off clear water.

Seeming to sense her stomach's unease, Sativola rushed her over to the side of the ship and put her down. She held onto the railings while her measly, partially digested breakfast went overboard. Sativola's large palm holding onto the back of her dress was a comfort. She had no desire to follow her breakfast into the choppy waters below.

When she was finished, Sativola guided her backward, then left her to sit on the wooden planks of the ship while he stood. "Take as long as ye need, lass," he instructed.

She feared she'd need a few years to regain herself, but didn't express her worries out loud. Instead, she glanced around the deck. There seemed to be few crew members, and only three that she could see at that moment: Sativola standing beside her, the brute who'd manhandled her, doing something with the sail, and a scrawny looking man doing something at the back of the ship. Kai and Anna were nowhere to be seen. She looked down at her hands in her lap. Her knuckles and the sides of her palms were swollen and bruised from banging on the door of her locked cabin. She had no doubt her arms would show similar bruises if she were to roll up her sleeves.

Feeling morose, she turned to say something to Sativola, but screamed instead as something came rushing down at her from the sky. The shape flipped around in the air erratically, before propelling itself straight for Finn.

Sativola began to rush forward with a shout, but was too late as the shape collided with Finn, knocking her from a sitting position onto her back.

Her hands reflexively gripped the creature. Her fingers touched upon damp feathers, and skin that felt malleable and loose, but rough and thick at the same time. The creature on top of her let out a small squeal, then buried its head next to her neck, caressing her skin with what felt like a large, sharp beak.

Finn opened her eyes slowly to see Sativola standing over her. He had his hands up in a cautioning gesture. "Don't move, lass," he said softly.

Finn's pulse sped. The other crew members had gathered around. "Kill the thing!" the scrawny man shouted.

The creature tensed, wrapping its wings around

Finn's midsection as much as it could with her lying on her back.

"It's got its claws near her throat," Sativola snapped. "Nobody move."

The creature began making mewling noises near Finn's ear. It didn't seem like it was threatening her, more like it was terrified. Some instinct deep inside her prompted her hands to begin gently stroking the creature's back. The creature wasn't large, perhaps just the size of Finn's torso, and probably only half her weight.

At her touch, the creature snuggled closer. "I don't think it means to hurt me," she said softly.

She tried to sit up, but the creature starting emitting short, panicked chirps.

"There, there," she soothed, as she moved one of her hands to stroke its bony head. She still couldn't see much of the creature with it nestled so close to her throat, but she could tell that its head rested on a long, thin neck, and its beak was mostly covered in the rough, thick skin, except for the very tip.

The creature made a sound like purring, and Finn slowly tried to sit up again. Sativola and the other men watched in silence. The creature let her move enough to sit, then released her torso to huddle in her lap. With its body facing Finn's belly, the creature folded its wings around its back, then turned its long neck to watch the gathered men with one of its eyes. The other eye, turned toward Finn, held a look of terror in its large, sea green depths.

"It's just a baby," Finn commented.

"A baby Faie creature!" the scrawny man whispered harshly. "Throw the thing overboard and be done with it."

Finn wrapped her arms around the creature and stared the man down. The creature's white feathers were soft against Finn's hands, in sharp contrast to its skin.

"Back to work," Sativola demanded.

The scrawny man opened his mouth to argue, but Sativola cast an impatient glare at him and he did as he was told. The brute, who'd watched the scene silently, walked back to his post without a word.

Sativola crouched in front of Finn. "It's probably not wise to keep that creature in your lap, lass," he whispered. "The Faie have never done us any favors."

Finn prickled at that. She might not really be Faie, but she was close enough. "Help me stand," she instructed, "we'll take the creature to my room where the other men can't hurt it."

He raised his eyebrows so high that they met his hairline.

"*Please*," Finn pressed, unable to bear the thought of the scrawny man tossing her new friend into the ocean.

Sativola let out a long sigh, then nodded. He went to crouch behind Finn, then gently grabbed the back of both of her arms and lifted while Finn gripped the creature against her. As they moved, the creature wriggled free from her grasp, but only to climb further up her chest, wrapping its dainty, taloned hands around her neck and its wings and lower feet around her chest.

"Quickly now, lass," Sativola instructed.

Finn looked in the direction of Sativola's gaze to find the scrawny man glaring at her. She nodded to herself, then hurried back to the trap door that led below deck, feeling much more steady on her feet with adrenaline spurring her on.

Within a few moments, Sativola, Finn, and the creature were all in Finn's room with the door shut behind them. With Sativola's help, Finn slowly lowered herself onto her straw mat. The creature instantly relaxed, seeming more comfortable in the closed space. With a curious coo, it finally detached itself from Finn to explore her bed.

Now that she could see it clearly, she stared in awe. The creature's body shape seemed almost cat-like, agile and fast, but its skin was more reptilian. Its glossy white feathers congregated mostly on its wings, and were sparse on its body, almost like a baby bird that was yet to fully fill out its plumage. The creature made a playful chittering sound with its beak as it buried its face in Finn's pillow.

Sativola stood on the other side of the room, as far away from the creature as possible. "Is that . . . " he trailed off, as if unsure what to say.

Finn turned questioning eyes to him as the creature returned to her lap, curling itself up contentedly, even though it was a little too large to rest there comfortably. "Is it what?"

Sativola shook his head at the sight of the creature, who was now making soft snoring sounds in Finn's lap.

"Well lass," he began again, "that thing looks a bit like a dragon."

Finn's eyes widened as she lowered her gaze to the creature. She knew about dragons, though she wasn't sure how. Yet, she was quite sure she'd never seen one before. As far as she knew, no one living had, though, given she'd been a tree for one hundred years, she was older than most of those who currently lived.

"I'm not sure what it is," she commented softly as she began stroking the maybe-dragon's little head, "but it seems friendly enough. It also seems too young to be away from its mother. I wonder what it was doing out in the middle of the ocean."

Sativola shrugged. "Perhaps it escaped from another ship, or perhaps it flew all the way from shore. Either way, ye probably shouldn't keep it."

Finn gasped and the little dragon tensed, sensing her sudden emotions. She felt an overwhelming need to protect the young life curled up in her lap, and not Sativola, nor anyone else would stop her.

Reading her expression, Sativola raised his hands in surrender. "I had to try. I suppose I'll have to go rummage up some food for the little scamp."

Finn smiled broadly. Perhaps she'd recruited a friend to her side after all.

BEDELIA RUSHED INTO HER ROOM, frantic to find Finn as the first light of morning peeked through the small window. She hadn't meant to be gone so long, but acquiring a ship had been more difficult than she'd guessed. While her *connection* to the Lady of Migris had held some sway with the guards at the gate, the docks were under different rule. The only thing that held sway there was coin, and apparently Bedelia did not have enough of it. Desperate, she'd searched through the day and night, unwilling to return to the inn empty handed.

Her heart jumped into her throat when she saw that the room was empty. Her already queasy stomach felt like it was doing handstands inside of her. Her supplies seemed to all be there beside her bed, neatly packed into her saddlebags. She took a step closer to the bed. Something small rested there. A glass phial. She reached out a hand toward it, then froze at the sound of footsteps behind her.

"That was here when I arrived," a voice said. "The innkeep must have left it."

Bedelia swayed on her feet at the sound of the voice, then turned slowly, not really wanting to look.

Óengus, a bitter smile on his lightly lined face, stood a few steps away. "You lost the girl," he accused.

Bedelia gasped. "No! She must just be down in the inn. Maarav would not have let her run off."

"The innkeep?" Óengus questioned. "He is missing too. Perhaps they have run off together."

"They wouldn't," Bedelia replied, hating the quaver in her voice.

Óengus snorted, then tossed his gray cloak back over his shoulder as he moved to look out the room's small window. With his back turned, he said, "Gather your things. I've a good idea where the girl is heading. We'll simply have to pick her up again before *your* fiery-haired lady finds out."

"Keiren sees all," Bedelia argued, knowing it wasn't entirely true, but wanting *something* to prove Óengus even the slightest bit wrong.

Still gazing out the window, he replied, "Not the girl, apparently, else she wouldn't need *us*."

Bedelia glared at his back, and seriously considered sticking a blade in it, but in the end, she would do as her lady wished. She had no choice but to work with the cruel excuse for a man standing before her. She began gathering her things mechanically. Finn had packed them well, so it only took a moment.

When Óengus finally turned around, he glanced down at the bed, and the glass phial that still rested there. "You might want to take that," he advised.

Bedelia glanced at the container, then back to Óengus. "What is it?"

He shrugged. "I've no idea, but if someone thought to leave it for you, it's probably important."

With a nod, Bedelia scooped up the phial of liquid and placed it in the pouch at her belt. "Where are we going?" she dared to ask.

Óengus breezed past her to open the door. Without turning around, he answered, "To my ship," then walked out into the hall.

Bedelia strongly considered her dagger again. *His* ship. *She'd* spent all day and night trying to acquire a ship, and Óengus made it sound like the most simple matter in the world. Muttering to herself, she followed him out, stepping lightly on her injured leg. It seemed to be getting worse, but there was nothing she could do about that now.

CHAPTER SEVEN

*E*alasaid had never heard a person curse so much in such a short span of time. Iseult had left them while the sun was still high over their heads the previous day, and now it was nearly dark for the second time around. Sensing that they would remain at their camp for another evening, she'd built a small fire for warmth while Àed alternated between pouting about being left behind, and glaring at the tall city walls.

She really didn't understand all the fuss about one single girl. She thought it would probably be quite embarrassing to have three men obsessing over you, though it might also be kind of fun. Still, she kept her thoughts to herself. Àed had not given her much information to go on, and for all she knew, this Finn person might be in grave danger. She would feel quite the fool if she spoke up, only to find that the men's urgency sprang from the threat of mortal peril.

So, she kept her mouth shut and tended the fire, while her elderly companion grumbled to himself.

As full darkness descended, the refugees began to mill about, looking to share a warm fire, or more importantly, a meal. She and Àed had little in the way of food, but she didn't doubt that they were far better off than most who camped around the city. She wondered how many had left their homes for similar reasons to hers, then shook her head. Very few, if any. Her gifts were unnatural, and were considered as such because few possessed them. She turned her attention back to Àed. He might have been a grumpy old man, but he was special, just like her. It made her feel a little less alone.

The sound of nearby footsteps drew Ealasaid's attention as a small, hunched form came into view, likely longing to share some warmth. Àed showed no signs of sensing the new presence, so she was startled when he announced, "We've no food to share, so ye best be on yer way."

The dark form halted, then a throat cleared. "I'm only lookin for a bit of warmth," a gravelly, female voice called back.

Àed didn't reply. Ealasaid, unused to the unwelcoming attitude of those who lived on the road, stood and gestured for the old woman to approach.

She hurried forward and plopped herself down near the fire, lifting her small, wrinkled hands toward the flames. The old woman's frizzy, silver hair glinted in the firelight, hidden partially by the hood of her cloak. Her eyes lifted to Ealasaid, revealing that one was clouded over, and didn't seem to move with the other one.

"Are you waiting to enter the city as well?" Ealasaid asked innocently, glad to have some hopefully less cranky company.

The old woman snorted and turned her good eye back to the fire. "I just left, actually, seeing as someone burned my home to the ground with me locked inside. It's lucky I'm small of build, else I'd never have escaped through the window."

Ealasaid gasped. "Why would someone do such a thing!"

The old woman laughed bitterly. "That's what happens when you're tricked into helping one of the Faie. The girl seemed so harmless, so I invited her right into my home." She shook her head. "Foolish of me, I know, but she seemed so innocent."

Àed perked up suddenly as the old woman spoke. "A Faie girl?" he questioned. "How could you tell that she was one of the Tuatha?"

The old woman shrugged. "I couldn't. A female guard enlightened me, and offered to take her away quietly. I thought that would be the end of it, but someone must have seen. I wouldn't have been the first to lose my life for interacting with one of the Tuatha Dé Danann."

Ealasaid could tell that the wheels in Àed's mind were spinning, but she wasn't sure why. She decided to wait and listen in hopes that the two elderly folk would give away more information.

"This Faie girl," Àed began slowly, "what did she look like?"

The old woman's expression turned suspicious as she gave Àed her full attention. "Why are you so interested in one of the Faie?"

Àed frowned and leaned back on his arms casually, though Ealasaid could still detect a measure of tension hidden just below the surface. "This isn't the first tale I've heard about a Faie girl summoning a storm into peoples' lives," he explained, "though I'm not sure if she's of the Tuatha, or something else entirely."

The old woman settled back on her haunches, seemingly satisfied. "This girl had long hair down to her waist, pale brown or dark blonde, depending on what you'd want to call it. Small of stature, with large brown eyes, and a very gentle way about her."

"The lass sounds harmless," Àed commented. "How'd the guard ye mentioned know she wasn't human?"

The old woman shrugged. "I didn't ask questions. I just wanted the Faie girl out of my house as quickly as possible. I've had enough trouble as it is simply peddling herbs to the city folk."

The old woman glanced in the direction of some ruckus coming from one of the other camps. It was only for a moment, but Ealasaid noticed the angry scowl that crossed Àed's face while the old woman's back was turned. Ealasaid sensed there was something to this whole situation that she was missing, and she would have given a lot to know what that thing was.

The old woman turned back to the fire, and Àed

resumed his pleasant expression. "What about the guard?" he asked.

The woman started, then looked at Àed in surprise. "What about her? Why are you asking so many questions? I simply wanted to warm myself by the fire."

"What did she look like?" Àed growled, finally losing patience.

The old woman stood abruptly, and glared down at Àed. "I don't know what you're playing at, but I've already had one attempt on my life, I'd like to avoid another." With that, she stormed off into the darkness.

Ealasaid turned wide eyes to Àed. "So is the woman you're looking for the guard she spoke of, or the Faie girl?"

Àed glared in the direction the old woman had gone. "The girl, though she's not of the Tuatha. Not really."

Ealasaid felt terrible. The girl they searched for was in mortal peril after all. She dreaded the words she had to say next. "If the city guard is anything like *An Fiach*, time might be growing short for your friend."

Àed turned his gaze toward the fire. "There's little chance that the woman who took her was a member of the guard. I only hope that our previous companion won't go back to his old ways when presented with both women at once."

Ealasaid wasn't sure if Àed meant Iseult or Kai, and she wasn't sure what he meant about *old ways*. She wasn't sure about a lot of things. The only thing she knew for certain, was that life was far more complicated out in the open world than she ever would have imagined from her safe, small bedroom, in her tiny little burgh, where she lived what seemed like several lifetimes ago.

She and Àed settled in for the night. Eventually they fell asleep after a long while spent gazing into the fire, sharing companionable silence, just like the night before.

THE NEXT MORNING, as Ealasaid boiled water over the fire for tea, she saw a wonderful sight approaching in the distance. She didn't particularly appreciate Iseult's silent, and oft times rude demeanor, but she'd take any excuse for a reprieve from Àed's cranky morning mutterings.

She noticed another tall man following behind Iseult as he approached, trailing a fully saddled, black and white dappled horse behind him. Àed was yet to notice their company, so deep was he in his dejected torpor. The second man looked eerily similar to Iseult, only he was dressed in a simple black tunic and breeches, not the more streamlined clothing of the warrior class worn by Iseult.

Iseult reached them first, not glancing back as the other man followed him. Ealasaid pushed a ringlet of hair behind her ear and stood to meet his gaze, waiting for an explanation. She felt somewhat deflated as he moved his eyes from her to Àed.

Àed didn't look up, and instead continued to poke at their fire. They'd kept it burning all night and into the morning, trying to keep away the cold. Ealasaid wasn't sure where the wood for the fire had come from, since the area had been long since picked over by refugees, but Àed always seemed to have more.

"She's gone," Àed commented, still not looking up.

Instead of responding, Iseult moved close to the old man and crouched by his side. He handed him a rough piece of parchment. Àed took it in hand, unfolded it, and read it quickly. From the motion of his bright blue eyes, Ealasaid could tell he read it several times over before aiming a meaningful glance at Iseult.

The unknown tall man stood back, casting his gaze over Ealasaid. She shifted her weight from foot to foot, feeling uncomfortable with the attention.

Àed went back to poking his fire. Ealasaid thought perhaps the parchment had carried bad news.

"We'll need a ship," Àed announced after several moments of silence.

The unnamed tall man stepped forward. "That's where I come in."

Àed turned to the man as if noticing him for the first time. "And where did ye come from?"

Ealasaid knew that Àed had to see the resemblance between Iseult and this new man, but he didn't remark on it. She tried to hide her disappointment.

"I'm kin to Iseult," he explained, "and we have similar goals."

Àed looked to Iseult. There was some mounting tension in the situation that Ealasaid didn't quite understand, but she wished it would end. They stared at each other for several moments before Àed asked, "Does yer ken have a name?"

"Maarav," the new man answered for him.

Àed's eyes narrowed as he continued to stare at Iseult. "Does yer ken have a purpose?" he asked gruffly.

"You need a ship," Maarav replied, "and I have one. It's docked a few day's journey North of here, but we should make your *meeting* in time."

Àed clenched his fist around the parchment Iseult had given him. Ealasaid was getting used to the old man's foul moods, but she had never seen him quite like this. She was beginning to think her journey with her newfound companions was about to come to an end, and wished she'd had the foresight to go with Kai. At least he was friendly. The thought of being on her own again with no destination in mind was almost too much to digest. Tears strained at the back of her eyes, but she refused to let them fall.

If she'd been able to remain in her small village, she would likely be planning her wedding by now, preparing to settle down and have children. She clenched her jaw. Her *gifts* had ruined that. Now she was doomed to wander the wilds alone, of no use to anybody.

Àed had fallen into a stupor, slouching down near the fire. Iseult and Maarav both waited, neither showing any emotion. Those two were family alright, though Ealasaid had been under the impression that Iseult had no family to speak of.

She cleared her throat, ready to announce her departure, when Àed suddenly stood. He stared at Maarav for a minute, as if peering into his very soul, then looked to Iseult and Ealasaid. "What are ye all waiting for?" he growled. When everyone stared at him in surprise, he clarified, "We have a meetin' to make."

Still too surprised by the sudden shift in atmosphere to move, Ealasaid stood motionless, watching as Àed left the fire to begin saddling his mule. Iseult joined Àed and saw to his horse, while Maarav waited with his already saddled mount, staring at Ealasaid with a curious expression. She turned her gaze downward, uncomfortable with the attention.

"What are ye waitin' for, lass!" Àed barked, startling Ealasaid out of her thoughts.

She looked to Àed and stammered, "B-but I thought-"

Somehow catching her meaning, Àed waved her off. "If I leave ye here among the refugees, ye'll be robbed, then ye'll either freeze to death or starve to death, whichever happens first."

Her stomach turning at the implications, Ealasaid nodded a little too quickly and rushed over to her horse. She thought she heard Maarav chuckle behind her. The idea of traveling with that man had her trembling with apprehension. She had to remind herself that she wasn't defenseless.

Her gifts may have ruined her life thus far, but in a pinch, they could also save it.

Iseult let out an irritated breath as he led the way on horseback. Once he found Finn, they could branch off on their own. He would fulfill his purpose, and he would protect her from her people. According to some, she was dangerous, but so was he. He'd made his choice, and she would be free to make hers.

He glanced over his shoulder at Maarav, his long lost brother. Long *dead* brother. Iseult was not unknown in these lands. The swordsman dressed in black, taller than most men, and faster, or so his reputation stated. Maarav could have found him sooner, so why now? Was it mere happenstance, or was it Finn? This was all based on the assumption that the man actually was his brother, but if he was, why had his mother told him he'd died? The world was turning itself upside down, and Iseult feared he was being swept up in the tides of fate. He had no use for fate. He would choose his own life.

He sucked his teeth as he came back to the present. As they traveled he'd seen numerous abandoned campfires, trampled greenery, and leftover refuse, signs of a large contingent of men, likely this ridiculous An Fiach they'd heard far too much of. He had chosen their route accordingly, far enough from the main road that they would not be spotted, but close enough that they would lose little time on their journey. He couldn't miss Finn when Kai brought her to the Archtree. *If* he brought her to the Archtree. He wasn't sure how Kai had figured things out to begin with, unless he'd snuck a glance at Iseult's map while he was sleeping.

"You noticed the camp, I see," Maarav observed as he rode up beside Iseult.

Iseult schooled his expression to remain impassive. He might not trust his *brother*, but he needed his ship. All of the questions he had for the man could wait. He *had* noticed the camp, off in the distance near the main road. He had no intention of moving closer to verify if it was An Fiach. It didn't matter.

"Aye," he replied simply.

Àed and Ealasaid rode behind them without comment. Iseult wasn't sure why the old man had really brought the girl along, but he thought it might have something to do with Àed's daughter. Some wrong of the past he was attempting to right, first with Finn, and now with this young girl.

Iseult drew his horse to an abrupt halt, noticing movement in the trees ahead. Catching on, Maarav stopped beside him, forcing Àed and Ealasaid to come to a halt behind them. No one spoke.

Iseult narrowed his eyes as the rustling foliage revealed a man. He swatted at a cluster of midges buzzing around his face as he walked on, not noticing the group of riders who watched him.

It would have been convenient to let the wanderer go about his way, never having noticed Iseult and his companions, except that Iseult knew the man.

He cleared his throat loudly, and the man whipped around. They were some distance off, but the man seemed to recognize Iseult instantly. They had travelled together for many weeks, after all.

"I never thought I'd say this," Anders said loudly as he approached, "but I am overjoyed to see you!"

Making no initial move toward friendliness, Iseult took in Anders' appearance as he neared. He wore the uniform of An Fiach, dark brown with crimson insignia, and his dusky red hair was tightly braided on either side of his scalp. He also looked tan and well-nourished, much more healthy than when they'd first met.

Anders' smile faltered as he reached the group and was met with no smiles in return. "Where's Finn?" he asked, as if just noticing that she was no longer there. "And Kai and Liaden?" he added.

"Where's yer sister?" Àed asked instead of offering an answer. "I don't imagine she's joined the Hunt as well?"

Anders' face fell even further. "I have searched for Branwen going on weeks now. She was taken by the Tuatha."

Finally Iseult dismounted, wanting to question Anders face to face. Once on the ground, he took a few steps forward to loom over the smaller man. "Why has An Fiach come this far North? What are they planning?"

Anders visibly gulped. "I think that's the most I've ever heard you speak in one sitting."

Still waiting for an answer, Iseult did not reply.

"Might I ask why we're harassing this soldier?" Maarav interrupted, still atop his horse.

"Perhaps we should just let him go on his way," Ealasaid squeaked.

She sounded farther away than she should to Iseult, as if she'd backed her horse up at the sight of Anders, though he did not turn around to confirm his suspicions.

Anders took a step away from Iseult and turned his attention to those still on their horses. Iseult watched as his gaze hesitated on Maarav for a moment, then obviously landed on Ealasaid, judging by the softening of his expression.

Anders paused, jaw slightly agape, then rallied himself. "I don't believe we've met," he began, still looking past Iseult to Ealasaid.

"I'm no one," she said quickly, finally drawing Iseult's eye. What was she hiding?

Ealasaid pushed her blonde curls behind her ears, only to have them fall forward again. She cast her eyes downward, uncomfortable being the new center of attention.

"Your mission," Iseult stated, turning the attention back to Anders. "What is it?"

Anders' skin flushed as he seemed to think things over, then he answered, "We're heading north to some old settlement that's been taken over by refugees. We seek to ensure their safety from the Tuatha."

"Ye seek to put innocents to the question, and to make the homeless doubly-so," Àed growled.

Anders appeared truly stricken. "We would do no such thing!" he shouted.

Iseult laughed bitterly. "Just as naive now as the day you chose to travel with any of us."

Anders took a steadying breath and turned his full attention to Iseult. "If you see my sister, please do your best to part her from the Tuatha. I beg you."

Iseult nodded. "If we meet again in the North, do your best to run the other way."

"I assure you we're not-" Anders began, but Iseult cut him off with the raise of his hand.

Anders let out a tired breath, then nodded, more to himself than to anyone else. "I should rejoin my contingent before they depart," he mumbled, thoroughly cowed. He cast a final glance at Ealasaid. "I wish we could have met under different circumstances."

As Anders began to walk away, Iseult turned to remount his horse, then instinctively turned to Anders again.

"I hope you find her," Anders said, a knowing, sad look on his face.

Iseult nodded, knowing that Anders wasn't talking about Branwen, but about Finn. Perhaps the young man wasn't as naive as Iseult had first believed.

"We need to warn those poor people," Ealasaid piped in, sounding braver now that Anders was almost out of sight. "I know just what An Fiach is capable of, and would not wish such a fate on anyone, let alone those who have already lost most everything."

Iseult grunted in acknowledgement. Few cities had ever existed to the north, and chances were likely that Iseult knew just where the refugees had set up.

"It's on the way to where we're going," Maarav announced. "We'll stop to offer a warning, then be on our way."

Iseult frowned as he kicked his horse forward without a word. Maarav spoke as if he too knew just where the refugees were. Chances were they were both right, and they would both see their ruined homeland quite soon.

ANDERS FOUGHT many conflicting emotions as he made his way back to the campgrounds of An Fiach. His once small contingent had joined up with many others. The crowd of men had made Anders anxious enough to take a walk in the woods by himself, despite any Faie that might lurk within. Now, with how Iseult and his companions had reacted, he was seeing the men in a different light. Could it be true what Àed had said? Anders trusted Radley, but could he trust the others? He'd been told they would make sure the refugees were safe from the Faie. They had no reason to harm innocent people, did they?

He felt close to tears as he reached a group of men sparring with practice swords. He imagined real swords in their hands as they chopped down innocent women and children. He shook his head. It couldn't be. Still, part of him wanted to rush back and join Iseult and the others, even if he was unwanted.

He gritted his teeth and moved past the sparring men. If they reached this settlement in the North and turned immediately to bloodshed, he would do exactly as Iseult had advised. He would run the other way.

Of course, if that lovely young lady, Ealasaid, was there, he might not be able to move his feet as fast as he would like.

He moved on past the cookfires, far away from the other men, to find an area where he could sit alone to think. Finding a spot, he sat on a moss-covered log, and stared out at the trees. He could hear the ocean not far off. Reviewing recent events, his heart ached. He'd argued when Radley first announced their new mission. They'd reached Migris, hoping to rest and resupply, but found the land riddled with poor and hungry people. He'd never seen anything like it.

Most travelers were turned away at the gates, but upon seeing the uniforms of An Fiach, the city guards had allowed Radley and his men into the city. There they'd gotten word that all men of An Fiach were to head north.

Anders had argued with Radley before they departed the city. His sister was in mortal peril, and he didn't want to waste any time checking on a small settlement of refugees. He didn't see what the harm was in letting the poor people stay as they were, but An Fiach planned to roust them, searching for Faie in the process.

Anders sighed, his budding doubts growing stronger. Feeling a chill, he began to build a small fire. He'd had little will to do anything after discovering his sister's bloody cloak, let alone the will to defy Radley. Never mind the fact that he stood no chance of rescuing his sister on his own.

As if sensing Anders' thoughts, Radley appeared from the direction of the main camp. His nearly bald head gleamed in the sunlight as he gave Anders a nod of greeting.

"Still down about your sister?" he asked as he took a seat in the dirt, opposite Anders. "She could still be alive. You shouldn't give up hope just yet."

Anders sighed. He was down about *many* things, but he couldn't confide them to Radley. "I should find some way to tell my parents what's happened, but I can't seem to find the nerve to send a letter."

Radley shrugged. "Few messengers are traveling the Sand Road these days. A letter wouldn't likely reach them either way. Perhaps our regiment will find reason to travel south after we see to these pikers in the north."

Anders held up his hands to warm them by the small fire he'd built, but it did little for the iciness that always seemed to be within him these days. He couldn't remember the last time he was truly warm. He appreciated what Radley was offering, but knew he couldn't accept. "I cannot return home without her. I swore to my parents that I would protect Branwen no matter the costs, and I've failed."

Radley pursed his lips in thought. As a military strategist, Radley was far more keen than most, but when it came to more emotional matters, he was often in the dark. "Well, you'll always have a home with An Fiach," he said finally, surprising Anders with his perceptiveness.

Anders forced a smile onto his face, though inside he felt ill. Though he did long for a home, a life with An Fiach wasn't exactly what he'd had in mind.

BRANWEN DID NOT RECALL much from when she'd been entranced, though Finn was prominent in her mind. She remembered briefly seeing her, but it was like she'd watched the scene from the end of a long tunnel. Her actions had not been her own.

She shook her head. It didn't matter now. None of it mattered. She was trapped in this . . . this *gray* place. She walked along endless corridors, sometimes bordered by stone walls, sometimes bordered by trees, but always with a relative feeling of *sameness*.

At first she'd thought that she wasn't alone. She'd seen other people, but when she approached them, they dissipated. *Illusions*. Yet, now she felt eyes on her all of the time, though she saw no one.

She wasn't sure how she'd gotten to that strange place. All she knew was that the voices that had instructed her since the Blood Forest had left her mind. She almost missed them. She would happily follow orders if it meant that she wouldn't be alone anymore.

Something on her side ached. A wound? She skimmed her hand along her side before she remembered that she'd already checked it several times over. There was no injury to be found. So why did it feel like she was bleeding?

CHAPTER EIGHT

*A*nna began to pace about her cabin as Kai left her. She'd explained what she'd been up to in their time apart, as had he. She'd lied about a great many things in her story, but once again, so had he. She stroked the hilt of a dagger, one of many in her belt. If only weapons could actually help her.

She continued to pace. The dreams had gotten worse. They began not long after Kai, Finn, and Iseult rescued her from the camp of the Ceàrdaman, but they had been sporadic back then. She'd brushed them off as nightmares. Who wouldn't have nightmares after her experience?

She still remembered wandering in that gray place for what seemed like weeks. The Travelers had put her there to search for their blasted tree. They didn't know how to find it, but Anna could see into the *gray*. The in-between place.

She hadn't wanted to admit it at first, but what the

Travelers had told her made sense. She *could* see things others could not. She'd always brushed it off as luck, something that helped in her trade, but she'd been lucky far too many times in her illustrious career as a thief, and sometimes mercenary. It was almost as if she could predict the pattern of fate at times, escaping from situations before they took a turn for the worse.

Where it had been convenient before, now it was driving her mad. The Travelers had increased whatever natural gifts she possessed, and she was beginning to have trouble telling the difference between reality and illusion.

Not long after leaving Port Ainfean, Óengus had tried to enlist her to hunt Finn *with* him, but her *gifts* had allowed her to be one step ahead. She didn't need to follow Óengus, or Kai, or anyone else to find that blasted tree girl. The woman shone like a captive star. They all shone, any who possessed innate magic, so brightly that at times Anna thought she might go blind. Just weeks ago, she'd believed that most magic was myth, but now she could see that many *normal* people possessed it, they just hid it, not wanting to be associated with the Faie.

Even with the magic users blinding her, and her dreams causing her to go mad, she wasn't one to be defeated. She would find that silly shroud and trade it to the Travelers, then they would make it all stop so things could return to normal.

She shook her head and lowered herself into the chair of her writing desk, then glanced over at her bed. She was exhausted, but too terrified to sleep. If she slept, she would go back to the gray place. She had seen many nightmares there. So many things she didn't understand. The previous night, she thought she even saw Branwen there with a bleeding wound in her side, but passed it off as subconscious guilt over what had happened to her.

The ship swayed comfortingly. She had never enjoyed sailing, but her distaste had recently changed. Out on the sea, you knew what dangers you might face, and you could confront them head on. Out on the sea, as long as she was awake, she was *safe.* Back on land, and in her dreams, the dangers were deceptive. They quietly closed in on her. She'd much rather drown in the ocean, than find a knife in the dark.

KAI HURRIED down the stairs that would take him below deck, clenching his jaw in irritation. Whether it was irritation at Sativola, Finn, or himself was anyone's guess. He'd just exited Anna's cabin, when Sativola caught him by the arm. The large man had held an unusually cowed expression on his face as he drew Kai aside, out of hearing distance of Anna or any of the men.

At first Kai felt terrified that something ill had befallen Finn, but then he realized Sativola was the one who'd fallen ill. Finn had charmed him, and he meekly requested that Kai ascend the stairs below deck to speak with her. Sativola had explained that he didn't want Finn to fall into trouble, and worried what might happen if Anna or one of the other men went to her first.

Kai shook his head as he reached the room where Finn was being kept. Sativola had refused to give him any more details, insisting that he just needed to go and see for himself. He raised his hand and rapped gently on the door.

No reply, except an odd scuffling sound, then a few animalistic chirps. Feeling suddenly worried again, he reached for the bolt that held the door in place from the outside, a special addition for Finn's stay, to find it already unlocked. He gritted his teeth, thinking of Sativola. Finn really *had* charmed him.

As if sensing that the door was about to open, Finn called out, "Do not come in! I'm not dressed!"

Kai shook his head. She had no idea who might be outside the door. Admitting such a thing to a man who might do her harm was unwise. Luckily, he hoped to never do her harm. At least, any more than he already had.

He let his hand fall, but a few more chirping sounds caused him to raise it again. "I'm coming in!" he called.

He opened the door to find Finn sitting on her bed with her loose hair mussed and a red flush to her face. She'd changed her clothes, and Kai was surprised to see her in dark colored pants like Anna wore, along with a loose, tan tunic topped by a deep blue corset. She seemed much smaller in the tight fitting clothes, but they suited her.

He would have liked to observe her for longer, but his attention was drawn behind Finn, where a bundle of blankets seemed to be moving of its own volition.

"What-" he began, taking a step forward, but Finn stood quickly, putting herself between Kai and the bed.

"Finn," he began in a lecturing tone as he peered around her shoulder. "Why is your bedding moving?"

She leaned to the side, paralleling his movements to block his view, smiling warmly at him. The smile was a dead giveaway that he really wouldn't like what was in that bed. Finn hadn't smiled like that at him since, well, *ever*.

He stepped forward and gripped her shoulders firmly, yet gently, then shifted her out of his way.

She grabbed his arm and tried to pull him backward. "You've no right!" she shouted, unable to move him as he continued looking down at the bed.

He'd only managed one more step, ignoring Finn's effort to pull him back, when the blankets exploded into motion. The fabric flew upward, revealing a feathered creature, who playfully pounced on the falling blankets like they were mice.

Kai stopped trying to move forward, and Finn let her hands fall from his arm in defeat. He stared at the creature in awe while it continued to play, not at all disturbed by his presence. As he tried to think of what to say, he finally took in the rest of the room, scattered with plates of fish bones, and a piece of bread that looked like it had been maimed, but was mostly uneaten.

He shook his head and turned back to Finn, who eyed him with a look of grim determination. She crossed her arms, as if daring him to take away her new pet.

He slumped in defeat. "Does it have a name?" he asked tiredly.

Finn's mouth formed a small 'oh' of surprise as the anger leaked out of her. "*She*," she corrected, "and her name is Naoki."

"Naoki?" he repeated, wondering at the strange name.

She looked back at the little creature still playing on her bed. "It means *tree of truth*," she explained, then frowned. "I'm not sure how I know that, but it seemed fitting none-the-less."

"It's nice," Kai commented.

Finn turned back to him, her frown deepening. "Being kind now won't get you much. I won't forgive you."

Forgive *him?* He'd traversed all across the blasted region to make sure she was okay. He'd endured Iseult's company, and put a serious rift in his relationship with Anna, *just* for Finn. Come to think of it, he wasn't really sure why he'd done all of that, when she had made it clear she simply wanted to be rid of him.

"What have I done that needs forgiving?" he questioned in exasperation. "I might have lied to you initially, but I more than made up for it by sheltering you in Port Ainfean while you waited for your *man* to rescue you. When those roots sucked you into the earth, I hacked them to pieces to find you, but you were already gone. *Then* I traveled all the way to Migris to find you, snuck onto Anna's ship, and convinced her that I was useful enough to stick around, *just* so I could make sure you were safe!"

Finn seemed to be growing increasingly angry. Naoki paused her activities to observe them. If Kai didn't know any better, he'd say the dragon-like creature was casting him a particularly venomous look on Finn's behalf.

After a few silent moments of staring at each other, Finn's anger finally boiled over. "You sheltered me *after* lying to me and kidnapping me! Then you did your absolute best to convince me that you only do things that benefit you. Now I'm to believe that you followed me after I found Iseult and Àed because you were worried? Or did you follow me because you had something to gain? And what do you mean *while I waited for my man to rescue me*? No man belongs to me!"

Kai grunted in annoyance. Of course, the one time he actually decided to do something moderately noble it would backfire on him. Iseult was clearly *hers*, but he wasn't going to point it out if she didn't already realize it. He threw his hands up in the air. "If you don't want my help, then fine!"

Finn took a step forward, her face flushed and her mouth twisted like she tasted something sour. "Not only do I not *want* your help, I don't need it! As far as I'm concerned, you can jump into the ocean right this minute!"

She looked so indignant at that moment that Kai could kiss her, though he'd likely get a slap if he did. Still, it was hard to hold onto his own anger when such a normally kind-natured woman was trying to appear imposing.

Her expression softened when Kai didn't reply.

He glanced around at all of the empty plates, to the dragon still watching them from the bed, then back to Finn. "I hope at least a portion of this food went to you," he commented.

Finn appeared suspicious at the subject change. "Don't pretend that you care if I eat," she replied petulantly.

Kai was too tired to be frustrated. This woman had somehow uprooted his entire existence, and now here she was, treating him like it all meant less than nothing. "Finn," he began patiently, "I traveled with Iseult and Àed to Migris. I've seen Iseult's map to the Archtree, and I know all about the much desired shroud of the Faie Queen. If that's all I was after, I could have boarded a ship immediately and set sail on my own. If I were still out to claim the bounty on your head, I could have told those looking for you that you were waiting in Migris. If I were out to harm you, I could have done it while we stood in this room, *alone*."

"Iseult and Àed were in Migris?" she questioned softly.

"And they'll be meeting us at the Archtree," he grumbled, slightly hating that fact.

Finn looked like she might cry.

Kai rolled his eyes. "What is it *now*?"

She bit her lip and shook her head as the first tears began to stream down her face. "I'm sorry I made such horrible accusations," she muttered.

Kai stood in shock for a moment. Was he actually getting an apology? He pulled her toward him and wrapped her in his arms as she continued to cry. His heart beat a little faster at Finn's nearness, then he felt something wiggling up between them. He pulled away from Finn to see Naoki peering up at him with her large, green, circular eyes, unhappy that Kai was touching her new-found mother.

Finn laughed through her tears, then pulled away from Kai to gather the dragon up in her arms, effectively ending the moment.

Before Kai could say anything else, a knock sounded at the door. Kai moved to answer it, suspicious that anyone else on the ship might have a need to call on Finn.

He opened the door to see Sativola's worried expression. "There's a reiver ship in the distance," the large man explained quickly, "we've veered off course, but if they want to reach us, they will."

Kai's thoughts raced. "What are reivers doing this far inland? They only raid the seas near the borders."

Sativola frowned. "The whole world has turned upside down if ye ask me."

Kai patted Sativola on the shoulder and turned to follow him out of the room. He thought better of it as he came to a sudden halt in the doorway. He turned to face Finn and pointed a reprimanding finger at her. "Stay here," he ordered, waiting for Finn to meet his eyes and nod.

He turned and raced out of the room with Sativola hot on his heels, slamming the door shut behind them.

Part of him wanted to stay and hide in the room with

Finn. Reivers weren't like normal bandits. They were more . . . feral. Normally they stuck around the borders where their small tribes dwelled, robbing any caravan that came too close. Now they were traveling the sea, well within the realm of Migris. If they boarded the ship, everyone was doomed.

FINN REMAINED in her room like she'd been asked. For quite some time things were silent. She would hear the occasional shout on deck as the men steered the ship away from the reivers, but little else. Iseult had mentioned reivers before. Finn wasn't sure who or what they were, but she knew they were to be avoided at all costs.

Naoki, sensing Finn's unease, prowled around the room, perking up each time one of the men shouted. After a time, Finn began to relax. Surely they'd escaped the reivers by now? She might have had her misgivings about Kai, and even more about Anna, but if she could trust in anything, it was their ability to stay alive.

Suddenly, there was a massive thud above deck, then the sound of too many voices. There weren't enough men on the ship to create such a cacophony. Finn glanced down at Naoki, who was eyeing her steadily, as if waiting for an explanation.

"We're supposed to stay here," Finn explained, not really expecting the little dragon to understand her.

Naoki cocked her head and made a chittering sound with her beak.

Finn jumped at a clambering sound on deck, like the sound of someone or something falling. She wrapped her arms around herself, feeling increasingly anxious. "We really must stay here," she muttered, speaking more to herself than to Naoki.

There was no more commotion up above. In fact, things were eerily silent.

Finn stood, then went to crouch over Naoki. "Maybe we can just take a peek," she whispered conspiratorially.

She walked past Naoki and opened the door, then went out into the narrow hallway. The sound of Naoki's talons on the wooden flooring behind her let Finn know that the dragon was just as curious as she.

Finn ascended the small stairway that led above deck, opening the wooden hatch that separated her from the open air just a crack. She angled her head so that she could peek out of the trap door without opening it any further. She could see the feet and legs of the men on deck, but nothing else. She recognized Kai's legs, and hated that she could recognize the blasted man just by his legs. Next to him stood thick legs that looked like Sativola's, followed by the rest of the crew. She didn't see Anna.

Opposite Kai and the crew were several other sets of legs wearing fur-lined black boots. The boots seemed clunky, and encased large feet attached to thick, well-muscled legs, also clad in black. As she watched, the black clad legs began to disperse around deck. She realized too late that one set of legs was headed her way. The man attached to the legs crouched down in front of the hatch and grabbed the handle, pulling it upward. Finn instinctively pulled back.

The man grunted, then gave a sudden tug, lifting both the hatch and Finn. They had a moment of looking at each other, stunned, then Finn loosed her grasp on the trap door and fell to the stairs. She scuttled down, then back in the direction of her room, seeing no other choice.

The man had been frightening in appearance, with wild, matted hair, and black smudged generously around his eyes. Finn reached her room before the man had even started coming down the stairs, but she stopped in horror when she realized Naoki wasn't beside her.

"What in Tirn Aill's name is that?" someone unfamiliar shouted above deck.

"The other world has nothin' to do with it!" another shouted. "That thing is of the Tuatha!"

Oh no. Naoki must have run on deck when Finn ran away. With a grunt of frustration, Finn left her room and ran back toward the stairs. The trap door was open, but no unkempt man hovered over it. She ran up the stairs without thinking, desperate to save her new little friend.

The sea wind whipped Finn's long hair into her face as she took in the scene that lay before her. Kai and the other men of the crew all stood near the middle of the deck with thick ropes around their wrists and torsos. There were around ten other men, though Finn couldn't keep count since most of them were moving, dressed like the one who'd opened the trap door. Those running about swung heavy axes and swords at Naoki as she deftly darted out of the way.

There was a ship moored up beside theirs with more of the intimidating men on board, watching as their comrades battled with the mighty little dragon. None of them even seemed to notice Finn as she came into view, except Naoki. The dragon ran toward her with a screech, terrified of the men chasing her, but she wasn't going to make it in time.

Just as Naoki was almost near enough for Finn to scoop her up, one of the reivers began an overhand swing of his sword. Spurred on by instinct, Finn lunged forward into the path of the blade.

Kai shouted her name, while Sativola shouted, "No!" but it wouldn't do her any good. She clenched her eyes shut as the sword raced down toward her shoulder.

A sickening feeling washed over her as she reached out her hands to ward off the blow that would strike any second. Dizziness struck her instead, then something hard knocked into her shoulder, but didn't slice her in half.

It still hurt. The blow was hard enough to knock Finn to the ground, sending a jolt of pain all the way down to her toes. The man had flailed forward at the last second, hitting her with the pommel of his blade. She curled up on the ground while she tried to remember how to breathe. She knew any moment the man might swing again, and she was sure this time he would not miss . . . but something was wrong. The man was whimpering in pain. Soon his whimpers turned into screams. Had someone attacked him from behind?

Finn still felt too stunned to move, and still couldn't figure out what was causing the man to scream in agony. Naoki nuzzled her beak frantically against Finn's face, making soft mewling noises.

"She's a sea witch!" one of the reiver's shouted, over his comrade's screams.

Finn's eyes remained on the downed reiver a few feet from her. Something was beginning to happen.

"She'll curse us all!" shouted another.

Finn took a deep breath and braced her good arm against the rough wood of the deck. The ocean somehow seemed louder than the men's shouts. With a grunt of pain, she was able to raise herself to a sitting position.

Numbly, she looked to everyone else on deck, her vision fading in and out of darkness. First, she saw the reivers all grouped together, backing away from her with looks of terror on their faces. Next, she turned to see Kai and the others, looking astonished or outright afraid. Finally, she forced herself to turn back toward the man who'd tried to kill her. At some point his screams had died down, but she hadn't noticed right away. She felt like she was in a dream. She knew everything was happening within a span of seconds, but it felt like she'd been sitting there for ages.

Finn's eyes widened as she stared at the felled man. First she focused on his tear-stained face, the salty water trailing through the black around his eyes, then her eyes moved down to his arm that had held the sword. The skin of his arm had turned a sickly yellow in places, a pallid green on his hand, and black at his fingertips. As she watched, the skin on the man's fingertips fell from his bones, rotting before her very eyes.

The man turned agony filled eyes to Finn. "Make it stop," he pleaded, his voice cracking with pain. "Please make it stop!" he shouted as the flesh began to fall from the rest of his hand.

Naoki curled around Finn and hissed at the man.

Finn began to cry, and shouted at the reivers, "Take him with you if you don't want to anger me further!" she shouted.

The reivers stood in silence, as if they feared touching their injured crewmate as he cried and rotted away before their very eyes.

She would make it stop, if she knew how, for she could bear the sight of him no longer.

She glared at them with tear filled eyes. "Help him or I'll curse you all!" She knew she should be feeling fear and revulsion, but all she could feel was rage. The reivers had made her do something horrible. It was all their fault. She couldn't have known what would happen.

The reivers jumped into motion and gathered the rotting man, then retreated to their ship, leaving Kai and the other men bound. As the reiver ship cast off, the remaining men looked to her as one.

She shakily got to her feet. Her shoulder was screaming, but it was a distant pain. Kai and the other men watched her wordlessly. She could practically taste their fear. She backed away while Naoki wove around her ankles like a cat.

"Finn-" Kai began, but that was all he got out as she turned on her heel and ran back below deck.

The Traveler at Maarav's inn had told Finn that she was a weapon, and now she was sure that he was right. She was made to destroy. To rot the flesh from her victim's bones. To call the earth up to swallow them whole. She deserved whatever the Cavari decided to do to her.

KAI POUNDED on the door to Finn's cabin. She'd run away so abruptly that he and the other men had been forced to wait for Anna to come out of her cabin to untie them. She'd hid when the reivers neared, as it was wise for any woman to do. With just the men on deck, there was a chance that the reivers would simply rob them and be on their way. Having women out in the open complicated things, as the reivers might try to steal them too, giving them as much regard as food or coin. Maybe less.

Anna had wanted an explanation to why the reivers were gone and they still had all of their belongings, but Kai left it to the other men. He couldn't erase from his mind the look on Finn's face right before she'd run away. Nor could he erase the sight of a man's flesh rotting from his bones. A few little gobs of flesh still dotted the deck above.

Kai pounded on the door again. "You can't stay in there forever!" he shouted.

There was no reply. There hadn't been any reply since he'd first started knocking. The room locked from both the inside and outside with a key, which Kai possessed, as well as the added bolt on the outside, but the locks did little good seeing as Finn had wedged something underneath the door to keep it in place.

Thoroughly flustered, Kai lowered himself to his stomach on the wooden planking. He peered underneath the door, but it was so dark that it was hard to make anything out. Either her lantern had gone out, or she'd intentionally snuffed it. At a loss, he pushed the long, iron key underneath the door and swiped it from one side to the other. It hit something about halfway across. Noting the location, he withdrew the key, then stabbed it back underneath the door where the blockage was. A wedge of wood came loose and skittered across the floor of the room's interior.

There was still no sound from Finn. Seriously starting to worry, Kai righted himself and opened the door. The only light in the room came from the open trap door down the hall, but he thought he could make out Finn's small form on the bed, her face turned toward the wall.

"Finn," he said, knowing he should say *something*, though he wasn't sure what.

"Will I be walking the plank then?" came a tear-strained voice from the bed.

Kai would have laughed if some of the other men hadn't suggested such a thing only moments before.

"Of course not," he assured. He still stood just inside the doorway. Normally he was skilled at easing the tension out of any situation, but here, he felt his normal tactics useless.

"You're afraid of me," she accused, if an accusal could be made with such an utter lack of emotion.

"That's not true," he argued, though part of him was. Who would have thought that sweet little Finn would be capable of something so horrifying? He'd been present what seemed like months ago, when she had called roots up from the earth to crush the life out of someone who'd been trying to kill him, so he knew she had the potential to be dangerous. Yet, this seemed different. This was the stuff of nightmares.

"Then why are you still standing so far away?" she countered, still bundled in her blankets with her back to him. "Usually you'll take any opportunity you can to invade my space."

Kai hadn't noticed at first, but Naoki was curled up in the bedding near Finn's feet. The little dragon's eyes reflected the small amount of light in the darkness as it blinked, then continued to watch him.

"Your dragon is standing guard," Kai joked trying to lighten the mood.

Finn finally turned over in her bed to look at him. Her puffy face stayed half in shadow, but the one eye he could see in the dim light accused him of a thousand wrong-doings. "I met one of the Ceàrdaman while I was in Migris," she explained. "He told me that I'm a weapon, and that's why the Cavari want me. I'm meant to destroy, and nothing more. You should probably kill me while you have the chance."

Kai grunted in frustration, then forced himself forward. If she did to him what she did to the reiver, well, then it was just his time to go. He sat on the bed near Finn's stomach, in the larger space created by her curled up form. Naoki shot up in protest and scampered up to Finn's shoulder, where she curled up and trained an accusing eye on Kai.

"That's like saying that I was born to be a slave, so that's all I'll ever be," Kai countered. Finn knew a bit of his ugly history. She was one of the very few people who did.

Finn buried her face back in her pillow. "It's not the same," she argued, the sound muffled by the bedding.

He lifted a hand to place it on her arm, but Naoki let out a low growl. Sighing, Kai moved the hand to the side of Finn's waist, still covered by blankets. It was probably too intimate a gesture, but he wanted to show her that he wasn't afraid to touch her. He wasn't sure why, really, but it seemed important.

"You shouldn't touch me," she muttered. "You saw what I did up there."

"To a man who was trying to kill you," he added.

"That's beside the point," Finn cut in quickly.

Not moving his hand, Kai continued, "Is it? Have you ever harmed a single person who wasn't trying to do you harm in the first place."

Finn sat up so suddenly that Naoki had to flutter her wings to maintain her balance on the bed. "That's just it!" she shouted, suddenly frantic. "I don't remember anything of my life before. Who knows what I've done? The Cavari destroyed Iseult's people! What if they used me to do it? What if they used me to do even worse?"

His mind simply couldn't wrap around the idea of Finn slaughtering innocents. She was good. Even after seeing her frightening powers at work, in his mind he still viewed her as purely good.

She was panting like she couldn't catch her breath, and somehow her face had ended up only inches from Kai's in her fervor. Her dark eyes stared into his, searching, but for what? Comfort? Absolution?

"We all have our own gifts," he stated calmly. "It doesn't matter what they are, because you are forgetting one very important part of being human."

"And what's that?" she breathed, her face still so oddly near.

"There's always a choice," he replied. "No one can force you to be something, if you choose not to be it."

She was silent, as if soaking in his words. Even with the grisly scene of the rotting reiver still fresh in his mind, Kai felt the overwhelming urge to kiss her. He leaned closer, and she didn't move.

Suddenly a beak appeared between their faces. The beak shoved forward until Naoki's entire head blocked Kai from Finn. He leaned back with a sigh. Blasted dragon.

Finn fell back to the bed as if the last ounce of energy

had left her. Naoki curled up in the crook of Finn's arm while Finn stared absently up at the ceiling. Not knowing what else to do, Kai stood, then crouched near the head of the bed.

"Get some rest," he said softly.

She nodded, though a few more silent tears fell down her face. She shut her eyes.

Kai stayed with her until her body relaxed into the thrall of sleep, and Naoki made soft snoring noises beside her.

He moved to leave, then thought better of it, and leaned down to kiss Finn's forehead. Her skin left the salt of sweat and tears on his lips, but he didn't mind. In that moment he finally realized why he'd been unable to just let Finn go. Why he'd followed her across the country-side, determined to prove to her that he wasn't the type of man she thought he was.

He straightened and shook his head. Once they reached the Archtree, she would be back with Iseult. They would run off like they'd always wanted, to save the world, or whatever else they had planned, and his life would go back to the way it always had been. It was better that way. He didn't deserve *good*. He'd continue to look out for no one, and no one would look out for him.

BEDELIA ROLLED the little glass phial around in her palm as the coastal air blew her hair back from her sweaty face. The liquid inside the vial was dark, not something she'd drink without knowing what it was. Her leg ached where the wolf had bitten her. At first she thought the wound would actually heal on its own, but the healing seemed to have halted. When she'd been brave enough to look, she'd seen that the skin around the wound was pallid, the veins underneath an unnatural black, showing through like ugly smudges of ink.

Part of her hoped the wound *would* kill her. She'd failed her mission and lost the girl. Óengus still seemed optimistic about finding her, and if anyone could, it was him, but Bedelia knew the chances were slim. If Finn had indeed boarded a ship, she would be almost impossible to track. The only way to find her was to know where she was going.

Bedelia cringed as she lifted herself off the railing she'd been resting on, lowering her feet to the wood of the dock. Óengus was attempting to find crewmen for the ship he'd procured, but it was proving difficult. It gave Bedelia a small amount of satisfaction, even though she would have liked to get on with things.

She stared out at the ocean, licking her cracked lips as the harsh, salty air coated her skin. She didn't want to believe that Finn had abandoned her intentionally. They were friends, after all.

She laughed bitterly at her thoughts, then shook her head. She didn't have friends. She had duty, and she liked to think she had her own version of honor, but not friends.

As Óengus came into view at the end of the pier, his silver hair glinting in the sunlight, she slipped the glass vial into her pocket. She tried to stand tall, belying her illness, but knew that it showed in the sickly sweat on her face, and the way she was forced to hold herself to avoid unnecessary pressure on her leg.

"It's time to go," he announced as he reached her, his abnormally pale eyes cold.

She nodded, feigning courage.

He looked down at her injured leg, as if sensing its disability through the thick fabric of her breeches. "Try not to be a burden," he grunted before turning on his heel, expecting her to follow.

She hobbled after him, once again strongly considering sticking a dagger in his back. Surely Keiren would understand that she couldn't suffer such an intolerable man to live?

Bedelia groaned against the pain in her leg as she continued to follow, not reaching for her dagger. Who was she kidding? Even if the world was coming to an end, Óengus would find a way to survive, and here she was, dying of a silly wolf bite.

innn squinted her eyes as she struggled to see through the fog. Unable to bear another moment within the confines of her cabin, she'd mustered the courage to go back on deck with Naoki as moral support. She still feared that someone might try harming her little dragon, but the men of the ship now seemed to be more frightened of Finn than they were of the Faie creature.

She sighed as she leaned her hands against the ship's railing, with Naoki curled around her shoulders. The young dragon was a touch too heavy for her small frame, but she hadn't the heart to shoo her away. It was comforting to have a friend, even one that couldn't speak to offer her any advice.

Of course, advice would have been useless in Finn's situation. There was nothing she could do to change who she was, just as she couldn't change the fact that she was stuck on an unmoving ship. The air was thick with fog, disorienting her more than the sway of the ocean waves already had. At least she no longer felt like she might lose her lunch.

Kai stood a few feet away, seemingly pretending not to notice her, but she knew better. He was either watching *her* to make sure she didn't jump into the ocean, or he was watching the crew to make sure they didn't push her in.

She had seen no sign of Anna. She must really be enjoying her cabin to be spending so much time within its confines. Anna's cabin *was* larger than hers, but she still didn't understand how someone could surround themselves with wooden walls for such prolonged periods of time.

Naoki chittered near her ear, indicating that someone was approaching, though Finn had already noticed the sound of boots on deck. Kai appeared by her side. Maybe *he'd* be the one to push her into the ocean.

"Feeling better?" he questioned, gazing out into the fog as he leaned his arms against the railing.

Finn inhaled deeply. Naoki's tight wrap around her was almost strangling. The dragon did not like Kai, and Finn couldn't say that she blamed her. "I'll feel better once we reach the Archtree," she replied softly.

Kai was silent for a moment, then asked, "What will you do once we're there?"

Finn glanced at him suspiciously, debating whether or not she should tell him the truth. She settled for being vague. "The Archtree's leaves have the power to answer your heart's most important question. If you are not tricking me, Iseult and I will find the answers to our questions, then we will decide what must be done from there."

Kai frowned. "That much I had gathered, just as I have gathered that Iseult searches for the shroud. What I don't understand, is what's in it for you?"

Finn frowned in return. At some point she'd shifted away from the railing to face Kai, and he'd done the same. He already knew about the shroud, and about the Archtree, so why was he trying to garner more information. Was this all a trick so he could steal the one thing Iseult wanted most?

Finn crossed her arms, then immediately had to uncross them to steady herself on the railing. Naoki made her top-heavy, throwing her off balance. "I'll know what happened to me. I'll know if my people are good or evil. I'll know if *I'm* good or evil."

Kai stood on his own, perfectly balanced, with no need to steady himself on the railing. He had a strange expression on his face, like he was biting his tongue to keep words from coming out of his mouth.

"*What?*" Finn asked sharply, already offended.

Kai sighed, glanced at Naoki, who was staring at him as hard as Finn was, then explained, "It just seems to me that all of those questions are irrelevant. It doesn't matter what happened in your past, because you're here now. I'd think it much more useful to ask questions of the present or future, of things you can actually change."

Finn crossed her arms again, this time spreading her

feet wide to maintain her balance. "And what will *you* ask the Archtree that's so much better?"

Kai seemed genuinely surprised. "I hadn't considered asking it anything, really. Especially given that it's probably just a regular old tree, and won't tell us a thing."

Finn felt her expression fall. Kai raised his hands up in a soothing gesture, as if to stop her trail of thoughts.

"I didn't mean to take away your hope," he said quickly. "Even if the tree isn't real, you can still find your answers."

Finn felt on the verge of tears. She had been struggling blindly toward the Archtree, comforting herself with the thought that if she could just make it there, everything would make sense.

"I'm sure the tree will tell you what you need to know," he amended. "Don't worry about it."

Finn shook her head. Why was he being so nice to her? "No," she replied softly. "No, you're right. I don't know anything, and that's not likely to change. I don't even know how to be a proper person. Even if I manage to get answers from the Archtree, I'll still be this . . . mess. A tool for others to use without me even knowing it."

Kai opened his mouth, but didn't seem to know what to say. Finn didn't blame him. Some of the other men on deck were glancing at them suspiciously.

"Finn-" he began, and she just knew that something comforting was about to come out of his mouth, and she couldn't bear to hear it.

She took a sudden step back, jostling Naoki, who let out a little squawk. With a final look at Kai, she turned on her heel and hurried away, as quickly as possible with Naoki on her shoulders, back toward the little trap door that would lead to her cabin.

As she descended the darkly lit stairs, she began to cry. She wasn't even sure why she was upset, or why it mattered so much that Kai thought the Archtree was a myth. She would still be reunited with Iseult and Àed, and *they'd* know what to do.

As she reached her cabin, she finally realized just what had really bothered her. She'd wanted the tree to tell her that she was capable and strong, and *good*. If it could not, then she would have to continue to depend on others. Unfortunately, she was far from realizing that the things she needed to hear were the types of things humans had to find on their own.

ANNA TOSSED AND TURNED, tangled in her bedding. She'd been spending most of her time in her cabin, if only to keep the crew from thinking she'd gone mad.

The dreams had gotten worse, and the lines between what was real, and what was in her head, were blurring. Though she only entered the *gray place* while she slept, she'd started seeing things in waking. The light that emanated from Finn and other magical beings was nothing new, but she was beginning to see a different type of light from the crewmen. Some were muted and dark, others more vibrant. Kai was a shade of serene green that she didn't mind as much as the others.

Anna hadn't wanted to go back to sleep, but her restless nights had left her unbelievably tired. Still, her brain, out of fear of what would happen, was keeping her awake.

Kai had been pestering her frequently, wondering what was the matter. He'd also informed her that Finn had adopted a baby dragon. The funny thing was, Anna had believed him immediately. If she could be held hostage by the Ceàrdaman, and could have her brain altered to the point where people shone like stars, then a baby dragon was entirely believable.

She flipped onto her back and thunked her arms down against the bed with a huff, blowing her tangled hair out of her face. Kai had assured her that he knew the way to the Archtree. He'd had a peek at a map that Iseult carried. It wasn't much to go on, but she trusted Kai's judgement in the matter, even if she could no longer trust his judgement on . . . other things.

The greedy survivalist in Anna still wanted to find the shroud of the Faie Queen, but perhaps that could be the question that Kai would ask the Archtree. She had too many other questions that needed answers.

She could just ask Finn in the meantime, but why would she help the person who'd twice kidnapped her? If Finn hated her, well, Anna felt she deserved it.

A knock on her cabin door made her groan. It was likely Kai again. Anna warred with emotions of annoyance and love. Kai was the only person in the world that actually cared what happened to her, even if he was a pest.

She rose from her bed and padded barefoot across the rugs that covered the wooden decking of the ship, withdrawing a key from her pocket to unlock the door. Opening it just a crack, she peeked out to make sure it was indeed only Kai waiting outside. She wouldn't dare let any of the crewmen see her in such a disheveled state. She was their leader, after all.

Kai stood outside the door, looking worried, and also surrounded by . . . was that fog? Anna had never seen fog so thick. It nearly obscured Kai's features from a few feet away.

She opened the door a little wider and ushered him inside, shutting it quickly behind him after he'd entered. After a moment, she locked the door as an added precaution, against what, she did not know.

Kai looked around Anna's cabin, as if searching for some sort of clue about her reclusion.

Anna, feeling tired and dizzy, still had enough gall to tap her bare foot impatiently while glaring Kai down for an explanation.

He smiled ruefully. "So you're really not going to tell me what's going on?"

"I'm ill," she snapped. "Nothing more."

Kai sighed. "As you might have noticed during that brief peek outside this room, fog has closed in upon us. It's too thick to even see the water directly below us, so we've been forced to come to a standstill. We can either wait it out, or move forward with the hope that we're lucky enough to avoid any reefs or ice. Just to throw in my opinion, I'm not feeling terribly lucky."

Anna nodded as panic clutched at her chest. She couldn't get to the Archtree soon enough. What was a short delay to some, was torture to her.

"I'm worried that there is something abnormal about this fog," Kai added.

Anna took a moment to actually *look* at Kai. His shoulder-length, chestnut hair was beaded with moisture from the fog. It clung to his cheeks and shimmered on the stubble that had formed on his chin and jaw. She'd always found him rather handsome, though men were not her preference. Plus, she'd take a best friend over a romantic partner any day of the week. She only had to look at what romance had done to Kai to back up that decision.

"What do you mean, abnormal?" Anna asked with a groan. Of course it was *abnormal* fog. Nothing was right in the world anymore.

"The way it formed," he explained, "and how dense it is. I've never seen anything quite like it. It almost makes it difficult to breathe."

Not quite meeting Kai's eyes, Anna asked, "What does Finn think?"

Kai snorted. "I'm surprised you'd ask her opinion on something."

Anna finally met his gaze, if only to glare at him. "She *is* a magical being, perhaps even of the Faie. It would make sense for her to know something about this."

Kai shrugged, his expression unreadable. "She doesn't even know who she is, not really. Plus, she just ran off and locked herself in her cabin again, so it's probably not the time to ask her."

Anna smirked, imagining Finn slamming the door in Kai's face at something he'd said. "She has a flair for the dramatic, I'll give her that."

Kai sighed and moved past Anna to sit at the foot of her bed. "Says the other woman who's locked herself in her cabin," he teased as he looked up at her.

Anna gritted her teeth. She wasn't fond of showing weakness to anyone, but sharing her troubles might help matters. Sharing them with someone like Kai was an added comfort. He would never view her as weak.

"Ever since I was taken by the Travelers," she began.

Kai sat up straighter, giving her his full attention.

Anna cleared her throat nervously, "Ever since my time with the Travelers," she began again, "I've been seeing *things*. At first it was just Finn and Àed. Finn shines like a captive star, and Àed like the soft golden light of the morning sun."

Anna let out a shaky breath. Kai wasn't looking at her like she was crazy.

"Now everyone is starting to shine," she continued. "Even you. You shine a soft green like light peeking through a canopy of leaves."

Kai seemed suddenly concerned. "So you've hidden yourself away, because we're all shining too much?"

Anna sighed. She had no idea how to explain things properly. "At night," she went on, wanting to get everything out before she lost her nerve, "I go to a place that's all gray and misty, with stone walls and long hallways.

I'm usually alone, though I'm quite sure I saw Branwen there once, of all people."

"So you dream that you're trapped in a place with long, lonely halls," Kai observed. "I'd say that perhaps says something about how you live your life. Maybe it's your subconscious thoughts coming through."

Anna stomped up to Kai, still seated on her bed, and glared down at him. "They're not just dreams," she chided. "It's like I really go there, but my body remains here. I went to such a place when the Travelers had me, when they made me look for the Archtree."

Kai stood so abruptly it almost knocked Anna off her feet. She had no idea what had suddenly excited him so much.

"Why would you wait until *now* to tell me the Travelers are looking for the Archtree!" he shouted. "What if they're already there when we arrive?"

Anna cringed, but remained calm. "I found it in my travels within the gray place, but I was unable to give them an exact location, as I wasn't traveling across normal terrain. I did find it though, and that seemed to satisfy them."

Kai slumped back down onto the bed, shocked. "So it exists then?" he breathed. "It's not a myth?"

Anna nodded. "Why do you think I believed you when you said you'd memorized a map to its location? I wouldn't have hired an entire crew to find something I believed a myth."

Kai glared at her. "Well, sorry for not assuming that you'd already traveled to the tree in your dreams."

Anna lowered herself to sit beside Kai, feeling drained from their conversation. They sat in silence for several minutes until she questioned, "What do you want to ask the tree?"

Kai frowned. "I thought you wanted to ask it how to find this fabled shroud."

Anna curled the corner of her lip. "I asked what *you* wanted."

Likely knowing that Anna would not cease her questioning until he gave in, Kai answered, "I think I'd like to ask it what happened to my family. If they were punished after I left."

"Everyone who knew you believes you to be dead," Anna commented, unsure of why *that* would have been Kai's question. "They would not have been punished for your disappearance."

"They would not have been able to keep up with the work without me," he explained as he rubbed a hand tiredly across his eyes. "They would have fallen even further into debt. Not being able to afford food is punishment enough."

"So go back there," Anna decided. "Don't waste your one question with the Archtree on something you could find out yourself."

"And if I'm seen?" he countered. "If they were not punished for me dying, then surely they would be if their *lord* learned that I had survived to run away."

Anna sighed. "When all of this is over, and we're free to live as we please again, I'll check for you. Do not waste your one question."

Kai seemed somewhat taken aback. He opened his mouth to speak, but no words came out.

Anna narrowed her eyes at him. "Do not act so surprised. I *can* be selfless."

Kai nodded, still seeming just as surprised, but not speaking. Anna couldn't blame him. Until recently, she wasn't sure she had a selfless bone in her body. Perhaps the Travelers had done more damage to her than she realized.

Suddenly feeling uncomfortable, she sighed. "I'm tired."

Kai raised an eyebrow at her. "Are you sure you don't want to come out on deck for a bit? The fog will soak you through, but it still might be good for you."

Anna looked down at her lap and shook her head. "I'd really rather not see anyone until we reach the Archtree."

Kai frowned, then accepted her answer with a nod. He patted her knee companionably. "I'll come check on you later."

Anna opened her mouth to tell him not to bother, but he'd already stood and headed for the door. She frowned after him as he left, wondering what had happened to make him so much nicer than he'd ever been before. She crawled the rest of the way onto her bed and lowered her head to her pillow, not intending to sleep, but feeling too weary to do anything productive.

Hours later, she lay on her bed, drifting in and out of consciousness, unsure if what she was seeing was a dream or reality. As her eyes fell shut once more, she found herself in a forest, enshrouded in fog, just like her ship.

She was hiding near a massive oak tree, using its thick trunk to conceal her cloaked form. She felt light, like she might float away at any moment, though the chill of the forest mist felt just as real as anything she'd ever experienced.

A moment later, her eyes found what she was hiding from. She shifted to peek around the tree's trunk, watching warily as the hooded figures came into view.

There were twenty or so, and they seemed to glide as they moved through mist so dense that it obscured the ground at their feet, if they even had feet.

The forest had gone silent at their approach, except for the trees, which seemed to move as the dark figures moved. It wasn't something that Anna could quite train her eye on. Instead, a branch that would have scraped across a cloak was suddenly bent backward out of the way. Any vines and brambles that reached up above the foggy ground seemed to twist away from the forms, rather than catching at them like they would with normal travelers.

Anna's eyes widened as she realized the forms were coming toward her hiding spot. A few more minutes and they would be upon her. Yet, something held her immobile. As the figures in the lead came near, she was able to see inside of their shadowy hoods. What she saw took her breath away.

Inside the hood of a more petite form, was Finn's face, at least, she thought it was Finn's face. Maybe it was a little more angular, not as soft, but otherwise the woman could have been her. Anna's eyes crept down the woman's face to see a lock of dark brown hair, far darker than Finn's, curling out from within the hood.

Anna's eyes snapped open as she shot up with a gasp. She wasn't quite sure what she'd seen, or who the cloaked figures were, but she knew it was important.

AFTER PACING AROUND in her cabin for what seemed like hours, thinking about the Archtree, about the fact that she was stuck on a ship in the fog and could do nothing to speed their progress, and about Kai, Finn simply couldn't take it anymore. She would have liked to believe that he didn't infuriate her on purpose, but he was so adept at it that there could be no other explanation.

Weary of pacing, she decided to take a peek above deck, to see if perhaps she could be alone outside the confines of her cabin. She left Naoki asleep on her bed, tired from a long day of *protecting* Finn.

Hurrying down the hall to ascend the stairs, Finn poked her head up through the trap door to find the deck mostly empty, save a crewman she'd yet to meet who was on lookout near the front of the ship. It seemed everyone else had retired, given it was nearly dark, and the fog was as thick as ever.

Finn climbed on deck, breathing in the salty ocean air. It felt like the fog flowed directly into her lungs with every breath, depriving her of pure oxygen and dampening her face, though it was still preferable to the stale air of her cabin.

She made her way to the railing at the side of the deck, and peered down where the water should have been. She could hear it, but the fog kept her from seeing much, except the occasional splash forced upward by the swaying of the ship.

She clung to the railing, fearful of slipping and plunging into the foggy waters without anyone to see her go.

Her fear had almost gotten the better of her, urging her to return to her cabin, when she heard one of the most beautiful sounds she'd ever encountered. It sounded like a chorus of voices, but instead of words, they emitted tones that no human throat could create.

She leaned over the railing once more to peer downward, but was once again met with only fog. She had a horrifying flashback to the Grogochs in Badenmar singing her to sleep, yet she felt no magical pull to the singing she was hearing now.

She jumped as someone appeared at her side. She had only a moment to register that it was the man who'd been keeping watch, then he leaned forward so far that he fell right over the railing into the water.

Finn screamed. She thrust her body forward to catch the man, maintaining a grip on the railing with one hand, while reaching the other out over the railing where his body had been just moments before. Her fingers grasped at empty air, then frantic splashing could be heard below. Next came the deafening silence of shock. Everything in

Finn's brain seemed to catch up as two more men appeared on either side of her.

One was Kai, and the other, the scrawny man who'd wanted to kill Naoki.

"Wha-" Kai began to ask, then his eyes snapped downward. The singing had begun anew, and Kai seemed enraptured.

Finn watched in horror as he began to lean further and further forward over the railings. Snapping into motion, Finn wrapped her arms around his waist and dropped her weight down to the deck. Kai continued to slowly pull forward as she heard another splash. The scrawny man must have jumped, though Finn's back was turned to him, so she couldn't be sure. She'd thought she'd heard him mutter something like, "Just one kiss," moments before.

She struggled against Kai's weight, begging him to hear her. She considered screaming again, but she seemed to be the only one immune to the eerie song. Perhaps it was her heritage, though that hadn't saved her from the Grogochs. She didn't want to wake the rest of the crew, luring them out to their deaths, but she wasn't sure how much longer she could hold onto Kai.

"Please, listen to me," she begged frantically. "It's magic, you must resist!"

The singing grew louder, as if the singers sensed Finn's struggle and wanted to bring it to a violent end. As her arms burned with effort, her grip around Kai's waist began to loosen.

She knew she was going to have to change positions

to tug him back, but the momentary shift might be all Kai needed to go overboard.

With a grunt of frustration, Finn stood, keeping her arms around Kai and wedging herself in between him and the railing. Her plan backfired as suddenly she was crushed by his weight as he bent her backward, perilously close to throwing them both overboard.

Unable to help herself, she screamed. She couldn't move, and she knew if they went crashing into the water, they would both die.

Moments later, footsteps thundered on the deck behind them, and Kai was pulled backward away from the railing. Finn went with him as he fell to the deck, placing her weight on top of him in an effort to keep him down.

She glanced up for a brief second to see their savior, Sativola, his curls damp from the fog, crawling forward to help her pin Kai down. She didn't have time to consider why Sativola wasn't affected by the song that filled Finn's ear louder than ever.

She looked down at Kai's frantic face as he muttered, "Just one kiss. I must have just one."

Finn's eyes met Sativola's once more as the large man pinned Kai's shoulders, taking some of the struggle away from Finn's small form.

"What in *Tirn Ail* is going on?" Sativola gasped as his damp ringlets fell forward into his eyes.

"Some kind of magic," Finn said through gritted teeth as she continued to put weight on Kai's lower half. "Two other men have gone over already."

"Just a kiss," Kai interrupted, his voice making it seem like he was in unbearable pain.

Sativola's eyes widened as he looked down at Kai, then up to Finn. "You better kiss him," he advised, "as I'm not sure that he'd thank me for being the one to save him."

Finn gasped. "How on earth would that help?"

Kai bucked against them, almost loosing himself from Sativola's grip, but with a grunt, the large man got a hold on him once more.

"They're Sirens, lass," Sativola explained. "The enchantresses of the sea, singing male sailors to their deaths. The only way to break their spell is with a kiss."

Finn looked down at Kai's enraptured face, then back to Sativola. "Why aren't you affected then?"

It was difficult to tell with the fog in the darkness, but Sativola seemed to blush. After a moment's hesitation he explained, "The Sirens only call to those interested in . . . females."

Finn's mouth formed an 'O' of comprehension as she turned her gaze back down to Kai. Neither she nor Sativola were affected because they were attracted to men, not women, which meant if Anna came on deck, she might go overboard just like the others.

"Kiss him already," Sativola grunted as he struggled to maintain his grip on Kai.

At some point Finn had wrapped her legs around Kai to keep him steady, and the thought of kissing him in that position made her entire face heat up with a blush.

"Now is not the time to be shy, lass," Sativola chided, raising his voice slightly as he struggled against Kai.

With a frustrated grunt, Finn plastered her upper half against Kai's, bringing her face level with his. His eyes stared right past her, searching blindly for the marine enchantresses. The dark stubble on his face glistened with moisture.

"Not exactly what I'd hoped for my first kiss in over a hundred years," she muttered as she lowered her face and pressed her lips against his.

For a moment nothing happened, then Kai began to kiss her back, lifting his arms to wrap around her waist. She felt Sativola's hands lift from Kai's shoulders, just as the singing abruptly halted.

Realizing that the spell was broken, and that she was still wrapped in a far too intimate embrace with Kai, she pulled away and rolled over to sit on the cold, damp wood of the deck.

Panting, Kai sat up and turned to look at Finn, astonished. "Not that I mind any of it," he began, his eyes wide, "but would you care to explain what in the Horned One's name is going on?"

Finn's face flushed as Sativola helped her to her feet. She was quite sure that her current blush would last a lifetime. She wanted to run away to her cabin, but was fearful that the sirens might return. Of course, if they did, she'd make Sativola kiss Kai back into awareness instead of her.

Seeming to sense Finn's loss for words, Sativola cleared his throat and explained, "Sirens. They've returned along with all of the other Faie, it seems. Finn claims we lost two men."

"Who?" Kai asked, speaking to Sativola, though his eyes remained on Finn.

As Sativola shrugged, Finn explained, "The man who was keeping watch, and the wiry man who tried to harm Naoki."

Kai nodded, his expression somber. Finn suddenly felt horribly guilty. If she'd known about the Siren's call, perhaps she could have saved the other men. Of course, even if she'd known, she wouldn't have had much of an opportunity.

Kai looked toward the nearby railing in thought, then turned back to Finn. "Sirens," he mumbled to himself in disbelief. "And *you* saved me?" he added, meeting her eyes.

Finn wrung her hands as she warred between embarrassment and irritation. "The proper response would be *thank you*," she snapped. She probably could have saved the wiry man instead of Kai, but she could admit, at least to herself, that she'd made the right choice.

Kai just stared at her, still surprised, as his damp hair dripped moisture down onto his unshaven face. Finn stared back, not sure what else to say.

"I'm going back to sleep," Sativola announced as he stood, looking back and forth between Kai and Finn, still sitting on the deck, then settling on Kai. "Let us hope that if the Sirens return while I'm gone, Finn will still find you worth saving."

KAI WATCHED Finn as she stood, continuing to wring her hands. Full darkness had descended upon them, making her look like some sort of ghost, outlined in fog and moonlight.

"Finn," he began as he got to his feet and took a step toward her.

"Stop," she demanded, raising her hand in defense. "If you make light of me right now, I will never speak to you again."

Kai halted. He'd had no intention of trying to embarrass her about their kiss. Quite the contrary, actually. "I was just going to say, thank you," he explained, wanting to move closer to her, but fearing she'd turn and run back to her cabin.

"I need you to bring me to the Archtree," she stated, lifting her nose into the air. "I couldn't very well just let you die."

Kai cringed. Finn really did know how to cut right to the bone when she needed to. He took another step forward, then stopped. "You should return to your cabin and get some rest," he said finally. "Hopefully the fog will clear by morning."

Finn nodded, but didn't move.

"Wha-" Kai began to ask, but Finn cut him off.

"I would prefer it if you returned to your cabin first. I would not like the Sirens to return while I'm away, making my efforts for naught," she explained haughtily.

Kai's heart did a nervous little flip. She was worried

about him. "I was going to check on Anna first," he explained. "Warn her of the Sirens, and notify her of the two men we've lost."

Finn nodded sharply. "I'll go with you."

Kai's instinct was to make a joke about Finn just wanting to spend more time with him in hopes of stealing another kiss, but he knew such a comment would backfire in a truly terrible way, so he kept his mouth shut. Instead, he nodded and gestured for Finn to walk ahead of him toward Anna's cabin.

She did just that. Kai followed behind her small form, wanting badly to reach out and touch her, but knowing he'd likely never get the chance again.

*U*í Néid was not the homeland Iseult remembered, the homeland he so often saw in his dreams. Nor was it where he imagined the refugees would set up camp. To them, it was simply a ruined city that offered the basis for new structures. To him, it was a legendary city, brought down by its own people's foolishness. Crumbling spires of stone were all that was left of what was once an impenetrable wall surrounding the small, seaside city, most of its buildings long since turned to rubble.

That wasn't to say that it was no longer habitable. New, wooden structures had been built, and the original walls had been patched. The road leading into the city was dotted with stands covered with small, hide canopies. The stands were the type that would be moved as soon as the sun went down, though since it was midday, merchants stood at attention, calling out their wares to those entering what was once Uí Néid, a name long since lost to most.

Iseult glanced at Maarav, who rode beside him down the bustling street. If he was as affected by the sight as Iseult, he did not show it. Of course, Iseult did not show it either, at least outwardly.

They rode onward, ignoring the street-side vendors as Àed and Ealasaid brought up the rear. Before they'd run into Anders, Iseult had hoped to leave the girl in this new settlement, but if An Fiach was on its way, it would not be an option. She feared them, of that much Iseult was certain. The only reason he could see, was that perhaps she hid powers of her own, and feared persecution. He did not blame her. Anyone who was *different* was wise to fear such a fate.

No, they could not leave her, nor could they stay. They would warn the settlers of their impending *visit*, then move on to Maarav's ship. They could not let themselves be caught in the middle of a budding war.

They dismounted as they reached the newly constructed gates, and the ill-dressed guards standing on duty, questioning any who wished to enter.

Iseult turned his attention to one of the *guards*, a boy that couldn't have been more than eighteen, yet before he could speak, Ealasaid rushed forward, dropping her horse's reins in her excitement.

"Seisyll!" she exclaimed as she threw her arms around the boy, nearly knocking him off his feet as she ruffled his short, red hair.

"Eala!" he shouted back, his green eyes lighting up

now that he realized who had attacked him. "I never thought to see you again. When you left-"

"How are my sisters?" she cut him off. "And my mother? Surely you've heard more news of them than I."

"Eala . . ." he trailed off, his expression falling.

Iseult knew something bad was coming. This young boy did not likely leave his village voluntarily like Ealasaid had.

"What is it?" she breathed, worry clear in her voice. She stepped away from the boy, but continued to clutch at his arms with her small hands.

Seisyll looked down at his feet. "Eala, they're gone. Few made it out alive."

Ealasaid swayed on her feet and Maarav stepped in to catch her before she fell. Seisyll stood there uncomfortably in his ragged clothing, looking lost.

After a moment of recovery, Ealasaid pulled herself from Maarav's grasp and stepped toward Seisyll again. Those entering the city behind them stepped aside to speak to the other guard, ignoring the scene Ealasaid had caused.

She smoothed her hands down her pale blue skirts, then lifted her gaze. Tears rimmed her eyes, but did not fall.

"What happened?" she demanded, turning that painful gaze to Seisyll. "Why are they dead, when you're standing here alive?"

Seisyll looked a bit like he might cry himself. "The Tuatha came first," he explained. "There were massive wolves that didn't quite look like wolves, and little creatures that huddled in the trees, singing people to sleep. The wolves killed a few, but eventually we managed to run most of them off with fire. Then An Fiach came, claiming they'd heard of the Faie activity. They started putting the townsfolk to the question, claiming there must be a *reason* why the Tuatha were congregating there."

Iseult noticed Maarav eyeing the passersby as Seisyll spoke. Turning back to their small group, he whispered, "We should not be discussing such things openly."

Iseult would have liked to argue with him just for argument's sake, but his alleged brother was right. In times where Faie sightings could cause the demise of an entire village, even speaking of the Tuatha was dangerous.

Ealasaid had finally started to cry with silent tears slipping down her flushed cheeks. Ignoring Maarav's advice, she shakily asked, "They killed my family, didn't they? An Fiach?"

Seisyll nodded morosely. "They were not good men, and took advantage of their power. Many tried to run, but few of us made it out alive. We were robbed, and many were burned alive after being put to the question. I fled along with several others, but we were chased into the woods. When I finally made my way out the next morning, I was alone. I met up with a caravan on the road. They'd heard of a place taking settlers. A place that would not allow An Fiach within its walls."

Ealasaid looked like she might collapse again, and was at an apparent loss for words. While Iseult sympathized, their time was short. He turned to Seisyll. "Who is in charge here?"

Seisyll looked up at Iseult, who stood a good head taller than him, and gulped. "C-conall," the boy stuttered. "He can be found in the tower within the gates."

Iseult nodded, and led his horse away from the others toward the gate. He could hear Maarav speaking softly to Ealasaid as he walked away, but did not take note of what was said. He needed to speak to this Conall, and warn him of the oncoming soldiers. Then he would find Finn.

Àed soon joined him as he walked through the small, ruined city, observing the ramshackle huts made out of coarse driftwood, along with the larger, intact stone structures that had been patched to make them functional once more.

Iseult did not look at anything too hard. Part of him feared that the ghosts of the past might look back at him.

Seisyll's vague instructions proved valuable as Iseult took in a large tower that hovered over the city ominously. Such a tower had not existed in Uí Néid previously. It was made out of wood, and did not seem structurally sound. Still, many men, and even a few women, patrolled the base of the tower. They were the city *guards*, most of them likely as green as Seisyll.

Before approaching the tower, Iseult scanned the busy street behind him for Maarav. It took him a moment to spot him, hunched over so that he could speak quietly with Ealasaid as they walked, leading their horses behind them, some distance behind where Iseult and Àed stood with their own mounts.

Not wanting to waste any more time, Iseult approached the nearest tower guard, a tall woman somewhere in her fifties, wearing rough hide armor that was likely just as old as she. It also seemed too large, and had probably been originally fashioned for a man.

Iseult looked down at her. "I must speak with Conall."

He'd expected resistance. No *lord* would ever agree to host a stranger without reason, but he received none. The woman waved an arm at the tower and said, "Up there."

A younger woman approached and took Iseult's horse and Àed's mule creature without a second glance. Iseult turned to Àed, who shrugged, just as confused as he.

With a final look back to Maarav and Ealasaid, Iseult began to approach the tower, though Àed did not follow.

At Iseult's questioning glance, Àed explained, "I've made it a habit in my later life to stay out of the affairs of cities and lords. I'll wait here for the others."

Iseult nodded and made his way into the tower, whose doors stood wide open for any to enter. He didn't know who this Conall was, but one thing was for certain. Conall was a fool.

The interior of the tower was circular, with piles of rough, decrepit armor, and shoddy weaponry stacked against the walls. Several attendants sorted the piles, prepared to outfit the settlers as best they could. A wooden staircase spiraled upward to Iseult's right, toward the upper levels of the tower. The stairs seemed just as unstable as the rest of the structure, making him question the soundness of the upper levels.

He sighed. Voices could be heard above, so he at least stood a chance of *not* plummeting to his death. Making up his mind, he took the stairs two at a time, leaving the small antechamber behind him.

The staircase spiraled along the outer wall with thin supports running downward, while the wooden floors of each level spanned the diameter of the tower to hold themselves in place. Looking up, one could only see the bottom of the next level, and not all the way to the top.

Three levels up, Iseult found who he was looking for. A man that had to be Conall, sat on a rough wooden chair, while several plainly dressed attendants served him food and wine.

None noticed Iseult initially, until he cleared his throat to gain their attention. Conall looked up immediately, perceptive gray eyes boring into Iseult as he stood impassive.

Conall's hair had once been blond, but most of it had faded to a whitish gray. His beard looked almost yellow, with streaks of white shooting through its unkempt mass.

He lifted one meaty palm up to Iseult in greeting, then plopped it back down onto his ample belly. "A visitor?" he asked, looking Iseult up and down. "No," he corrected before Iseult could speak. "Too well dressed for a refugee, yet your weapons are not those of a soldier."

Iseult gritted his teeth, annoyed with the entire display. "It doesn't matter who I am," he cut in. "I've come to warn you that An Fiach will arrive within the day. I know not what they intend for the people here, but I imagine it will not be to anyone's liking."

Conall frowned for a moment, then began to laugh. This brutish, fat man was clearly mad. Iseult waited for the laughter to die down. Conall's attendants seemed uncomfortable, and most showed eyes wide with fear. They knew the reputation of An Fiach.

"Let them come!" Conall shouted, seeing that no one would be joining in his mirth. "We are prepared to give them a taste of what they have already bestowed upon many of those who dwell within this city."

Iseult had the overwhelming urge to stride up and punch the man, but was not in the habit of striking the witless. "If you resist, they will slaughter you," he explained calmly. "If you cooperate, many will be tortured, many will die, but some may live. Your best option is to disperse before they arrive."

Rage crossed Conall's lined face. "We will not run from those fiends!" he shouted.

Iseult stared him down, and soon Conall's face fell. "Will you stay and fight, or not?" Conall asked, surprising Iseult.

He inhaled deeply, then let it out. He did not like the idea of leaving the settlers to their deaths, but there was little he could do to change it. "I have prior obligations," he answered.

He had just decided to leave and warn the other settlers as best he could, when Ealasaid came charging up the stairs behind him. Maarav was hot on her heels, trying to stop her, and failing.

"I will stay and fight!" she shouted. Her eyes were a bit wide, but the set of her mouth was firm. Her curly hair was a wild mess, as if she'd been tugging at it in frustration.

Iseult turned his attention to Maarav, who stood behind Ealasaid, looking slightly embarrassed. "What on earth did you say to her?" he asked.

Ealasaid moved to stand in front of Conall, who watched the scene with a bemused expression.

"I simply told her to focus her emotions toward vengeance, as crying would do her no good," Maarav muttered, then lifted his gaze to Ealasaid and Conall.

Maarav groaned as Conall said, "You're welcome to fight, lass. Your bravery far outweighs that of your companions." He cast a bitter glance at Iseult, then looked back to Ealasaid. "Journey back to the base of the tower and choose your weapons."

Ealasaid nodded, seemingly satisfied with herself.

Shouts erupted outside, soon followed by the thudding of footsteps racing up the tower stairs. One of the women that had been seeing to the makeshift armory crested the stairs and skidded to a halt beside Maarav.

"They've been spotted," she panted. "An Fiach. A larger contingent than I've ever seen."

Conall stood abruptly and thrust a fist into the air. "Let them come!"

Iseult shook his head and muttered, "Fools," under his breath.

Conall raced down the stairs after the female messenger, moving much faster than Iseult would have suspected for a man of his girth. His attendants followed shortly after, leaving Maarav, Ealasaid, and Iseult alone in the room.

With a frantic look to Iseult and Maarav, Ealasaid tried to rush out of the room, but was deftly caught by Maarav as he reached out a hand to grab her upper arm. He pulled her back toward him.

"We should be leaving," Maarav announced, looking to Iseult while ignoring Ealasaid as she struggled against his grip.

Iseult replied with a sharp nod. "If we can."

Maarav suddenly retracted his hand from Ealasaid with a gasp, and the young woman dashed away and down the stairs.

Iseult looked a question at him.

Maarav's eyes were wide. "It felt for the life of me like I'd been hit by lightning," he said, astonished. He looked down at his hand, flexing his fingers as if afraid they no longer worked.

Iseult let out an irritated breath and chased after the girl, figuring she'd used whatever *gifts* had caused her to flee her village. They needed to leave. They should have never even stopped in the ruined city. Now it might be too late.

He sped down the stairs, skipping several with his long legs until he reached the landing. The sound of steel on steel accosted him as he rushed outside, confusing his senses. Yet more jarring still, were the various eruptions and waves of magic holding the greater numbers of An Fiach back near the gates. In some areas, fire scalded the men, in others it was as if great torrents of wind manifested out of nowhere to knock them off their feet.

From the looks of things, the men of An Fiach had not expected resistance of any nature, let alone destructive magic. Yet the settlers attacked them ferociously, leaving the soldiers with time only to defend, not to attack. Many of the soldiers charged onward, dispersing amongst the settlers to make themselves less easy targets. The fighting spread out toward the tower, and into other areas of the city.

Amidst the chaos, Iseult spotted Àed, fending off attackers with little bursts of magic, while obviously just trying to escape. Legend had it, and yes, Àed the Mountebank was a legend in his own right, that the aged conjurer had stood up against his daughter and lost, becoming magically crippled in the process. That weakness showed now, as the old man barely made it past his attackers and toward Iseult.

Once they were together, the two retreated from the main area of the fighting, and back toward the tower.

"That Conall has amassed every conjurer and sorceress in the land!" Àed screeched as they ran for cover.

Iseult didn't respond, though he'd been thinking the same. Perhaps Conall was not as foolish as Iseult had originally thought. Magic users were easy targets for An Fiach when only one or two might dwell in a single village, but gathered together, they were a force to be reckoned with.

The tide of battle seemed to be turning in favor of the

settlers as many continued to use their magic. Iseult and
Àed retreated further, not wanting to get caught up in
any stray bursts.

"Let's find yer brother and the girl," Àed grumbled,
eyeing the now distant fighting with distaste. "Perhaps
we can use this opportunity to make our retreat."

It went against Iseult's very being to retreat from
battle, but he followed the old man as he began to search
for Maarav and Ealasaid, not voicing that leaving would
likely be more difficult than Àed hoped. Even if the
settlers pushed back the first wave, they were just that,
the *first* wave. The remaining troops of An Fiach would
gather not far off to wait for reinforcements. Any who
tried to flee the ruined city would be cut down. Yes,
Iseult was no stranger to the ways of war. A group
fleeing the city with hopes of boarding a ship stood little
chance.

Àed stomped down a nearby alleyway, never calling
out, but seeming to know just where he was going.
They'd left the fighting completely, though small groups
of both settlers and soldiers either fled, or chased others
down the crisscrossing city streets. Àed made his way
deftly through the maze of streets, easily avoiding any
soldiers, while never pausing to consider where he was
going. Perhaps he could *sense* others just as he sensed
Finn.

Iseult followed silently, keeping to the shadows while
wracking his brain for some way to leave the city. Àed
was right, they needed to reach Maarav's ship as soon as
possible. If Kai fulfilled his promise and brought Finn to

the Archtree, only to have no one there to meet her . . . Iseult shook his head. He shouldn't waste time thinking about the possibilities. They had to find a way out.

MAARAV HAD RUSHED down the stairs of the tower behind Iseult. He had no intention of fighting amongst the ill-equipped settlers, rather, he hoped to quickly gather the girl and the old man so they might be on their way.

He groaned as he reached the bottom of the stairs and stepped out into the sunlight, realizing that it was too late to slip out quietly. The first wave of An Fiach had arrived, and the settlers had rushed out in an attempt to bar the gates against them.

Maarav shook his head, eyeing the scene dispassionately. Iseult had almost instantly disappeared in the chaos, but Maarav was not worried about him. If his brother knew anything, it was how to stay alive.

Maarav watched as the men of An Fiach descended upon the city quickly, not put off by the hastily assembled gates, though it was obvious that the men of the Hunt were unorganized. After their initial siege, they dispersed to fight in clusters within the city, weakening the efficacy of their initial attack. If they'd had a proper general, they would have taken the gates down at once, marching into the city in full force. The sight alone would have likely caused the settlers to throw down their weapons in fear. Instead, the disorganized soldiers were scampering about as waves of magic threatened to overcome them. Maarav wasn't suprised to see the magic being used, he was no stranger to the unusual, but he was surprised by the utter destruction of the scene. Nearly half of the settlers seemed to possess magic in one form or another.

He shook his head as the fighting neared the tower. If only the townsfolk would have peacefully submitted to questioning, he and the others might have been able to slip away. As it was, the immediate attack of the settlers had spurred An Fiach into action, cutting down any who opposed them just as they were cut down themselves.

Maarav's ship was moored not far off with people he trusted, unrelated to the settlers, but reaching it would be a gamble. He did not want to risk leading An Fiach to the ship, or those who protected it.

He caught sight of Ealasaid darting around swinging blades, a look of determined fury marring her normally soft features. With a grunt of annoyance, he raced forward. If this foolish girl got him killed now, he would haunt her in the afterlife.

He kept his eyes open for Iseult and Àed as he ran, but both were nowhere to be seen. He would need them with him to find Finn, else she would never trust him, but he would have to find them later. First, he needed to stop the girl from getting herself killed as a direct result of what he'd said to her. He'd only meant to stop her from crying, not throw her into a blood-thirsty battle frenzy.

He reached her side just as she neared the more organized bodies of An Fiach, marching through the downed gates. He was about to pull her aside and down an alleyway to hide, when she thrust an arm skyward.

Brilliant lightning bolts rained down from where her fingers pointed, erupting in the middle of the troops, casting the men aside like they weighed nothing. There were shouts of confusion until some of the men left standing caught sight of the young, blonde girl in a highly visible blue dress, her fingers still stretched skyward.

"A Faie witch!" one shouted. "Kill her!"

"Well, I was not expecting that," Maarav mumbled to himself before taking hold of Ealasaid and pulling her away from the oncoming men.

At first she struggled until Maarav chided, "Do you really think you can hold them all off at once?"

Seeming to realize how stupid she was being, Ealasaid went momentarily limp, then allowed Maarav to guide her away. They ran together through alleyways and corridors created by the new, roughly assembled buildings, not taking the time to look back over their shoulders.

"We must fight them," Ealasaid panted as she jogged beside Maarav, having to hold her skirts up above her knees lest she trip. "They deserve to die like my family." The last came out more like a sob as tears began to stream down her face.

Maarav had a feeling she would not keep up with his pace for long. Really, he should have just left her to ensure his own survival, but given her newly revealed powers, she might prove quite useful. Plus, he might have felt a bit guilty if she died.

He stopped and pulled her into an alcove, where hopefully they would not be spotted.

She looked up at him, suddenly frightened as if *he* were the one who meant her harm.

Maarav rolled his eyes. Their position in the corridor was awkward, as Ealasaid was much shorter than him. He pressed his back against the wall to look down at her. "You may kill a few, but their arrows will cut you down quickly. Better to stay alive now, and enact vengeance when you stand a better chance of success."

She continued to cry. "I have nothing to live for," she whispered.

Maarav smirked, not because her words were humorous, but because many years ago, he had said the same thing.

"You will find purpose in time, but you must give yourself that time to find it," he explained.

She nodded, then turned suddenly as several men ran down the street adjacent to their alcove. They were An Fiach, evident by their dark brown uniforms, but did not notice Maarav and Ealasaid as they remained in the shadows.

A few painful heartbeats later, the men passed. Maarav began to urge Ealasaid out into the alley so they might retreat behind the men's turned backs, when a final man came running, trying to catch up with the others.

Ealasaid had stepped out a moment too soon, and the

man came to a skidding halt. With a heavy sigh, Maarav stepped out behind her, ready to draw his sword.

The soldier swiped his sweaty red hair away from his face as he peered at Ealasaid and Maarav in disbelief. It was the man they'd met in the forest, who'd introduced himself as Anders.

"My lady," Anders breathed, focusing on Ealasaid as his chest rose and fell with exertion, highlighting the red insignia of the wolf.

"Murderer!" Ealasaid shouted, launching herself at him before Maarav could stop her.

They went tumbling to the ground. Coming out on top and straddling the poor man, Ealasaid lifted her arms skyward.

"I've never killed anything!" Anders shouted, cringing away from Ealasaid's fury.

She hesitated, then looked down at him, her arms going slightly slack. "Your men murdered my family, my *entire* village."

Anders shook his head. "I've only travelled with a small contingent. We haven't killed anything but rabbits since our journey began!"

Maarav shook his head. What a miserable little whelp, this Anders. Now that Ealasaid wasn't going to kill him, Maarav helped her to her feet, pulling her away from him. More members of An Fiach appeared further down the street, spotting them.

Ealasaid looked between Maarav, Anders, and the oncoming men, as if deciding what to do.

Sensing that she was about to pull away from him,

Maarav glared down at her. "You cannot find your vengeance if you're dead," he hissed.

Nodding to herself, Ealasaid allowed Maarav to move her further down the street. She glance over her shoulder at Anders as he called out to them to wait, but Maarav continued their forward motion.

The girl would probably prove more trouble than she was worth, but Maarav had never been one to leave behind a promising opportunity.

They continued running deeper into the city to find it had not all been repaired. Many of the buildings were no more than rubble, offering few places to hide.

While Maarav scanned the buildings, Ealasaid looked behind them. "I don't think they're coming," she commented.

Maarav paused to listen. The now distant rumble of battle seemed to be dying down, and he heard no signs of immediate pursuit. *Good.* Now to find the others, and a way out of the city. He and Ealasaid had left their horses stabled outside the tower before venturing up to meet Iseult. They would have to act quickly if they wanted to retrieve them before An Fiach gained control of the ruined city. It would be risky going back for them, but the journey to his ship would be a long one on foot.

"Over here," said a familiar voice from somewhere behind one of the nearby buildings.

Maarav smiled as first Àed, then Iseult came into view. "The battle is all but over," Àed announced as they approached, "though I've a mind to be on our way. I dinnae think An Fiach will be held back for long."

Maarav frowned. There was no way the ill-equipped settlers could have held back such an onslaught.

Had the magic users been enough to hold off An Fiach? He thought back to Ealasaid's lightning bolts. She was capable of holding a small contingent off all on her own.

The gears in Maarav's head began to turn. With more folk like Ealasaid, they could not only protect their own city, they could lay siege to others. Perhaps Conall was not as foolish as he seemed.

Iseult gave a subtle nod as his eyes met Maarav's. Conall had not only taken in the destitute. He'd formed an unnatural army.

"We'll fetch our horses, then we'll depart," Iseult ordered.

Maarav and Àed both nodded, while Ealasaid seemed conflicted. Perhaps she'd like to remain among others of her kind. Maarav hoped not. It was better to live a life of solitude, than as someone's pawn.

THE BUGLING of horns as they walked back toward the tower signaled the early retreat of An Fiach, followed by the cheers of the settlers. They'd turned the soldiers back before a true battle could take place, but many lives had been lost in the process. Iseult shook his head at the cheers as the settlers came into view, knowing An Fiach would simply return with greater forces. Men like that, blinded by the idea that they were doing *good*, would not give up so easily.

Maarav jogged ahead to retrieve their horses, as Iseult paused to watch the spectacle before him. Conall's people continued to cheer, taking final stabs or casting final bursts of magic at the last few stragglers to make their retreat. It would have been an amusing spectacle if it weren't for the dead lying at everyone's feet. By the looks of it, both sides had suffered heavy losses in the short span of time.

Now that the enemy had retreated, those left alive didn't seem to know what to do with themselves. Many stared blankly in shock, while others ran to fallen comrades, searching for signs of life.

Àed spat on the ground near Iseult's feet, then muttered, "Fools."

Iseult smirked bitterly. He was not naive to the ways of war, and saw the first assault for the disaster that it was. "Which ones?" he asked, honestly wondering if the old man was referring to An Fiach, or those who followed Conall.

"All of them," Àed growled. "Including us. We should have never stopped to warn them."

Iseult nodded his agreement, though they'd no way to know what type of situation they were walking into. Still, if they would have continued on their way, they likely would have reached Maarav's ship already. By Iseult's estimates, Finn and her *captors* would only be a day or two away from the Archtree by now, if Kai managed to navigate the course correctly. If Maarav's ship was far enough north, it would mean a more direct route to the island, but they would still likely arrive after the others, unless the elements interfered.

Maarav returned with three horses and a mule in hand. "Not that our mounts will do us much good with no way out of the city," he commented, handing Iseult his reins.

Iseult nodded, taking the reins. Leaving through the gates was no longer an option, but there may well be other ways out of the city. The perimeter created by the city wall was only a blurry memory to him, but it would be easy enough to check for a breach on his own. The settlers were all consumed with tending to the injured and dead, and Conall seemed to have locked himself inside his tower.

"Wait here," Iseult instructed his group.

Àed nodded to Iseult, then turned to Ealasaid. "Come lass, we'll tend the wounded." He turned a glare up to Maarav. "Ye too."

Maarav gave Àed a sarcastic bow, then followed the old man as he led Ealasaid toward the impromptu battlefield.

As Iseult retreated from the crowd, darkness slowly descended. They'd lost an entire day in the city. An entire day in which they should have been making steady progress toward a ship.

Once away from any onlookers, he lifted himself onto his horse and galloped toward the western edge of the city. If he could find a breach in the wall somewhere along the coast, they might be able to slip out, unnoticed by An Fiach. They'd quite possibly be leaving the settlers to an ill fate, but the fools had gotten themselves into their mess to begin with. It wasn't his job to save them. Or so he kept telling himself.

By the time he'd reached the edge of the ruined city, darkness had fully engulfed the sky. He dismounted and looked up at the city wall, illuminated only by a sliver of moonlight. He began to pace the length of the wall, feeling at home in the shadows, glad he'd left the others behind. He thrived on solitude. So many weeks spent traveling with a party had left him feeling uneasy. He needed both Àed and Maarav if he was to find Finn, but in another reality he would have by far preferred to find her himself. She trusted him, and was waiting for him to save her. He would not let her down.

Iseult paused to look back up at the wall with a sigh. The city of his early childhood had become surprisingly fortified. Not that it hadn't been when he was a child, but the stone walls had been long since ruined. Conall's people had patched them with wood, which wouldn't be terribly effective at keeping people out, should their enemies come bearing torches, but it was effective at keeping people *in*. Especially people who would need their horses to reach their destination in a timely manner. He continued walking for some time.

Nearly an hour later, he paced along the final stretch of wall, finding no breaches wide enough to fit a horse. In fact, he found no breaches at all. It was quite a nice wall.

He debated going back to the tower right away to

meet up with the others. He would have preferred some more time alone, but time was of the essence. He would not waste a minute of it on his own well-being.

His mind made up, he remounted and wove his way through the various, vacant alleyways and back toward the tower. The remaining settlers were all gathered there, torches illuminating their nervous faces as they waited for Conall to emerge and address them. Iseult had no desire to hear whatever blustery speech Conall had prepared, but he needed to know the man's plans before he could make his own.

He dismounted and led his horse through the crowd, quickly picking out the shadowy forms of his companions, standing on their own. As his companions were yet to notice him, he waited a moment, observing them. Maarav stood whispering to Ealasaid. He'd watched over her during the battle, something Iseult found both surprising and confusing. He was usually an excellent judge of character, but his *brother* was difficult to read. He was a man of scheming and war, of that, Iseult was sure, but he could deduce little else.

With a glance behind to make sure no one was watching *him,* he approached his party. They acknowledged him, but had no time to speak as Conall finally appeared from within the tower.

"This should be entertaining," Maarav muttered, barely loud enough for Iseult to hear.

Conall, massive in girth, but less so in height, stepped onto a small, roughly assembled podium. His full beard reflected the firelight like it was made of flame, a fitting image in comparison to some of the magic that had been used in the battle. Scorch marks seared the earth, along with scores of badly burned bodies, now all neatly stacked together for a final burning. Iseult had seen some of the fire first hand, leaping from the arms of several wielders. It seemed magic users were not as rare as he'd been led to believe. It was frightening to consider the implications of so many working together, especially under the lead of Conall.

As Conall cleared his throat, all fell silent. "Today, we were victorious!" he began, his voice booming.

"*Today*," Maarav said sarcastically under his breath as the settlers let out a cheer.

"Tomorrow," Conall continued, "our chances of survival are slim."

All fell silent again.

Iseult shifted his weight impatiently from foot to foot, anxious for the speech to reach its end so they could continue searching for a way out of the city without being seen by the regrouped troops of An Fiach.

"As many of you know," Conall said, his voice taking on a softer tone, easily heard in the utter silence, "I am not a man of these lands. I hail from the borders of the North. In the past, you would have called me a reiver. A mindless, killing bandit, feared, and never befriended."

Murmurs of acceptance echoed throughout the crowd, letting Iseult know that this was common knowledge. That the settlers were so accepting of Conall proved how desperate they'd been. It was unheard of for reivers to live amongst the more civilized folk.

"These men, calling themselves An Fiach, would judge you as I've been judged," he went on. "They would put you to the question, but would never be satisfied of your answers. There is no peace to be had, save the cool embrace of death." He paused for dramatic emphasis.

Maarav sighed.

"And so we must fight!" Conall shouted.

The crowd cheered.

Iseult shook his head. Without a plan, they would fight and die, even with their magic to bolster them. With the next onslaught, An Fiach would be prepared for what they faced. They had thought the ruined city an easy victory, and so had not come equipped for true battle.

As the cheers died down, Conall continued. "An Fiach may have reinforcements on the way, but so do we, and no man of this land can fight with more fervor than my kinsmen!"

As the crowd cheered once more, Maarav groaned, likely coming to the same conclusion as Iseult. Conall had formed an army of magic users, not out of benevolence, but to bolster his own invasion. The Northern reivers were at an advantage, as the greater cities were distracted by the chaos brought on by the returning Faie. They would strike while everyone was on guard against the Tuatha, never realizing that the more immediate danger came in human form.

Maarav leaned in close to Iseult's shoulder. "If we needed to leave this place before," he murmured, "it was nothing compared to the need for escape now."

Iseult nodded. They would stand better chances against An Fiach than they would against the reivers, who were great in number, and ferocious in combat. The settlers who'd proven themselves in battle would likely be forced to join the reivers cause. They would have little choice but to turn traitors against their kin, a worthwhile opportunity to some, considering many of their kin betrayed them first, but not all would agree.

Iseult glanced at Ealasaid, who stood on Maarav's other side, to find her hanging on Conall's every word as he continued to speak. Not *all* would agree, but some would jump at the opportunity.

Maarav leaned close to Ealasaid's shoulder and muttered something, though all Iseult could make out was, *lightning bolts*.

He looked to his other side to see how Àed was taking the speech, but the old man had vanished. Iseult frowned, wondering what he was up to, then turned his attention back to Conall.

Iseult's eyes narrowed as the reiver continued to bluster on, though he'd already stated the most important fact. Reivers would be joining them in the city. They would come from the North, either along the coast, or through the forest, and would be unable to use the front gates because of the placement of An Fiach. This all meant one very important thing to Iseult. There *was* another way out of the city. One that would allow a large group of fighters, along with their horses and supplies, to pass into the city unnoticed. Now all Iseult needed to do was find it.

"I THOUGHT we were going to save people!" Anders cried out. He was bruised, dirty, and had blood on his shoes. He didn't even know whose blood it was. The woods had grown dark, making him jump at every sound.

"Quiet," Radley hissed as he led the small group of men back to the larger camp.

Anders stumbled to keep up. Radley had found him shortly after Ealasaid ran off with that man who looked eerily like Iseult. Anders hadn't had the heart to tell his commander that he'd been attempting to run away from the fighting. He had no business killing humans. It was the Faie who took his sister.

On a surge of adrenaline, he grabbed Radley's beefy bicep and spun him around. Once they reached the larger contingent of men, there would be no time to talk, and Anders would be trapped once more.

Radley gave Anders such a look that he was surprised his hand didn't melt on the spot.

Swallowing the lump in his throat, Anders asked, "What are we doing killing innocent humans? That's not the purpose of An Fiach."

The few men who accompanied them nodded in agreement. They were what was left of Radley's entire crew. The others had all been killed by the magic users in the ruined city.

Radley sucked his teeth, then spat, pulling his arm away from Anders in the process. "We're following orders," he said gruffly.

"Whose?" Anders asked, more surprised than anyone at his own gall.

Radley shook his head like Anders had asked a very silly question. "An Fiach."

Unwilling to let the subject go, Anders immediately asked, "But who leads An Fiach? Until a few days ago, I thought *you* were our leader."

"I am," Radley growled, puffing out his chest, "but in war, there are generals, and there are *kings*."

"But who's the king?" one of the other men piped in.

Radley narrowed his eyes at the man, but didn't answer.

Anders' jaw went slack with realization. "You don't know, do you?"

Radley turned his withering gaze to Anders. "Are you coming, or not?"

Anders seriously considered saying no. He'd seen far too much death that day, and Ealasaid's rage-filled eyes still haunted him. The Hunt had killed her family, and Anders was a member. She hated him, and would so long as he remained by Radley's side.

"A deserter then?" Radley asked, sensing Anders' hesitation.

Anders felt so anxious that he thought he might pop. "I joined this cause to find my sister and the monsters who took her. I saw no monsters today, except maybe An Fiach."

The men around them went utterly silent. No one insulted An Fiach in front of Radley. No one.

Radley pursed his mouth and let the silence draw out.

Finally, just when Anders thought he couldn't take another moment, Radley spoke. "Perhaps you're right. Who am I to judge men from monsters? All I know is that I took an oath, and I will uphold it."

Mustering every ounce of bravery he could, Anders replied, "I took no such oath."

Radley smirked, then thumped his hand against Anders' chest, near the red wolf insignia. "You took that oath the moment you put on the uniform of An Fiach."

Flustered, Anders quickly removed his coat with the red wolf insignia and threw it on the ground. If he left the Hunt, he had nowhere else to go, but in that moment, he didn't care. He never wanted anyone else to look at him the way Ealasaid had.

Radley glanced at the coat on the rocky ground, then turned on his heel and walked away. The other men, who'd just moments before seemed to be on Anders' side, gave him a wide berth as they walked around him.

"You're just going to leave?" Anders shouted at their backs.

"An Fiach has no time for deserters!" Radley shouted without turning around. "The wolves will be around for you soon!"

Anders watched in shock as the men he'd considered friends faded into the darkness. He'd somehow deserted An Fiach without really thinking about it. He looked back over his shoulder, then forward to where the men had disappeared, not knowing which way to go.

If he tried to return to the ruined city, surely he would be killed, and now the same fate likely awaited him with An Fiach. He looked down at his coat again, not wanting to put it back on, but knowing he had to if he didn't want to freeze. He might freeze regardless.

He crouched down and lifted the garment, then donned it reluctantly. He shifted his shoulders to straighten the coat, and something crinkled in his breast pocket.

Holding his breath, he tentatively reached his fingers into the pocket to pull out a crumpled piece of parchment. He unfolded it to read the words, *Meet me on the coast, two hundred paces north of the city.*

Anders read over the note again, but there was no hint of who'd written it. Had Radley slipped it into his coat pocket, or perhaps one of the other men? He shook his head. He had no idea who'd written the note, but in his current condition, he'd be a fool not to cling to any ray of hope that was offered.

CHAPTER ELEVEN

ightning crashed overhead, startling Finn awake. Confused, Finn took in her surroundings, finally realizing that she'd fallen asleep in a chair in Anna's cabin. Her chair teetered dangerously as the ship swayed in the storm. The lantern that hung from the ceiling swung about erratically, casting dizzying shadows around the room. The only other light came through the room's sole window. Its shutters had been closed against the storm, but dim light and water still seeped through.

Finn glanced at Anna's bed. She was still asleep, motionless and quiet, though that hadn't been the case when they'd first arrived in her cabin.

After the incident with the Sirens, Finn had accompanied Kai to check on Anna. She wasn't keen on doing *anything* nice for Anna, but she also wasn't about to let Kai get drowned by any Sirens who might return, not after all she'd done to save him. She shivered as she thought about the two men who hadn't been saved, basically strangers to her, yet their deaths stung all the same.

Anna hadn't answered her door when Kai pounded on it, so he deftly picked the lock while Finn watched in awe, thinking it was a skill she'd like to learn.

Once the door was open, they'd found Anna tossing about in her bed, drenched in sweat and muttering nonsense. Kai had attempted to shake her awake, but no matter what they did, Anna stayed in a deep, fitful sleep.

They had waited with her, hoping that she'd wake on her own, and at some point Finn had fallen asleep in her chair, and morning had come, along with a storm. Kai had been there last she saw, but was now missing, likely on deck given the shouting she could hear through the door whenever the thunder died down.

With a final glance at Anna, she stood, then nearly lost her footing as the ship lurched violently, sending her now vacant chair crashing to the floor.

Extending her arms for balance, she made her way to the door, glad that the larger pieces of furniture were bolted to the deck.

She turned the handle and tugged at the door, but it wouldn't budge. The wind roared outside, followed by several more thunderclaps. She tugged again as the storm fought her for control of the door, then a sudden gust in the opposite direction tore the handle from her grasp and opened the door outward to slam against the exterior wall of the cabin. Anna's papers whooshed up from her desk, creating their own little whirlwind, but still Anna didn't wake.

Finn forced her upper body through the doorway, clinging to the jamb as the rain pelleted her. Judging by how long she'd slept, it was daytime, but it almost seemed like night with the darkness of the storm.

The deck was in utter chaos. Kai, along with the remaining crewmen, hustled about, getting drenched while they tried to maintain control of the ship's sails. Sativola was nearest to Anna's cabin, and seeing Finn, he shouted for her to get back inside.

She lingered long enough to watch in awe as a brilliant lightning bolt lit the gray sky, then she struggled against the wind to pull the cabin door shut, sealing herself and Anna inside.

She took a few steps away from the now closed door, feeling like electricity was dancing across her skin. Her face felt numb from the cold rain and wind, or perhaps it was from shock. She'd never seen such a ferocious storm, at least that she could recall. It was unfortunate that such a phenomenon would occur while they were in the middle of the ocean.

Feeling off kilter, as if lifting her feet too high would make her launch into the air, she made her way to Anna's bedside. Throughout all of the motion and noise, the woman still slept, clinging to a pillow with her long, dark hair plastered to the sides of her face with sweat.

Finn glared down at her. "I'm going to be very upset if you're the person I have to die with," she muttered.

Another gust of wind violently swayed the ship, and she took a quick seat on the side of Anna's bed, clutching the small, wooden headboard for balance.

Wanting something, anything to distract herself from the image of Kai or the other men being thrown overboard in the storm, she grabbed Anna by the shoulder and shook her. A futile attempt, as the woman had already proven herself unresponsive.

Yet, to Finn's surprise, Anna's eyes opened just a sliver, then opened more to reveal only the whites, with her pupils rolled back into her head.

Finn leaned away from the eerie sight, but didn't stand, fearing she'd just fall right back onto the bed. Anna's hand lifted from the bedding, making slow progress toward her.

Finn froze, unsure of what was happening. Anna's hand found Finn's cheek and cradled it gently, as Anna's lips muttered, "Mo gealbhan beag milis."

Her hand dropped back to her side as her eyes rolled forward. Then she began to scream.

Finn screamed right along with her.

"Get out of my head!" Anna shouted, as her hands batted at Finn.

Finn stumbled up and off the bed, only to trip and fall on the floor. "I'm not in your head!" she shouted as she scurried further away from Anna.

The door to Anna's cabin flew open, and the next thing Finn knew, a sopping wet Naoki had pounced on her chest, knocking her back flat on the ground. The little dragon shivered and made mewling noises in its throat, deeply afraid.

Finn clutched Naoki to her chest, then craned her neck to see Kai closing the cabin door behind him. He was just as dripping wet as Naoki, and seemed almost as concerned. She had caught a brief glimpse of the sky through the door, and though it still rained, it seemed the worst was beginning to pass. She noticed with a start that at some point the ship had stopped swaying so violently, but she'd been so caught up in Anna's actions, she hadn't realized when it happened.

Kai walked past her and approached Anna, who was clutching the sides of her head and rocking back and forth with her eyes shut tight. She was mumbling something, but it wasn't loud enough for Finn to hear.

Kai looked unsure of what to do to help her. He glanced back toward Finn as she struggled back into a sitting position on the floor, forcing the wet dragon to her lap.

"She was muttering in her sleep," Finn explained as she stroked Naoki's damp feathers. "I went to her, and she said something to me. Something like, *mo gealbhan beag milis.*"

Kai looked to Anna again. "What does it mean?" he asked softly.

Finn bit her lip. "It means, *my little sparrow.* I'm not sure how I know that, but I feel like I've heard it before."

Kai moved toward the bed and laid his hand gently on Anna's shoulder, but she didn't seem to notice.

"She hasn't been herself since the Travelers took her," he explained, his gaze remaining on Anna instead of Finn, "and I think it's getting worse."

He turned and looked to Finn hopefully.

Finn frowned. "If you expect *me* to talk to her, you're

madder than she is," she grumbled. "Anna has not had a kind word to say to me since she became *Anna* instead of Liaden. Not to mention, I'm on this ship because she *kidnapped* me. She can lose her mind entirely for all I'm concerned."

Kai gave her a patient look and waited.

Finn glared at him as the ship gave another gentle lurch in the wind. "Stop looking at me like that. I mean what I said."

Kai tilted his head and looked at her a little harder. His sopping wet hair dripped water down his face in steady rivulets onto his already soaked through clothes.

Naoki began to chirp and chitter in Finn's lap.

"*No*," Finn stated again. "Even if I knew how to help her, she doesn't deserve it."

Kai sighed and sat down by Anna's unresponsive form. He patted Anna's back comfortingly, though she still didn't seem to notice. He turned back to Finn hopefully.

"*No,*" Finn stated.

Kai sighed again. "If not for Anna, then do it for me."

Finn stopped petting Naoki and crossed her arms, much to Naoki's chagrin. "With that in mind, I want to help even less."

Kai rolled his eyes. "Then do it because you want to find out why the Travelers are so interested in *you*. If you can get Anna to talk about her experience with them, then maybe you can glean some valuable information."

"I can hear you, you know," Anna cut in miserably. She finally opened her eyes, aiming them directly at

Finn. "And if talking about what happened to me will make it go away, I will tell you absolutely anything you want to know."

Finn's eyes widened. Her mind raced for what question she should ask first.

"What did they do to you?" she asked, hoping to understand Anna's situation better before delving into more useful questions.

Anna took a deep, shaky breath.

Too nervous to maintain eye contact, Finn looked down at Naoki, who had gone to sleep in her lap.

"They told me that *old blood* runs in my veins," Anna said finally.

Kai had righted Finn's chair near the desk, and sat, somewhat removing himself from the situation without actually leaving Finn and Anna alone. Finn glanced over at him, but his eyes were on his long-time partner.

"Clan Liath," Anna clarified, then laughed to herself. "It's funny, I often used the name Liaden when posing as someone of noble blood. I was simply drawn to it, though I know little of my ancestry."

"And that's why they wanted you," Finn commented.

Anna swallowed audibly, then nodded. "Yes, more specifically because of my ancestors' associations with divination. It was said they could see into *the gray*."

Finn nodded, remembering her conversation with the Travelers, what seemed like months ago. "They called you the *Gray Lady*."

Anna met Finn's eyes for a brief moment, then looked down at her hands resting in her lap. "I'm not entirely sure what they did to me once we reached their camp," she explained. "I was in some sort of trance, lost in a gray place of never-ending mazes. Most of the time I was in stone corridors that all looked the same."

Anna went silent. Finn sensed that now was not the time for her to speak, so instead she waited patiently.

Eventually Anna looked up again. "I've been going to that place in my dreams ever since. Sometimes I'm in the stone corridors, or sometimes in a misty forest. It's gotten to the point where I'm having difficulty distinguishing what I see in front of me from what I see behind my eyelids."

"Why would they put you there?" Kai interrupted, sounding almost angry. "What was the point?"

Anna glared at him. "They wanted to find the Archtree, to see if it even still stood. It was much faster for me to look for it than it would have been to physically scour the land."

Finn held her breath at the mention of the Archtree. If the Travelers wanted to find it, perhaps it wasn't just a regular tree, as Kai had suggested. Maybe her answers were nearer than she thought.

"Did you find it?" she asked, unable to contain herself.

Anna gave her a calculating look, then answered. "Yes, and you found me before the Travelers could scour all of my thoughts. Traveling through the gray place is different than traveling in the real world. The directions don't match up. As far as I know, the Travelers still have no idea where the Archtree is."

Finn's heart began to beat more quickly. "So it's real?

You found it, and it's the tree of legend, the one that can answer all of our questions?"

Anna narrowed her eyes at Finn. "Is the shroud of the Faie Queen real?"

Finn felt slightly deflated, she really didn't want to give Anna any unnecessary information, but it seemed they were all in this together now. "I'm not sure. Iseult believes that it is. His people came in . . . contact with it near the end of the Faie war. Still, we are unsure of what it *does*."

Anna sighed, as if resigning herself to the unwanted partnership with Finn. "There's one more thing," she added hesitantly.

Finn nodded for her to go on, glad to have the subject off the shroud. She wasn't about to let Anna steal it when Iseult wanted it so badly, temporary partnership or no.

"Right before I woke with you hovering over me," Anna began, making it clear that she hadn't appreciated Finn's presence in that moment, "I saw a woman. I've seen her before too, and she seems to recognize me. She's always in a forest with many cloaked figures. They seem to almost float above the earth, else their gait is unnaturally fluid. The trees and brambles appear to move with them, never snagging at the fabric of their cloaks."

Finn's heart was beating quickly again. The words *my little sparrow* repeated in her brain. Where had she heard them before?

"Finn," Anna began again, "I think I saw your mother."

Still in his chair, Kai turned his upper body to Finn,

his jaw slightly agape as if he knew the impact such information might have on her.

He was the only one. In that moment, Finn had no idea how she was supposed to feel. It made sense for her to have a mother, though since no one seemed to know where the Dair came from, she wouldn't have been surprised if she didn't.

"I'm sure you're mistaken," she replied calmly, doubting what Anna had actually seen.

Anna shook her head. "She looks so much like you, it's eerie."

"Perhaps it's her sister," Kai chimed in, but Anna shook her head again.

"You don't understand," she snapped, frustrated. "This woman has been in my head." Her eyes met Finn's. "I've *felt* what she feels for you. And-" she cut herself off.

Finn inhaled sharply as she realized she'd stopped breathing. Naoki jumped at the sound, then settled back into Finn's lap contentedly. *"And?"* Finn pressed, feeling like she wanted to run out of the room and end the conversation right there.

Anna's eyes gazed past her as if seeing something in the distance, though there was only wood planking behind her. "I-" she began, then cut herself off again. She took a deep breath, then bravely stated. "I think she's dangerous. She's looking for you, and letting nothing get in her path."

Kai leaned forward in his chair, gazing at Anna. "What does she intend?"

Anna shook her head. "I don't know. We . . . *connected*

in the gray place, though really only our eyes met, but I feel like in that moment, she saw everything in my head. She wants to find Finn, but is hiding things from those who are with her. That's all I can tell."

Finn gathered Naoki in her arms and stood abruptly. "It doesn't matter," she said quickly, feeling panicked, yet determined. "Our plan remains the same. We will find the Archtree, and have all of the answers we need." She turned to Kai. "Are we near?"

He nodded as he eyed her cautiously, as if waiting for her to burst into tears. "Judging by what I copied from Iseult's map, we should reach the island within a day."

Finn nodded, then turned her attention to Anna. "I do not know specifically what the Travelers did to you, but they spoke to me previously of the *old blood* returning to the land. I think these visions would have begun to accost you regardless of their interference."

Anna's face fell. "But how do I make it stop?"

Finn almost felt her face slipping into compassionate lines, then forced herself to harden. Anna did not deserve her compassion, even after the information she'd shared. "You don't. It is a part of you. Just as I cannot stop myself from melting the skin from men's bones, or from stirring up the earth to swallow creatures whole. These things are a part of who we are, and only we can deal with them. There is no help, save that which we give ourselves."

Kai and Anna both seemed slightly stunned by Finn's assertive display. *Good.* Turning from them, she confidently strode to the door, bracing Naoki against her with one arm as she opened it. The rain still drizzled outside, but rays of sunlight broke through the dense clouds in places, making the moisture glisten on the wood of the rough deck like broken glass.

She stepped outside, feeling strong, yet also like she might fold in on herself any moment. She closed the door behind her. Naoki chirped happily, wriggling out of Finn's arms to perch on her shoulders.

Sativola and one of the other men were on deck checking over the damage caused by the storm. It seemed minimal, though Finn knew little about ships. The fact that they were still floating was enough for her.

She walked across the deck, then walked a little faster as she heard Anna's cabin door open and shut behind her. She doubted it was Anna chasing after her, and she wasn't ready to face any questions about her mother. She had no recollection of her mother. To Finn, she was just another person that left her as a tree for one hundred years.

Kai caught up to her shoulder a moment later, just as she'd reached the trap door that would lead down to her cabin. Deciding that she'd rather not continue their discussion in an enclosed space that would leave her nowhere else to run to, she veered from her path toward the railing that bordered the deck.

Kai followed and stood beside her as the rain drizzled on them both.

She gazed out at the now calm ocean, amazed at how quickly things had settled after such a violent storm. "I don't want to talk about it," she said before he could say anything.

"I wasn't going to ask," he replied.

She turned her head, and raised an eyebrow at him. "Liar."

He winked at her, then pointed out at the sky. "Take a look."

She looked to where he pointed, and saw a weak little rainbow had formed on the distant horizon. Her eyes lingered on the faint arch, marveling at the soft hues.

She turned her head back to Kai with a look of bemusement. "I've never thought of you as a man that would appreciate rainbows."

He smiled softly. "You speak as if you've known me for years."

She laughed. "I've known you almost my entire life, at least, what I can remember of it."

Still smiling, he turned his eyes back to the rainbow as the ship gently rocked. "I suppose that's true."

They both gazed off in silence for a long while. Finn had thought that she didn't want to talk, but there was a question burning in the back of her mind. If they were going to be reaching the island tomorrow, she needed to know something, though she wasn't sure *why* she needed to know it.

"What will you do after we find the tree?" she asked. "Will you still try to find the shroud?"

Finn wouldn't let Kai or Anna take the shroud from Iseult, and she really didn't like the idea of *competing* for it.

He shrugged. "I imagine I'll return to Migris, or perhaps Port Ainfean. I'm sure I'll find something to pass the time."

"But Anna-" Finn began.

"Wants answers from the tree far more than she wants any shroud," he finished for her.

Finn was at a loss for words. Finally she asked, "So once we find the Archtree, and Àed and Iseult, you'll simply leave?"

He shrugged. "I said Anna wants the tree *more* than she wants the shroud. I would not be surprised if she still tries for the latter."

"And what will you do when she tries?" Finn asked suspiciously.

Kai sighed and turned to Finn with a look of frustration.

Naoki chittered her beak at him, not liking that look aimed at her new mother.

Finn came to a sudden realization. "You haven't thought any of this through, have you?"

Kai seemed to deflate. "Isn't that quite obvious?"

Finn shrugged, jostling Naoki. "You always seem to have a plan."

Kai laughed. "Well then you're not very observant. I've been grasping at straws from a haystack ever since I met you."

Finn smiled, glad she wasn't the only one that had no idea what she was doing. "And which straw are you grasping at now?"

He waggled his eyebrows at her. "If I told you, you'd slap me."

Finn shoved his shoulder playfully.

"About your mother-" Kai began, but Finn cut him off with a sharp look.

Unperturbed, Kai continued, "I was just going to say, don't waste your question for the Archtree on her. If she left you as a tree for all those years, she doesn't deserve it."

Finn couldn't restrain her smile. "I wasn't planning on it."

It was the truth. She didn't want to find her people *or* her mother until she understood her true purpose. She wasn't about to take the word of the Ceàrdaman on the subject, nor anyone else for that matter. Her *gifts* might point in the direction of her being merely a weapon, but the tree could tell her for sure.

Naoki began to snore on her shoulders as she and Kai continued to gaze out at the distant horizon. Despite the circumstances, Finn thought she rather liked being out at sea.

BEDELIA LAY IN HER BED, feeling about ready to die. Her illness had gotten worse since she and Óengus had set sail, along with a small crew of men. The bite on her leg was tender to the touch, and appeared infected. Her body was plagued with alternating bouts of shivering, and feeling like she'd been placed in a furnace.

She rolled the little glass vial across her palm, observing its dark contents in the lamplight. It had obviously been left for *her* in her room back at Maarav's inn, but by whom? Maarav, Finn, and Óengus were the only ones that knew she was there, unless someone had seen her without her knowing. It was all just too suspicious since Maarav and Finn had disappeared at the same time. Perhaps someone had kidnapped the pair, or perhaps Maarav had run away with Finn. They didn't seem an ideal match, but who knew?

Another wave of nausea wracked her entire body, not helped along by the sway of the ship. She clenched her fist around the little vial to keep from dropping it.

"You should probably drink that," a voice said from across the room.

With only the dim light of the lamp, the corners of Bedelia's cabin were left entirely in shadow. Even so, she had searched the room thoroughly upon entering, and had locked the door behind her.

"Keiren?" she questioned, recognizing her mistress' voice, but not understanding how she came to be on the ship.

Keiren stepped into view until the lamp illuminated her soft features and long, fiery red hair. Her bright blue eyes sparkled by the light of the flame, full of secrets.

"What-" Bedelia began, but Keiren cut her off with the raise of her hand.

She stepped forward to sit on the bed beside Bedelia, smoothing her ornate, black dress and matching cloak beneath her. "I see you have failed in your task," Kieren commented lightly.

Bedelia cringed. "I apologize. I did all that I could."

Keiren smiled. "Yes, you did," she replied, speaking like one would to a cherished pet, or perhaps a child. "You gained her trust, a trust that will likely prove useful in the future."

"We'll find her still," Bedelia assured, attempting to sit up, then falling back to the bed as another wave of nausea and pain hit her. "Óengus will know how to track her," she added through gritted teeth.

"Yes, you will find her, but only to observe. You are no longer going after the girl," Keiren explained nonchalantly as she glanced around the room.

"But why-" Bedelia began, but was cut off once more.

"Your new task is to find my father before she does. There are too many forces at work, either hiding the girl from my sight, or stealing her away to point her in entirely new directions. My father knows this girl, as do many others. They are helping her. We must take away her support, making you her only option."

Bedelia stared up at Keiren wide-eyed, unsure of what to say.

"I know you care for her," Keiren stated bluntly. "She must be quite the enchantress to have swayed a heart like yours."

Bedelia shook her head against her pillow as much as she was able. "I only seek to please *you*, my lady."

Keiren shot Bedelia such a venomous look that she thought she might die on the spot, if she wasn't dying already. "Lies do not become you," she replied coolly, "and it matters not, as long as you remain loyal to me in the end."

"You have my word," Bedelia assured, feeling on the brink of tears, "as you have always."

Keiren stood abruptly. "Good." She walked toward the door. "The girl is on her way to a special island. You are in luck, as her ship has been delayed by storms and other nuisances. You should reach the island shortly before her, but you are to remain *unseen*, do you understand?"

Before Bedelia could reply, Keiren continued, "You are to wait there to intercept my father. He must not reach her . . . " she trailed off, as if deep in thought. "And listen to Óengus," she added suddenly. "He knows much more about the ways of subtle schemes than you, while you are the superior soldier."

Bedelia nodded, not feeling like the superior anything.

Keiren put her hand on the door, then looked back over her shoulder. "Oh, and drink that tincture you've been fondling all evening. You've contracted a disease from that nasty bite on your leg. It may be too late to save you, but the liquid in the vial may at least prolong your life."

With that, Keiren silently let herself out of the room, shutting the door behind her. Would she speak with Óengus next? Tell him what a failure Bedelia was?

Bedelia uncorked the vial still in her hand and stared down at the liquid before taking a swig. It didn't really matter *what* Keiren told Óengus. He already knew every weakness Bedelia had to offer.

She lowered her head back to her pillow as the liquid seared a bitter line down her throat. She felt no immediate effects, and wondered if Keiren had lied to her, though why would she? Bedelia was on the verge of death either way.

As she waited to feel better, she thought about her new orders. Finn had spoken highly of her friends, and seemed to have unyielding faith in them. Now Bedelia was supposed to take them away, starting with Keiren's father. She'd only heard her speak of him once or twice previously, and it was always with apathy in her tone. Keiren's father had tried to limit his daughter's powers, and that was something Keiren simply could not accept. She was destined for greatness, and no one, not even her own father, would stop her.

Bedelia rolled onto her side, knowing she should try to rest, but doubting it would happen. Was Keiren still on the ship? Maybe she could convince her of a different course of action.

Bedelia stood abruptly, then closed her eyes as she was overcome by dizziness. Her leg screamed at her, but she forced herself forward. She was vaguely aware of the fact that she smelled like an unmucked stable, but didn't want to waste time scrubbing herself with the lidded basin of fresh water that sat near her bed.

She stumbled toward her door and groped in the dim lighting for the handle, then realized she wore only her underpinnings. Groaning in frustration, she left the door to struggle into some tan breeches and a loose, white cotton tunic, taking care as she slid the fabric over the dressing on her wound. With a sigh, she stumbled toward the door again and let herself out.

The journey to the deck above seemed to take ages. Her movements were sluggish, hinting that she really shouldn't be moving at all, but she really wanted to speak with Keiren again before she left. There had to be *something* she could say. Surely she'd think of a brilliant monologue by the time she reached Óengus' cabin.

She ascended the stairs to the deck, lifting an arm to shield her eyes from the sting of the sun. The cool, sea breeze made her already sweaty face feel sticky as it toyed with the unwashed clumps of her shoulder-length hair.

She took a quick look around, and noticed Óengus, standing on his own near the mast, which meant Keiren was gone. Bedelia instantly deflated. She'd probably spoken to him first, viewing him as more immediately important to her plans.

Bedelia frowned, as she realized that some of her dizziness had subsided. Perhaps the tincture had worked, or perhaps it was the fresh air. Regardless, she felt good enough to stumble to the railings along the deck, far from where Óengus stood, to gaze out at the glistening sea.

She jumped as Óengus appeared at her side, then scowled. Had it not been obvious that she wanted to stand alone?

"Feeling better, I see," he observed without emotion.

Bedelia nodded, wanting to question their new plan, but at the same time, wanting nothing more than for Óengus to go away. She might have stood some chance of swaying Keiren to a new set of goals, but with Óengus, well, mermaids were more likely to jump up from the calm waters to sweep Bedelia away to their undersea kingdom.

"We will reach our target location within a day," Óengus continued as he gripped the railing beside her. "*Your Lady* hast forseen it," he added with a smirk.

Bedelia shivered. Most would never dare make fun of Keiren, or her unusual gifts. "What will we do to him?" she asked, thinking of Finn, and what a nice man Keiren's father must be to be valued so highly by her.

Óengus smiled wickedly. "All you need to know, is that the old man will not be leaving the island."

A pang of guilt unsettled her stomach, as she remembered how excited Finn was to introduce her to all her friends. If only Finn knew her mission now . . . She shook herself away from guilty thoughts. Finn was *not* her friend. She'd run off, leaving her sick and alone. *No.* Maybe, she hadn't run off. Maybe Finn was taken against her will, and was waiting for Bedelia to save her.

Bedelia shivered again as Óengus clapped his hand on her shoulder, bringing her attention once more to his face. His silver hair seemed darker with the ocean's moisture clinging to it, and his cheeks showed signs of sunburn from his time spent on deck.

"I trust you'll follow orders?" he questioned.

Bedelia nodded as she turned her gaze back to the

horizon, feeling sick at Óengus' touch. She sighed. She would do what she needed to do. If Finn found out, she would never forgive her. Yet, Bedelia knew if she faltered, she might lose Keiren's attentions forever. It was a price Bedelia was simply unwilling to pay.

CHAPTER TWELVE

*A*nders never thought he'd actually make it to the coast on his own. He'd walked all night to keep from shivering, giving the ruined city a wide berth. He didn't want any lookouts to accost him with arrows or bolts of magic, thinking he was still part of An Fiach. While he'd run into a few other soldiers of An Fiach on his way, none had questioned him, given he was still wearing his uniform. He was just another soldier searching for the rest of his contingent after the catastrophe of their first battle.

He sighed in exasperation as he stood alone on the sandy beach, the first rays of sunlight peeking over the horizon. How could he have been so stupid? To blindly follow An Fiach into battle, thinking it would somehow bring back his twin sister? She was *gone*. He had to come to terms with that fact. Until she'd gotten kidnapped, there had never been a day that Anders had not spent with her. They were inseparable, even though they fought more often than they got along.

Now it was all over. Anders was now an only child, and as good as an orphan. He could never go back to his family in the Archives, even though all he wanted in that moment was to bury his nose in a good book, warm beside a fire. Well that, and to see his twin sister's face again.

Now, to add to his troubles, someone had led him to the coast by way of a mysterious note, most likely a joke to take up his time until someone or something killed him. He would probably be better off dead, though he would have rather avoided the humiliation of waiting on the beach for someone who would never come.

Was he even in the right place? The note had not been terribly specific, but the beach was wide and open. He could see a long distance in either direction. While darkness had been clinging to much of the land, he'd convinced himself that he'd be able to see whomever he was meeting as soon as the sun fully rose. Now the sunlight was beginning to sparkle on the calm waves of the ocean, and Anders was still alone.

It was this surety that caused him to nearly fall on his face when someone tapped his shoulder. He gathered his wits and turned around. His mouth fell open, astonished. The note had not come from Radley, or Iseult, or anyone else Anders could have suspected.

The Traveler raised one of his unnaturally long, boney hands to his mouth as he laughed at Anders' surprise. Instead of the flowing, white robes Anders remembered seeing upon their first meeting with the Ceàrdaman, this one wore charcoal gray. His bald head was bare to the cold morning air, emphasizing his unusual translucent skin and large, reflective eyes.

"What do you want?" Anders demanded, finally gathering himself enough to take a step away from the Traveler.

"Something quite similar to what you want," the Traveler answered puzzlingly.

Anders wasn't sure what to say. Part of him wondered if he'd fallen asleep back in the forest, and was now trapped in some strange dream. "I doubt that," he answered finally.

The Traveler smiled, revealing sharp teeth. "You want information on what happened to your sister. You long to know if there's any chance of saving her."

Anders' eyes widened in shock. "If you know where she is, you must tell me," he begged. "Does she live?"

The Traveler tilted his head to the side, observing Anders like he was a small, entertaining child.

"Tell me!" he shouted, at his wit's end.

The Traveler smiled again. "You know the price," he warned. "My information is only given in exchange for a great boon."

Anders' heart thudded in his chest. He really had nothing else to lose. "Anything," he agreed. "I'll give you anything."

The Ceàrdaman grinned wickedly. Anders felt like perhaps he would learn to regret his decision, but he couldn't bring himself to care. If he could find his sister, he'd at least have some hope of his life going back to normal. It was more than he'd had just moments before.

The Traveler nodded, satisfied. "Your sister has become what my people call Éagann. Her senses have been taken over by an unseen force. They use her body like a puppet."

"Who?" Anders pleaded. "Who has done this to her?"

"The Dair," the Traveler answered simply. "They have returned to this land. I believe you are even acquainted with one, the girl who calls herself Finn."

"Finn would never harm Branwen," Anders defended. "She saved her from the Blood Forest. She swore to help her further if she could."

The Traveler raised the skin where his eyebrow should have been, though there wasn't a single hair upon it. "I did not say that Finn harmed your sister, only that her people did."

Anders was exhausted and cold, and found that he'd lost any patience he might have had for word games, even from someone as imposing as the Traveler. "Just tell me how to find my sister," he demanded, placing his hand on the pommel of his sword for emphasis.

The Traveler chuckled. "She is in a place that is not a place. The in-between, many call it. Trapped between the worlds of the living and the dead. At least, that is where her mind resides. Her body is cold and alone, quite near death."

Hot tears stung Anders' eyes. His emotions felt out of place on such a calm, sunny morning. He glanced at the ruined city in the distance, wondering if he could enlist

Iseult to help him find his sister instead of the Traveler, but quickly dismissed the thought. Iseult had his mission, and it had nothing to do with Branwen. Of course, if he could find Finn, perhaps she could help.

The Traveler laughed again. As if reading Anders' thoughts, he taunted, "Though others may be able to help you in returning her mind, no one else knows where to find the physical body of your sister."

He glared at the Traveler. "You found her, and you left her near death? You couldn't have helped her?"

The Travelers eyes narrowed. "It is the Ceàrdaman's place to watch, and to record. We have been watching the Dair closely since their return. Your sister's condition was a secondary observation."

Anders had the urge to throttle the Traveler, but resisted. If this monster really was his only hope of finding his sister, he needed him alive.

He clenched his jaw, wishing he could just turn away without speaking, but he had no choice. "What do you want in exchange for my sister's life?" he asked.

The Traveler tsked at him. "Our deal was for information. I said nothing about helping you fetch your sister."

Anders felt rage like he'd never known. In fact, he previously thought he hadn't been capable of such intense anger. Branwen had always poked fun at him for being far too soft.

His fists clenched and unclenched as he resisted drawing his sword. "You *will* help me find her, or I will do my very best to kill you here on this beach. I have nothing left to lose."

A strange look crossed the Traveler's face. Anders almost thought it was a look of respect, but quickly dismissed the notion.

After several silent moments, the Traveler nodded. "I will have my people tend to your sister, and you will get her back after you've led me into your family's Archives."

Anders' jaw dropped. When he'd promised he'd do absolutely anything, he never expected *that*. It was unheard of. The Archives were well protected, as many of the tomes were ancient and irreplaceable. While many had no respect for history or literature, there were enough lords and ladies that deemed the Archives a valuable enough venture to fund. Anders' name alone would gain him entry, but the Traveler would be cut down as soon as he appeared.

"Deal," Anders agreed, knowing he at least had to try.

The Traveler nodded. "Then let us depart." He turned on his heel and began to walk away down the beach.

Anders had to jog to catch up. "I suppose I should at least know your name," he grumbled. "We have many weeks of travel ahead of us."

Never slowing his pace, the Traveler replied, "You may call me Niklas, and do not fear. There are modes of travel known to my people that your mortal brain simply cannot comprehend, and I have no desire to remain by your side for *weeks*."

Anders bit his tongue to keep a snide remark from escaping his mouth. He could admit, if only to himself, that the prospect of learning how the Travelers seemed to move around faster than anyone else was more than enticing. In fact, it would be one for the books.

Iseult waited not so patiently in the lowest chamber of the tower. Upon finishing his speech, Conall had retreated to his chambers to rest, leaving Iseult no opportunity to question him on the way out of the city. Àed had never reappeared. Impatience eating at him, Iseult had once again considered escaping the city on his own, leaving Maarav, Ealasaid, and their horses behind. Àed was probably already on his way to Finn, having had the same idea as he. Still, he needed Maarav's ship to reach her. He couldn't waste the time it would take to employ someone back in Migris. He had no other option than to stay with the party.

At first light, having slept little, Iseult, Maarav, and Ealasaid entered the tower to speak with Conall. The attendants did not send them straight up as before, but rather, instructed them to wait in the common area. Iseult clenched his jaw in annoyance as he watched the attendants, several young women and one man, outfitting any settlers who'd damaged their decrepit gear in the battle. He had no time for any of it. Where in the horned one's name was Conall? Iseult would either fight the man, or be shown a way out, but he would not wait around for the reivers to *join* them.

He had left his party's three remaining horses with one of the settlers, promising payment if the man agreed to remain with them outside the tower, just in case. Àed's mule creature was nowhere to be found, confirming Iseult's suspicions that the old man had left them permanently. He only wished Àed had shown him the way out first. He would have gladly escaped with him.

Iseult rested his back against the rough, wooden wall, shaking away his thoughts of Àed. If the conjurer indeed was gone, his only hope of finding Finn was to meet her at the Archtree. If he missed her, he would have trouble locating her again without Àed's unnatural senses to guide him.

He scowled at the unsavory thought. He had shunned the chair offered to him by the tower's attendants, choosing to remain ready to leap into action. Beside him, Maarav had taken a chair graciously, as had Ealasaid, who remained unconvinced of Conall's ulterior motives. Iseult himself was not entirely convinced. His judgement was speculative, after all. Hopefully the forthcoming meeting would clarify things.

Maarav, sitting in the chair nearest Iseult, glanced up at him with a raised brow. "It's quite odd that we've been asked to wait this time around. It makes a man wonder who our glorious leader might be meeting with currently."

He'd made his statement loud enough for the attendants in the chamber to hear. Rather than looking at Maarav, they glanced warily at each other, upping Iseult's suspicions. They knew something, and were afraid to give it away.

Iseult nodded at Maarav, then turned his attention to

the pair of female attendants descending the stairs. He recognized them as the ones who'd been assisting Conall with his meal the day before, though they seemed far more fearful now.

One of the pair, a woman around twenty, with icy blonde hair, approached and offered Iseult a slight bow of her head. "Lord Conall will see you now," she said softly.

"Ah," Maarav muttered behind Iseult as he rose to his feet, "so he's a *lord* now."

Iseult followed the attendant as she turned to walk back up the stairs, leaving the dark-haired woman who'd accompanied her to come up the stairs after Maarav and Ealasaid. Those remaining in the room watched the whole scene with wide eyes.

By the time Iseult had reached the top of the long, spiraling staircase, a quiet rage had begun to simmer in his gut. It was not his job to save the people who remained in the city, hoping their great *lord* would protect them, but he found it difficult to remain uncaring. He knew what it was like to be left defenseless, and without a home.

He stepped away from the staircase as he entered the throne room, moving to stand in front of Conall, who now eyed him from his wooden dais. As Iseult looked down at the aged reiver with his full beard and wily eyes, he knew he could not simply leave the city as it was. He might be able to chill his emotions toward those ignorant enough to believe that any leader really did things for his or her own people, but he could not chill his fresh hatred for the man before him.

Iseult's life had been a long stream of watching the innocent lower class as they repeatedly fell beneath the boots of the upper. It was an entirely new insult to see refugees fighting for a man who would ultimately sacrifice them if it suited his needs.

Cold realization shone in Conall's eyes as he stared at Iseult, unspeaking. He had recognized one of his own, a predator, unwilling to be ruled.

Maarav strolled up to stand beside Iseult. He flashed a smile at Conall's remaining female attendants, then turned his gaze back to Conall. "I must advise you to dismiss the extra ears in the room, *Lord* Conall," he began happily. "There are things, I'm sure, that you would not like them to hear."

Conall smirked, then nodded his head toward the stairs. The small gesture was enough to dismiss the women, who hurried from the room as if flames licked at their heels.

"I find it fair to warn you," Conall began, his smirk remaining, "since you assisted my people in yesterday's battle, that we are not as alone as we appear. I would not make any sudden movements."

Iseult glanced around the room, really *looking* at it. The wall behind the throne came too far into the space, far enough to not simply be a divider between the room and the staircase. It had been roughly assembled for a reason, he realized. The mismatched planks of wood hid the seam of a door. *Anyone* could be hiding behind it.

Iseult looked back to Conall, feeling an odd mixture of respect and hatred. "We've come only to talk," he stated blandly.

Conall's pudgy face broke into a crooked smile. "To talk?" he questioned. "Or to make *false* accusations?"

The reiver really wasn't as stupid as Iseult first imagined. He knew not all would believe his story of being a magnanimous ruler, and he was fully prepared for any accusations that might come his way.

Ealasaid, who'd been listening to the exchange silently, took a subtle step toward the stairs, giving herself a clear line of escape. Perhaps the girl wasn't as naive as Iseult had originally believed either.

He gritted his teeth. What he wouldn't give to just skewer Conall, ending things quickly and cleanly. Unfortunately, such an act would likely bring reivers rushing out of the walls.

"You have made enough use of the settlers," Iseult stated. "Let them go in peace before the rest of your men arrive."

Conall raised a bushy eyebrow. "You really jump right past pretenses, don't you?"

Ealasaid looked around the room nervously, making Iseult worry that the girl might do something stupid, but at a quick look from Maarav, she stilled.

He turned a stern gaze back to Conall, unwilling to be led away from the subject at hand by useless observations of ceremony.

"No, I will not release the settlers" Conall answered

simply. "We have many magic users among our ranks. The settlers will prove useful."

Iseult glared. "Not all of them have such skills to offer. Many were simply forced to leave their ruined villages. Let those ones go. They are of no use to you."

Conall rolled his eyes. "And when the ones I want to keep ask why their family members are being sent away?"

Iseult's expression remained impassive, though his anger was growing. "You've proven yourself skilled at manipulation. I'm sure you'll think of something."

Conall snorted and cast his hand into the air, dismissing the thought. "Lead the people out to meet An Fiach, if you wish."

"There must be another way out of the city," Iseult said instantly, undeterred. If more men from the north would be joining Conall's ranks, they had to get in some way.

Conall seemed to think about what Iseult said, then he raised a pudgy finger into the air as if he'd just had a grand idea. "There is a way out," he said with a snide grin. "And I will have someone guide you to it, if you agree to leave quietly, under guard."

So that was his plan after all, Iseult thought. Conall would sneak the rest of his men into the city, unbeknownst to the settlers or An Fiach. Before the refugees knew it, they would be surrounded by savage warriors, left with only two choices. Fight against their own countrymen, or die.

Iseult pondered his options. He could easily leave

quietly, continue on his mission to find Finn, and eventually absolve his ancestors of their mistakes. Yet, he knew if his mother would have been alive to see that moment, she would have cursed the promise she forced him to make when he was young. These were living, breathing people on the line. His ancestor's honor could wait.

Just as Iseult had made up his mind, Maarav answered, "We could leave quietly, that's true, but what would be the fun in that?"

At Maarav's words, Conall lifted a hand into the air. The hidden door behind the throne burst outward, revealing several men, large and stocky like Conall, dressed in hides and fur, wielding either massive axes, or greatswords that likely weighed more than Ealasaid.

Within seconds, Iseult had his short sword in one hand, and a parrying dagger in the other. He glanced to see Maarav with daggers in either hand. They were probably both about to die trying to save people who should have meant nothing to them, but at least they'd die with honor.

As the warriors approached, Iseult cast a quick glance toward the stairs, wondering if he could reach them to warn the townsfolk before he got sliced in two, but more warriors had come from somewhere below to block the way. Conall had planned the moment well.

The warriors charged, and Ealasaid screamed. Then the room filled with what Iseult could only call lightning, though they were indoors. He dropped to the ground as a bolt shot toward him. Many of the slower, bulky warriors weren't as lucky. The lightning hit them, blasting them off their feet to the ground.

"Like trying to control the Earthen Mother herself!" Maarav shouted happily as he rushed past Iseult toward Ealasaid. The uninjured warriors gathered themselves and charged while their comrades shakily got to their feet. None in the room had been killed, but those on the stairs had been knocked backward to tumble from whence they came.

Thinking that forcing the unharmed warriors to follow them into the street seemed like as good a plan as any, Iseult followed as Maarav hurried Ealasaid toward the landing. The three of them ran as footsteps thundered behind them. Iseult expected an axe to find his back at any moment, but the blow never came. The trio took turns leaping over the body of a reiver who'd fallen down the stairs, landing halfway down the flight with his neck twisted at an unnatural angle.

They reached the bottom of the stairs, only to be met by more warriors, one of whom had fallen all the way down from the top, yet was somehow already climbing to his feet. Maarav, holding onto Ealasaid by the backs of her arms, thrust the poor girl toward the reivers like she was a weapon to be wielded. Lightning shot from her hands, knocking the men aside. The three of them made their way to the tower doors and burst out into the sunlight.

Many settlers had gathered around the exterior of the tower, no doubt curious about the commotion from within. Iseult and his companions joined the relative safety of the crowd, then turned to face Conall's men. The crowd's curiosity turned to terror as the pack of reivers poured out into the street.

Iseult wracked his brain as he scanned the townsfolk around him. Spotting the man with their horses, he approached and quickly took the reins, then placed several coins in the man's trembling palm.

As he handed the reins of their horses to both Maarav and Ealasaid, he pondered his options. He could lead the settlers out the front gates, but An Fiach would be waiting not far off. He needed to find the other way out of the city, but how?

"Conall has lied to you!" Ealasaid shouted, now safely hidden within the crowd. "These men have come to invade our great land!"

The reivers had come to a standstill, only now aware of their folly. There was no telling how many within the crowd wielded magic much more devastating than Ealasaid's.

"Is it true?" an unknown face in the crowd asked.

"Where is Conall?" another inquired.

"Let him answer for himself!" another shouted.

A moment later, Conall appeared within the doorway of the tower. He sauntered out amongst his men, belly jutted outward in confidence.

"My dear people!" he shouted. "Had I not told you that reinforcements were on the way? These men are here to protect you. *They*," he began, throwing a finger toward Iseult and Maarav, who towered above most of the crowd "would see you handed to An Fiach, the true enemy."

"He's buying time until the rest of his men can arrive!" Maarav shouted. "We must find another way out of the city!"

The settlers looked around, confused.

Conall smiled. "Leave if you like!" he shouted. "If you believe An Fiach will treat you more fairly than someone who has been persecuted, just as you have, then I beseech you to run willingly toward their waiting swords!"

More murmurs sounded amongst the crowd.

"There is another way out of the city!" Iseult announced. "One that Conall has kept hidden from you all!"

The murmurs grew louder. Conall looked nervous once more.

"There is no other way out," he argued. "You people rebuilt this city yourselves."

"Not the walls!" someone shouted. "The walls were in place when I first arrived!"

Many mumbled their assent. It seemed none present had taken part in assembling the walls.

Conall's face was beginning to turn red. His men shifted uncomfortably around him. "Search the walls if you so choose!" he snapped, "but the fact remains, you have nowhere else to go! Together we are strong, we can fight An Fiach. Alone, you will be cut down one by one."

The crowd went silent.

Maarav leaned in close to Iseult. "I believe now is our cue to search for this apparent secret passage."

Iseult nodded. There was no way of knowing how much time they had until the other reivers arrived, and he was sure that if he departed from the crowd, Conall would send his men after him, even if it meant exposing himself as a wanted criminal.

"Any who would like to avoid death may follow me!" Iseult shouted. "I will show you the way out, and leaving will be *your* choice."

Maarav smirked and whispered, "So now you know the way out?"

Iseult did not respond. He had an idea, but there was no surety. Still, he was willing to stake his life on it. Given that the only other options were to wait for the reivers, or confront An Fiach outside of the gates, it would have to do.

EALASAID COULDN'T BELIEVE she had been such a blithering idiot. To blindly believe Conall's intentions, simply because he was an outcast just like her.

She was lucky to have Maarav and Iseult, two men who were not blind, looking out for her, though she didn't particularly like either of them. Still, following them was better than following the other magic users who'd been just as gullible toward Conall's preachings.

Regardless, she wasn't happy to be clinging to her horse as they rode through the streets, her pale blue skirts hitched high above her knees, following Iseult toward the East end of the ruined city.

Many of the other settlers had followed, though some surprisingly stayed behind with Conall and his men, likely hoping that swearing allegiance to the reivers would mean protection from An Fiach. Ealasaid doubted that would be the case for them. Reivers had no respect for the more civilized folk. Those who stayed behind would be little more than slaves, surviving only as long as they served a purpose. A purpose that would require they kill their own country-men, likely not limited to An Fiach. While Ealasaid would have liked to see the men of the Hunt skewered, she would not willingly venture forth to attack innocents.

She nearly ran into Maarav's black and white horse as he brought the animal to a skidding halt. They had reached the portion of wall that separated the city from the coast, and Iseult had dismounted to examine the structure.

They had enough magic users among them that they could probably blast down the wall, but it would take time. Most of the planks of wood were thicker than tree trunks, anchored deep within the ground. The wall had been built to withstand a siege. They could burn it, but it would take hours. Time was not on their side, especially if more reivers were on their way.

Ealasaid laughed to herself as she imagined a door opening within the wall, only to reveal a massive host of armed, brutish men, ready to herd herself and the others back to Conall. The fact that she was laughing at such a thought made her feel like she was losing her mind, which actually seemed a nice alternative to the current circumstances.

Maarav watched Iseult thoughtfully, then dismounted to join him. The two men looked so similar it was eerie, though their demeanors could not have contrasted more. Iseult seemed angry, while Maarav seemed merely curious. Ealasaid could not identify with either emotion, as she was simply scared out of her wits.

A few of the many settlers who had joined them had horses, and stayed mounted while Iseult inspected the wall. Ealasaid huffed and climbed down from her horse. She might be a follower just like the others, but she could at least be a *useful* follower.

Holding tightly to the reins of her horse, she approached the wall and began walking along it, opposite the direction of Iseult and Maarav. She thought back to the secret door within Conall's tower as she paced. The only evidence of the door was the straight seam, slightly more prominent than the other joints within the wall.

Anxiety ate at her gut. Conall had confirmed that there was a secret passage within the city, but what if it wasn't in the wall? They could be searching blindly until the reivers came to enslave them. They might as well start blasting away at the wall for the time it might save.

Steeling herself against her thoughts, she began to look at things logically. The land to the north of the ruined city was mountainous with dense vegetation. A large force of men would be greatly hindered coming from that direction, and coming from the east would put them too close to the camps of An Fiach. The western coast was the only option, something Iseult had obviously already figured out. The northern end of the coast in particular would be the best point of entry, as they would be far from An Fiach. Any men who chose to attack the incoming reivers would have to funnel along the narrow coast, making their ranks vulnerable.

Ealasaid began to look not only along the wall, but at the sparse buildings nearest them. Many were little more than ruins, but some had been built up to house settlers. One in particular was extremely well put together, solid and without any lower windows. The building was taller than average, and had small openings near the top of its walls, large enough for a man to fit through, but more likely made for those inside to look out across the city, given the window's height.

She approached the building that had caught her attention, feeling vulnerable venturing a bit away from the waiting settlers. A reiver could jump out of the shadows to carry her away, and her companions would be none the wiser. Still, something about this building was giving her pause.

She circled the structure until she found the double doors that would lead inward. She grabbed one of the handles and rattled it, but the door didn't budge. It seemed to be held in place from the inside.

Ealasaid jumped, then clutched at her chest as someone appeared at her side. Maarav raised his free hand in a *calm down, it's only me* gesture, while his other hand remained on his horse's reins.

Ealasaid turned back to the building in front of her to hide her blush. Doing her best to steady her breathing before speaking, she said, "The doors seem to be barred from the inside. It's suspicious, isn't it?"

Maarav nodded, handed Ealasaid the reins of his horse, then walked away toward the back of the building. A little rush of anger made Ealasaid's face flush. He hadn't even listened to her, then he'd just demoted her to horse holder. She had discovered something useful, but since she was a sheltered, young, village girl, no one would listen.

A moment later, as she stood still seething with quiet anger, there was a sound right on the other side of the door. She stepped backward, ready to scream that the reivers had arrived, cursing Maarav for not listening to her, then something heavy hit the ground inside, and the door swung outward, revealing a lone man, looking down at her with a mischievous smile.

As soon as she'd gathered her wits, she glared at Maarav. "You could have told me you were going inside! How in the blazes did you manage that?"

"The windows," Maarav said simply as he reclaimed his horse's reins, not elaborating on the fact that said openings were placed in a wall four times taller than Maarav himself.

Before Ealasaid could question him further, he ordered, "Gather the others. I'll scout the way ahead."

The way ahead? Ealasaid thought, dumfounded for a moment. Then it all became clear as Maarav led his horse inside the building to a massive open cellar in the middle of the floor. The rest of the interior was barren, except for a ladder that led to one of the windows, crafted as a lookout perch.

Trusting that the cellar was a way out of the city, Ealasaid hurried to find the others.

Within a few minutes, she had everyone willingly following her. She felt a surge of excitement as she led Iseult and the settlers back to the hidden exit. She remained on foot, dragging both her and Maarav's horses behind her. Maarav had returned to the opening to meet them, and nodded that the way was clear as soon as Ealasaid and the others came into sight.

Relief washed through her. They might make it out of this alive. Though what she would do after that, she wasn't sure.

Maarav began ushering the settlers through the underground tunnel while Iseult watched silently. Ealasaid wanted to rush ahead through the large, beam-supported tunnel, mounting her horse on the other side to rush away from everything, but steeled herself against her urges. She wanted to be one of the rescuers, not the rescued.

"They have nowhere to go," Ealasaid heard Maarav comment quietly to Iseult.

"We've done what we can," Iseult replied.

Ealasaid felt a shiver of fear. If Iseult and Maarav were planning to leave the settlers on their own, they might leave Ealasaid with them. If she was going to avenge her family, she needed to be amongst warriors, not common folk, magical abilities or no.

Maarav's eyes met hers, as if sensing her thoughts. "You should catch up with the others," he advised.

Her reply was cut off by the sound of a horn, somewhere outside the gates. Ealasaid's eyes widened just as several figures moved into view from deeper within the city.

"You are too late," Conall called, looking smug as he took a few steps forward, flanked by his men. "Though I admire your cleverness. A passage near the coast really was the only option."

It all clicked into place. Conall's reinforcements had arrived. That's who had sounded the horn, and now the settlers would be trapped between the city and the oncoming reivers.

"We must warn them," Ealasaid breathed, ignoring the fact that Conall and his men might try to bar their way.

Conall chuckled. "Warn them all, for what good it will do, but let them know they may still return to the city to be part of a cause greater than they could have ever imagined." Conall winked in Ealasaid's direction. "You too, lass, though I fear your ill-chosen companions must die."

Not thinking twice about the consequences of her actions, Ealasaid handed the reins of both horses to Maarav, then mustered what little strength she had left to summon a bolt of lighting. It struck in front of Conall and his men, temporarily scattering them.

"Run!" she shouted.

Iseult and Maarav did not question her. The three of them hurried into the secret passage. It was wide enough for five men to run side by side, and more than tall enough for their horses to trot behind them. They probably stood a better chance against Conall and his men than they did the incoming reivers, but at least outside of the city, they wouldn't be trapped. Perhaps they could gain enough of a start up the coast to outpace the reivers, even if it put them in uncharted lands.

The air of the passage was stale, but Ealasaid could smell the salt of the ocean filtering through. They were close, though the supporting boards forming the tunnel seemed to go on forever. Her horse whinnied behind her, unhappy to be in a dark tunnel, led along beside two other horses. Ealasaid would have ridden her, but feared that areas of the tunnel would not be tall enough.

Suddenly, they had cleared the end of the tunnel. Cold, salty air hit Ealasaid's face uncomfortably as the bright light burned her eyes. The first thing she noticed as her vision cleared was the fleet of ships in the distance. The second, was the group of settlers, huddled together and arguing what to do.

The first few settlers to spot Ealasaid seemed relieved, as if she would have a plan. She had a brief moment of pride before realizing that they were probably looking to Iseult and Maarav behind her.

Conall and his men hadn't followed. There was no need. They were as good as trapped.

She looked to Maarav and Iseult. As much as she wanted to be a leader, she had no idea what to do.

"Too many mouths to feed," Maarav muttered.

Iseult nodded. "We can lead them North, then they will have to survive on their own."

Ealasaid wondered which side of that statement she was included in, but didn't have time to ask questions as Iseult and Maarav approached the settlers.

"Conall's ships will reach the shore within the hour," Maarav announced. "Your only choice is to head north."

"That's no choice at all!" someone shouted.

Maarav shook his head. "You were not forced to believe the lies of a reiver. Your choices were your own then, just as they are now. You can choose to follow us, or remain here to wait for the ships. There may be a place in the North where you will find refuge, or you may die. Either way, at least you won't be waiting around to be slaughtered."

Iseult had mounted his horse, and seemed impatient to get moving. The passageway still stood wide open behind them, leaving the threat of the reivers still within the city for all to dwell upon. Most of the settlers were ill equipped, with only the clothes on their backs to aid in their survival.

Maarav and Iseult kicked their horses into motion, heading north up the coast to where Maarav's ship, and this settlement, allegedly waited.

"We may have room for a few on my ship," Maarav commented quietly to Iseult as they rode ahead of the settlers, "a few magic users could not hurt to have around."

Iseult shook his head. "We cannot take some, and not

the others. They stand better chances if they stay together."

Ealasaid glanced back at the settlers who all had begun to follow, the ones on horses staying back with those who walked.

Maarav smirked, then turned to Ealasaid. "There's room at least for you."

Ealasaid frowned, unsure of what to do. She didn't actually *know* any of the settlers, but could she really leave them? She felt her face flush. It wasn't like she could do anything to help them. She was a young, village-sheltered girl. She had no idea how to survive in the wilds.

ÀED TIRELESSLY LIFTED the oars of the small boat, plunging them back into the water to propel himself forward. Across from him rested his shaggy, brown mule, leaning back on its haunches to lower its center of gravity.

It had been a tedious task instructing the mule to sit in the boat, and more tiresome still to cast the small vessel out to sea, but he had managed. He'd had enough magic in him for that small feat, if little else.

He regretted leaving Iseult behind. He was a useful companion, and highly protective of Finn. Still, Àed only had enough magic to conceal himself as he departed from the city gates, his mule in tow.

Happening upon the little rowboat had been sheer

luck. It had likely been used by the settlers as a fishing vessel, never meant to travel into deeper waters, but Àed had little choice. If Kai managed to bring Finn to the Archtree, and there was no one there to meet them, they would eventually leave. Who knew where that man would take her after that?

No, it had to be now. Àed would make it to the Archtree no matter what. He only had what Iseult had told him to guide his way, but it would have to be enough. Hopefully, he would be able to sense Finn when she was near, guiding him the rest of the way to the island.

He couldn't fail her like he'd failed his daughter. She had so much power, so much potential, that could easily be turned toward darkness. He could not stand by and watch as such a bright light once again turned dim.

CHAPTER THIRTEEN

he island had come into sight around dawn. It was enough to finally draw Anna out of her cabin amongst the remaining crewmen.

She approached Finn and Kai as they stood side by side near the front of the ship. Anna wasn't sure at what point Finn had gone from prisoner to partner, but the shift had definitely taken place. She should have seen it coming the moment she allowed Kai aboard.

Still, she found she actually didn't mind the new dynamic, as Finn was somehow entwined in the mystery of what was happening, with the gray place, and the hooded figures. If she wanted to figure things out, it would serve her to keep Finn close, and on the same ship was close enough, regardless of whether Finn was in shackles, or roaming freely.

Anna went to stand on Kai's other side as they gazed out at the nearing island. He acknowledged her presence with a nod, but didn't speak. His directions had proven true, if the mass of land ahead of them was in fact the correct island. According to the sea maps Anna had brought along, this island didn't even exist, so the likelihood of it being the right place was promising.

Kai shifted his weight from foot to foot beside her, seeming nervous. Anna shared the sentiment. It wasn't every day you went searching for a tree out of legend that would answer your most profound questions.

At one point, the tree probably would have led Anna straight to the shroud, as money was her driving force. Now, she could only hope that it would tell her how to fix herself so things could go back to normal.

She would have liked to think that she could depend on Kai to ask the tree about the shroud, as his motivations were similar to hers. Yet, she had a feeling that his heart was now concerned with other things, and whatever answers the Archtree might have for Kai, they would do Anna little good.

Then there was Finn. The tree might tell *her* where the shroud was, but it would be another thing to force the information out of her. Still, given the opportunity, she would try.

"How will we reach the island?" Anna heard Finn ask from the other side of Kai. "There's no dock."

"We'll take a smaller boat," Kai explained.

Anna watched Kai as he spoke to Finn, noticing the sudden change in his stance. His face was turned away from her view, but she had little doubt that his expression had softened as he spoke to Finn.

She took a deep breath, then looked out to the island.

They would soon board the small rowboat to head ashore, just her, Kai, and Finn. Sativola would stay to watch over the remaining crew members, just two men now, given the other two had passed. She trusted Sativola to prevent any mutiny while they were ashore.

"We should prepare ourselves," Anna announced.

Finn jumped as if she hadn't even realized Anna was there, or maybe it was just her nerves.

Finn leaned forward to see Anna around Kai. Their eyes met, communicating all that was unsaid between them. Anna felt somewhat guilty that she'd had so little information to give Finn on her mother, but she knew less about what the hooded forms might mean than Finn did. Then there was what Finn had told *her*. That these visions were as much a part of her as her personality. Now that they'd started, they couldn't be stopped. Anna shivered. Finn had to be mistaken.

The trio moved apart from each other to return to their cabins and gather their things. The island was large, and might take a day or two to traverse as they searched for the tree. They would bring enough food and supplies to camp comfortably if need be.

Anna returned to her cabin, going over a mental list of what she needed: food, flint and steel, extra clothing, water, and weapons. Every weapon she owned.

A sickening feeling of foreboding had curled up in her gut. She would have liked to just pass it off as nerves, but there was something strange about this island. She had sailed these oceans before and never caught sight of it, though it was relatively large. Could it be that to see it, you must be looking for it?

Anna shook her head as she sheathed the blades at her waist. It couldn't be just that. If the island could be found that easily, the Travelers wouldn't have needed Anna to seek it out in the gray place. She sighed. Kai had been the one who'd spotted it when it first came into view, so it wasn't some special ability on Finn's part.

She supposed the why of things didn't matter. The island was in front of them now. They would find the Archtree and use it how each of them saw fit. The shroud was only a secondary thought. She had to fix her mind first.

She lifted her heavy coat from her bed. It was black, like the rest of her outfit. They had no idea what might be waiting on the island, and Anna would rather not stand out when darkness fell. After donning her coat, she topped off her outfit with a black cloak. Only the paleness of her face would stand out amongst the monochrome of her clothing and hair. That, and the shine of her blades, though hopefully they would remain sheathed.

With her clothing firmly bundled around her, and a satchel of supplies across her shoulder, Anna exited her cabin. Her boots felt too tight with the double layers of wool socks she'd worn, but they had no horses with them. They might be walking many miles on the island, and the last thing she needed was blisters.

Of course, if blisters were all she received on their upcoming adventure, she'd willingly accept that fate.

FINN PUSHED herself as far to one side of the rowboat as possible. Unfortunately, it was a small boat. Anna looked pale and morose in her solid black clothing, pressing herself against the opposite side of the wooden vessel.

Kai sat in the middle, manning the oars, dressed in his usual gear of tunic, breeches, and coat, all in dark neutrals that would blend in well with the woods. For some reason, as she observed him, her mind wandered back to their forced kiss. She found she was still angry about it. It had been her first kiss, as far as she could remember, and from what she'd gathered, it was supposed to be romantic. She *wanted* it to be romantic. She might be of the Dair, but it didn't mean that she couldn't want human things too. As far as she was concerned, she wanted *only* human things. Not to be some sort of weapon.

Kai caught her frowning and raised an eyebrow at her as he continued to row. His dark chestnut hair had gotten long enough in the time she'd known him to skim just past his shoulders, slightly more curly with the added effect of the salty sea air. Feeling uncomfortable, she turned away. Soon she would be back with Iseult and Àed, and Kai would go on his way. She placed her hands in her lap, wishing Naoki rested there.

She'd felt it best for her little dragon to remain on the ship with Sativola. She trusted him to care for her, though she wasn't sure Naoki shared her sentiments. They'd had to lock her in Finn's cabin, something that gave Finn a painful feeling in her heart every time she thought about it. Still, they had no idea what they might face on the island. It was too risky to bring any more lives into the equation than necessary. She would go back for her before leaving the island with Iseult and Àed. She stifled a shiver. There was always the possibility that her friends had met some ill fate. They might have even fallen prey to the Sirens.

Kai's eyes looked past her to the island. The sea was calm, and the sun was obscured by fluffy clouds, making their journey swift and easy. At least, Kai made it look easy. Finn couldn't help but wonder what he'd be asking of the Archtree. Probably where to find the greatest riches in the world, if she had judged him correctly.

He glanced downward and their eyes met again, but he quickly looked the other way. He'd been acting odd since that morning. It was the first time she could remember going any period of time without him teasing her, or making some flirtatious remark. She almost preferred the old Kai to this new . . . discomfort. The feeling was hard to describe, but it was as if he was shutting himself away, no longer leading with his true thoughts.

Finn frowned and looked over the edge of the ship into the calm waters. She sincerely hoped there were no Sirens lurking beneath them. She didn't want to have to kiss both Anna and Kai to keep them from abandoning her in the small boat.

"I see many trees," Kai commented, once again looking past Finn to the island, "but they all look the same. I hope the Archtree will stand out from the others in some way."

"I'll know it when I see it," Anna mumbled, not sounding happy about the fact.

"Then we just make a tea of its leaves?" Kai questioned. "I know the legends, but it seems a bit far fetched."

Finn peered around Kai to see Anna's expression darken. "The Travelers kept much from me."

Kai frowned. "So even if we can find the tree, we're not sure what to do with it?"

"Iseult believed making a tea of the leaves was the way," Finn cut in. "I trust his judgement."

"Of course you do," Kai muttered.

Finn glared at him, feeling her face heat. "What exactly are you implying?"

Kai snorted. "Simply that you've known the man as long as you've known me, and have spent less time with him. You're naive to trust him so."

Finn sucked her teeth in irritation. "Trust is earned," she snapped, not sure where her sudden anger was coming from. "His actions have earned him that trust, while yours have broken it."

Kai fell silent, and seemed to Finn's surprise, almost . . . abashed? The moment was quickly ended as they reached the breakwaters near the shore. The boat rose and fell with the waves, sometimes lifting partially out of the water, and landing hard enough to rattle Finn's bones. The ship they'd left behind seemed as small as their rowboat in the distance.

Kai pushed the oars against the waves, doing his best to keep the small boat steady long enough to reach the shore. Finn lurched forward as another wave shook her, then turned her back as she landed at the base of the boat with her shoulder blades against Kai's knees.

He didn't comment, and instead kept rowing until the edge of the boat hit the sand of the coast. Finn scurried to her feet and leapt from the front of the boat onto solid land, feeling shaken. She was beginning to realize that maybe she didn't like the water. Some part of her feared the ocean's depths. That realization was emphasized by how suddenly grateful she was to be on dry land. It hadn't been bad on the larger ship, but the small row boat made her feel vulnerable. Her boots sunk into the sand, and her legs felt like they were made of pottage from all of the days at sea, but the feeling of solidity was glorious none-the-less.

Finn stepped back as Kai exited the boat, then pulled it more firmly onto the beach. He offered Anna a guiding hand as she walked gracefully across the small boat, then stepped down deftly onto the shore. Finn blushed, feeling like a fool for scrambling off the boat so quickly. Normally Kai would have poked fun at such a moment, but he remained silent, not even looking in Finn's direction.

Instead, he pulled the now vacant boat even further onto the shore where the water wouldn't touch it, then handed each woman one of the satchels they'd brought along from the vessel's floor.

Finn had been surprised when she'd first discovered

she would have a satchel of her own. Her elation had soon quieted when Anna commented that if they were separated, it would at least be a day or two before Finn starved.

"We should hide the boat," Anna commented.

Kai nodded. "I sincerely hope there is no one here to steal it, but better safe than sorry, I suppose."

Kai and Anna dragged the boat further away from the shore to the foliage that began where the beach ended. The trees here were strange, not what Finn was used to at all. Their bark was smooth and shiny, and their broad leaves were a vibrant green, as opposed to the more muted, dark green of oaks and firs.

Finn moved forward to help as Kai and Anna moved the large leaves of the ground covering plants to obscure the boat, then watched as Anna tore one of the leaves free to obscure the footprints leading up to the hiding place. The area would still be obvious on the otherwise pristine beach, but a light rain or heavy evening mist would reset the sand.

The trio stepped away from their handiwork, but did not move in any other direction.

Both Kai and Finn looked to Anna, the only one there who'd visited the Archtree, even though she had never seen it physically.

Anna frowned and closed her eyes. "The coast doesn't feel familiar," she said after a time. "I don't think the tree was near the ocean. We should move inland." She opened her eyes and looked back and forth between Finn and Kai as they nodded their assent.

Finn appreciated that Anna looked to her for agreement, and not just Kai. Perhaps she didn't believe she was a blithering idiot after all.

"Try not to do anything stupid while we're here," Anna commented as she walked past Finn toward a narrow opening in the foliage.

Finn scowled as she moved to follow Anna down the path, with Kai bringing up the rear. A blithering idiot after all.

They walked along the tree line until a narrow footpath was found, seeming like an animal trail, given it was barely wide enough to place two feet upon. Kai took the lead, bending the branches that barred his way until Anna took hold of them, then Finn, letting them snap back into place after she'd passed.

It took Finn quite some time to realize why the island seemed so strange to her. The ground beneath her feet felt solid, the trees, though foreign, seemed normal enough, and the breeze that occasionally picked up a lock of her hair felt like any other breeze, but suddenly it hit her. It wasn't her sense of sight or touch that found something amiss, it was her hearing. All she could hear was the occasional rustling of the wind in the leaves, and the crunch of her party's boots on the gravely path. There was no sound of birdsong. No crackling branches to alert them to other wildlife. If it weren't for the subtle wind, the island would have been perfectly still.

It was odd, Finn thought, that you never really realized how much sound surrounded you until you were without it. Well, almost without it. The sounds of their footfalls seemed startlingly loud in contrast.

"There are no birds," Finn commented softly as they walked, not wanting to be the only one dealing with the startling realization.

"No," Kai replied as he continued on down the path. "There doesn't seem to be much of anything here."

"It doesn't matter," Anna commented, not turning to look at them as she passed Kai to take the lead on the path. "As long as we can find what we're looking for, we can question the rest later."

Finn bit her lip. *If* they could find what they were looking for. They'd been walking for quite some time, and everything looked the same. Anna paused, making Kai and Finn stop behind her, then looked side to side, as if searching for any other paths, but there weren't any. Finn had been looking too.

Kai glanced back at Finn to see her worried expression. He turned and patted her shoulder in comfort as he opened his mouth to say something, then seemed to think better of it. He withdrew his hand quickly to his side, and turned away from her.

Finn looked down at her feet, feeling dejected, as they walked on.

THEY WALKED ON AND ON. Many times, Kai thought he smelled a whiff of smoke along the way, but it was always gone a moment later. He was sure the smell was just his senses playing tricks on him. The island was clearly void of life, at least the part they were exploring.

The path had widened enough that Finn was able to walk by his side, though she didn't so much as glance at him. No one had spoken after discussing the lack of noise on the island, and Kai would not be the first one to break the silence. In fact, he would do his best to not contribute to any conversations at all, at least where Finn was concerned.

He needed to distance himself from her. If everything went according to plan, Iseult and Àed would be waiting somewhere on the island to take Finn away from him. Even though he'd travelled with them all before, Kai doubted he would be invited along. He couldn't abandon Anna regardless. No, he would return to the ship with Anna, and they would sail away, forgetting that the strange "tree girl" ever existed.

Kai's heart gave a little leap as he remembered Naoki. Surely Finn would at least like to return to the ship to fetch her new friend. Kai shook away his thoughts. Even if the island wasn't their final parting, Finn wanted nothing to do with him, and he had no part in her world. He was a mortal man, and knew little about Finn's people or her purpose. It was better this way.

He caught a whiff of smoke again. He looked to Finn to see if she smelled it too, but she was studiously ignoring him, and Anna had ventured further ahead down the trail, and would disappear around bends in the path until they hit a straightway.

He glanced at Finn again and frowned. It would all be over soon.

FINN SCOWLED. Over the past hour, Kai had continuously glanced at her. She noticed, but chose to ignore it. There was a strange smell in the air, like woodsmoke, but with the scent of some sort of herb she couldn't quite place. Many times she thought to ask Kai if he smelled it, but she resisted. If he was going to turn up his nose at her, she would do the same to him.

To increase her discomfort, her feet were beginning to ache, and the satchel she carried felt heavier by the moment. In it, she had two water skins, flint and steel for lighting fires, and enough food to last one person several days.

Anna came into view as they continued walking. She had stopped in the middle of the trail to wait for Finn and Kai, looking dangerous with blades at her hips.

She pursed her lips in thought as they reached her. "Do either of you smell smoke?"

Kai nodded, looking relieved for some odd reason.

"Does it mean there's someone else on the island?" Finn asked, knowing that it did. Perhaps Iseult and Àed had arrived. If not, then perhaps the party should be worried. She had no desire to find out what sort of people might dwell on such a remote island.

Anna frowned and looked up at the darkening sky. "We should make camp."

"With no fire," Kai agreed.

Finn's heart sank. The air was already chilly, and the sun hadn't fully descended. Come nightfall, they'd freeze.

Anna nodded her agreement and walked away from the path, presumably to find a camping spot. Finn's feet screamed as she followed, wishing they could just camp right by the path.

Of course, people like Kai and Anna knew what they were doing, so Finn didn't argue as they walked for twenty more minutes, until Anna found an area she deemed suitable. The clearing was small, as the trees were closely spaced, but there was enough room on the even ground for three bedrolls to be set up.

It was just starting to get dark, but Finn was more than ready for sleep. She was no stranger to long journeys, but something about being on a ship for such a prolonged period of time, followed by the long walk, had her legs feeling ready to give out.

Wordlessly, the trio unfurled their bedrolls. Anna took the middle spot, with Finn and Kai on either side of her. Finn felt uneasy being so close to her would-be captor, but given her only other choice, she accepted her fate.

Soon enough, Finn was in her bedroll, shivering and waiting for sleep to take her. She tried to calm her nerves as her mind remained active, but to little avail. Kai had sworn that Iseult and Àed would meet them on this island. Finn longed to see them. To feel safe again. Nothing about her latest journey had felt safe, though she could admit, it had all been rather exciting. She could have done without the visit from the reivers, as she was still uncomfortable with what she'd done, but the rest hadn't been terrible.

She pushed away the horrifying memory of the man's flesh rotting from his hand, then her mind leaped to what Anna had said about seeing Finn's mother. She had never considered the idea of having parents, though she supposed they must have existed at one time. Still, she had no desire to meet them. Perhaps Anna's vision had been a memory of the distant past, and Finn would not have to worry about her parents either way.

She shivered, and not just from the cold. If her parents were Cavari, she hoped to *never* find out about their existence.

She tossed herself onto her back, unable to find comfort on the hard ground. She turned her head to glance at Anna, but all she could see was a mess of dark hair sticking out of her bedroll. She could make out Kai's shape lying on the other side of Anna, but little else.

She turned her eyes up to the sky as another whiff of smoke filtered into her nostrils. It was stronger than before. She waited motionlessly for Anna or Kai to comment, but they both seemed to be sound asleep.

With a grunt of irritation, she struggled out of her bedding. She'd gone to sleep fully clothed, with her cloak wrapped around her for extra warmth, so there was no need to get dressed. She paused just long enough to slip into her boots, lacing them up tightly around her ankles.

She'd just go for a short walk, remaining near enough that Kai or Anna would hear her if she yelled. Then she'd be able to sleep. She would close her eyes, and before she knew it, the sun would be up and they'd hopefully have just a short walk to their final destination.

She moved in the direction of the path, taking care to step lightly. The moon was full enough to provide ample lighting, though she still worried about tripping in the leaf-strewn soil. The air around her was hazy, and the smell of smoke was becoming consistent.

She continued walking, curious as to what could create such a strange smell. The smoke grew thicker as she moved onward. It stung her eyes and made her feel slightly dizzy. Nervous, she was about to turn back when she heard a voice.

At first, it was just the barest of whispers, almost imperceptible, but it sounded like it was saying her name.

Finn looked over her shoulder, through the dark trees that surrounded her, yet something had changed. The trees seemed different, and there was no sign of the sleeping Kai and Anna in the distance.

Finn, the voice whispered again.

Finn found herself walking forward, as if compelled by something unseen. The smoke grew thicker as she walked. Her vision began to blur. She trudged onward as the voice called to her once more. She *had* to find the source. There was no other choice.

She pushed through the vegetation that stood in her way, barely noticing as it snagged at her clothing. A distant fire came into sight. It had to be what was creating all of the smoke.

Mo gealbhan beag milis, the voice said again. Finn's eyes began to water, partially from the smoke, and partially from some long-forgotten memory, tickling at the edge of her senses.

She continued onward until the fire came into sight once more. The fire towered above the tree line, perhaps fueled by a tree that was taller than all the others. She knew with a sudden surety that she'd seen such tree before, standing above all that surrounded it, in some distant past life she could not fully recall.

The fire filled the dark night air above it with smoke, illuminating the outpour with its flames. If it was a tree on fire, and she was quite sure that it was, it should have been burning faster, and the flames should have been catching onto the foliage around it. Yet, the fire remained stationary.

She stared at the flames in awe as a sudden gust of smoke-filled wind blew toward her. The acrid stench filled her lungs and she began to cough. Realizing that perhaps the burning tree was the Archtree, she lifted her arms to cover her nose and mouth with the loose fabric of her sleeve. She knew she should go back to Kai and Anna, but she felt disoriented, like the smoke had muddled her thoughts. She pulled her eyes from the distant fire to her immediate surroundings, wondering which way she should go. Perhaps she'd come from the area to her left? No, that wasn't right. Hadn't she been following a voice? As she continued to grow increasingly dizzy, she was overcome by smoke once more. She bent forward and coughed, as her remaining senses seemed to leave her entirely.

BEDELIA WATCHED in the darkness as Finn coughed and tried to cover her mouth and nose with her sleeve, surrounded by the smoke of the Archtree. She held the damp cloth around her mouth a little tighter, though she had to admit, the idea of inhaling the smoke was appealing. She wouldn't have minded a few illuminating answers, but her orders did not include interacting with the tree, except to light it on fire.

To her way of thinking, it would have made sense to grab Finn right there. She was Keiren's actual target, after all, but Keiren claimed she was protected by unseen forces. Bedelia did not doubt the claims, recalling when Finn brought the earth up to swallow the wolf creatures whole. Anyone *protecting* someone with such a fearsome power, was someone she had no desire to interact with.

She shifted her weight from foot to foot as she continued to peer into the darkness. Her wound had healed in record time, though the veins beneath the skin of her leg still flowed with black, as if inundated with Faie poison. She glanced down at her leg instinctively, though it was covered by her tall leather boots, over black wool breeches. When she glanced back up, she gasped.

Finn was gone.

CHAPTER FOURTEEN

Finn instinctively reached for her chest as she was jerked backward by the collar of her shirt. Someone pulled her from the trail into a dense thicket surrounded by trees. It was all Finn could do to keep her feet on the ground as she was pulled farther backward, then jerked down to a crouch.

Anna's face came into view inches from hers. "Someone was watching you," she hissed, voice barely audible.

Finn looked back to where she had been standing, but her movements felt slow and clumsy. She didn't see anyone or anything out of place, except for the smoke. Turning back to Anna, she said, "I don't think anyone else is there," keeping her voice down.

Anna's face was paler than usual, especially in the cool light of the moon, and her eyes were bloodshot. She held a rag up to filter the smoke from her airways. With her sleep mussed hair, she looked a bit mad. She glared at Finn. "I can see things others cannot, remember?"

Finn nodded, not wanting to argue. The smoke was making her feel dizzy. "The fire-" Finn began, her words muffled as she covered her mouth once more.

Anna cut her off with a nod. "I know. I believe it's the Archtree."

Finn took a shaky breath, then held her throat, overcome with the need to cough. "The smoke-" she sputtered, trying to remain quiet.

Anna nodded again, and gestured for Finn to follow her in a low crouch away from the trail as she explained, "I know. If drinking a tea made from the leaves can answer ones most burning questions, it stands to reason that inhaling the smoke would do the same. We need to hide before we're overcome with whatever is going to happen."

Finn hurried after Anna silently, glad that at least one of them seemed to still have a hold of her wits. The memory of the voice she'd heard when following the smoke echoed through her head, though now the words seemed fuzzy. She couldn't quite remember what the voice had said.

Once they had gained some distance, they stood upright and hurried back to where they'd made camp. Kai was up and about with a worried look on his face. He heaved a sigh of relief as first Anna, then Finn came into view in the moonlit darkness. His hair stuck out at odd angles, and his shirt was askew, as if he'd just then climbed out of his bedroll, realizing the women were gone.

"Thank you for scaring me half to death," he chided. "Where were the two of you? What's all this smoke?"

Anna and Finn closed the distance between themselves and Kai.

"It's the Archtree," Anna explained as she crouched to begin rolling up her bedroll. "At least, I believe it to be. Someone has set it on fire, and perhaps that same someone was just watching Finn as she stumbled about by herself on the trail for who knows what reason."

Kai took a step toward Finn and looked her up and down, as if to assure himself that she was well. "The smoke-" he began.

"Yes," Anna cut him off. "We're not sure what magical properties it might have, but I'm not going to miss my chance for answers. We must make for the tree. Either we try to put it out, or the smoke will have some sort of effect on us."

Kai and Finn both began rolling their bedrolls as Anna finished hers. Finn felt nervous as Kai glanced at her.

"Why did you wander off?" he asked far too gently. Wasn't he supposed to be mad that they'd left him alone while he slept?

Finn frowned, once again recalling the voice, though the memory seemed even more distant now. "I-" she began, then stopped. "I'm not sure," she explained. "I remember not being able to sleep, then I smelled the smoke. After that, I didn't quite feel like myself."

Kai tightened the cinches around his bedroll and stood. Seeing Finn's bedroll freshly secured, he offered her a hand up. She took it gratefully, feeling somewhat unsteady. What had the voice said? Trying to remember was driving her mad.

"Let's go," Anna demanded, seeing that Kai and Finn were both ready.

They gathered the remainder of their supplies and began to walk in the darkness toward the scent of smoke. Anna led, avoiding the path, which was probably for the best if someone really had been watching Finn.

Finn stumbled continuously as they plodded along through the darkness, boots catching on hidden roots and clothing snagging on brambles. She was at least grateful that she no longer wore skirts. Breeches provided such ease of movement that she wondered why any woman would choose to wear skirts, though most that she'd seen did. In fact, the only women Finn had seen in breeches were Anna and Bedelia. Her thoughts turned to her lost friend, and she felt momentarily ill. Was Bedelia even still alive? For the hundredth time she cursed Anna for kidnapping her before she could give Bedelia the tincture that might save her life.

The smoke grew thicker as they walked. From the low point of view, with foliage obscuring their sight, it was difficult to catch a glimpse of the actual blaze, but Anna seemed to know where she was going. She had been there before, after all, if only in her mind.

They pressed onward. Finn felt a mixture of elation

and fear. Soon she might have answers, if the tree didn't burn completely to ash by the time they reached it. Perhaps they could make a tea from the leftover powder. She still wasn't entirely sure what she would ask. She wanted to know just where she came from, why she'd been turned into a tree, what the Cavari really wanted from her, and also about the shroud. If Iseult had not made it to the island yet, he might miss his answer, which meant Finn would need to ask it for him. She sighed as Kai helped her over a fallen log. She wasn't sure she could bring herself to use her one question on the shroud, and she didn't think Iseult would blame her if she didn't. Surely there was another way to find it?

She flinched as she stubbed her toe, teetering awkwardly with her overstuffed satchel bouncing against her hip. The smoke was becoming unbearable, making her dizzy. Perhaps they'd have their answers even sooner than they thought, else they would die from lack of oxygen.

THE SETTLERS GROANED about lack of food as they journeyed onward. Maarav had claimed that his ship, along with a small settlement, was only two day's worth of riding away, but Iseult doubted the claims. There was no settlement this far north to be found on any map, save the reiver camps, which tended to not remain in one place for an extended period of time.

They'd been lucky enough to happen upon a fresh spring for water the previous evening. With the threat of the reivers nipping at their heels, they hadn't much time to explore for resources. Iseult felt it safe to say that they weren't being followed, as the well-supplied reivers would have caught up by now, but wasting time was still a risk. He tried to clear his mind of what might be happening to those who'd stayed behind. Though more troubling still, was the thought of unsuspecting burghs eventually falling under attack at Conall's command. An Fiach had to be taken care of first, but with the magic users, and the addition of the reiver fleet, Iseult would not be surprised if the troublesome faction soon ceased to be.

The settlers, who'd had the wherewithal to drag a few horses along, took turns riding, giving extra time to the women and older folk among them. Iseult had offered his horse up a few times, though the animal was bred for war, and many feared riding him. Even with the help of the horses, there wasn't a single person among the group who wasn't tired or hungry. Ealasaid seemed hardly able to keep her feet as she walked along, the hem of her dirty blue dress dragging in the coastal sand. An elderly woman rode Ealasaid's horse, and had fallen asleep upright in the saddle. Her loud snores, the occasional hungry grumble, and the sound of the ocean kept an odd rhythm as the sun slowly made its way across the sky.

"There," Maarav pointed, riding up beside Iseult to get his attention.

Iseult saw nothing but black stone jutting up in the distance. The far off rocky outcropping had been worrying him for a while. If they were unable to find a way around it, they might have to journey deep into reiver territory to continue onward.

Ealasaid had looked up as Maarav pointed. "I see only rocky mountains," she commented.

"Precisely," Maarav replied smugly. "The settlement we seek is guarded by those rocky mountains."

Excited chatter erupted amongst the settlers, hopeful that they would soon have hot meals and a place to rest. Iseult narrowed his eyes at the distant spires, but could see no way in. They jutted up against the coast, probably forming a cove in the middle, impassible on either side.

"I hope you are correct," Iseult said simply, not caring about the settlement itself, as long as there truly was a ship inside.

"I am," Maarav replied. "Where do you think I went when I *died*?"

Iseult's breath caught in his lungs. It wasn't often that he showed surprise, but he was sure that it showed now. He and Maarav had not had any further discussion on why their mother had told Iseult his brother was dead. Iseult still hadn't quite convinced himself that Maarav truly was his long-dead kin. To hear that he'd been living in some hidden settlement this far north was absurd. Ridiculous. Yet, he couldn't help but be curious.

"You lived there?" Iseult asked evenly, hoping to keep Maarav talking.

"Aye," Maarav replied, "but that is a tale for another time, when prying ears are not near."

Iseult frowned as he continued to scan the distant rocky escarpment, wondering what sort of people would live in such a remote, hidden location, and why his brother would be sent to live among them. If he truly had, what eventually brought him to Migris? There were too many unknowns, and he was trusting this man to aid in one of the most important tasks of his life.

He glanced at Maarav, who smiled happily, content atop his horse even though they'd had little food in the past two days.

One of the settlers, a man of around sixty years, dropped to his knees in the sand, unable to go on any longer. The man had refused any time in the saddle, too prideful to take the offered help, and now it was catching up to him. Iseult dismounted gracefully and hoisted the man up by the shoulders. With the help of Ealasaid and one of the other settlers, they helped the man onto the saddle of Iseult's horse. The man apologized profusely, but took the offered help, saying, *his legs weren't working quite right, but he'd be able to walk again soon.*

Iseult shook his head as he took the horse's reins to lead him. How had he ended up in the position to take care of this flock of people, and at what point had he begun to care about failing them? He shook his head again. He was growing soft. In the treacherous world he knew, the soft did not survive for long.

As they neared the rocks, Iseult continued to scan their surroundings for some sign of inhabitance. A sharp whistle cut through the air, coming from the direction of the massive rock wall.

Maarav lifted his fingers to his mouth and whistled back at the exact same pitch, first low, then with a high lilt at the end.

After that, there was silence.

"Someone will meet us at the gates," Maarav explained.

"What gates?" Ealasaid asked as she walked beside Iseult.

Maarav grinned. "You'll see."

The settlers chattered amongst themselves as they marched onward. The sun continued its slow creep across the sky. By the time they reached the base of the rocks, the sun had nearly disappeared beyond the horizon, leaving them in the looming shadow of the rocks, with no entrance that Iseult could see.

Suddenly, as if by magic, a woman appeared from within the rock wall. She was short, with long, graying hair, and tight black clothing encasing a form slender and strong for her age. She eyed the settlers cooly until her eyes found Maarav.

"You know better than to bring foreigners here, boy," she said tartly.

The settlers shifted nervously. If they were turned away, there was nowhere else to go but to their deaths.

"Oh come now, Slàine," Maarav replied as he dismounted, "you know I can't resist helping those in need."

The woman, Slàine, let out a hearty chuckle, then spread her arms wide. "C'mere and give your ma a hug."

Maarav did as he was bade, wrapping the small woman in his arms. Even if they did not *allegedly* share the same mother, Iseult would have suspected the term "ma" had come from a shared bond, rather than blood, as the woman looked nothing like Maarav.

As they pulled away from each other, Slàine's eyes found Iseult. Her expression softened as she turned back to Maarav. "It seems we have much to discuss," she said quietly.

The settlers continued to shift uncomfortably, though all remained silent, hoping they would not be turned away.

Slàine eyed them all in turn, including Ealasaid. "You must all know, there is no turning back from here. Once you are inside, there is no leaving these walls." Her eyes shifted to Iseult. "Of course, any ken to Maarav may come and go as they please."

Iseult nodded, and a few nervous murmurs passed through the group. Eventually the old man climbed down off Iseult's horse and stepped forward. "I accept your terms. Even if I wanted to leave, only death awaits me at the hands of my own countrymen."

Slàine nodded, not bothering to ask *why* the only other option was death. The remaining settlers talked amongst themselves, but they soon all agreed to Slàine's terms. All but Ealasaid.

The girl, still standing beside Iseult, shifted from foot to foot before stepping forward. "I'm afraid I cannot agree to those terms. An Fiach murdered my family, and I must have my revenge."

Maarav grinned at that. "I will vouch for the girl," he told Slàine.

Slàine gave him a knowing look, but nodded. "Well, come on," she said tiredly as she turned back to the stone wall, waving them all to follow her.

Iseult's curiosity got the better of him as he stepped ahead of the settlers to see the entrance. Not only that, if there was some sort of trick to going inside, he wanted to observe it firsthand.

Slàine walked into an alcove in the stone that turned sharply to the right. She took a lit torch that had been mounted on the wall, then turned to the left, followed by another sharp right, like switchback trails on a steep mountain. Iseult followed behind her and Maarav, then came the settlers with the horses. The switchbacks were just tall enough and wide enough for the horses to pass through easily, though the close quarters elicited various degrees of concerned whinnies. After the switchbacks came an open cavern that seemed manmade, as the walls were smooth, forming a perfect dome, though Iseult had no idea how such construction was possible. Several more torches mounted into the stone lit the space.

Everyone filtered into the cavern before Slàine ventured onward, into another narrow crevice, once again with only the light of her torch to guide them. At that point, the path split off into several, then the path they chose eventually split into several more, like some sort of maze. Finally, just as many of the settlers were beginning to panic, they reached a solid stone wall, with no paths leading away except the one they'd taken.

Slàine stepped forward and knocked on the stone in an intricate pattern composed of quick knocks, light knocks, and slow, heavy ones that likely bruised her knuckles.

Iseult watched in awe as the stone began to rumble, then a segment of the stone separated and swung inward. Slàine led the way through, followed by Maarav. Iseult followed next, inspecting the door as he passed, but not spotting any mechanisms that would give him a clue how it worked. Regardless, it was the perfect cover. Anyone venturing into the maze-like corridors would undoubt-edly get lost long before reaching the doorway, but if they did make it that far, they'd only be met with a dead end.

Inside, the sight was even more spectacular than the entrance. An entire village was built into the massive cove, complete with stone walkways in between the buildings. They'd entered on an upper tier, providing a view of the distant, calm coast within the cove. The rocks jutted far enough into the ocean to form a bay, protecting the narrow coastline from the more violent waves that hit the rest of the shore.

Many of the buildings in front of and below them were constructed of the same dark stone of the cliffside, reminding Iseult of Sormyr, the Gray City.

People still milled about the streets, even though darkness was quickly descending. Iseult would have liked to stay atop the tier to observe things further, but the refugees began to filter in behind him, along with the nervous horses. Ealasaid had taken up the reins of Iseult's horse, and now handed them to him without a word.

He followed Slàine and Maarav down wide stone steps as the two chatted happily.

Ealasaid walked down the steps beside Iseult. "What is this place?" she whispered as her gray eyes darted about nervously.

Iseult glanced again at the stone buildings as he continued down the steps. "It's a place not on any maps, with a hidden entrance, requiring that any who enter may never leave again. Whatever this place is, I doubt that it's good. Most things this hidden, are hidden for a reason."

Ealasaid frowned as they reached the base of the steps, and a wide walkway that seemed to be the main street of the village. Although, village was not the correct term. It was more of a city, all hidden away inside an impossibly large cove.

"I imagine your friends are hungry," Slàine said loudly so that all could overhear.

Appreciative murmurs sounded behind Iseult. He was starving too, and was curious about the city, but he'd forgo food and information if they could board a ship and sail for the Archtree.

Slàine led them past several smaller residences to a large building that appeared to be an inn, though there was no sign to hint at a name. The bottom portion of the structure was composed of dark stone, while the upper two stories were whitewashed wood. The lack of actual color in the hidden city was jarring.

A young boy dressed in a too large tunic took Iseult's reins, and the reins of the other horses as the party was led into the inn. The few passersby eyed the newcomers curiously. Iseult sensed no animosity from any of them, though he still felt nervous to be trapped in such an odd place.

The scent of roasting meat and fresh bread overcame Iseult's senses as he followed Maarav into the inn's warm interior. Soft lantern light illuminated the space, accompanied by tall white candles on many of the small, wooden tables. Normal looking folk filled many of the tables, while a rotund barmaid carried a large tray of food and drinks to disperse. A slender, aged barkeep stood behind a narrow wood bar, looking sullen.

Slàine left them to approach the barkeep.

Maarav stepped to Iseult's side and leaned in. "Slàine's husband," he explained, nodding in the direction of the barkeep. "Poor skunner."

The refugees, along with Ealasaid, all huddled near the door, obviously out of place. Maarav moved to take a seat at a vacant table, and Iseult joined him. Taking this as a signal, the refugees began to seat themselves, often at tables with the locals since there was a limited number of seats. Slowly the atmosphere became more comfortable as conversation grew. Food was passed around, along with sweet wine, whiskey, and fresh water.

No one sat at the small table with Maarav and Iseult, though there were two vacant seats. Ealasaid continuously glanced over at them, as if wanting to usurp one of the chairs, but unsure if she was welcome.

Iseult turned his attention away from the rest of the room to Maarav as food was placed before them. The thick slab of pork and fresh bread made Iseult's mouth water, but there were important things to discuss before any comforts could be had.

"What is this place?" Iseult asked quietly, his words easily hidden from prying ears in the loud din of conversation.

Maarav had torn into his pork with bare hands and teeth, and had to put the greasy hunk down to reply, "This is where I was sent when I *died*."

"Explain," Iseult demanded, frustrated. If Maarav really was his brother, why had his mother told him he was dead? Why was he sent to such an unusual place?

Maarav pulled apart his bread and filled it with ham, then took an enormous bite. Once he'd swallowed, he replied, "Our mother sold me off, so that you and she might live. I was put to work within these walls, and once I'd earned it, I was trained. Once I was trained, I was put to work some more."

"That's a lie," Iseult interrupted. It was preposterous. His mother had loved both her sons. She'd cried for months when Maarav had succumbed to illness.

"I do not blame her for it," Maarav said happily. "We were destitute when we left Uí Néid. We had no way to survive. Our mother's decision saved all of our lives."

"Except hers," Iseult growled.

Maarav nodded. "I heard when it happened. I'd

assumed you were dead too. Then a few days ago, a friend of mine walks into the inn with Finnur herself. Ma had shown us that picture so many times, I'd recognize that face anywhere. My friend leaves Finnur in her room, asks me to make sure she doesn't leave, and explains that some men may be looking for her. One, quite old and not very tall, and the other, taller than most men, with black hair, and eyes like a hunting cat, rumored to be unbelievably fast, an expert swordsman. The man sounded like someone my brother could have grown into, or at the very least, someone hailing from Uí Néid. Still, I was quite surprised to see you outside of my inn."

Rage washed through Iseult. Maarav's final explanation had rushed by his ears as he considered the character traveling with Finn. This *friend* must have been who'd originally taken her. Was this person Cavari, or something else? The roots that had taken Finn and had nearly suffocated Iseult and Àed had been of the Dair, there was no mistaking it.

"Who was this *friend*?" he demanded. "How had she known we would be looking for Finn?"

"I'll not give this person's identity up willingly," Maarav answered after taking another bite and a swig of whiskey, "but suffice to say, she likely knows just as much about Finnur as either of us. I do not know her motivations, but she's a soldier in with the Lady of Migris herself. That is all I will say on the subject."

Iseult frowned. Maarav had said *she*. This woman had travelled with Finn, and knew his description. Perhaps

Maarav referred to Anna, previously known to him as Liaden, but she was no soldier. She was a con-woman and a thief, but no warrior. Anna must have taken Finn from this other woman at some point.

"And you just happened to be around to witness all of this?" Iseult asked. "To witness my arrival in Migris?"

Maarav shrugged. "Finnur's arrival was a surprise, though I admit, after I'd spotted her, I'd intended to follow wherever she went, just to see what she was up to. I witnessed her abduction, and recognized the woman who took her. I also knew that woman had recently acquired a ship, and had been spreading word that she was looking for crewmen. That's how I knew to lead you to the dock, though I had not expected them to cast off so soon."

All that Maarav said made sense, but Iseult still found it difficult to trust. His brother still hid a great deal.

"You never answered," Iseult said calmly, casting a glance around the room. "What is this place?"

Maarav raised an eyebrow. "No reply on anything else I've told you? Not even a thank you for all of the valuable information?"

Iseult eyed him cooly. "Thank you."

Maarav sighed. "This is a place that acquires men and women of special talents. Those acquired are trained, and put to use, just as I was. Eventually, I payed off the coin given to our mother, and earned quite a bit more. At that point I left and opened my inn, wanting to be more involved in the world, though I remain loyal to those dwelling within these walls."

Loud laughter filled the room. Many of the refugees were becoming intoxicated.

"Trained to do what?" Iseult asked.

"Kill," Maarav replied simply. "We all have our individual talents, suited to individual cases, and there are always people who need other people killed."

"You're assassins," Iseult observed. He personally didn't care for the vocation, but held greater distaste for those who made the vocation necessary. If you wanted to kill someone, you should do it yourself.

Maarav nodded.

"And magic users," Iseult added, thinking of the stone door into the city.

Maarav nodded again. "Some of us, but not me, if that's what you're asking."

Iseult finally began to pick at his food. Nothing he'd been told so far would interfere with his task . . . as long as they boarded a ship soon. "What will become of the refugees?"

He noticed Ealasaid hovering nearby, pretending not to look at them. He ignored her.

"Those with appropriate skills will be trained," Maarav explained. "Others will be given other vocations and will live normal lives. They will receive pay, have homes, and will be safe from both the reivers and An Fiach."

"And this ship you promised?" Iseult asked after taking a sip of his whiskey. He rarely indulged, but after the week he'd had, he felt like it was justified.

"We'll cast off in the morning," Maarav replied. "It's

nice to be home, but it is far too easy to get wrapped up in the way of things around here. I would not wish for our visit to go on any longer than necessary."

Iseult nodded. "What of a crew? We'll need a few men."

Ealasaid chose that moment to plop herself down in one of the vacant chairs. "Count me in," she announced.

Iseult and Maarav both stared at her, Iseult's expression cold, but Maarav with a hint of a smile.

Ealasaid seemed to wilt under the pressure. She pushed her dirty curls behind her ears, only to have them fall forward again. "I mean, I've never sailed before, but I'm sure I could be of use. I'll do anything you ask of me . . . within reason."

Maarav looked to Iseult, as Iseult weighed the benefits of the girl joining them. She wouldn't be much use in sailing the ship, but her magic was nothing to scoff at. She might be useful should an altercation occur. He felt he could trust her to fight by his side, and more importantly, he suspected Finn would like her.

His mind made up, Iseult nodded.

Ealasaid slumped in relief. "You won't regret it," she assured.

Iseult turned back to his meal without a word. He had many regrets in his life. The decision to let a young, naive girl join on his travels would never measure up to the others, even if she somehow managed to sink the ship.

~

EALASAID WAS WILDLY curious about the hidden city, but not curious enough to stay there. The woman, Slàine, made her feel on edge. She didn't like the calculating glances the older woman was throwing her way as she stood at the bar conversing with the rail thin innkeep.

The rest of the city dwellers seemed normal enough, though she was glad she'd mustered the courage to join Maarav and Iseult at their table. While she related to the refugees, she could not remain among them. She needed to find out which men of An Fiach had been responsible for her family's deaths, then she needed to kill them.

Traveling the open seas with two knowledgable warriors seemed a much better way to eventually meet her goals than leaving the hidden city on her own, even if she hadn't a clue to what their ultimate destination might be. She assumed Iseult was still looking for the girl Àed had mentioned, and Maarav seemed to want to do whatever Iseult wanted to do. She hoped they would find the girl soon, as spending yet more time alone with Iseult and Maarav was unnerving. They were pragmatists, of that she was sure, which meant she would only be kept around as long as she was useful. Another woman amongst the group might show her more sympathy than the men.

She shook herself and looked down at the food the barmaid had set in front of her once she'd joined the men at the table. Sitting around feeling sorry for herself would do her no good. She might not particularly like Iseult and Maarav, but the two *had* ensured her safety, at least to an extent. In fact, if it weren't for Maarav, Ealasaid would still be huddled in a heap crying about the loss of her family.

The thought made her eyes suddenly sting with unshed tears, but she pushed the tears back down. There would be time for crying later. Later, after she'd had her vengeance. Perhaps then, she could return to this hidden city and make a life for herself, far away from those who would persecute her for her *gifts*. The doorway into the city had been disguised by magic, which meant there were others like her here, in addition to the refugees, many of whom possessed terrifying magic, far exceeding Ealasaid's.

She picked at her food. She'd been given a mug of wine to wash things down. She'd never had a full mug before, only sips from her father's. The thought of her father made her eyes tear up again.

Seeming somehow uncomfortable, perhaps because he sensed she was about to cry, Maarav excused himself to speak with Slàine. Iseult watched him go, expressionless. The man showed as much emotion as a rock.

She took a sip of her wine, attempting to gather some composure. Once she was sure she could speak without her voice breaking, she asked, "What will happen to the settlers when we leave?"

Iseult took a sip of his whiskey. "As it has been explained to me, they will be able to live as they would in any other city, with added protection from An Fiach and the Faie. Whether this is actually the case, only time will tell."

Ealasaid frowned. "So you don't know if they'll be okay?"

Iseult sighed and pushed his dirty black hair out of his face. Normally it was held back by a leather clasp, but the coastal winds had pulled much of it free, giving him a wild appearance.

"I do not know this city," he answered blandly. "To say that the settler's safety is guaranteed would be a lie."

"Maybe we can bring them with us," she said hopefully.

Iseult shook his head. "We will bring only those needed to crew the ship, one or two extra men in addition to the three of us. It is not wise to outnumber yourself with strangers."

"They're not strangers," Ealasaid pouted. "They fought beside us, and fled the reivers with us."

Iseult's eyes narrowed. "You've no idea of their pasts or motivations. To trust so blindly is folly, especially for a young girl like you."

Ealasaid frowned and thought back to her village again. She'd trusted most everyone there, and had never thought much about someone taking advantage of her until she was on the road alone. Her first instinct was still to trust. She supposed she'd have to break herself of that habit.

Her eyes filled with tears again.

"It will get easier," Iseult assured, the hint of sympathy in his voice surprising her.

"Learning not to trust?"

"All of it," he clarified. "The pain of loss will fade,

and you will find new people to connect with. People that will make you feel like you have a family again. You will not always feel as alone as I imagine you're feeling now."

Ealasaid's jaw went slack with surprise. She'd been under the impression that Iseult was incapable of saying nice things. "Do *you* have those sorts of people?" she asked, then instantly bit her tongue. The question had been far too forward. She was a fool.

Iseult's expression set into its normal stony lines. "No," he answered. "My life has other purposes."

Ealasaid frowned. She knew she should not ask any more, but he was actually talking to her, and she didn't want to miss the opportunity. "Not even the girl you seek?" she questioned.

His expression softened just a touch for the briefest moment. "She is part of my purpose," he said simply.

"You want to save her," she clarified.

"For a purpose," he replied. "I made certain promises, and they must be fulfilled."

Ealasaid bit her lip. This man was absolutely exhausting to speak with. She wasn't sure what gave her the bravery to say what she said next. Perhaps it was fatigue, or perhaps she just realized that she had little to lose. "Àed claimed you're in love with her."

If Iseult's face was stone before, now it was ice. Ice so cold that it would burn your skin if you touched it. "I know nothing of love," he replied, then stood. "Get some rest. We leave at first light."

With that, he walked out of the inn. Noticing his

departure, Maarav excused himself from Slàine and hurried after him.

If Ealasaid's foot could reach her mouth, she would have shoved it right in. As it was, she stared down at her food with no appetite, wondering where she was supposed to sleep, and wondering even more if she would even be capable.

CHAPTER FIFTEEN

They boarded Maarav's ship at first light. Two crewmen had been chosen to accompany them. Maarav had offered up their compensation, as Iseult was running low on coin.

Iseult now stood at the mast of the ship, charting out their journey in his mind. His map detailed a route to the Archtree in relation to Uí Néid, but it shouldn't be hard to navigate from a little farther North. In fact, their current location put them even closer.

He glanced over his shoulder at Ealasaid, who huddled near the center of the ship, looking petrified. She'd only just seen the ocean for the first time within the last week, and now she was about to cast off into the middle of it. Someone, presumably Maarav, as he seemed to enjoy caring for the girl, had provided her with a new dress to replace her dingy blue one. The bodice was a dark red, edged with black, that made her pale coloring and blonde hair stand out in contrast. The black skirts were divided for riding, though Ealasaid had been forced to leave her horse behind. Both Maarav's and Iseult's horses were trained to remain calm on ships. Ealasaid's gentle village horse, was not. She'd cried when she parted with the animal, her last remnant of home. Maarav had assured her it would be waiting for her should she return.

Iseult turned his thoughts back to their course. It should only take half a day to reach the island. If the winds were right, they might reach it by noon. If not, then the evening at the latest. If all went according to plan, Kai would be waiting on the island with Finn . . . and Anna . . . and likely whomever crewed Anna's ship.

He knew it would have been wise to bring more men to fight, but he had no one he could trust. Finn was valuable, as was the Archtree. He could not risk the possibility of mutiny with a larger crew. Maarav had assured him that the two men they brought along had been trained from childhood within the hidden city, and would gladly fight as ordered, but Iseult had his doubts.

One of the men, Tavish, appeared around thirty years of age. He was small of build, with red hair and dark eyes, reminding Iseult of a fox. His lighthearted demeanor made him seem innocent, and not at all dangerous, though Maarav had promised Iseult otherwise.

The other man, Rae, was older with dark skin, hair, and eyes. He was tall and lanky, and would have almost seemed weak and clumsy if he didn't move with such graceful efficiency. Iseult could tell Rae would be useful in a fight. Of Tavish, he was not so sure.

Ealasaid gave a little yip as the ship cast off, and Maarav went to stand next to her. He must have told her a joke, because the girl laughed nervously.

Iseult shook his head as the wind caught the ship's sails. If Kai came through on his end, he might very well find Finn that day. It was both an exciting prospect, and a terrifying one, for reasons Iseult would not admit to anyone. For at times, he could not even admit them to himself.

FINN and her companions had walked through the remainder of the night, and well into the morning. The smoke surrounded them continuously, never seeming to ebb. A normal tree would have burnt to ash in such a long expanse of time, but this was obviously no normal tree. Finn felt they were getting close, just judging by the blaze she'd spotted the night before, but it stood to reason that the fire should have spread. It should have spanned outward, meeting them before they reached the tree, but all they encountered was smoke.

Her lungs ached from the impure air, though she kept her mouth continuously covered. Still, no visions had come upon her from the tree, nor had she fainted from lack of oxygen. Perhaps drinking a tea from the leaves was the only way, and the smoke was useless. She glanced to her right at Kai. His eyes were downcast, and sweat beaded on his face as he held his sleeve up to his mouth. This was the warmest weather Finn had encountered since she'd first awoken from her long spell as a tree. Or perhaps it was just the heat of the smoke.

"There," Anna said as she crested a large hill ahead of them. She looked just as bedraggled as Kai, her dark clothing damp with sweat. Little particles of ash danced around her slender form as a gust of wind rushed over the hilltop.

Finn and Kai hurried to catch up to her, and Finn gasped at what she saw. An enormous tree stood on its own. Barren ground surrounded it, as if no other vegetation could grow near its massive roots. Its trunk was as thick as Kai, Anna, and Finn put together, twisting upward to branch off into what was once likely grand foliage. Now it was a solid wash of flame. The tree burned from halfway up its trunk all the way to the smallest branches, but the flame did not seem to eat away at it. It was like a giant candle, blotting out the morning sky with smoke.

Kai coughed as he stood beside her, staring at the fiery spectacle. "What do we do now?" he asked. "I don't imagine we'll be able to pluck any whole leaves from the inferno."

"I feel dizzy," Anna commented.

"Too much smoke in your lungs," Kai replied, still staring at the tree.

"No-" Anna began to argue, then fell to her knees.

Finn moved to catch her, but then nearly fell over herself. Her vision went gray, and she slowly crumpled to the ground. She felt someone's hand gripping hers. She thought it was Kai's. Then she lost consciousness.

~

FINN COUGHED and sputtered as she fought her way into wakefulness. Everything around her was gray and misty. She vaguely remembered following the smell of smoke and finding the tree, but the smell was gone, as was the awe inspiring spectacle of the fire. What surrounded her now felt more like fog, dampening her loose hair and chilling her skin.

She sat up, not remembering when she'd fallen, and looked down at her legs. The dark fabric of her breeches was covered in soil. Upon closer observation, so were the sleeves of her shirt. It even stuck in her hair. Her breath came too quickly as she began to panic. She glanced around, but the mist was too thick for her to see anything more than a few feet in front of her. She vaguely remembered Kai's hand in hers, but there was no sign of him now.

She stood, thinking again of the tree's smoke. They'd inhaled so much that she thought it had no magical properties at all, but then, what had happened? Had she simply fainted, and now she was stuck in an illusion as her body shut down, or was this all a smoke-inspired dream where she would find the answers she sought?

Though she felt shaky on her feet, she hurried forward, not sure where she was going, but wanting to find her answers as soon as possible. She could not accept that perhaps she was dying. She'd come too far. Suddenly her boots splashed into water and she cursed. The fog was too thick for her to even see the ground at her feet, but she must have run into some sort of pond or bog. She'd seen no bog anywhere near the burning tree.

"I wouldn't go in there, if I were you," a voice said from behind her.

Finn jumped, then stepped back out of the water to face the voice, though no figure was apparent in the fog.

"This is not a normal sort of place," the voice continued. "Who knows what creatures may lurk beneath the water's depths?"

Finn took deep breaths as she tried to slow her heart from leaping out of her chest. "Who are you?" she questioned bravely.

The voice did not answer.

"Are you the Archtree?" Finn asked impulsively, knowing her question likely sounded crazy.

"No," the voice answered, "but you were in danger. Someone was watching you while your helpless lungs filled with the tree's smoke. I had to remove you from the situation, even if it meant taking away the answers the tree could have given you."

Finn froze. If she had been in danger, that meant that Kai and Anna were too. She hated that she cared, but she did. "Where am I?" she demanded. "I need to go back."

"I will send you back when it's safe," the voice replied.

Anger and desperation overcame her fear, and she stomped forward through the fog. A dark shape came into view, roughly her size, and cloaked in black. As she continued forward, the figure did not move.

Soon they stood face to face, though Finn could see nothing beyond the dark cowl. She lifted a hand to push it back, and the figure grabbed her wrist, lightning fast.

Finn looked down at her wrist in shock.

"I fear I'm not ready for your reaction," the figure stated.

"Too bad," Finn growled. She'd had enough of being kept in the dark, and now her answers that she'd worked so hard to find had been stolen from her. She jerked her wrist free.

As if resigned, the figure removed its cowl. Finn's face stared back at her, outlined in fog, only it wasn't Finn's face. The jaw was sharper, the eyes smaller, and blue, compared to Finn's dark brown. The hair was also different, a brown as dark as Finn's eyes.

Finn wasn't terribly surprised.

"Anna told me about you," she stated apathetically.

The woman, possibly Finn's mother, frowned. "The one you've been traveling with? I'd wondered how I could see her."

"Why am I here?" Finn demanded.

Her mother's face fell. "Out of all of the questions you could ask, that's the one you choose?"

Finn glared. "There's no point in asking questions if I choose not to believe the answers. I've traveled all this way to find the Archtree for answers. I do not want them from *you*."

"I've been protecting you since you were on your

travels," she argued. "Why do you harbor me such ill will?"

Finn snorted. "Protecting? Who was protecting me when I was left as a tree for one hundred years? Who was protecting me when I awoke, naked in a field, with no recollection of who or what I was?"

"*I* was," she insisted. "You could not come to terms with your guilt."

"My guilt over what?" Finn demanded. "What did I do?"

Her mother's face might as well have been made of stone, for all the answers it gave her, but suddenly her stony pall broke as her eyes shifted nervously. "I will send you to the one who can protect you from our people," she said, voice suddenly urgent. "You *must* stay by his side. He's the only one who can truly guard you against what is to come."

"Who?" Finn questioned as her mother began to drag her by the arm. "Protect me from what!"

She paused and leaned her face close to Finn's. "I travel with the Cavari. They *cannot* know I have access to you. *He* can shield you from them, from *me*." She continued walking, dragging Finn along. "The seasons are changing," she chanted. "The lines are faltering, undoing the old and bringing life to the new. Trees will fall, and changed earth will be left in their place. A storm is coming."

Finn recognized the Traveler's words instantly, though she did not understand them any better than she did upon first hearing them. "Please, wait!" she begged.

Her mother stopped, but only to crouch near the ground, dragging Finn down with her. She met Finn's eyes intently as she kneeled beside her. "The ghosts of our past deeds haunt us. Stay *away* from the Dair. I can say no more."

She pushed Finn to the ground as roots snaked up around her. They spiraled Finn's limbs, binding her to the earth. "Please," she cried. It had all happened so fast. She still had so many questions. "What am I?" she sobbed.

"You've brought the earth up to swallow entire cities," her mother whispered as she hovered over her. The roots continued their progress, encasing Finn in their leathery embrace. "Nations have trembled at your feet," she continued. The roots wrapped around Finn's neck, and began to crawl across her face. "You are both an anomaly, and a force of nature, but you are still my daughter, and I will not let our people use you. I will not let them make you into a monster *again*." There was a moment of silence, then her mother added. "I buried the object you seek beneath your roots. There it still lies. If that is truly the path you wish to take, go back to where you began."

Finn continued to cry, but could do nothing else as the roots encased her entirely, obscuring her mother from view.

"I will find you again, *mo gealbhan beag milis,*" her mother whispered somewhere near her ear, then was gone, leaving Finn alone in the darkness to be swallowed into the earth.

❧

KAI KNEW HE WAS DREAMING, or at least, something like it. As he'd collapsed from the smoke, he'd taken Finn's hand in his, not wanting to somehow lose her, though he didn't feel her hand now. He hoped it was just a product of the dream, and not an actual lack of her presence.

He opened his eyes and sat up, finding himself in a dimly lit room. The walls were composed of stone, and there seemed to be no doors, nor windows. Were Finn and Anna in similar situations in their own dreams?

He blinked, then startled as he reopened his eyes. Three cloaked figures stood in front of him.

"Ask your question," one said.

"Are you the Archtree?" he blurted without thinking.

"We are spirits of the past," one said.

"Nothing more," added another.

"But I do not suspect that was the question you wanted to ask," added the third.

His mind went blank. All he could think about was whether Finn and Anna were okay.

"The Gray Lady is finding answers of her own," one explained.

"The Dair child is communing with her kin," said another.

Kai's heart leapt into his throat. Communing with her kin? Did that mean Finn had not been taken over by the tree's smoke? Or had she succumbed, only to be snatched away through the earth, just as he'd witnessed before?

Regardless, she was in danger, and he needed to get out of this dream.

One of the cloaked figures laughed. "You cannot save her from herself."

"I don't want to save her from herself," he growled. "I want to save her from everyone else."

It was true. In that moment, all he wanted to do was leave the dream to make sure she was okay. There were a million questions he could have asked, but he couldn't seem to just think about himself. It was a first.

"Ask your question," one form said.

"And you may leave," said another.

Kai smiled in sudden realization. "I don't need to ask a question."

"And why is that?" asked the third form.

Kai smirked. "Because the most important questions in life, we have to answer for ourselves, and I think I already have mine."

"That's a first," one of the forms said, sounding amused.

All three laughed, then snapped their fingers.

Kai sat up with a start. Anna was unconscious beside him, but Finn was nowhere to be seen. The tree in front of them continued to burn, just like the sudden rage that was inside Kai. He wasn't sure just *who'd* taken her, but he was going to get her back.

FINN'S HAND shot up through the earth as her body

surged upward. It had all happened so fast. She'd been face to face with her mother, and now she was being sent . . . somewhere. It had to have been her mother who'd stolen her away from Iseult and Àed previously, but if she was trying to protect her, why did she deliver her into the hands of the half horse, half man creatures? Then, the same roots had saved her. Had the first location been a mistake? Had her mother never planned for her to be taken into custody and led to the Cavari? She'd claimed that she'd been protecting her, and that the Cavari could not know, so was she working against them? Perhaps her mother had stolen her away upon the Cavari's orders, only to save her when they were not looking.

Her hand flailed as the roots slowly lifted her upward. Finn's scream was muffled by the earth as someone gripped her hand and began pulling, speeding her progress. Soon she was free from the earth, and someone was lifting her to her feet.

Strong arms wrapped around her, and she began to sob, suddenly feeling safe for the first time in a long time. "I knew you'd find me," she whispered.

Iseult's arms tensed around her, then relaxed as he continued to embrace her.

Finn wiped at her eyes as they eventually pulled away. So many emotions were flowing through her, she wasn't sure which one to address first. Iseult looked her up and down, as if doubting she was real. She brushed the dirt from her breeches, and shook it out of her loose hair before observing him.

He wore his usual black attire, with his hair back in a clasp, making the light salting of white at his temples evident. He watched her as if unsure of himself, an expression she'd never seen on him before. Aways behind him stood a young girl with blonde curls, and a man that looked startlingly like Iseult.

Finn gasped. "You!" she shouted, recognizing Maarav.

Maarav gave a little bow, while the girl beside him looked confused.

Before an explanation could be offered, Kai came crashing through the underbrush, followed by Anna.

Kai's relieved expression when he saw Finn was tempered only by his disappointment upon seeing Iseult. Finn was not sure why Kai would look so disappointed. Hadn't the plan been to meet Iseult all along?

Anna's eyes widened in shock as she took in Iseult and his companions. Finn thought she saw Anna hesitate as she noticed Maarav, but then she moved on to turn a glare to Kai. "YOU," she growled as her fists flexed near her daggers.

Kai shrugged as he offered Anna an apologetic smile. "Yeah, sorry partner."

Anna's mouth formed a thin line, and her eyes glared daggers, but she remained silent as Kai approached Finn.

"What happened?" he asked. "The Archtree said-"

"You spoke to the Archtree?" Finn interrupted as she moved to meet him halfway. She glanced again at Maarav, desperately wanting an explanation for his presence, but it could wait.

"Well, to three cloaked figures," Kai explained, "that I

assume were somehow related to the Archtree. They told me you were communing with one of the Dair, which sounded much more interesting, so I rushed out of that foolish dream straight away."

Finn couldn't help but smile. "So you didn't get to ask your question?"

He shrugged. "I never really had one to ask to begin with."

Suddenly remembering herself, and the whole point of their entire journey, Finn took a step back from Kai and looked to Iseult. "The tree," she began, then looked around to get her bearings, "if it's still burning, perhaps we can reach it once more."

Anna frowned as she moved to stand beside Kai, and Finn's heart fell. She'd been around people long enough now to know the face of bad news. "The fire went out shortly after we woke. The tree is now nothing more than ash. Judging by the sun we were only unconscious for a few hours, so it should not have burned so quickly given its previous rate, but somehow, it did."

Finn was wracked with immense guilt as she turned back to Iseult. "You didn't get to ask your questions."

Iseult's face was expressionless, which Finn knew meant he was probably hiding powerful emotions. "We will find what we seek another way," he said evenly.

That reminded Finn of something her mother had said. She'd said that which Finn sought had been buried at her roots, and to go back to the place where she'd begun. Was she referring to the shroud? Had it been back in Greenswallow, where she'd stood as a tree, all along?

She wanted to tell Iseult immediately, but then glanced nervously at Anna, effectively giving herself away, she realized too late.

Anna narrowed her eyes at her. "What is it?" she demanded.

Iseult took a step toward Finn as if to come to her rescue, but there was no need. Anna had been entranced by the Archtree's smoke just as Kai had. She'd probably already learned what Finn was trying to hide.

Finn turned back to Iseult, glancing nervously at the two companions he'd brought, who still stood aways back, removing themselves from the reunion. "I know where it is," she said softly, gazing up into Iseult's eyes.

He stiffened in surprise, then his mouth formed a small smile. Finn had rarely seen him smile, and she thought that she rather liked it.

"We have a ship waiting," Iseult explained.

"You can't just take her!" Anna snapped, moving forward aggressively, despite being outnumbered.

Finn put a hand on Iseult's chest to stop him from moving toward Anna. "I still must retrieve Naoki," she announced.

Kai seemed once again relieved. Anna just seemed angry, then her face suddenly fell. If Finn didn't know any better, she'd say that there were unshed tears in Anna's eyes.

"I need the shroud to fix myself," she blurted. "It can fix-" she cut herself off to glance at Iseult and the others, "what we talked about in my cabin," she finished vaguely. "Please, I won't try to sell it."

"And why should we trust a single thing *you* say?" Iseult growled.

Anna ignored him, and turned pleading eyes to Finn.

Finn took a deep breath. She'd sworn to herself that she would not feel sorry for Anna. The woman had been nothing but cruel to her, and did not deserve her help.

"Fine," Finn agreed, surprising everyone, especially herself.

Anna was so relieved that she swooned and nearly fell. Finn thought the sight was almost worth helping her. It wasn't often Anna showed such weakness.

Finn turned back to Iseult. "I must retrieve my . . . friend from the ship before we can depart."

He nodded, back to his cool, stony demeanor.

"You can't just take your dragon and leave us," Anna cut in. "I'm sorry, but a promise is not enough for me. How do we know we'll ever see you again?"

"Dragon?" Iseult questioned, his eyebrows raised.

Before Finn could explain, Kai turned to Anna and offered, "I'll go with them, to make sure they meet you wherever we plan."

Anna scoffed. "And I'm supposed to trust *you*, traitor?"

"Finn stays with me," Iseult stated, his tone inviting no arguments.

Maarav stepped forward. "I've an idea," he announced.

Ignoring him, Finn turned to Iseult, but glanced at Maarav. "Why is *he* here? I met him in Migris."

Iseult nodded, assuring her that he knew about the

meeting. "I will explain everything to you later."

Everyone turned their attention to Maarav to hear his *idea*.

"Eala," he began, gesturing to the girl, "and I will go sail with these two," he gestured to Kai and Anna. "And Finn will go with Iseult. If Iseult does not meet us once we make port in Migris," he looked to Anna, "you can kill us."

The girl, whom he'd called Eala, gasped.

Anna thought about it for a moment, then nodded. "Deal."

Pleased that they could come to an agreement without bloodshed, Finn looked up at Iseult. "Does Àed await us on your ship?"

"*My* ship," Maarav murmured.

Iseult's expression went blank. "He disappeared several days ago, I assumed to find you. Perhaps he hasn't arrived yet."

"Then we must wait for him," Finn said instantly. Àed had been the first person to help her, and he'd remained by her side as much as he could ever since. She would not desert him now.

"Are you sure he's on his way?" Kai interjected. "He would not be able to sail a ship on his own. Perhaps he's in Migris attempting to hire one."

Iseult seemed to think, then nodded. "That is a possibility. We were several days north of Migris when he left us, but he could have returned on his own."

"But An Fiach," the girl Maarav had referred to as Eala cut in. "How would he have gotten past them?"

"He has his tricks," Iseult replied. "I've little doubt he left on his own because it was his best chance of remaining undetected."

The girl's face seemed to fall for some reason that Finn had no way of understanding, unless it was simple concern for Àed. Finn felt that too.

Iseult looked to Finn. "Àed can sense when you're near. If we return quickly to Migris, we may be able to catch him before he sets sail."

Finn felt tears building up behind her eyes. It felt wrong just to leave the island when Àed might arrive any moment, but Iseult was probably right. They could not just wait there when he might never arrive, especially when they stood a chance of finding him in Migris before he could set sail. Still, it was a gamble, but there was little choice. Feeling like a traitor to her friend, she nodded.

"So we all sail for Migris?" Kai asked.

"You're sure the Archtree is entirely gone?" Finn asked, glancing back at him. She still felt guilty that Iseult didn't get to ask any questions. She knew where the shroud was, but she also knew there were many other things Iseult would like to ask. Why his people stole the shroud in the first place, dooming themselves to eradication, for one.

Kai nodded. "It's nothing but ash now. Perhaps the ash could be used somehow . . . " he trailed off.

"No," Iseult interjected. "We'll not waste time for me." He looked down at Finn. "I have everything I came here for."

"Then we should go," Anna agreed. "Now that I know what can *help* me, I'd like to get it over with."

"But how can it help you?" Finn questioned, knowing they should part ways and head to their respective ships, but having trouble with making the final decision.

Anna sighed and glanced at Maarav and the girl by his side, then turned back to Finn. "The shroud is powerful because it can absorb magic from others, and grant them to the possessor. It can take this curse away from me, enabling me to live a normal life once more."

A sharp intake of breath caught Finn's attention. She turned to see the girl standing tight-lipped, looking pale as a ghost. "C-can it really do that?" she stammered.

Anna nodded.

The girl said nothing more.

Iseult placed his hand gently on Finn's arm. "We should go."

Finn nodded, and looked to Kai. Their relationship had been tumultuous at best, but sometimes, she perhaps considered him a friend, and she felt an odd, sick feeling in her gut at their parting.

"Finn-" he began.

For some reason, she didn't feel prepared for whatever he had to say, whether it would have been too much, or too *little*. Instead of facing his words, she cut him off. "Naoki!" she exclaimed. "I almost forgot."

"What in the dark lands is a Naoki?" Maarav asked.

Finn turned to Iseult, feeling like she might cry. "She's just a baby," she paused, searching for the term that would seem the most innocuous.

"Dragon," Kai finished for her.

"We'll keep her safe until Migris," Anna interjected, "though how you'll smuggle her into the city is anyone's guess."

Finn frowned, wondering why Anna would be willing to do her such a favor.

Anna rolled her eyes. "I've a feeling you don't care for either of the hostages you've offered, but you care for the dragon. You'll want her back. You can keep the human collateral."

Finn's frowned deepened as the girl in question squeaked, "Hostages?"

"So you'll take Naoki hostage instead?" Finn inquired, not liking the idea in the least.

"I'm still stuck on the *dragon* part," Maarav cut in.

Finn glared at him, then turned back to Anna.

"I swear to you that I will keep the dragon safe," Anna assured, "and with her in my possession, I know that you will not fail to meet us in Migris."

Finn still felt unsure, but as long as Anna could guarantee Naoki's safety, she could stand to be without her friend for a few days. She nodded.

"Does anyone else have the feeling we're being watched?" Maarav cut in.

"Yes," Iseult answered simply.

Finn's eyes widened. Why had they not said anything earlier?

"We should go," Maarav announced.

Iseult nodded, and it seemed to be settled.

Before Maarav could walk past her, Finn grabbed

his arm, then instantly recoiled at the odd look he gave her.

"Bedelia," Finn began, mustering her courage. "When I was *taken*," she glared at Anna, "she was ill. I had procured a tincture for her, but was unable to deliver it. Do you know if she's alright?"

Maarav nodded. "I might have seen you drop the tincture," he said with a subtle smile. "It might have ended up in your room at my inn."

Finn gasped. "You saw me being kidnapped and did nothing to aid me?"

He offered her a wry grin. "I'm here now, aren't I? And with your noble rescuer, no less," he nodded in Iseult's direction. With that, Maarav walked past her, followed by the girl.

"I'm Ealasaid, by the way," the girl said quickly to Finn as she passed. "I don't know why Maarav insists on shortening it."

Finn nodded, but had time to do nothing else as Iseult began to guide her after the others. She looked over her shoulder at Kai, who looked back at her, seeming to want to say a million things. Instead, he offered her a smile and a wave.

Finn paused as a sudden thought came to her. She looked to Anna, who raised an eyebrow at her.

"I need you to deliver a message to Sativola," Finn explained.

Anna shrugged her okay.

"Tell him that if any Sirens come about, that I demand that he kiss Kai firmly on the lips."

Kai balked, and Anna laughed. "That is a favor I will gladly grant," she assured, then turned to saunter away.

Finn still felt worried, and obviously Iseult could tell.

"We'll sail around the island and follow them to Migris," he assured her.

Finn let her breath out in relief as she nodded.

Kai met Finn's eyes, then turned and followed after Anna.

Finn watched them go, then was suddenly alone with Iseult as Maarav and Ealasaid had already gained progress down the trail.

"Are you well?" he asked.

She turned and looked up at him. "Yes. I'm just nervous, I suppose. I have many things to tell you."

Iseult was silent for a moment, then nodded. "There are some things I should tell you as well." He peered through the trees, as if he'd noticed something. "But not here. We should return to the ship."

Finn looked where Iseult was gazing, but saw nothing. She nodded and allowed him to lead her away. If someone was indeed watching them, perhaps it was whomever set the Archtree on fire. She would have liked to know who it was, but pushing an altercation with an unknown pursuer with many a possible power, seemed unwise.

They walked on in silence. Finn was exhausted, and hoped Iseult's ship was nearer than Anna's. Those who'd gone the other direction would have a solid day of walking ahead of them, if not two.

Finn thought again to what her mother had told her,

that she wouldn't let her become a *monster* again. What had she done in the past, and who else might know about it? She gazed at Iseult's back as he walked down the narrow path, wondering what things he would tell her once they reached the privacy of the ship.

BEDELIA LET out her breath as the party broke apart to walk to their respective ships. She'd never been much for the covert arts, and those two men had nearly spotted her. Óengus had given her the task of observing all who came to the island, while he waited for Keiren's father. It rankled that Óengus was in charge of the more important task, but Bedelia was just glad to be away from him for a time.

She followed a good distance behind Finn, figuring her the most important target to track. Bedelia had hardly believed her ears when Finn asked Maarav about her. She'd had no idea the lifesaving tincture had been Finn's initial doing, even if it was Maarav who'd finally delivered it. They'd both saved her life, and she was thanking them with endless betrayal. Still, that line of thinking brought up a troubling question. What was Maarav doing traveling with Finn's companions? She shook her head and continued to follow the party.

All of this intrigue was too much. She should have just let the poison of the wolf's bite take her.

She cringed as she stepped wrong, straining her wounded leg. Perhaps it still would.

CHAPTER SIXTEEN

*I*t only took an hour's hike to catch sight of the ship. The vessel was a bit smaller than Anna's, but seemed well made. There was a rowboat near the shore, which Finn, Iseult, Maarav, and Ealasaid took out to the waiting ship.

Iseult had remained silent for most of their walk, and it had Finn feeling nervous. To increase her unease, she couldn't stop thinking about who else might be waiting on board. Even though the ship they rowed toward was small, it would still need a few men to sail it. Since Maarav had initially offered himself and Ealasaid as collateral, there had to be other men waiting on board, else how had they expected Finn and Iseult to sail to Migris? The thought made her nervous. The thought of sailing with Maarav made her even more so.

The little rowboat bobbed in the water as Iseult brought it parallel with the ship. He offered Finn a steadying hand as she grabbed onto the rope ladder that

355

would lead her up to the deck. Iseult came after her. Then, two men from on board threw ropes down in preparation of hoisting the rowboat up. Ealasaid and Maarav remained below to secure the ropes.

Once she reached the deck, Finn eyed the extra men nervously. One was small, with bright red hair, while the other was tall and lanky, with dark skin and dark eyes.

"Hirelings of Maarav," Iseult explained as he came to stand beside her. He frowned at them, then turned his attention back to Finn. "One of the many things I will explain," he added.

Finn nodded, then allowed Iseult to lead her toward the captain's cabin above deck. She glanced back at Maarav and Ealasaid as they climbed over the ship's edge to join the two men dealing with the rowboat.

"I would speak to you privately before we cast off," Iseult said softly, drawing Finn's attention back to him.

Realizing she'd paused mid-step, she jumped into motion again. She wasn't sure why she was such a bundle of nerves in that moment. She knew part of it was leaving Kai and Anna behind, and entrusting them with Naoki's care, but that was only a fraction of her worry. How would she explain to Iseult what her mother had told her? How could she tell him that she'd been a *monster*, and had been made into a tree for her own good. Or, did he already know?

There was no malice in his expression as he held the cabin door open for her. She went inside, feeling somehow safer to be out of the open air.

Iseult closed the door behind her, and they both

moved to sit on opposite sides of the cabin's single bed, beneath a small, shuttered window.

Finn glanced around at the rest of the cabin's interior, from the small writing desk, to the multiple storage trunks, then to her hands in her lap. "Your room?" she questioned, not knowing what else to say.

Iseult smirked. "Maarav's," he corrected, but did not say anymore.

Finn felt like she needed to cry, or laugh, or perhaps to just explode. She bit her lip and turned wide eyes to Iseult. She could take the silence no longer. "How much about me do you really know?" she questioned. "You recognized me back in Garenoch, yet you've harbored me no ill will. From what I've gathered, I deserve ill will."

Iseult smiled sadly. "You're correct. I know more than I've let on, but you are mistaken in how I should be feeling toward you."

Finn frowned. "I do not know the specifics, but I was told that I was a-" she cut herself off to take a deep breath, "a monster," she finished.

Iseult shook his head ruefully. "I'd like to tell you a story. A story perhaps I should have told you from the very start."

"Why didn't you?" Finn interrupted, almost irritated that he'd withheld information that could have been useful to her.

He sighed. "I did not want you to doubt my motives for helping you. I truly do want to right my people's wrongs, but there is more at stake than the honor of my ancestors."

Finn wrung her hands nervously, not meeting his eyes as she asked, "What more could be at stake?"

"Their souls," Iseult replied flatly. "And mine."

There was shouting outside the cabin as the sails were raised, and the ship began to pull away from the island. There was a sudden pounding at the door.

Iseult sighed. "What is it?" he called.

The door opened and Maarav popped his head in. "Are we really going to meet the others and follow them to Migris? We need to chart our course. We could always return to . . . " he eyed Finn as his words trailed off, then turned his gaze back to Iseult, "where we departed from," he finished.

"And confront the reivers on our way south?" Iseult asked, making it clear he thought the idea ridiculous.

"Reivers?" Finn interrupted, as the memory of what had happened during *her* reiver encounter jumped forward in her mind. She felt suddenly ill.

Iseult sighed, his gaze on Maarav. "I'll be right out," he said evenly.

Maarav nodded and shut the door, then Iseult turned to Finn. "I apologize. I was anxious to speak with you, and did not consider that I would need to guide the men in the correct direction."

Finn nodded a little too quickly, glad for a reprieve from the intense conversation. "Speaking of Maarav," she said as she stood, glancing over her shoulder to assure herself the man hadn't popped back in. "How *do* you know him?"

Iseult stood and walked past her toward the door,

then turned to offer her a small smile. "He's my brother, or so I'm told. Cursed right along with the rest of us."

Finn's mouth formed an 'oh' of surprise as Iseult opened the door and went out onto the deck to speak with his *brother*. She followed him out, and watched as the men began to expertly maneuver the ship to sail around the perimeter of the island. She wasn't quite sure where Anna's ship was moored in relation to theirs, but they would likely have time to circle the entire island before Anna and Kai finished their long walk.

Ealasaid came to stand beside her as the men continued their work. "So you're Finn," the young girl began kindly. "I must admit, I've heard next to nothing about you." She aimed an eye roll in Iseult's direction.

Finn laughed as she cast her gaze upon Iseult as he directed the other men. "Yes, he tends to keep his words to himself."

"I'm on a mission to avenge my family, by the way," Ealasaid added casually.

Finn's eyes widened in surprise as she turned her gaze away from the men to observe the innocent looking young girl, her blonde curls a puffed up mess from the sea air. "I'm on a mission to stay *far* away from mine," Finn replied.

Ealasaid shook her head, bobbing her curls back and forth. "I imagine you have a reason for that, but you might want to reconsider."

Finn frowned, thinking of the evils the Cavari had committed. "And why is that?"

Ealasaid gazed out at the ocean. "Because once they

are *gone*, you will no longer have a choice."

Finn went silent as the ship picked up speed. What the girl had said might have been true, but some part of Finn told her that if she rejoined her family, she would have no choices at all.

She turned her gaze back to Iseult, wondering what choices *he'd* made to lead him to where he was today.

Maarav kept Iseult busy for some time, and eventually Ealasaid moved to help. Finn, feeling utterly useless with no way to help, retreated below deck. It was probably best for her to simply remain out of the way.

She peeked briefly in each of the rooms, hoping to find one that appeared unoccupied. Each chamber, however, had various belongings strewn about, and two appeared to be storage for food and other supplies.

Finally, she reached the last room. There was a bed and a stool, but no other belongings. With a sigh, she entered, thinking the space seemed rather lonely without a dragon sleeping on the bed, or without Kai banging on the door.

She was looking down at the small, lonely bed, feeling morose, when a knock sounded on the doorjamb behind her. She turned to see Iseult waiting in the doorway, a kettle of tea and two empty mugs in hand. "I see you found your room," he observed.

She nodded, then waited wordlessly as he came in. She was anxious to hear the rest of his explanation, but also terrified.

She sat on the bed and took the mugs Iseult offered, and held them while he poured the steaming tea. He set the kettle on the floor, then sat beside her. She offered him his full mug, then they sipped the hot liquid in silence, neither meeting the other's eyes.

Finally, just when Finn thought she couldn't take the silence a moment more, Iseult turned to her and spoke. "When I was a small boy, my mother told me a story," he explained. "She said it was very important to remember every detail."

He paused, and Finn nodded for him to go on.

"She told me of the events that had led to the start of the Faie war. There was a clan called the Cavari, and we stole a special shroud from them, the shroud of the Faie Queen. To get it back, they not only killed many of our people, but their high priestess cursed us."

Finn gasped. Did he mean *her*? Cursing sounded just like something a monster would do, and that was apparently what she was. Iseult surveyed her face, and Finn wondered what he saw there. Did he sense her terror and repulsion at what she might have done? Did he think that she remembered doing it?

"What kind of curse?" she asked weakly.

Iseult looked down into his mug of tea, but did not speak.

"Please tell me," she begged, her voice a strained whisper.

He met her eyes. "Finn, you took away our souls."

She jumped and spilled scalding tea all over her lap. Quickly setting the mug on the floor, she stood and brushed at her legs, but the hot liquid had already soaked into her breeches. Tears began to stream down her face, not from her scalded skin, but from what she had allegedly done. Such an act didn't even seem possible.

Her body began to shake as she wrapped her arms around herself and cried. Iseult set down his cup of tea on the bedstand and stood, then surprisingly, embraced her.

She tensed. "Why haven't you killed me?" she sobbed.

He rubbed small circles on her back, attempting to soothe her. "I was not alive at the time, but there's more to the story."

She pulled away slightly so she could see his face, though they remained in a loose embrace. His grayish green eyes held sadness. "I do not think the rest of it matters," she mumbled. "If I truly did such a thing, there is no excuse."

Iseult guided her to sit back down. He sat beside her and took her hand. "Remember, this is how the story was told to me," he began, "I cannot account for all circumstances, but there is one very important memory you seem to have lost, and I am reluctant to return it to you."

She met his eyes as her tears continued to flow. "You've already told me the most terrible thing possible. Nothing can harm me more than this."

He glanced down at his lap, then seemed to force himself to meet her eyes. "Finn," he began again, "you were a mother. My people killed your child. Your grief was so great, that you used all of your energy to curse us. You used the Faie Queen's shroud to do it."

Finn felt like she might vomit. "I don't have a child," she murmured. "Your mother told you wrong."

Iseult took a deep breath. "I did not want to tell you, for fear that you would hate me. Perhaps my people deserved to lose their souls, but I cannot stand the idea of leaving them trapped. When I die, my soul will remain trapped as well. None of us can ever move on."

Finn shook her head over and over. None of it could be true. She'd never had a child. She didn't have the power to steal people's souls.

Worry tensing his eyes, Iseult continued his explanation, "When I told you the shroud was a way to contact my ancestors, it was not a lie. Anna is correct in her belief that the shroud can take away magic. Souls are a type of magic, and you used the shroud to claim them from the living, and to curse any borne of the blood of Uí Néid. Most who survived the original curse refused to have children, lest they pass the curse on to innocents. As far as I know, Maarav and I are the only ones left, though there could be others."

Finn took a deep breath. Her emotions all seemed to desert her at once, leaving her utterly numb. She met Iseult's earnest eyes. "I must ask you again. Why have you not killed me?"

Iseult took her hand. "I do not believe you deserve to die. In fact, quite the opposite. My ancestors believed you were the only one who could remove the curse, and you needed the shroud to restore our souls. Only, you disappeared, along with the shroud. The stories were passed down to the few children borne to my original clan after the curse. Eventually they were passed to me."

"You need me to lift the curse," Finn said, feeling silly

for not coming to the conclusion sooner. "And after I lift it, you will kill me."

Iseult flinched as if she'd slapped him, then he suddenly looked angry.

Finn cowered in the face of that rage.

"I will *not* harm you," he said through gritted teeth. "All of the sacrifices made would mean nothing if this were to end in bloodshed. I want to right the wrongs of my people."

Finn felt so many emotions at once, it was over-whelming. "And I want to right the wrongs of mine," she said shakily. "We will find the shroud, and I will lift the curse. I swear it."

Iseult nodded and squeezed her hand, but looked suddenly sad.

"What is it?" she asked softly.

He lifted his free hand to wipe a tear from her cheek. "I only wish I could restore what you lost in return."

Finn's mind went blank. It was like a mighty stone wall barred her memories of her *child* from sinking in. She could not remember a thing.

"If I truly had a child, they are lost to me in every way," she explained. "I do not know if my memories were warped by my grief, or if my people took them away, but I do not want them. I want to help you, and I want to be a *person*. I do not want to be a monster, a member of my clan, or even a tree."

Iseult laughed suddenly. Tears strained his voice, but did not fall from his eyes. "As I recall, when we first met, you wanted nothing more than to be a tree again."

She smiled as she felt a measure of her will to live return. "That was before I went on an adventure. I escaped an enchanted forest, visited one of the grand cities, and braved mighty storms on a ship in the middle of the ocean. There's simply no going back from that."

"Well there's more where that came from," Iseult assured. "Our journey has only just begun."

Finn's smile widened into a joyous grin, though tears still stained her face. Iseult knew everything about her, and he still wanted to travel by her side. She'd done terrible things, but she might have the chance to right them. They would meet Kai and Anna in Migris, and hopefully Áed would be there too. Then they could all set out on yet another adventure, and this time, they would all know each other's true stories.

Finn continued to grin. She may have been a monster in the past, but Kai's words echoed in her head. *There's always a choice. No one can force you to be something, if you choose not to be it.* She could *choose* what she wanted to be in the present, just like any other human. In that moment she chose to be a friend, and someone who would keep her promises. No matter what.

It had taken Kai and Anna longer to catch sight of their ship than they had hoped. They were both utterly exhausted from the previous day, making it a necessity to rest frequently along the way.

They had spoken little on their journey, and it was

only once they'd pulled their rowboat back out of the bushes, and had dragged it across the sandy beach toward the shoreline, that Anna finally brought up the discussion he'd been dreading.

"You knew all along that Iseult would be here," she commented as she stepped into the little boat for Kai to push it into the water. "You tricked me."

His boots were already soaked, and next came his breeches and the edge of his tunic as the boat's bottom lifted away from the sand. He quickly pulled himself in, than sat sodden and unhappy across from Anna as he took the oars in hand.

"Yes," he admitted as he began to row. "I traveled with Iseult and Àed to Migris to find Finn. When I ran into Sativola, and he claimed you were his captain, I surmised what you were up to. I had to act quickly, so I left a note to be delivered to Iseult."

Anna shook her head, tossing her tangled, dirty hair from side to side. "Why would you help him of all people?

Kai sighed. *Why*, indeed. "It's what she wanted," he explained.

Anna narrowed her eyes and pursed her lips in thought. "No, that's not why you did it. You did it because you're trying to be something you're not."

Kai raised an eyebrow at her. "And you're not? The Anna I know would have fought the situation till the bitter end, and Finn would be back on this rowboat with us."

Anna seemed suddenly sad. "I'm not trying to be something I'm not. I'm trying to not be what I am."

They went over a particularly choppy wave, then landed hard, spraying salt water in their faces.

Kai spat water out of his mouth. "I don't follow."

Tears suddenly rimmed Anna's eyes, or maybe it was just the salt water. "I'm a magic user, Kai," she said softly enough that he almost didn't hear her over the sound of the surf. "I can see things that I shouldn't. I can *see* all of the other magic users too, but I don't want any part of it. I just want Finn to use the shroud to remove my curse, then she and Iseult, and *you* for all I care, can go on your ways."

Kai fell silent, thinking of Finn and Iseult. They had promised to meet them in Migris, but who knew if they actually would. He had no doubt that Finn would do her best to keep her promise, but of Iseult, he was not sure.

As they crested a gentle wave, another ship came into view past Anna's. It was small, with a black sail. He had to squint his eyes to see much else, but he was quite sure he saw several people milling about on deck.

"It looks like she's keeping her promise," Kai muttered, speaking of Finn.

Anna turned around so quickly that she almost rocked herself out of the boat. Clinging to the edge of her seat, she peered at the distant ship, then turned around, slumping in relief. "We still have to find the shroud," she said shakily, then lifted her eyes to meet Kai's gaze, "but this is at least a start."

Kai nodded, thinking much the same thing. The fact

that Finn was on a ship in the distance, and not an ocean away, was a start. A start to what, he did not know. All he knew was that she had become the one thing in life he simply couldn't let go of. If that meant becoming something he was not, then so be it.

Maarav smiled to himself as he stood near the mast of his ship. He thought he spotted Anna and her companion rowing toward their vessel, though it was hard to tell in the distance, especially with the sunlight reflecting blindingly off the water. Things hadn't exactly gone according to plan, but perhaps they'd gone even better. Anna had not outed him as the one who had led her to Finn, and Finn still believed that he was a simple innkeep, as well as Iseult's brother.

At the thought of his brother, he frowned. His appearance had been the largest deviation from his plan, though it had proven beneficial thus far. Iseult had already made contact with Finn, and had managed to gain her trust, something that he had failed at. Now it was up to him to decide whether his loyalties lay with those who raised him, or with his blood.

He laughed at his own thoughts. His loyalties would lie where they always had. With *himself*.

Slàine saddled her horse, preparing for the long ride

to Migris. Her messengers had returned from the grand city to report that the tree girl had eluded them, and many guards had died in the process. If Slàine could not depend on highly skilled assassins to get the job done, then there was only one person left. Herself.

She was not worried about slipping past the reivers Maarav had spoken of, nor was she worried about An Fiach. She had trained her entire life to embody a mere shadow in the night. Her enemies would only see her the moment she stuck a dagger through their hearts.

The rumors in Migris of cloaked shapes roaming the city streets, leaving rivers of blood in their wake, were about to increase tenfold. She'd been hired to find a certain girl, a girl she thought Maarav and his brother might know something about, and no one would stand in her way.

ÀED GROANED as he forced the oars upward, only to circle back down into the water, propelling his small boat forward. The salty air stung his sunburned skin, and sweat soaked through his ragged, gray robes. His burlap hat had saved his scalp from the burn he felt on his face, but his long silvery hair was still matted with salt. He scowled at his mule sitting across from him, wishing the heavy creature could contribute to the rowing. His mule looked back at him, thoroughly abashed.

An island had come into sight early that morning, right where it should have been according to Iseult's maps, yet he could only distantly sense Finn. It worried him. More worrisome still, was the small ship in the distance, moored as close to the island as it could be without running into any sandbars. He took a deep breath, tasting mildly of smoke. He'd been catching whiffs of it since that morning. Now that he was near, he could see smoke trickling up from the treeline of the island. It was a small amount, just enough to be a camp-fire, or something larger that had long since burned through.

Determination coursing through his tired arms, he lifted the oars and plunged them back downward. Just a few more minutes and he would reach the sandy beach. Perhaps he'd arrived early, and was sensing Finn on a distant boat, or perhaps she was somehow being shielded. Either way, he needed to investigate.

The oars lifted. The oars came down. Sweat stung his eyes. Just a bit more.

His entire body jolted as the bottom of the boat hit sand. His mule creature let out a startled whinny, then clambered to its hooves to leap out of the boat. It splashed down into the shallow water and trotted onto the shore, followed by Àed, who wearily dragged the boat behind him onto the sand. He tried to drag it out of the water entirely, but found he did not have the strength. In fact, he hardly had the strength to stand. Wait. When did he fall down to his knees?

He sighed, knowing he'd pushed himself too far. He was no longer a young man, it seemed. His mule looked down at him, waiting patiently.

"Ye could help me stand!" Àed huffed.

The mule seemed to sigh, then turned its body sideways. Àed was suddenly overwhelmed with gratitude that he'd left his mount's saddle on, as one of the stirrups dangled near his face. He grabbed hold of it, and slowly pulled himself to standing. With a final sigh of exertion, he hoisted himself into the saddle, then hunched forward, the last bit of his energy gone.

His mule stumbled a few times as it began to walk, but seemed no worse for wear after the long journey. There was a distant smell of smoke in the air, though now that Àed was on the island, he could no longer see the smoke to pinpoint the fire's location.

Resigned to the fact that he'd have to wander a bit, he rode inland, letting his senses guide him. There was a hint of magic on the island, perhaps the Archtree, though he'd expected it to shine much brighter than it was. Unfortunately, he now sensed nothing else, not even Finn. Had his senses lied to him? Was she nowhere near the island? If Kai had failed in his mission, and if Iseult hadn't escaped from the ruined city, that might mean that *no one* was coming to meet him at the Archtree. He might have rowed all of that way for nothing.

He shook his head as he rode, unwilling to give up so easily. If anything, he could find the Archtree, and it could tell him anything he needed to know about Finn, and how to find her.

He rode on for several hours, following the distant shine of magic, that was soon accompanied once more by the faint scent of smoke. Eventually he happened upon the source, which was little more than a charred chunk of ground. In the middle of the black scar, were the smoldering remains of a tree trunk.

He dismounted, still feeling horribly weak, to examine the ashes.

"Hello, old friend," a voice said from behind him.

Àed straightened abruptly, then hunched over from a sharp pain in his old, weary back. He turned slowly to find the owner of the voice.

The man stood tall and strong, though he was in his later years. His silver hair glistened in the sunlight, matching several days worth of silver stubble. His pale eyes looked white in the midday brightness.

"Travelin' once together dinnae make us friends," Àed growled, attempting to hide his surprise. Óengus was perhaps the *last* person he expected to see in that moment. He'd thought they were done with the man after recovering Finn in Port Ainfean.

Óengus shrugged. "You're right, and it's a good thing, because that means I don't have to feel guilty over what's about to happen."

Áed looked around, feeling fear for the first time in a very long time. Óengus was a well-trained killer, and Áed had weakened himself to the point of utter exhaustion.

"Hello father," a voice slithered from the tree line.

Áed's heart stopped. He had never expected to hear that voice again.

Keiren stepped into view. The green leaves surrounding her contrasted with her fiery red hair, flowing freely to her waist. Black clothing encased her tall, slender form. Eyes the same color as Áed's gazed coldly at him.

"Keiren," he breathed, reaching a hand toward her helplessly, though she was far out of reach.

"This is no heart-warming reunion," she said icily. "I simply need you out of my way."

Tears formed in Áed's eyes. He knew he should run, or try to hide, or *something*, but his daughter had always been his weakness. That day, so many years before, he'd felt the same. She'd attacked him viciously, and he was powerless against her.

Óengus stood aside as Keiren strode forward. She came to stand directly in front of Áed, towering over him. She reached a long fingered hand forward to caress his face, then he was suddenly overcome with dizziness. Startled, his mule began to prance and whinny from where it stood near the tree line. Agonizing pain shot upward from Àed's feet to his head, searing through his brain. His body seemed to stretch and contort. He tried to scream, but he no longer had lungs or a mouth.

The tree that was once Áed stretched upward, forming itself from the Archtree's roots. Its perfect, green leaves unfurled as it reached its full height. Áed was still somehow able to look outward, though he could not move, nor could he speak. His heart stilled as his entire being transitioned into wood pulp and bark.

Keiren looked up at the tree and grinned wickedly. "Sorry father," she whispered, "but you always were my weakness."

ABOUT THE AUTHOR

Sara C Roethle is a fantasy author and part time unicorn. For news and updates, please sign up for her mailing list by visiting:

www.saracroethle.com

GLOSSARY

A

Àed (ay-add)- a conjurer of some renown, also known as "The Mountebank"

Anders (ahn-durs)- a young, archive scholar.

Arthryn (are-thrin)- alleged Alderman of Sormyr. Seen by few.

B

Bannock- unleavened loaf of bread, often sweetened with honey.

Bladdered- drunk

Boobrie- large, colorful, bird-like Faie that lures travelers away from the path.

Branwen (bran-win)- a young, archive scholar.

C

Cavari- prominent clan of the *Dair Leanbh.*

Ceàrdaman (see-air-duh-maun)- The Craftspeople, often referred to as *Travelers.* Believed to be Faie in origin.

À Choille Fala (ah choi-le-uh fall-ah)- The Blood Forest. Either a refuge or prison for the Faie.

Ceilidh (kay-lee)- A festival, often involving dancing and a great deal of whiskey.

D

Dair Leanbh (dare lan-ub)- Oak Child. Proper term for a race of beings with affinity for the earth. Origins unknown.

Dram- a small unit of liquid measure, often referring to whiskey.

Dullahan (doo-la-han)- Headless riders of the Faie. Harbingers of death.

F

Finnur (fin-uh)- member of Clan Cavari.

G

Garenoch (gare-en-och)- small, southern burgh. A well-used travel stop.

Geancanach (gan-can-och)- small, mischievous Faie with craggy skin and bat-like wings. Travel in Packs.

Glen- narrow, secluded valley.

Gray City- See *Sormyr*

Grogoch (grow-gok)- smelly Faie covered in red hair, roughly the size of a child. Impervious to heat and cold.

Gwrtheryn (gweir-thare-in)- Alderman of Garenoch. Deathly afraid of Faie.

H

Haudin (hah-din)- roughly built homes, often seen in areas of lesser wealth.

I

Iseult (ee-sult)- allegedly the last living member of Uí Neíd.

K

Kai- escort of the Gray Lady.

Keiren (kigh-rin)- daughter of the Mountebank. Whereabouts unknown.

L

Liaden (lee-ay-din)- the Gray Lady.

M

Meirleach (myar-lukh)- word in the old tongue meaning *thief.*

Merrows- water dwelling Faie capable of taking the shape of sea creatures. Delight in luring humans to watery deaths.

Midden- garbage.

Migris- one of the Great Cities, and also a large trade port.

Muntjac- small deer.

N

Neeps- turnips.

O

Óengus (on-gus)- a notorious bounty hunter.

P

Pooks- also known as Bucca, small Faie with both goat and human features. Nocturnal.

Port Ainfean (ine-feen)- a medium-sized fishing port along the River Cair, a rumored haven for smugglers.

R

Reiver (ree-vur)- borderland raiders.

S

Sand Road- travel road beginning in Felgram and spanning all the way to Migris.

Scunner- an insult referring to someone strongly disliked.

Sgal (skal)- a strong wind.

Sgain Dubh (skee-an-doo)- a small killing knife, carried by roguish characters.

Slàinte (slawn-cha)- a toast to good health.

Sormyr (sore-meer)- one of the Great Cities, also known as the Gray City.

T

Travelers- see *Ceàrdaman*.

Trow- large Faie resembling trees. Rumored to steal children.

U

Uí Néid (ooh ned)- previously one of the great cities, now nothing more than a ruin.

TREE OF AGES READING ORDER

ALSO BY SARA C ROETHLE

The Bitter Ashes Series

Death Cursed

Collide and Seek

Rock, Paper, Shivers

Duck, Duck, Noose

Shoots and Tatters

The Thief's Apprentice Series

Clockwork Alchemist

Clocks and Daggers

Under Clock and Key

The Xoe Meyers Series

Xoe

Accidental Ashes

Broken Beasts

Demon Down

Forgotten Fires

Minor Magics

Gone Ghost

The Moonstone Chronicles

The Witch of Shadowmarsh

Curse of the Akkeri

SNEAK PEEK OF BOOK THREE, THE
BLOOD FOREST

CHAPTER ONE

Finn peered at the distant coast from the ship's railing, though it was difficult to see through the fog, or was that smoke? The acrid scent in the air seemed too strong to be put off by cook fires alone. She brushed a lock of her long, dirty blonde hair away from her sunburned face, cringing at the feeling of grit beneath her fingers. Her entire body felt covered in a thin layer of salt from the sea.

Iseult stood next to her, gripping the railing tight enough to make the wood creak. She turned to ask him if he thought a bath was in their near future, but kept her mouth shut at his expression.

He was all tension, standing by her side while she leaned against the railing more casually. His black hair, flecked with gray at the temples, was partially held back in its customary clasp, leaving loose tendrils around his face for the sea air to play with. His gray-green eyes were serious, his mouth set in a grim line. He'd been almost relaxed during their time out at sea, but it seemed that had ended now.

Finn turned her gaze back to the distant city. Once they reached land, they'd begin their long journey back to her beginning, where she once stood as a tree. Part of her hoped they'd find Àed there, back in his small hovel, tired from traveling, but she knew it was only wishful thinking. Her aged conjurer friend would not give up on finding them so easily.

She glanced away from the distant city to the other passengers on the ship. At one time, the fast movement while out at sea would have made her lose her last meal, but she'd eventually gotten used to the ship's gentle sway, and now almost found it comforting . . . almost. She could never quite put out of her mind the fact that Sirens dwelled in the sea, waiting to sing sailors to their watery graves.

Finn watched as Iseult's long lost brother, Maarav, and his men manned the sails, guiding the ship steadily toward Migris, where they would dock to meet Kai and Anna. Finn couldn't help but wonder how everyone would get along. She held no warm feelings toward Maarav, and knew he'd likely anger some of the others before long. It was simply in his nature.

She was more worried, however, about how Kai and Anna would behave. Neither of them were particularly good at making friends. Hopefully they'd at least taken good care of little Naoki, Finn's adolescent dragon, though the small creature did present another problem.

The people of Migris were terrified of the Faie, and would not take kindly to a dragon in the city. Finn comforted herself with the idea that Kai would think of a way to smuggle Naoki out unseen. He was good at that sort of thing.

Footsteps across the deck preceded Ealasaid's appearance at Finn's other side. Her curly blonde hair had seemed to grow in size the longer they were out to sea, foaming into a snarled mass around her delicate freckled face and pale gray eyes. She wore the same burgundy dress with black accents Finn had first seen her in, causing her to assume it was the girl's only one.

Not that Finn could say much different. She still wore the tight breeches, loose white blouse, and corset she'd been given aboard Anna's ship. Her deep green cloak, beginning to fray heavily at the edges, was secured around her shoulders, shifting gently in the breeze. The people of Migris would likely stare as much at her state of attire as they would a baby dragon, but she was loath to change back into a dress, especially if they'd be riding. Sitting on the saddle wasn't the issue. Her previous skirts had consisted of enough fabric to still cover her ankles, but lifting her leg over the horse always caused a blush. Of course, they'd have to find horses to purchase first, which likely wouldn't prove easy.

Ealasaid stepped forward and leaned her arms against the railing beside Finn. "I've never actually been to Migris. I've never been to any of the great cities, for that matter."

Finn tilted her head, confused, squinting her eyes

against a harsh blast of sea air. "I thought you traveled with Iseult to find me."

Iseult had told her everything that happened while they were apart, including how they'd come to travel with Ealasaid. She knew he'd narrowly missed her in Migris as she sailed away, locked in a cabin on Anna's ship, and had just assumed Ealasaid and Àed were with him.

Ealasaid nodded. "We reached the gates together, but no one was allowed inside the city. Iseult found his own way in, while Àed and I waited with the refugees."

Finn's heart gave another nervous patter at the thought of Àed. Though it was doubtful he'd be waiting for them at the end of their journey in Greenswallow, he might very well be waiting in Migris. He'd parted ways with Iseult somewhere north of the large city, supposedly to search for her on his own. Her only hope was that he had not traveled all the way to the Archtree, only to find it burned to a stump with her nowhere to be found.

"Ah, yes," Finn replied, stuffing her nerves back down, "my travel companion at the time had been able to gain us special entrance to the city. I'd almost forgotten."

The thought of Bedelia brought her nerves right back up. Was she even still alive? Maarav had claimed he'd delivered the potion that would cure Bedelia's illness, brought on by the bite of a Faie wolf, but Finn did not fully trust a single thing he said. He'd stood idly by while Anna kidnapped her, after all. She took a deep breath to settle her anxiety, then nearly gagged on a sudden whiff of smoke in the air, not the pleasant smell of wood burning, or even food, but a sickly sweet stench that made her gut clench.

"Something is wrong," Iseult muttered, drawing her attention.

She followed his gaze to the distant port. It *was* smoke surrounding the city, not fog, though she saw no flames over the city walls. They were still too far out to see anything else.

"Is the city on fire?" Ealasaid questioned.

Iseult nodded. "So it would seem." He smoothed his hands over his clothing, all in shades of his customary black, as if preparing himself for a confrontation.

Finn squinted her eyes in the direction of the city, but could not tell if men still guarded the walls or the dock. She turned her gaze out toward the open ocean, then pointed, "There's Anna's ship. It seems they will arrive shortly after us."

She turned to see Iseult nod. "Yes, if we decide to dock at all. The smoke might mean Migris has been attacked. It may now be inhabited by enemy forces." He frowned at the thought.

Finn knew he was likely thinking of Conall. He'd regaled her of his visit back to the place of his birth, now just a ruined city. It had been taken over and fortified by Conall, a Reiver commanding magic-using refugees. Reivers were the wild people of the borders, bandits by most accounts. Finn had encountered such a group while she was on Anna's ship. The altercation resulted in disturbing repercussions. She could still clearly picture the man's skin melting from his bones at her touch.

She shook away the memory, focusing on the current situation. She had no desire to encounter Reivers *ever* again. If they inhabited the city, they would simply have to dock elsewhere.

Maarav came to stand at Iseult's other side, leaving his men, Tavish and Rae, to tend the sails. He peered out across the water. "Can't say I like the look of that. I'll not be pleased if my inn is no longer standing."

Finn chewed her lip in consternation. She'd almost forgotten about Maarav's inn, *The Melted Sea*, named after the ocean they now sailed.

"I don't think your inn is necessarily a priority right now," Ealasaid sniped back.

Maarav only chuckled. The pair often seemed to be at each other's throats, but spent more time together than apart. Finn suspected Ealasaid enjoyed Maarav's company more than she let on, though she also seemed constantly irked by the man.

"I'd say it was burned at least a full day ago, judging by the lack of visible flames," Iseult commented. "The remnants of the city will likely smolder for a while longer."

Ealasaid let out a shaky exhale, muted by the sound of lapping ocean waves, more rough now that they were closer to shore. "The whole city?" she asked. "Are you saying the *entire* city was burned?"

Iseult nodded, then gestured toward the sight. "Look

at the smoke. That's not the smoke of a single building, or even several."

Unease blossomed in Finn's gut. Migris was only the first stop of many on their journey, but they would still need to resupply. Weeks out to sea had depleted their provisions, and they only had two horses, belonging to Iseult and Maarav. Not to mention that whoever had burned the city might still be in the area.

"Should we still dock?" Finn questioned, searching the sea again for Anna's ship to find it was making steady progress toward the shore. It seemed they planned to dock despite the smoke.

"Aye," Iseult replied. "The nearest ports to Migris are Sormyr, far south, and," he hesitated, "*another* far north." He glanced at Maarav.

Finn supposed he was alluding to the hidden city Iseult had secretly told her about. All on the ship had departed from there, save Finn, who'd been on a ship with Kai and Anna at the time. She couldn't help but be a little jealous. A city completely concealed within a rocky wall, forming a secret cove, sounded like quite a sight, and it irked her that she wasn't supposed to know about it.

Maarav and Iseult turned away to aid the men with the sails, prepared to guide the ship toward the docks, leaving Finn and Ealasaid alone.

"Do you think it was the Faie that burned the city, or was it the Reivers?" Ealasaid questioned distantly, still leaning against the ship's railing. She turned her gaze to Finn. "Or perhaps even An Fiach?"

Finn took a shaky breath and pushed her waist-length hair behind her ear, unsure which option was worse, though it wasn't necessarily any of the three. The Cavari, her tribe, could have been to blame, or perhaps even the Ceárdaman, the *Travelers*, relinquishing their role as watchers to twist the strings of fate.

"Let's just hope whoever it was did not decide to linger," she replied. "And let's hope there are supplies left to find, lest we starve before anyone has the chance to kill us."

Ealasaid's face scrunched up like she might be sick. Finn could not blame her, she was tempted to lose her breakfast herself.

"Bladdered, cursed dragon," Kai growled, giving a final tug to the blanket.

Naoki perched on the bed, digging her talons into the straw of the mattress. She clasped the other end of the blanket in her beak, refusing to let go, while fluffing up her sparse white feathers to make herself appear larger than she was. He tugged again, making her wings flap chaotically as she tried to maintain her balance, sending loose papers fluttering around the room from the bedside table.

Kai let go of the blanket with a huff. "We can't just go walking about with a dragon out in the open," he explained tiredly. "If you'd just wear the blanket, perhaps we could pretend you're something . . . else."

Dropping her end of the blanket, Naoki craned her long neck to the side, blinking spherical lilac eyes at him. She'd been a handful since they'd parted ways with Finn, Naoki's *mother*, as far as the little dragon was concerned. He'd been forced to keep her in Finn's vacated cabin, lest Naoki attempt to fly away in search of her.

He sighed, then took a seat on the bed beside the dragon. Finn would never forgive him if he managed to lose her friend, not to mention Anna would be furious with losing her collateral.

Naoki made a chittering sound in her throat, then retrieved the blanket and dropped one end in Kai's lap.

He snorted. "It's all just a game to you, isn't it?"

She chittered again.

"Are ye almost done with that dragon!" Sativola called down the stairs leading to the cabins. "We're about to dock, and it looks like the city has been burned."

Burned? Well that didn't sound good. Pushing the blanket aside, he stood, then hurried out of the cabin, shutting the door before Naoki could bound after him. He cringed as her weight hit the closed door, then proceeded to jog down the hallway. He reached the stairs and raced up them two at a time to find Sativola waiting on deck, his massive form partially blocking out the sun.

As soon as Kai was at his side, Sativola pointed a sausage-like finger at the nearby city of Migris. Sure enough, it was giving off large amounts of smoke, and no men could be seen around the gates.

"No signs of life?" Kai questioned, not spotting any,

but wanting to verify that whoever had burned the city was not around.

Sativola shook his head, tossing his golden curls to and fro. "None that we've seen yet. Looks like the fire has died down, leaving only the smoldering remains."

Kai snorted. *Smoldering remains.* An apt description for his life at the present, or so he felt. He had no idea where he stood with Finn, and now she was back with Iseult on their little quest. Not to mention Anna's troubles with seeing into the *gray*, the in between places. Her nightmares had only grown worse, sometimes crossing into waking so that she jumped at shadows at the oddest times. Now they somehow had to make it all the way back to Garenoch, and a meadow somewhere beyond that, where Finn used to stand as a tree. It would have all been hard to believe if he hadn't seen too many odd things with his own eyes, including the Faie of the Blood Forest.

"Well at least we won't need to hide the dragon when we dock," Sativola sighed, drawing Kai out of his thoughts.

Kai nodded. There was that, at least. Perhaps he could just keep Naoki in her cabin, and leave it to Finn to draw her out without a fight.

Thinking of Finn, he scanned the sea for the ship she was on, finding it not far off from his own. He squinted his eyes, attempting to make out the figures on the deck, but they were too far away to see clearly.

Sativola jumped as the door to Anna's nearby cabin burst open, slamming against the exterior wall with a loud *bang*. Anna exited the cabin and approached, looking dangerous in her tightly fitted black attire: breeches, tunic, and corseted vest. Twin daggers, her constant companions of late, swayed at each of her hips. Her straight, black hair, pulled into a tight braid, accentuated her sharp, hawklike features and dark eyes.

"It seems someone has laid siege to Migris," Kai explained as she reached them.

She nodded, her eyes taking on a distant look. "It was the Faie, or something like them."

Kai frowned, waiting for further information.

Instead of answering, Anna glared at Sativola until he raised his hands in surrender and walked away. Turning back to Kai, she explained, "I saw it in a dream last night. I don't know who led them, or why, but many powerful creatures gathered together to conquer the city." She frowned. "They wanted to send a message," she added distantly.

Kai suppressed a shiver. He'd stood witness as the Faie attacked the Ceàrdaman, slaughtering them to break the barrier trapping them within the Blood Forest. He couldn't imagine what the people of Migris must have felt when the Faie descended upon them. Even if some managed to flee, they would not likely last long in the wilds. The roads were already crowded with refugees searching for a safe place to dwell. At least, that was how it had been when they'd departed on their search for the Archtree, over two weeks prior.

"Are the Faie still within the city?" he questioned,

hoping Anna had gained more useful information from her dream.

She shook her head. "I do not know, and I didn't say they were Faie for sure, just something like them. Something . . . magical. Perhaps some remain, but I doubt it. They accomplished what they set out to do."

"And that was to send a message?" Kai asked, feeling uneasy as they neared the docks. "What kind of message, and to whom?" This close to the city, he was quite sure there were no signs of life, but he'd prefer to avoid any stragglers who might remain.

"If I knew, I would have said," Anna snapped. "I don't know why I dreamed of it at all. The only thing I can say for sure is that our troubles will only increase from here."

She'd grown flustered as she spoke, darting her eyes around the ship. Was she seeing things again? Kai tried to follow her gaze, knowing he couldn't see what she saw, but unable to keep himself from trying.

Giving up, he left Anna's side to help the other men with the sails. Just a moment before, he'd been thinking his life couldn't get any worse, but if hoards of Faie, or something perhaps even worse, were sacking the great cities, all men would have many more troubles to come.

Iseult watched as Finn carefully stepped down the slatted plank connecting the ship to the dock. The smell of smoke was stronger this close to the city, coating the chill air hitting his lungs. His gaze lingered as Finn paused to wrap her ratty green cloak more tightly around her, catching her snarled hair in the fabric around her shoulders. She stared down the length of the dock, her feet not moving.

He stepped up behind her on the plank and gently touched her shoulder. She jumped at his touch, then turned her worried gaze back to him.

"There's nothing to be concerned about," he assured her softly. "I will keep you safe."

He looked past her, observing Maarav and Ealasaid already down onto the dock, both watching as Anna's ship drifted into the harbor. Maarav's hired men, Tavish and Rae, also waited below, securing the ship to the large wooden beams of the dock with heavy lengths of rope, in addition to the already lowered anchor.

As Finn nodded and started forward again, Iseult briefly wondered where Tavish and Rae would go from here. He watched Rae, the older of the two, grimly checking each of the ropes they'd secured. Sunlight glinted off his dark skin as he glanced up at Finn and Iseult as they passed by. He hadn't spoken much on their journey, and Iseult had found himself increasingly uneasy around the man.

Tavish, however, had rarely stopped blabbering. He'd excused his lively demeanor as an accompanying trait to his bright red hair. An idiotic thought as far as Iseult was concerned, though the man's dark brown eyes reflected a certain cunning.

Maarav stepped forward and offered Finn his hand as she reached the dock, but she ignored him. Just as Iseult had found it impossible to trust Rae, so Finn had found Maarav. Though, he couldn't blame her for being wary of his long-lost brother. Iseult was wary too.

Finn stepped onto the dock with him close behind. Roughly sixty paces away, a plank was lowered from Anna's ship. Peering in the direction of the sun, it was difficult to decipher who managed the plank, but judging by the man's massive size, Iseult didn't think it was Kai.

He turned to witness Finn nervously chewing on her lip. Noticing his gaze, she asked, "Do you think there's anyone left in the city? Anyone who might harm Naoki?"

Iseult pursed his lips in thought. He was still skeptical that Finn had actually adopted a *real* baby dragon, though Kai and Anna had both seemed to agree that's what it was. He flicked his gaze to the nearest ruined building, a small shack that would normally store extra lengths of rope and spare planks. "I doubt anyone is left here. Perhaps a few looters hoping to salvage some goods, but our party is large enough that we should not be bothered."

With a nervous nod, she began walking toward Anna's ship. Iseult followed after her, continuously scanning their surroundings for hidden threats. It was unnerving that the city seemed so empty. When they'd first noticed the smoke, he'd thought it likely that Conall was responsible, but now he wasn't sure. If Conall had taken Migris, he would have left men in place to claim it for his people. Now that they were able to observe things more closely, Iseult thought the Faie were more likely to blame. Only the Faie would attack a city simply to lay it to waste, abandoning what could be a useful commodity. It would also explain why any survivors would be hesitant to return. Though most alive had only been around to experience the aftereffects of the Faie War, stories were still told of the horrific occurrences.

Leaving Maarav, Ealasaid, and the other two men behind, Iseult and Finn reached Anna's ship just as Kai was making his way down the plank toward the dock. He seemed tired, and a little thinner than usual, not to mention the pair of angry red gashes across his cheek. Upon closer observation, Iseult noticed more gashes on his hands, and a few tears in his dark green tunic and gray woolen breeches.

Kai's gaze remained on Finn as he finished his descent. Anna could be heard shouting orders up on deck, but was yet to appear at the top of the plank.

"Where's Naoki?" Finn demanded, taking a step toward Kai. She seemed to have noticed the gashes on his face, taking it as a sign her dragon had been harmed.

Kai narrowed his eyes at her. "Well greetings to you too," he grumbled. "Your dragon is fine. *I*, however, have borne the brunt of her tantrums during this last leg of our voyage."

Finn's expression softened. Iseult's did not.

The trio stood in awkward silence for a moment before Kai gestured toward the plank leading back up to the ship. "I'll leave it to you to retrieve her," he said to Finn. "And you're *welcome*."

Not responding, Finn hurried past him up the plank.

Kai gave Iseult a quick nod in greeting, then turned to

walk back up the plank after Finn. A half-second later, Iseult was at his side, boarding the ship. By the time both men reached the deck, Finn had disappeared from sight. Anna stood on the other end of the deck near a pile of supplies, ordering three men around as they carried things out of the main cabin.

Kai sighed, then gestured toward the hatch leading below deck. "Protect any areas you'd rather not have sliced open," he explained. "The little dragon has talons as sharp as any blade." He absentmindedly touched the wounds on his cheek, then led the way forward.

Iseult followed Kai to the hatch, then down a narrow set of wooden stairs. At the bottom, they walked down a short hallway, then turned right into one of the small, windowless cabins. Iseult widened his eyes in surprise as he observed Finn, seated on a small bed, being nuzzled by what appeared to be a baby dragon.

With only the light streaming in from above deck to see by, he couldn't make out all of the creature's details, but he noted a sharp beak, large, round eyes, likely lavender or blue in color, and a sparse sprinkling of glossy white feathers, densest around the edges of the creature's wings. It was making a soft purring noise deep in its throat as its beak rubbed against Finn's face.

At Kai and Iseult's appearance, Finn bundled the creature into her arms and stood, disregarding the sharp talons resting perilously close to her throat. Iseult would have liked to tell her bringing a dragon on their travels was not a wise idea, but her glowing smile forced him to silence. He hadn't seen her smile like that since before he'd told her she was responsible for stealing his people's souls.

"Let's check the city for supplies," he muttered instead, "then we'll move on."

He turned and led the way back out of the cabin, as Kai whispered, "A man of few words, eh?" to Finn behind his back.

Their footsteps followed his a moment later, and soon they were all on the dock, along with Anna and her three crewmen, including the massive one with curly hair he'd heard referred to as Sativola.

They met Maarav, his men, and Ealasaid further down the walkway. Maarav now held the reins of both his and Iseult's horses, brought down from the ship. Once everyone was gathered together, Iseult repeated his plan.

"What about the ships?" one of Anna's men, with deeply tanned skin and short yellow, hair argued. "We can't leave them behind."

Iseult sighed. He didn't have time for these men. Greenswallow was a long way off, and they needed to arrive there before anyone else discovered the location of the Faie Queen's shroud, buried where Finn once stood as a tree.

"I had hoped to leave my ship in a safe harbor as well," Maarav cut in smoothly. He raked his fingers through his black hair, peppered with a few strands of white, just like Iseult's. "But we must adapt to the current situation. Many of us have places to be inland, and those left can hardly manage to sail two ships on their own. We'll have to leave them, and hope for the best."

"Or someone can stay to guard them," the yellow-haired man spat.

"Are you volunteering?" Kai questioned. "I'm sure a *brawny* man like yourself can hold off an entire army of Faie on your own. We'd be much obliged if you'd watch the ships for us."

The yellow-haired man snarled his dry lips, but didn't speak again.

Iseult took a step closer to Finn, still holding the dragon in her arms with its limbs curled around her. Tavish, Rae, and Ealasaid were all staring at the creature, but said nothing.

"We'll divide into two groups, search for supplies, then meet at the front gates," Iseult instructed.

No one argued. Instead, all glanced warily at the smoldering city, wondering what dangers might still lurk within its walls.

Finn straightened her satchel strap across her chest, trying to balance its weight with the awkward addition of Naoki on her shoulders. It seemed the dragon had grown a bit in their time apart, but still insisted on her chosen perch.

Finn suppressed a grunt of effort. Her legs already felt like pottage transitioning from the ship to dry land, and the added weight made her feel even more off balance. It would not do to topple over and land on one of the corpses, visible now that they'd entered the city.

Iseult prowled at her side, his eyes keen on the surrounding buildings, all showing signs of being touched by fire. At their backs walked Ealasaid, Maarav, Tavish, and Rae. Maarav still held the reins to his and Iseult's horses. The animals remained eerily quiet, as if sensing the ghosts of the dead. Kai, Anna, and Anna's crewmen had taken another route. They would all search for supplies, then reconvene at the city gates to begin their journey.

They now walked in the direction of Maarav's inn, since he'd insisted they check in on the establishment. Finn didn't know what he was hoping to find, it seemed most everything had been destroyed, but she supposed if he had a cellar some goods might remain.

She quickly averted her eyes from the ground as she stepped around another charred corpse. It wasn't the first body they'd come across, and it surely would not be the last. Many had been killed.

She hurried forward, only to have Iseult reach out a hand to stop her. "Don't look down," he instructed, but the warning came too late. At their feet lay a child, badly burned like many of the other bodies.

She raised a hand to her mouth, afraid she might be sick.

Seconds later, from behind her, Ealasaid gasped. Naoki hissed at the noise, prompting Ealasaid to then let out a surprised yip.

Iseult put an arm around Finn and led her forward.

Surprisingly, Naoki did not seem to mind his presence, or else found him more frightening than Kai, and so refrained from hissing at him.

"Are you sure you want to walk all the way to your inn?" Iseult grumbled, looking over his shoulder toward Maarav.

"We need supplies," Maarav replied simply, "and our best chance of finding them is my inn. With any luck, the cellar will be intact."

"I think I'm going to be ill," Ealasaid muttered as they passed another body. "This is far worse than Uí Néid."

"The dead there were freshly killed," Maarav explained. "It's different once they've been lying around for a while, but you'll get used to it."

Ealasaid snorted. "I'd rather not get used to seeing corpses at all."

Finn attempted to take a steadying breath, but inhaled too deeply. Her stomach convulsed, forcing her to bend forward. The smell of the charred corpses was too much for her, and she found herself expelling what little food was in her belly. Naoki hopped to the ground and chittered nervously at her side as Iseult kept a hand on her back, waiting for the moment to pass.

As Finn's nausea began to wane, she heard someone else retching behind her, and turned to see the red-haired man, Tavish, had also lost his morning meal. The sight somehow made her feel slightly better.

"Perhaps some of us should go ahead to the gates," Maarav sighed, glancing between Tavish and Finn. "Rae and I can gather the supplies on our own. With only two of us, we can ride the rest of the way."

"And what if you encounter whoever killed all these people?" Ealasaid gasped.

Maarav gestured to the desolate streets. "Take a look around you, my girl, no one is left in this cursed place."

Finn crouched to allow Naoki back onto her shoulders, then looked to Iseult for his opinion, secretly hoping he'd agree with Maarav so she wouldn't have to continue looking at the bodies.

Iseult nodded in understanding, then turned his gaze to his brother. "I'll take the women . . . and Tavish, to the gates," he agreed. "But be quick with your tasks, I'd like to be far from this place come nightfall."

"We all would," Tavish muttered, then gestured for Ealasaid to walk ahead of him toward Iseult and Finn.

The four of them changed directions, making their way toward the gates, while Maarav and Rae climbed atop the horses and continued on toward whatever might remain of Maarav's inn.

Finn walked beside Iseult in silence for some time, deep in thought, keeping her gaze upward to avoid looking too closely at any more corpses.

"Do you know what's odd?" Tavish blurted suddenly.

Finn jumped, realizing the man was walking close to her other side, though she noted he was peering around her toward Iseult.

Iseult did not reply, but Tavish still continued, "It's odd that we seem to only be seeing the corpses of towns-folk and the city guards."

"Why is that odd?" Ealasaid questioned, walking a few paces behind them.

"Because in any battle there are casualties on both sides," Iseult answered grimly.

"So you *did* notice," Tavish commented, seeming relieved that he wasn't the only one to find the situation strange.

"Yes," Iseult replied simply.

Finn wished she could be so observant, but she'd been too busy trying to pretend they weren't surrounded by *any* corpses, let alone only those of the townsfolk.

"So what do you think happened?" Tavish continued, once again looking past Finn at Iseult.

"Either the bodies of the opposing forces were taken," Iseult explained, "or the townspeople were killed by a force so great they all died where they stood. Now keep your mouth shut. Dangers may still lurk."

Wide-eyed, Tavish snapped his mouth shut and glanced around warily. Finn couldn't say she was glad for the silence. It seemed to bring out the eeriness of their surroundings. As far as she was concerned, they couldn't reach the gates soon enough.

Naoki let out a sudden *squawk* from her perch on Finn's shoulder. Finn stumbled, but Iseult's hand darted out to catch her arm before she could fall.

Maintaining his grip on her, Iseult glanced around for what had alerted Naoki. Finn looked too, until her eyes caught a hint of movement a few feet away. She pointed, just as Tavish seemed to notice the same movement.

It was the corpse of a young woman, less burned than

the rest, but still just as dead. Her limp body was wriggling back and forth, though none of her limbs seemed to be responsible for the movement.

"The dead are coming to life!" Tavish gasped.

"No," Iseult said coolly, then released Finn's arm to step forward.

He withdrew his sword, lowering the tip toward the woman's still wriggling body. At first Finn thought he might use the sharp edge to skewer her, but instead he slid the point beneath her torso, then flipped her body over, revealing a small creature that had been trying to free itself from the trapping weight of the corpse.

It struggled to its clawed feet, checking over its craggy, rock-like skin for injuries with its spherical eyes. One of its bat-like wings seemed to be broken.

"It's a Grogoch," Finn gasped.

The Grogoch jumped at the sound of her voice, then trembled in fear as it looked up at Iseult. Naoki hopped off Finn's shoulder and crouched on the ground, prepared to pounce the Grogoch.

"Wait!" Finn cried, then knelt beside Naoki to halt her pounce. However, Iseult looked just about ready to pounce the small creature himself, and Finn couldn't blame him. They'd met Grogochs before. Not only had many townsfolk danced themselves to death, but both Finn and Iseult had been rendered unconscious long enough for Kai and Anna to kidnap her.

The Grogoch blinked up at her, still trembling.

"What happened here?" she demanded. "Did you sing

the townsfolk to sleep so the other Faie could murder them?"

Naoki let out a low growl.

The Grogoch was trembling so violently she thought it might wet itself. "N-no, lass," it sputtered in its humming voice. "I was only here to have a bit of fun, then *they* attacked. I was knocked down and my wing was broken." It gestured pleadingly with its taloned hands at the drooping wing.

"We know these creature's tricks," Iseult muttered. "We should kill it and move on."

"No!" it rasped. "I did no wrong!"

Finn held up a hand toward Iseult, halting his sword arm.

"Tell me what happened," she instructed. "Who attacked?"

"Other Faie," the Grogoch whispered. "Elementals, led by someone powerful. The elementals *never* meddle in the world of humans. They must have been forced."

Something tickled at the edge of Finn's memories. She knew something about these elementals, but couldn't quite place what it was. "Tell me more about the elementals," she urged. "Tell me everything you know and you will not be harmed."

"Finn-" Iseult began to argue, but she silenced him with a pleading look.

"Cannot be killed," the Grogoch explained. "These ones were made of pure fire. Whoever commanded them did not reveal themselves. Many of the townsfolk fled, but others tried to fight. Silly men. Stood no chance."

Goosebumps broke out across Finn's entire body. She knew she'd encountered elementals in her previous life, but could not quite recall the event, just like all her other memories. She knew they were there, buried somewhere deep within her subconscious, but she had no access to them.

The Grogoch was eyeing her suspiciously, as if wondering whether she'd go back on her word.

Several pairs of footsteps sounded behind Finn's back. She turned for just a moment to see Kai, Anna, Sativola, and the other two crewmen jogging toward them, carrying sacks of supplies over their arms, but when she turned back, the Grogoch was gone.

"We should not have let it go," Iseult muttered as the others reached them.

"What are you all standing around for?" Kai questioned upon arrival.

Finn frowned and turned back to Iseult. Their eyes met, and she tried to silently let him know there were things they needed to discuss. He seemed to understand her silent meaning, as he nodded, then turned his gaze to everyone gathered around them.

"Let us leave this place," he instructed. "Hopefully Maarav and Rae will have already made their way to the gates."

Soon Naoki was back on Finn's shoulders, and the party continued onward. Finn hardly noticed the corpses they passed, her mind entrenched in trying to recall her memories.

She was not sure who would be able to command the

elementals, but she felt it was critical she find out. If elementals could not be stopped by human means, perhaps they could be stopped by one of the Dair. If they could, she needed to figure it out fast, lest they come for her and her friends next.

To be continued...

26230653R00237

Printed in Great Britain
by Amazon